THE UNFORGETTABLE
HERO OF
THE BLUE MAX
RETURNS IN
THE BLOOD ORDER

"A compelling novel . . . combines powerful political intrigue with a sharply detailed study of the times and characters involved in Hitler's ascent to power."

—*Publishers Weekly*

"Bruno Stachel is a nervy, appealing antihero . . . a solid entry for those who prefer their Hitler & Company . . . more gritty than fanciful."

—*Kirkus Reviews*

THE BLOOD ORDER

JACK D. HUNTER

To Tommie, with love—
Again . . . Of course . . . And always.

This low-priced Bantam Book has been completely reset in a type face designed for easy reading, and was printed from new plates. It contains the complete text of the original hard-cover edition.
NOT ONE WORD HAS BEEN OMITTED.

THE BLOOD ORDER
A Bantam Book / published by arrangement with Times Books

PRINTING HISTORY
Times Books edition published August 1979
2nd printing .... August 1979
Bantam edition / June 1980

ISBN 0-553-13549-X

Published simultaneously in the United States and Canada

PRINTED IN THE UNITED STATES OF AMERICA

0 9 8 7 6 5 4 3 2 1

The wicked are wicked, no doubt, and they go astray
and they fall, and they come by their deserts; but
who can tell the mischief which the very virtuous do?
—Thackeray

With Prussian officers, correct behavior
had been a point of honor. With German officers,
it must be a point of honor to be sly.
—General Werner von Blomberg
Chief of Truppenamt in Weimar Republic, 1928
Minister of Defense in Third Reich, 1933–38

A note of fond thanks to:

Eleanor Wood, who champions;
Marcia Magill, who perceives;
Doris Craig Austin, who persists;
Bernhard Weickert, who counsels.

And a reminder:

In the words of the late James Jones, "readers should remember that the opinions expressed by the characters are not necessarily those of the author. . . ."

J.D.H.
Chesapeake Isle
November, 1978

CAST OF CHARACTERS

Hans Berger	SS Sturmbannführer
Martin Bormann	Politician
Friedrich von Boetticher	General; military and air attaché, Washington, D.C.
Karl von Brandt	Major, Air Intelligence
Georges Doubet	Major; French military attaché, Berlin
John M. Duncan	Captain; U.S. air attaché, Berlin; later, U.S. senator
Reinhardt Funk	Oberst; an aide to Chef der Heeresleitung
Josef Goebbels	Politician
Hermann Göring	Reich Commissioner for Aviation; Politician
Elfi Heidemann	Widow of World War ace; nurse; church worker
Adolf Hitler	Politician
Emil Klaus	Church worker
Adalbert Kleine	Major, Air Intelligence
Anna-Marie Elsbet	Society matron
Karlotte, the Baroness von Klingelhof-und-Reimer	
Rudi von Klingelhof-und-Reimer	Her son and Sturmabteilung trooper
Theodor von Kolberg	General; assistant chief for air, the General Staff
August Kratzer	Inspector, Berlin police
Dieter Laub	Conspirator
Alfredo Laumann	Assassin
Siegfried Lehr	SS Untersturmführer
Ludwig, the Baron von und zu Lemmerhof	General; chief of aviation services
Friedl Lockermann	Landlady
Polly Loomis	Secretary, U.S. Embassy, Berlin
Viktor Lutze	Obergruppenführer, Sturmabteilung; politician
Erhard Milch	Chief of Lufthansa; later, Göring's deputy
Karl-Heinz Nachtigal	Aviation mechanic; farmer

Fritz Pohl	SS Obersturmführer
Ernst Randelmann	Oberleutnant, Fliegerzentrale
Willi Schneider	Oberst, Air Intelligence
Hans von Seeckt	General; Chief der Heeresleitung
Bruno Stachel	World War ace; Luftwaffe officer
Kaeti Stachel	His wife; publisher
Ludwig and Emilie Stachel	His parents
Harry Taylor	U.S. Department of State
Ernst Udet	World War ace; technical chief, Luftwaffe
Anson Whitlow	Superintendent, Curtiss Aeroplane Co., Buffalo, N.Y.
Alice Williams	Farm girl, Coley's Corners, N.Y.
Hans Wohlheim	Hotel manager
Bernhardt Ziegel	Salesman, church worker

Court-martial Principals

Hauptmann Oswald Diestl; Major Alfred Klausser; Gefreiter Heinrich Ludke, Baron Wolf von Menzing; Franz Koch; Alfred Gunther

Industrialists

Putzi von Berthold; Otto von Stolz; Graf Kurt von Zeumer

Refugees

Herren A, B, C,; Siegfried Effelmann and wife; Rudolf Munser and wife; Alois Steiner, his wife and children; Gerda Rolf; Sophi Wilke

GLOSSARY

Abteilung	Section, unit (military)
Abwehr	Intelligence branch
Bierstube	Beer parlor
Blue Max	Soldier's slang for Pour le Merite medal
Bundestag	Federal parliament
Burgerbräukeller	A Munich beer hall
Coco	Slang for Communist
Feldherrnhalle	A Munich landmark
Fliegerzentrale	Flying Center
Forschungsamt	Research Department
Gasthof	Inn
Gauleiter	Nazi party district leader
Gestapo	Secret State Police
Graf, Gräfin	Count, countess
Heeresleitung	Army Command
Jagdgeschwader	Fighter wing (Luftwaffe)
Jasta	Squadron
Junker	Nobleman
Junkers	(Professor Hugo) aircraft designer
Kaiser	Emperor
Landräte	District governors
Luftwaffe	Air Force
NSDAP	Nationalsozialistiche Deutsche Arbeiterpartei (Nazi party)
Oberpräsidenten	Provincial leaders
Platz	City square
Putsch	Uprising, coup d'etat
Quatsch	Nonsense (American: baloney)
Regierungspräsidenten	National presidents
Reichskanzler	Chancellor
Reichstag	Legislature
Reichswehr	National Defense Force
Schloss	Castle
Schutz Staffel (SS)	Guard Echelon (elite troops)
Sondergruppe	Special Group
Staatsbibliothek	State Library
Staatsnervenheilanstalt	State Clinic for Nervous Disorders
Sturm Abteilung (SA)	Storm Troops
Truppenamt	Troops Office
Vierjahreszeiten	Four Seasons (Munich hotel)
Wehrmacht	Armed forces

MILITARY RANKS

German Army	SS	*U.S. Equivalent*
Schütze	SS-Mann	Private
Oberschütze	Sturmmann	Private first class
Gefreiter	Rottenführer	Corporal
Unteroffizier	Uterscharführer	Sergeant
Unterfeldwebel	Scharführer	Staff sergeant
Feldwebel	Oberscharführer	Master sergeant
Oberfeldwebel	Hauptscharführer	First sergeant
Stabsfeldwebel	Sturmscharführer	Sergeant major
Leutnant	Untersturmführer	Second lieutenant
Oberleutnant	Obersturmführer	First lieutenant
Hauptmann	Hauptsturmführer	Captain
Major	Sturmbannführer	Major
Oberstleutnant	Obersturmbann-führer	Lieutenant colonel
Oberst	Standartenführer	Colonel
(no equivalent)	Oberführer	(no equivalent)
Generalmajor	Brigadeführer	Brigadier general
Generalleutnant	Gruppenführer	Major general
General	Obergruppenführer	Lieutenant general
Generaloberst	Oberstgruppen-führer	General
Generalfeldmarschall	Reichsführer	General of the army

ACHTUNG! NUR FÜR DEN EMPFÄNGER!

10 April 1920

For the sole attention of:	Funk
From:	Chef der Heeresleitung
Subject:	Stachel, Bruno

I have received your nominees for Fliegerzentrale appointments and will be making my initial selections by Monday next.

I am curious as to why your list does not include Oberleutnant Bruno Stachel, who was, after all, one of our most celebrated combat fliers.

Please refresh me on his personal history and advise me of his current status.

Von Seeckt

Von Seeckt
General

ACHTUNG! NUR FÜR DEN EMPFÄNGER!

11 April 1920

For the sole attention of:	General von Seeckt Chef der Heeresleitung
From:	Oberst Funk
Subject:	Stachel, Bruno

Re your inquiry of 10/4/1920, subject officer is the only son of Ludwig and Emilie Stachel (nee Niederauer) who together own and operate a small pension-hotel in Bad Schwalbe im Taunus, north of Wiesbaden.

Upon completion of public schooling, subject Stachel joined the infantry regiment in Frankfurt and, after a tour of garrison duty, was transferred to the Imperial Flying Corps and trained as a fighter pilot at Jastaschule 1, Köln. He was posted to the Western Front in January, 1918, as a member of Jasta 77, commanded by the late Hauptmann Otto Heidemann, and soon won wide attention for his aerial exploits. In September, 1918, when Heidemann died in the crash of an aircraft under test at Johannisthal/Berlin, Stachel was named his successor as Jastaführer. A month later, at the special request of Hauptmann Hermann Göring, commander of the Richthofen Geschwader, he was transferred to Jasta 11, core unit of the Flying Corps' most illustrious group. In the 11 months of his front-line service, Stachel was credited with the destruction of 58 Allied aircraft.

Stachel's awards include Pour le Merite (the Blue Max); the Iron Cross first and second classes; Hohenzollern Medal with Swords; Saxe-Coburg-Gotha Medal for Bravery; the Hessian Cross; and numerous medals and citations from Austria-Hungary, Turkey, and lesser powers friendly to the Kaiser.

The press of many nations publicized Stachel's undeniable proficiency as a combat flier. However, he was not generally accorded the respect received by such luminaries as Boelcke, von Richthofen, Udet, and others, primarily because of his abrasive, volatile manner. Those who know him best (see source list attached hereto) assert that Stachel is ruthless, opportunistic, wily, and often intemperate. Yet these same sources unanimously note that he is capable of selfless, compassionate impulses, citing as a prime case in point his heroic rescue of a drowning French child—an act which propelled him to international popularity during the war's final summer.

Since his retirement to inactive duty at war's end, Stachel has become one of Café Society's more notorious profligates. Moreover, it is no secret that Stachel's marriage to Kaeti von Klugermann (nee Wolff), widow of the famed surgeon, the Graf Hugo von Klugermann, is tempestuous and marked by casual infidelities. The Gräfin, herself willful and occasionally less than discreet, owns the Fatherland's largest and most successful publishing venture. Informants are unwilling to speculate as to whether the marriage will last.

In light of the confidential and delicate nature of your plans for Fliegerzentrale, I considered it inappropriate to recommend an officer of such mercurial characteristics and dubious reputation.

Funk

gez: Funk
Adjutant

Enclosures: Officer's Service Record
Officer's Performance Reviews
Source List

1

The room was cold. He stood at the casement, pressing his forehead against the icy glass and trying to focus his gaze on the street below. The dawn was without character, still and empty and gray, and a spittle of snow eddied across the housetops.

He was in a hotel, of course, one of the bleak, impassive places that dotted the Old City near the Marienplatz. He blinked his eyes and tryed once again to identify the street, but Munich's ancient core, a webwork of cobblestone canyons faced in medieval gloom, could be perplexing under the best of conditions; shuttered and opaque, dim on the steel-colored rim of day as it was now, it told him nothing.

The anxiety and guilt were, as always, the stuff of nightmares. He continued to peer down at the deserted pavement, willing himself not to confront the bed behind him, because to avoid the fact was to prolong the fiction that he knew who she was. In awakening, he'd seen only a cloud of dark hair and the pale shoulders of a woman who slept uneasily in a snarl of bedding, facedown and clutching her pillow.

Eyes shut tight now against the gathering panic, he probed the night before, seeking a bench mark that would explain this day's portion of the familiar remorse.

He had left Sonnenstrahl in the Mercedes. After lunch. He'd driven to—where? Rudi's place? Or had it been Karlo's? There had been agreement to meet somewhere, and he was almost certain that Rudi and Karlo were to have been there with Friedl and Lisa. But where? Karlo favored Der Goldene Ritter, an inn near the Andechs monastery beside the Ammersee; Rudi doted on the intimacy of the Kabaret Odeon in the artists' quarter of Schwabing. The woman in the bed would not likely have been attracted by the pastoral beauty of the Andechs, so he must have found her in or near the other place. Such women were as available as beer in Schwabing. So it had probably been the Odeon. There were little tables, all connected by telephones, and when the dances and skits were under way it was acceptable practice to glance around the cabaret for attractive women to ring up. They would always answer, and he would always make the same outrageous proposition, and for all the shocked faces—all the angry slamming of receivers—there would be occasional laughter and acceptance.

But what difference did it make? The fact was that she was here, and he was here, and the barren room was a simple statement of the duplicity and degradation that had become his lot.

He tried to think of Kaeti, because he had found over the years that self-reminders of her arrogant tyrannies had routinely served to ease the wretchedness that always followed his binges. But on this gray morning its therapy failed, and he saw instead that recitals of his wife's little savageries were no justification—they represented, rather, rationalization of his own propensity for the rotten life.

In his fit of private honesty he recognized that Bruno Stachel was where he was not because of Kaeti's shortcomings but because of his own.

He knew, too, that it was absolutely fundamental that he begin—at this very moment—the effort to regain control of himself. An hour's delay could be fatal; in an hour he could resume his drinking and that would be that. He'd had his last spree months ago, a gross, demoralizing thing that had lasted for seven weeks, and he'd promised himself never again. So there was no explaining this new one, whose beginning had been worst of all. The drunkenness had come swiftly, fiercely, storm-like, despite his every will to the contrary. There had been none of the initial incandescence; none of the mellow Gemütlichkeit which, in the better times, had characterized the twenty minutes following the first drink.

The woman stirred, and there was a rustling, and he heard her step on the worn carpeting. He simply could not turn to face her.

"Morning, Liebchen." Her voice was dry, and without emphasis.

"Go back to bed," he said, his breath making a fog on the window.

Her arms encircled him from behind, and he could smell the female smell and the stale perfume and yesterday's tobacco and alcohol. He vowed he would not be sick.

"Why?" she murmured against his ear. "You have something in mind?"

"I have some thinking to do."

"You're a strange one."

"I'll say." (Why did he feel such panic? Why was he so frightened? And of what?)

"War hero. Flier. Playboy. Lover. And now—thinker."

"Go back to bed, I said." The realization that she knew who he was stirred an anger.

"Come with me. It's so early, and I'm cold—"

"No. Leave me alone."

"You'll freeze, standing here."

"Will you please shut up and leave me alone?" The anger surged, hot and barely contained. He knew he would have to get out of this place at once. His mind showed him tabloid headlines: "Woman Strangled in Old Town Hotel." (Oh, Jesus God, what was he doing here? What was his life, that he could materialize in this grubby corner of a rotting city, contemplating the murder of a whore? Who was he? Why?)

"Well, then," she said neutrally, her arms releasing him. "The party is over, I see."

"Right. So put on your clothes and go. If I owe you anything, take it from my wallet there on the table."

He sensed her hesitation, a kind of incredulous silence followed by a hard little laugh. "Owe me?" she said. "Why, you ridiculous whelp. I could buy and sell you with my lunch money."

That voice. That sudden imperiousness. He turned, unbelieving. "My God."

"You don't remember a thing, do you." It was more than a statement; it was accusation, mixed with contempt.

"I don't know what to say—"

"What does one say, Liebchen, when he awakens in a fleabag with the mother of his best friend?"

He felt an absurd need to correct her. Rudi had never been—could never be—his best friend. Rudi, heir to the Klingelhof-und-Reimer riches, for all his money, was a vacuous little bore. And his mother, for all her castles and manor houses and shiny automobiles and winters in Turkey and social renown, had the mind of a trollop.

The night just gone began to take shape in the gauze of his mind. Rudi had been in one of his intellectual poses, a pretense of interest in things artistic and academic, although in truth Rudi had the intellectual capabilities of a glowworm and endured concerts and galleries only as a means to some earthier end. (He loved to boast of the afternoon he'd had Monika von Diessen behind the biography stacks in the Staatsbibliothek—a dubious conquest at best, since Monika could be had by a cretin in the lobby of the Vierjahreszeiten at high noon.) There had been some preliminary drinking at the Kleinhesselohe, of all places, because Friedl said William Langhorn, the famous American actor, was rumored to be among the current crop of tourists who favored the place. Actually, the only actor they had seen there was the waiter, who pretended to be delighted with Rudi's beggarly tip. From the Englischer Garten they'd gone on to Brakl's Kunsthaus on the Beethovenplatz, where Rudi's mother was sponsoring the paintings of a fellow named Delocke, whose work, Rudi confided, had caught his Mutti's attention while slumming in Montmartre before the war.

Stachel had never met the Baroness von Klingelhof-und-Reimer, current custodian of billions amassed in generations of shipbuilding and colonial exploitation. Rudi talked about her a lot, of course, and he and Stachel had staged some rather spectacular parties at Schloss Löwenheim, her main home, where a hundred rooms had been piled atop a Bavarian hill by her medieval forbears. But the lady herself had always been in Italy, or South America, or Greece, and so Stachel's knowledge of her had been limited to Rudi's rambling anecdotes and the rather gaudy (and tastelessly flattering, it turned out) portrait hanging over the library fireplace in the Schloss' west wing. And so, with their introduction in the indirect lighting of the perfumed gallery, Stachel had felt that he was meeting a stranger who was no stranger.

There had been much talking, much laughing—that he could remember. And the later evening was marked by a champagne supper. But nothing, beyond the candlelight and a string quartet made up of old men with boiled shirts and drawn faces, was clear about supper or its aftermath.

She had dressed and was at the door, her expensive furs wrapped primly about her, her hair covered by a felt hat dotted with sequins. Her eyes were dark and oblique.

"Will I see you again?" she asked.

"I doubt it."

"Ah. You are feeling guilty, eh? You have betrayed the Gräfin von Klugermann. And adultery doesn't become you."

"She's not a von Klugermann. She's my wife."

She laughed softly.

"What day is it?" he said, rubbing his eyes.

"Friday, November 9, 1923."

"God. What happened to 1922?"

"Call me tomorrow, eh? I'll be at the town house. I'll be there through Christmas."

"I'm busy tomorrow."

"Mm-hm. You're a real adventure, my little war ace. But do cut down on your drinking. You drink entirely too much. It's bad for your stomach."

He closed the door behind her and went to bed, and falling across it, drifted into a feverish half-sleep full of half-dreams.

There was much singing and shouting. Noise. A drumming of thousands of feet on pavement. Horns sounding. Cheering.

His eyes were lacquered at the corners and filled with brine. His mouth was thick with a sourness, and it was difficult to lift his head from the pillow. In time, though, he managed to roll over and sit erect, struggling for breath and awareness, eventually to make his way unsteadily to the washstand.

Only after he was dressed did he venture a look out the window.

The mean little street was teeming with people, all jostling and waving red and white flags with black swastikas in the centers. Many of the men were wearing steel helmets—the kind issued to the army in '17. (Or had it been '16? In the latter half of the war, anyhow. He wasn't sure, since the Imperial Flying Corps hadn't taken steel helmets seriously until shortly before the Armistice, when the Allied bombers had been so thick overhead.) Whoever they were, and whatever they were up to, they were a ragged bunch, and angry, and shouting slogans.

He remembered the Mercedes, and suffered a spasm of alarm. He must have parked it somewhere nearby, and if it was in the way of that mob it could be reduced to tinfoil in minutes.

He pulled on his camel's-hair overcoat, settled the fedora on his head, and made for the stairway. The man at the desk was absorbed in the goings-on outside and barely glanced at him as he entered the tiny lobby.

"How much do I owe you?"

"Forty billion marks," the man said, his eyes fixed on the crowd seething past the front windows.

"Your sign says ten billion."

"That was yesterday. This morning it's forty. Our fabulous German inflation waits for no man."

"I've got only twenty-eight billion with me. Will you take a check?"

"No."

"Well, then. What do I do? Wash dishes or something?"

The man, a suety fellow with blue jowls, shrugged. "So I'll take the twenty-eight. It doesn't make any difference anyhow. Money is worthless."

"Not if you have it in Swiss or American, like our beloved aristocracy has it."

The man humphed and said nothing, his bitterness beyond words.

"What's all the row outside?" Stachel said, placing two ten-billion mark notes on the counter.

"I'm not sure. Otto Dittmann—he's the policeman for our street—Otto says it's those Nazi fellows. They're marching on Berlin, or something."

Stachel, blinking his aching eyes, counted out the remaining eight billion. "That's a hell of a march, I'd say. Think they'll make it before 1925?"

"I wouldn't joke about them if I were you. I hear they're a bunch of tough customers."

"What do they want?"

The man coughed dryly. "Who can say? The newspapers are all confused and they contradict each other. But Otto says they want to take over the government and end the inflation and kick the Jews out of the country."

"Well, I wish they'd do it more quietly. My God, what a din."

"Hung over?"

"A bit."

"Who was the lady? Your mother?"

"Yes. We're visiting the art galleries."

"Well, then, you'd better fill out another police card. The one you signed last night says you're mister and wife. From Wiesbaden."

"Can't we just let that one stand as it is?" Stachel sighed.

The man held out a pudgy hand, palm up. "That'll be another forty billion."

"I have only the twenty-eight."

"I'll take a check for the rest."

Stachel sighed again. "Such inhospitableness. With an attitude like that, you'll never win high ratings in the tourist guidebooks."

"Say it isn't so." The man laughed openly this time and Stachel wrote the bank draft with the scratchy desk pen, his hand trembling badly.

"Is there a back door to this place?"

"Down the hall, through the kitchen. The alley leads to the Rezidentsstrasse."

"Thanks. Here's your check."

"Keep it. I was only kidding. An extortionist I'm not."

"Take it. I feel charitable today."

"All right. So do I, as a matter of fact. I'm my favorite charity." The man laughed again, overwhelmed by his own wit.

The Mercedes was in the alley, aloof and unruffled by the clamor echoing in the streets beyond. Stachel went to the end of the narrow way and found that the Rezidentsstrasse was even more choked by crowds than the other street, which must have been Weinstrasse or one of its tributaries. He was about to return to the car—where he could at least sit in comfort while waiting out the carnival—when a face caught his eye.

The street, lined on both sides by applauding crowds and vicarious demonstrators, was only wide enough for eight men to march abreast. General Ludendorf, the World War brass hat, was leading the marchers, his famous scowl severely in place, his hands thrust in High Command arrogance into his overcoat pockets. But Ludendorf's was not the face that caused Stachel to pause. It was, rather, the broad face of a man in the van of the column, marching briskly in a leather coat whose open collar revealed the pale cross of the Blue Max.

Göring, of all people. Marching with a bunch of rabble.

Stachel hadn't seen him since the day Jagdgeschwader 1 had flown its Fokkers to Darmstadt, rather than surrender them to the French. Göring had been the last to lead the Richthofen Jasta and its JG 1 units, and, typical of the man, he had ordered the pilots to wreck their planes so that "those Frog swine" would have "nothing but splinters to play with." Stachel had wanted to keep his own machine and had plans to land it in the meadow behind his father's little hotel in Bad Schwalbe, where he could dismantle it and hide it under the hay in the cow barn. But Göring wouldn't hear of it—not that he was against hiding an aircraft, or even risking its being found by the French, but because he'd prided himself on never changing his mind after having given an order. So Stachel had flown dutifully to Darmstadt and, upon landing, steered his airplane directly into the side of a warehouse. It was a satisfying crash, even though he had split his lip in the impact.

The business of remembering gave way suddenly to an old soldier's reflex awareness of impending danger. There was a brittleness in the air, an electric tautness, and the subtle smell of fear seemed to emanate from the marching column. It was soon all around him, this feeling that something important and quite dreadful was about to happen.

He was standing at the curb, evaluating the sensation, when the sound of a shot, oddly muffled by the crowd noises, came from the Odeonsplatz. Almost at once there was answering fire—the thin crackling of rifles and the deeper thumping of a heavy machine gun.

He heard screams and the crying of women, the pounding of running feet, motors racing, the keening of richochets.

Ahead, toward the Feldherrnhalle, he could see the turbulent scrambling of panic. People were falling, some to remain still, others to crawl, moaning, for the cover of buildings. Ludendorf had disappeared, but huddled in a gutter, rocking slowly in ponderous agony, Göring clutched his leg and mouthed soundless curses.

Stachel, responding to some peculiar shade of anger, fought the human surf—shoving, elbowing, kicking. Somehow he got through to where Göring sat in a pool of blood, his gashlike mouth a zigzag of pain.

"Here. Hold on to my arm. I'll get you to a doctor."

"Stachel?"

"Hello, Captain. It's been a long time, eh? Five years, at least."

"You are with us? I didn't know—" Göring's voice fell off. "Oh, God, it hurts," he managed a moment later.

"Hold on, I said. I've got a car."

"The Führer—is he dead?"

"Führer?"

"Adolf Hitler. Our leader—"

"I don't know. Everything is very confused." Stachel peered toward the Odeonsplatz. "There are a lot of casualties. People lying in the street. Ludendorf must have got his. He was out in front."

"I'm in great pain, Stachel. My leg—"

"Put your arms around my neck. I'll lift you."

"I must know if the Führer is dead."

"We'll find out later. Now hang on."

"Watch out, for God's sake—I—" Göring's smoke-blue eyes stared fearfully over Stachel's shoulder.

Stachel glanced to his rear and saw a policeman coming at them in wild-eyed lynching madness, waving a riot club in furious anticipation and shouting unintelligibly.

Rising to his feet, Stachel held up a hand and bellowed, "Hold on, you idiot. This man's been hurt."

The policeman swung the club in a great, lopping arc, and Stachel, falling back, heard the hiss of its passing.

"What the hell are you trying to do? We're not—"

The club rose again, suspended for a tiny interval, then came down. This time it brushed Stachel's arm below his shoulder, and he could feel the shock even through the heavy sleeve.

Hotly angry now, Stachel launched a savage kick, which caught the policeman solidly in the crotch. The scream was lost in the cataract of noise that caromed through the Old Town labyrinth, but Stachel could see the man's pain and the club's impotent spinning on the pavement.

The policeman crouched, clutching his violated body, and Stachel snarled, "Have another, chum."

With the second kick the man went down, sinking beyond sight under a wave of mindless humanity.

Stachel turned to help Göring once again, but several men and two women, one who appeared to be a nurse, were half-dragging, half-lifting the big man to safety in the vestibule of a house.

Stachel brushed the gutter grime from his coat, adjusted his hat, and headed for his car. He sat behind the wheel for a time, numbly waiting for the streets to clear.

Somewhere in the interval a thought formed. *Führer?*

Any man who'd have Göring on his roster was no Führer. He'd be a follower. Göring tolerated no ideas, no directions, but his own.

2

Politics had never interested Stachel, primarily because of his father. Ludwig Stachel, a fastidious man who made a religion of hard work, was contemptuous of bureaucrats and their "parasite mentality." There were times, when the day's chores were done and a stein of beer had worked its mellowing effect, he would lecture his wife and son on the evils of the German system, in which, he said, the Bundesrat was the Kaiser's plaything, the Reichstag was nothing but a debating society, the Prussians dominated things by their vicious "circle system" of voting, and the Landräte, the Regierungspräsidenten, and Oberpräsidenten ruled, not from the people upward as claimed, but through edicts—from the Junker class downward. He would also—in remarkable departure from the mute acceptance that prevailed among the majority of Germans—rail against the "hidden government" of the military caste and the nobles who dominated it.

Stachel, from his fourth birthday, had been taught in school that Germany's government was the only good and effective form. Yet, even in his earlier years, he was able to see—thanks to his father's iconoclasm—that it was natural for his teachers to push this idea; they were, after all, government employees regulated by principles established by the state's rulers. And the message was always the same: There must be continuing reverence and awe for the Fatherland's military heroes, past and present. Even on Saturday nights, after six straight days of such indoctrination, he was turned over by the state-paid teacher to a state-paid clergyman who would, carefully and elaborately, put God's imprimatur on the German system and its warriors.

If the truth were known, only his mother's cool humor and closet intellectuality had saved Stachel from atrophy of the mind. Emilie Stachel was rather well educated for a woman of her time; in fact, there were some in the village who still spoke openly of her having married below herself. And, although she was warm and supportive in her attitudes toward her husband, Frau Stachel was not the kind to let his parochial biases go uncontested—especially if they threatened to stunt her son's mental growth. So, along with her often amusing and insightful commentaries on the arts and the philosophers—usually delivered when kneading bread dough, making beds, or washing windows—she had done her best to teach him what she knew of politics, which, as it soon developed, was precious little. But Stachel had listened to them both, eventually deciding on the basis of his own ruminations that his father had been right in the first place: Politics and politicians were a thoroughgoing pain.

Yet, when the World War came, Stachel had fallen in quickly with the system, since it was obvious to him that, if he was ever to break away from the inflexible condition that made an innkeeper's son ineligible for better things, he would have to become one of the military heroes Germany admired so much. So, in his way, he had used the system against itself, and with his success as a flying ace had come the fame that bridged the chasm between middle-class drabness and the upper-class good life. He had not used politics, he had used airplanes and guns to move from nowhere to somewhere. (The thought caused him to snicker. *God Almighty. This is somewhere?*)

Presumably, Göring had followed the same route.

And that was why it had been so ironic, so terribly sad, to have witnessed that ridiculous affair of the morning.

To see Göring heading up a column of slogan-shouting malcontents had been embarrassing—as if he had watched Genghis Khan leading the hymn singing at an evangelical welfare home. Göring was a pigheaded snob. He was arbitrary, ruthless, arrogant, and dangerous. Stachel had disliked him from the first, but later, in the squadron, he'd come to respect the man as one hell of a soldier, full of guts and sense of mission. So now, to have Göring striking absurd postures in a band of hooligans was to feel the old dislike giving way to a new and indefinable pity.

But who am I to pity anyone, he thought in sudden, savage self-contempt. *Göring may have degenerated into a street-corner anarchist, but I am a drunken poodle on a rich woman's string. At least Göring is trying to change the world. I can't even change my own mind.*

Steering the Mercedes through the main gate at Sonnenstrahl, he wanted a drink very badly; but, for the hundredth time since dawn, he vowed eternal abstinence.

Brass Buttons, the insufferable butler with the Roman nose and adenoids, took his hat and coat and informed him, in elevated Prussian tones, that Madame was in the sitting room.

Stachel strode the length of the baronial corridor, concentrating as he went on assembling a coolly sober expression. This, of all the bad parts, was the worst: to confront authority and pretend that all was well and under control and what, for heaven's sake, was everybody so upset about? And he particularly hated to confront Kaeti, since it was humiliating to play the penitent before a female authority whose own private life was so wretched.

She was standing at the large window, gazing at the blue hills across the placid expanse of the Ammersee. Reflected daylight traced her profile in a series of delicate arcs, and her hair, soft in a new bob, shone glossy and golden. She did not look at him, but said, with detachment, "You'll be pleased to learn that I plan to visit Sofie in Berlin."

Stachel tried to decide if the news pleased him or not. He found that it left him unmoved.

"When will you be back?"

"I'm not sure."

"Well, there's nothing for you here. The big city might be just what the doctor ordered." He wondered if he sounded as silly as he felt.

She turned and gave him a direct stare. "Where were you last night?"

"With Rudi and his mother. We took in an art show she's sponsoring."

"Lotte von Reimer?"

"The Baroness von Klingelhof-und-Reimer. Frau Croesus, so to speak."

"I can't imagine Lotte spending ten minutes with you. She's droll, even daring sometimes. But her tastes in people run considerably beyond you and your kind."

"Call her up and ask her. She'll send you an affidavit. On a silver tray."

"Why didn't you come home?"

"Why should I? You weren't here. And it wouldn't make any difference if you had been. We're not exactly great pals, are we."

"I came home early," she said in what seemed to be an irrelevance. "Maria took ill, after dinner, poor dear."

Stachel considered telling her what he knew of her dinner party at Maria's. He might, for instance, express surprise that Maria's illness had any bearing on Kaeti's evening, inasmuch as he understood—on good authority—that Maria was taking the waters at Bad Homburg and had turned over her guest cottage to Kaeti for her liaison with Sigmund Riefschneider, the soccer star. But he decided against it, suspecting that the Riefschneider matter was too high a trump simply to throw away in a routine confrontation like this. "Oh?" he said with careful sympathy. "That's too bad. I like Maria."

Kaeti crossed to a side table, where she selected a cigarette from a lacquered ebony box. Lighting up, she blew a long stream of smoke at the ceiling, then said, again without looking at him, "You look terrible. Why don't you get some new clothes—or something?"

"I've got three cabinets full of clothes I haven't worn yet. I look terrible because I feel terrible."

"You were drunk again last night, I take it."

He saw no reason to deny it. But he was angry nonetheless. "Well, a man has to have some kind of career and we can't all be soccer stars."

(*Damn, damn, damn.*)

"What's that supposed to mean?" she demanded in a carefully modulated voice.

"It's not supposed to mean anything. I happen to be a professional drinker, that's all. Inebriation is my career. My natural state."

"You're disgusting. There's no need for you to drink the way you do."

"There's no need for us to live the way we do."

She examined the end of her cigarette, her manner pensive and oddly taut. "Please don't start all that again," she said. "It would not suit me to give you your freedom."

He sank into a chair and considered her. This, too, was part of the system, he sighed inwardly. The social castes still prevailed, even though the war was long over and the monarchy and its noblemen and courtiers and satraps had been disenfranchised by Weimar's ridiculous republicanism. A mere glance at any first-class hotel register would tell the story. When a woman entered her name as a guest—today, as before the war—she would declare her husband's title as her own: Mrs. Bank President Schmidt; Mrs. Second Lieutenant Klaus; Mrs. Factory Owner Schultz. The relative social positions among such a trio were never in doubt. Mrs. Factory Owner Schultz might own a dozen villas, travel in a private railroad car, sail in her personal steam yacht, and have a husband who developed products of stupendous importance to a grateful mankind, but she would be forever compelled to play second fiddle to Mrs. Second Lieutenant Klaus.

Kaeti, widow of the great surgeon, the Graf Hugo von Klugermann, was herself, as a commoner, a creature of imperial times; in those days, if a girl had the chance to marry three equally attractive men—a rich scientist, a successful merchant, or a destitute army officer with a "von" in his name or a Blue Max at his throat—she wouldn't hesitate a moment in taking the military man. And once the Graf was dead, leaving her his aristocracy and his millions, Kaeti had been free to acquire the ultimate, the definitive trophy: Bruno Stachel, who in that ancient time had been an ace—a warrior acclaimed from the North Sea to the Dardanelles.

"I could walk out and go to South America," he suggested finally, for lack of anything better to say.

She glanced at him, sarcasm in her small smile. "Oh, could you now," she said. "That would be a day among all days, wouldn't it."

"Don't be so smug."

"I know too much about you, darling. I know you don't have the nerve."

"You want to see my war record? The Kaiser himself had praise for my nerve."

She sighed, giving sound to her indifference. "Please, Bruno, don't belabor me with that old song. I probably know more about your war record than anyone else—including the fact that you killed my nephew, and that you were given the Blue Max for an action you were too drunk to remember to this day."

"Willi flew into a factory chimney in a fog. Which I almost did myself, right after him."

"That's not what my informants say."

"To hell with your informants. They're liars. And, since Willi was your lover, it suits you to romanticize his death."

She gave him an exasperated glance. "I simply can't go through all this again." She turned deliberately to study herself in the large wall mirror, patting her hair. "I'll be in Berlin for at least a month," she said.

"Is the soccer player going with you?"

She crossed to the hallway arch, her heels tapping on the parquet flooring. In the alcove, she paused to sift through the mail, her blue eyes clouded with preoccupation. Then, with no further comment, she went upstairs, humming a little tune.

By nightfall Stachel had ridden through the stormy urge to drink himself into a state of forgiveness. Ironically, a high alcoholic content would always provide him with a special benignity in which it was possible to deny that Kaeti meant him ill. With drunkenness came a peculiar willingness to see her sins against him as unintentional slights.

But not this night. Tonight he would cultivate his rage by remaining determinedly sober.

3

The newspapers made much of the Nazi Putsch. Hitler had not died in the street, as rumored, but had been arrested and held for trial. Göring, while known to have been wounded, had not shown up among the fourteen dead and was presumed to be hiding in the Austrian Tyrol.

Stachel had read most of the accounts with the ambivalence of one who simultaneously gloats over having put a police bully in his place and worries over the potential punishment for the deed. But none of the thousands of words gave note of a policeman's violated groin, and so he eventually grew bored with the whole matter and reverted to pacing through the silent halls of Sonnenstrahl and sending sullen glances at the wine cabinets.

As he often did in the slough of his loneliness, he fell into recollections of the war days. A mere glimpse of a patch of sky, a tuft of cumulus in the blue, and his mind would call up the racket of straining engines, the snapping of machine guns, the sighing of an enemy airplane spinning out of control. In the midst of the dying all around, the world of those times had been paradoxically alive, with its sights and smells and tastes intensely immediate, insistent. But today's memory, benumbed as it was by the intervening six years of dissipation and aimlessness, offered no sensation, and his mental re-creations of the days aloft were now akin to the moody woolgathering of the withered roué.

He went into Munich one day after New Year's, possibly in reflex to Kaeti's suggestion that he do something about the seediness that was taking him over, inexorably and vinelike. But the streets were still chaotic, and the better shops were closed and shuttered against the starving, who wandered aimlessly and waved useless currency in the winter air, and so he had returned to Sonnenstrahl and his solitary ruminations.

It was on a blustery, snow-swirling morning when Brass Buttons drifted, wraithlike, into the study to announce a caller.

Stachel, his slippered feet thrust toward the fire, stirred in the big leather chair, yawned, put down his magazine, and said, "Who in hell visits people on a day like this? And before noon, for God's sake."

"He did not present a card, sir," Brass Buttons sniffed. "However, he did say his name is Bormann. Herr Martin Bormann."

Stachel yawned again. "Never heard of him."

"Shall I say you're not in, sir?"

He gave in to curiosity. "No. Bring him in. And fetch some coffee."

The butler disappeared, and Stachel went to the diamond-paned window, pulling his smoking jacket closer against the chill. His gaze wandered over the lawns, which spread, white and cold and dead, to the sweep of frozen lake. A bird, dark and forlorn, circled in the wind, called a thin cry, then settled disconsolately onto a branch of an uneasy yew—an incursion of poverty on the preserves of the rich. He thought of the government buildings in Munich, and how their fussy elegance had been so mocking of the beggars who huddled at their gates.

Bormann proved to be a chunky man wearing a nondescript trenchcoat and carrying a velour fedora, as if he'd been unwilling to grant its custody to Brass Buttons for fear of losing it. There was a crescent scar on his forehead and his nose was bulbous, and there was an air of obsequiousness about him. Stachel disliked him at once, recognizing in him the bourgeois who'd found a home in some bureaucracy and was as dull and utilitarian as a barn door.

Bormann smiled fatuously and bowed slightly. "I'm calling

at the request of Captain Ernst Röhm, who is, if you please, under temporary arrest."

"Arrest? For what?"

"Perhaps you've heard of the recent incident at the Odeonsplatz."

"Who hasn't? You're one of those Nazis, then?"

"May I sit down?"

Stachel nodded toward the stiff-backed chair by the fireplace. He didn't want this clod to get too comfortable. He was sorry now that he'd asked that coffee be brought in.

Bormann sat on the edge of the chair, as uneasy as a schoolboy in the headmaster's office. His eyes, oddly vacant, roamed about the paneled room and its towering tiers of books.

"So if the Nazis are under arrest, what are you doing here?" Stachel said, sinking into his armchair.

Bormann smiled primly. "I am not an important person, Herr Stachel. And our jailers are old comrades. They let us come and go. Besides, the authorities don't know exactly how to handle us, or the whole counterrevolution, for that matter. They put us in jail, but not too firmly. Or for too long."

There was a long pause, and Stachel realized the man was waiting for him to say something. Lacking anything better, he said, "What about Göring? He's one of you, I understand. And he was hurt in that thing at the Odeonsplatz. I know. I saw him there."

"Yes," Bormann said, nodding with elaborate sincerity. "The wound was a bad one. But he managed to escape to Austria, and Karin—his wife—has sent a message saying he'll recover."

"How did he get mixed up with a bunch like you?"

There was no evidence that Bormann had been offended by the question and its bluntness. He maintained his air of earnestness and polite attention. "It's a natural result of the officers' class struggle, I suppose."

"Struggle? What struggle?"

At this, Bormann's placid façade showed the tiniest of readjustments, a flicker suggesting an inner astonishment. But then it was gone, and Stachel sensed irritably that he'd revealed himself to his caller as the uninformed ass he truly was.

"Surely," Bormann said, his tone just short of condescension, "you are feeling its sting yourself, Herr Stachel. A man of middle-class heritage, your education interrupted, for a brief time living high and lordly as a German officer and aviation hero, then to be thrown into nothingness—uselessness—when the generals gave up and sent you running home. I'd guess you're feeling the sting worse than any of us"—he glanced about him—"for all your, ah, affluence."

Stachel sniffed. "I'm not aware of any struggle. Unless you mean the fight to keep from dying of boredom."

Bormann smiled again. "That's part of it, of course. But I'm speaking of the larger struggle, in which the junior officers—the lieutenants, the captains, the majors—are giving the old fellows, the doddering brass hats, the elbow. When this idiotic Weimar Republic disbanded the army, the brass wasn't hurt a bit.They either kept their jobs or retired on fancy pensions. But what happened to you and Göring? To Röhm? You are the German army. You represent its spirit, its tradition. And what have the generals done to all of you? They make you night watchmen, hotel detectives, bill collectors, or they put you in the Fatherland's attic to gather dust."

"So who is Röhm, and what does he want?"

"Captain Röhm," Bormann said blandly, "is adjutant to Colonel von Epp, commander of the Reichswehr's infantry force in Bavaria. It's a stupid, demeaning post, but the captain manages to use it to larger advantage."

"What's that mean?"

"Let's put it this way," Bormann said in the manner of one who has made the same speech many times. "The spurts of revolution we've been witnessing since '18 aren't uprisings of the German people—they're symptoms of a larger battle to control the source of power in a modern society—the middle class. The middle-class worker is really the guts of any military organization; without him, the military will fold. The army needs the middle-class worker to survive, so it's fighting against the revolutionaries who would destroy the middle class. In other words, it's not fighting to protect the government or the bankers and the capitalists, but to protect itself. And—"

Stachel broke in, recognizing solid ground for a change. "Protect itself with what? The Versailles Treaty has stripped Germany of every weapon it ever had."

Bormann turned the hat in his hands, studying it with coinlike eyes. "I'm not speaking of weapons alone—although we've plenty of those hidden away. I'm speaking more of the effort to capture and hold on to the army's greater need, its greater resource—the hearts and minds of the working middle class that makes up its center of gravity."

"Weapons? You've hidden some?"

"Of course. A gigantic arsenal doesn't simply evaporate when generals surrender, my friend."

Stachel thought about that for a time, and Bormann waited, seeming to listen to the ticking of the clock, the crackling of the fire, the hissing of the snow at the windows.

"Sort of tricky, isn't it?" Stachel said finally. "Don't the Englishmen and the Frenchies patrol these kinds of things?"

"Indeed they do, Herr Stachel. Their control commission runs all around the country, making a lot of fuss about finding blunderbusses hidden in this barn, fowling pieces discovered in that cellar. But the good stuff, the machine guns and the mortars and the rifles—they do a lot of looking the other way."

"Why?" Stachel asked, incredulous.

"They're as unhappy with the Communists as we are. The world revolution is moving west, from Russia through Germany to the Rhine. The Allied army types are in the same struggle we're in, so to speak, and our hidden armored cars and Mausers could make a difference to them. Captain Röhm gets along quite well with some of the Englishmen, as a matter of fact. Even some of the Frogs and their spaghetti-bender pals from down below."

"What a world."

"Yes."

"What do you mean—Röhm gets along with them?" Stachel said, following his curiosity again. "He's in charge of the hidden weapons?"

"Only in Bavaria," Bormann said.

"What else does the captain do? I mean, he sorts papers for a colonel, he's pals with some enemy officers, he rides herd on a weapons cache. What else does he do? Play piano in a whorehouse?"

Still unoffended, Bormann smiled, "He has also secretly enlisted a hundred thousand men in a volunteer army he's named, ah, the Gymnastics and Sports Division of the German Workers Party. Ostensibly, they've nothing to do with the official, the legal, Reichswehr, but actually they're an extension of the Reichswehr and they're all under Captain Röhm's command."

"God. He's a busy rascal. What's this secret army supposed to do?"

"Stand by for directions from the Führer."

"Oh, that Hitler fellow again. He's a former corporal, and, from what I hear, a real nut, to boot. What influence does he have with your brave officer types?"

Bormann was about to answer when the tall, varnished doors whispered open and Brass Buttons brought in a tray with coffee and an assortment of cakes. They watched in silence while he poured. When they were alone again, Stachel gave Bormann a long stare and, sipping his coffee, said across the rim of the cup. "Well?"

"Adolf Hitler," Bormann said, "is destined to save Germany."

Stachel snorted. "And I'm to be Queen of England."

"You may scoff, Herr Stachel, but it's true nonetheless."

"It seems to me that Röhm's in a better position to save Germany than Hitler is. Röhm's got the men, the guns."

"But the Führer has the Geist—the spirit. He will give the German people a new strength, a restructuring of their noble character. Men and guns will implement his will, translate his holy spirit into deeds and accomplishment."

"Oh, come now, Bormann. You're talking to Bruno Stachel, not some Boy Scout."

"I hope," Bormann said evenly, "I'm talking to a fellow worker. A collaborator in the cause."

"Don't be ridiculous. I'm no politician."

"But you are—were—a German Officer. One who comes most highly recommended by Hermann Göring. Who, incidentally, has told Captain Röhm of how you saved his life in that shambles at the Odeonsplatz."

"I didn't save his life. I saved my own. That policeman was getting ready to beat me to death."

Bormann drained his coffee cup in three gulps, then set it carefully on the table. "Göring said you're a tough, brave man."

"Well, Göring was never known for his brilliance."

"You won't help us, then?"

"I told you—I don't like politics. I don't know anything about politics. I don't want anything to do with politics."

"Captain Röhm is not asking you to be a politician, Herr Stachel. He's asking only that you make your talents available to us."

"Talents? Hell, I'm a flier. That's all. You want me to ring doorbells and kiss behinds for votes, you've got the wrong customer."

Bormann shifted in his chair, preparing to rise. "Well, Herr

Stachel, I might have put it badly. Instead of talents, perhaps I should have said 'associations'. We'd very much appreciate your representation among the, ah, well-to-do circles in which you travel."

Stachel was scornful. "You're wrong again, chum. My wife's the one with the class, the one who travels among the la-de-da. I'm just along for the ride."

"Göring said you're often self-deprecating. I can't believe that a hero of your stature is without friends and influence in high places."

"You want me to try to sell your Hitler and Röhm to the swells, so that they might cough up some cash to pay for your doorbell ringing? Is that it?"

"Something like that."

"Forget it, chum. It's out of my line."

Bormann stood up, turned his hat in his hands again, and, after another of his protracted pauses, made for the door. With his hand on the knob, he glanced back. "I'm sorry you feel that way. We might have accomplished a lot together. Captain Röhm will be disappointed. Göring, too."

"By the way, Bormann, how do you know you can trust me? I mean, you pop in here, tell me about secret armies, weapons caches. How do you know I won't call the authorities?"

Bormann smiled dimly. "You won't, Herr Stachel. Because, your supercilious ways notwithstanding, you need us more than we need you. You'll find that out, someday."

The large doors closed behind Bormann, and Stachel stood for a long time, staring into the fire.

4

Anna-Marie Elsbet Karlotte, the Baroness von Klingelhof-und-Reimer, emerged from her bath and dried herself by the large window that overlooked the tree-lined reaches of the Maria Theresa Strasse and the Isar River beyond. The twilight was a time of blue-shadowed snow and pink sky and golden traceries across Munich's distant horizons, and she gazed at it absently, preoccupied with her recollections of last fall's encounter with Bruno Stachel.

Winter was almost gone, and she hadn't seen him since, but she felt once again the glow of self-congratulation—a flutter of relief mixed with secret triumph. The episode had taught her that she was still a woman capable of attracting a lusty young goat, by God, despite the conventional Quatsch that consigned females who had passed forty (or had marriageable children) to a sexual limbo as bleak and arid as the Gobi. With Stachel—the turbulent, inscrutable, angry-eyed, sardonic, wonderfully sensual bumpkin—there had been the sense of collision, a slamming together of elemental forces. And she'd not been found wanting, having given the arrogant hayseed a combat to remember.

She dropped the towel and turned to examine herself in the mirrored wall. Her skin and teeth were the best features. Her figure was still trim, and her eyes were rather striking, too. But there was a smooth, golden quality to the skin, and the teeth were strong and even and white, a combination that suggested hygiene and vigor.

She dressed slowly, thinking of years that were gone. Men had rarely given her problems—even in Berlin, where everything conspired against one's powers of self-control. Through birth and circumstance, she'd grown up in the aristocratic Berlin of high walls, ornate gates, and the blasé nobility. But some ingrained wariness (her native sense of the politic?) had helped her hold off the dandies who set the social tone for that citadel of pomp and egocentrism. Pride of birth seemed to be the only fire those men possessed, and she'd learned early the folly of playing moth to their flame. The lesson came when little Erika von Loden was seen accepting a carriage ride home from her hairdresser's. The Graf von Brismantier was one of the most lofty and mannered of all the Prussians, but he was also known (to all but Erika, apparently) for certain proclivities, and in no time at all the whispering had begun behind the high, polished windows. She herself knew for a fact that Erika was a naïve, fastidiously moral person who wanted nothing more than someday to be a good wife and mother to some decent man and his brood. But the innocent ride with the Graf had cost her: from that day on Erika was known among the elite as the wanton who performed fellatio in cabriolets. Not that the world-wise Berliner had anything against such exotic forms of dalliance;

it was simply fun to gossip about its occurring in a horse-drawn carriage at high noon. Nonetheless, Erika was hardly a dinner-party fixture after that, and the last anyone had heard of her was that she'd gone to live with an aunt in Chamonix. And Lotte, learning the lesson, held free of sordid entrapments—much to the relief of her parents, who had raised her in the immutable mores of the true aristocracy and had nothing but contempt for the democratic permissiveness sweeping the Continent.

Descending the stairway, she decided that her preference for older men had dwindled in direct proportion to her own advance through the years. She had been attracted to her husband because he'd had that mature air of calm good will and the level eyes and black hair graying at the temples and the sensitive hands and the mouth that hinted of passion under rein. Her early lovers had been similarly set up. But in time he'd become fat and cranky, and Rudi, their only child, had turned out to be a rotten little poop, and one day came the realization that she was considered middle-aged and beyond passion. She'd begun to believe it herself, until Stachel.

Georg, the butler who supervised the town house, came from the salon to give her a frosty smile. Opening the door for her, he intoned, "Your cab's outside, madam. Alois reports that your car should be operable again by tomorrow morning. Some prankster has apparently tampered with it."

"Such a nuisance. Tell Alois to look into a new car, will you?"

"Yes, madam."

"I'm dining with the Von Ellenders and the Mecklenbergs at the Vierjahreszeiten. If Rudi calls, tell him I'll ring him in the morning."

"He's been here and left, madam. He picked up some caviar for a supper he's having at his flat."

"He could at least have said hello."

"Yes, madam."

In the doorway, she hesitated. "Georg—"

"Yes, madam?"

"If a Herr Stachel calls, ask him to have me paged at the hotel." She didn't really expect a call. There hadn't been a word from Bruno in three months, and there was no reason to believe there'd be one tonight. But it never hurt to hedge.

Pulling on her gloves, she entered the purpling evening, her nose tingling at once from the dry winter air. She went carefully down the steps and, nodding at the cab driver, who stood impassively at the vehicle's open door, said, "Vierjahreszeiten, please."

"Of course, madam."

As the car moved off, she settled against the cold leather and resumed her daydreaming. Her mind went to Berlin again, and there was the realization that she didn't miss it at all. For years now, Berlin had been a political and military steamboiler, bulging and hissing with rumor and intrigue, and here in Munich, in this gloomy and defeated city, life managed to drone on unchanging, soft and quiet and undemanding. From the great court ceremonial of Schleppencour, the ultimate gala in the court of Wilhelm II, to the Bogenhausen town house and the country estate: from Bedlam to Eden. From frost to incandescence.

Good God. That Stachel adventure was making her moon like a schoolgirl. She laughed aloud.

At the circle, where the Maximiliansbrücke arced off from Maria Theresa, the cab slowed to a halt at the curb and the driver climbed out, without a word, to disappear behind the monument. Incredulous, speechless, she watched as another man appeared, seemingly from nowhere, to take the wheel.

"Vierjahreszeiten, right?" he said over his shoulder.

"Now look here," she said testily, "what's this all about?"

"Please, dear Baroness. Don't be frightened. I simply want to talk to you for a few moments."

"Who are you, anyway? I mean, after all—"

"My name is Bormann. Martin Bormann. But that's not at all important. I'm only a messenger, and this was the best way to deliver the message. For your safety and mine."

"Safety? Safety from what?"

The man, lumpish and square in his overcoat and slouch hat, eased the car into the thinning traffic and headed south on the boulevard.

"Where are you taking me?" she said, anger building. "I'm to meet friends at the Vierjahreszeiten, and you should be driving me across the bridge."

"Relax, Baroness—I'm simply going by way of the Ludwigsbrücke. It'll give us a few more minutes to chat."

"I have nothing to chat with you about, you clod."

The man held up a hand, a small gesture demanding silence. "Please. Just be quiet for a moment or two, eh? I have a message. When you hear it, you might have some questions. That's what I mean by chat."

She sank back against the seat, her anger mixed with a

rising sense of excitement, and adventure. Unbelievable, she thought; I must be more fatally bored than I suspected. First Stachel, then abduction, and all I can do is enjoy the pitty-pat of my schoolgirl heart. The next thing you know, I'll be breaking out in pimples and pressing flowers in musty books. She wanted to laugh again, but instinct told her that this would be a mistake, in view of the man's intense seriousness.

"Very well," she said, putting on her most lofty Prussian air, "deliver your message."

"Are you acquainted with General Hans von Seeckt, commander of the Reichswehr?"

"Of course."

"Do you have ready access to him?"

"No. He has ready access to me."

The man nodded, as if approving her answer. "Good. Even the most mighty are putty in the hands of a lovely woman, eh?"

"Your gallantry is as awkward as your language is trite, Herr Bormann."

"We'd like you to contact the general. We'd like you to ask him to do you a favor." Bormann, for all his somber earnestness, seemed privately amused.

"We? Who's we?"

"Just say we're friends of Hermann."

"Hermann? Hermann who?"

"Göring."

"Ha. I'm not surprised. So what do you and Hermann want of Hans?"

Bormann made the turn onto the Ludwigsbrücke, blowing the taxi's horn at a van that wallowed uncertainly in the snowy lane ahead. The ruts were too deep and icy to allow him to pass safely, so he gave up the effort.

"Von Seeckt," Bormann said, "as the officer appointed to head the Reichswehr under the Versailles Treaty, has set up—without authorization—a so-called Fliegerzentrale, or a kind of secret cadre for an air force that will, unhappily, remain on paper for some time to come. Göring, because of his political activism is no favorite of von Seeckt's and therefore can't expect the old man to appoint him to this cadre. Göring plans someday to be commander of the German Air Force, so he wants to plant a friend who, when von Seeckt retires or dies, will be able to facilitate his return to the service."

"What has all this to do with me?" the Baroness broke in irritably. "I know nothing of armies and politics and air forces. You and Hermann are wasting your time."

"Patience, Baroness. We simply want you to contact von Seeckt and propose that he appoint an officer to the Fliegerzentrale."

"What officer, may I ask?"

"Oberleutnant Bruno Stachel."

"Oh?"

"Simply remind the general that Stachel, as a demonstrated expert in aerial combat—a national hero, and all that sort of thing—would be indispensable in the effort to organize the future German military air arm."

The Baroness sneered elegantly. "Come now, Bormann. You underestimate Hans von Seeckt. He is a paragon of military virtue. He is unwavering in character and devotion to duty. He would as soon take my advice on military matters as I'd take your advice on questions of etiquette."

"So I understand. But that should only make the challenge greater for a lovely lady, eh? I daresay you'll find a way."

Her anger was returning. "Just what makes you think I'll do what you ask, anyhow? You burst into my cab, insert yourself in my personal life, and expect that I'll simply comply with your demands. Well, let me inform you, Herr Bormann"—she gave a deliberately contemptuous emphasis to the title—"that as soon as you deliver me to the Vierjahreszeiten I propose to have you arrested for kidnapping."

Bormann nodded. "Very well. And with my arrest, you'll be shot."

It pleased her in a strange way to realize that the man's threat did nothing but stimulate her. The thought: *My God, with the prospect of my own murder, I've never felt so alive.*

"What if I speak to Hans and he refuses to appoint Bruno? Will I be shot anyhow?"

"That's for you to worry about, Baroness."

"Are there any other conditions?"

"No," Bormann said reasonably, "not really. Except, of course, it's most important that you don't tell Stachel about this discussion. We'd prefer to have him think that von Seeckt sought him out, so to speak. . . . Now, here we are at the hotel, all safe and sound. If you'll wait a moment, I'll help you out."

But as the cab pulled to the curb, she opened the door herself and stepped to the snowy sidewalk, then leaned into the cab's window to smile her most winning smile.

"I'll help you, Bormann. But meanwhile there's one thing you can do for me."

"What's that, Baroness?"

"You can kiss my rosy ass, you son of a bitch."

She turned and, laughing, allowed the doorman to escort her to the lobby.

5

He had been in Berlin only once before, and he hadn't liked it then, either. It was too big, too gray, too heavy with stone and iron, too stilted with fussy trees and brick walls and gas lamps and formal gardens and snappish, haughty people. It had been in the last year of the war, when he and his squadron leader, Otto Heidemann, tested the new fighter planes in the official tryouts at Johannisthal. Heidemann had died when the Adler entry broke up around him at two hundred meters, and there had been a lot of subsequent drinking and days of melancholy wandering along the lonely streets. For Bruno Stachel, Berlin was not a happy place.

The new republican government was located at Weimar, since Berlin had become a hotbed of Communist agitation and was therefore considered an unsafe home for the embryonic democracy. But the real government—the system in which the landed squires and the noble families and the professional militarists collaborated in their subtle perpetuation of feudalism—was seated here in Berlin, rooted stolidly and immutably in the monuments and heroic fluted columns and towering statuary. And, as if reflecting the fact, there was a sooty gloom that seemed to mute the sunlight and freeze the city in an everlasting sulk. The effect was particularly oppressive in the headquarters building of the Truppenamt.

"The general will see you now," the Oberst said, his pomaded hair glistening in the pale light from the high windows. "He will give you eight minutes."

Stachel was wondering, of course, why the general was giving him any time at all. The summons, coming out of nowhere, had carried no clues:

"Oberleutnant Bruno Stachel, formerly of the Imperial Flying Corps, will report to the office of Chef der Heeresleitung at 13:30 hours, 14 April 24. Officer will be reimbursed at per diem rate, plus travel allowance. Signed: Funk, Adjutant."

He had read it many times during the train ride from Munich.

The Oberst led him through a pair of tall, enameled doors to a spartan and unfriendly anteroom. While Stachel waited, the man tapped politely at another door, then swung in to announce, "Stachel is here, sir."

"Send him in, Colonel Funk."

Stachel, ill at ease in his tweed suit and celluloid collar, wondered if he should salute. Von Seeckt was a prepossessing man, monocled, mustached, with a dancer's waist and a head of white hair, carefully barbered. He stood by the window, erect and inscrutable in his faultless uniform and glistening boots. He appeared to be the kind of man who would expect a salute.

"Oberleutnant Bruno Stachel reporting as ordered, sir."

"At ease, Stachel."

"Thank you, sir."

"I've read of your exploits on the Western Front, of course."

Stachel said nothing, standing stiffly in the center of the room, sensing the old man's condescension. He hated himself for his own sense of inadequacy, the odd defensiveness that invariably took over when he came up against men whose major claims to superiority were time on earth and money in the bank. The feeling was not helped in this case by the general's reputation for intellectual agility, administrative genius, linguistics, and mastery of the military sciences. Rudi had told him the night before his departure that von Seeckt was a long-time friend of his mother, the Baroness, and anybody who entered the general's presence had better have his wits about him because the old man was a tiger, icy with social graces, elegance of mind and purpose, and a total unforgiveness for stupidity and inefficiency. To Stachel's mind, this had to be true, since Rudi had confided—with high good humor and indifference—that the general considered him, for all his mother's wealth, to be a thoroughgoing clod.

"What would you say is Germany's greatest problem these days, Stachel?"

Even for one so poorly informed as Bruno Stachel on the political and economic forces that were tearing Germany to shreds, there could be only one answer to the question. Hans von Seeckt, the archetypal aristocrat and career officer—despite his renown for broad-gauge perceptions in literature, the performing arts, and philosophy—would be almost guaranteed to suffer a basic narrowness when it came to the Fatherland and its destinies.

"The Versailles Treaty, sir."

The general turned to regard the metallic day outside, and Stachel thought a flicker of approval might have crossed the old man's frozen features.

"The treaty is a poison that threatens the very life of our nation, Stachel. There is virtually not a single problem among the many that belabor Germany today that doesn't stem from that atrocious document."

Stachel congratulated himself on his successful guess. He wondered why this pleased him.

"What do you think we ought to do about it, Stachel?"

Again, for a man like von Seeckt, there was only one answer. "Ignore it, sir."

"But to ignore it would invite full-scale occupation of Germany by the French and English."

"Perhaps, Herr General. But there should be many ways to get things done without the French and English knowing about it."

"Oh?" The general's tone was soft, almost baiting. "What about Germany's word of honor—the Fatherland's scrupulous adherence to agreements made and signed?"

Stachel sensed that von Seeckt was probing his capacity for deceit. Well, interviews with General Staff officers were never the time for faintheartedness:

"The treaty is not a document drawn in good faith, I'd say, Herr General. It seems to me it's a deliberate, sly attempt by our enemies, not to ensure world peace but to enslave Germany. Despite its high-toned moral posturing, it's a license to tyrannize and plunder. It was not drawn in good faith, and so Germany need not consider itself bound by ethics missing in the character and aims of the other signers. After all, even the most righteous of men wouldn't hesitate to cancel a promissory note he'd written to the order of a convicted extortionist."

There. That should hold the old bugger.

"Sit down, Stachel."

"Thank you, sir."

Von Seeckt removed the monocle from his left eye and polished it with a snowy handkerchief, his gaze still centered on the gray sprawl of buildings beyond the window. "We have no air force, you know."

"Yes, sir. I know."

"We must build a new one."

"Of course, sir."

"It so happens that I agree with your assessment of the Fatherland's position as a signer of the Versailles madness. The treaty is an exercise in ruthlessness and deceit, and Germany is no more bound by its excesses than I am bound by the Torah. Our single most urgent duty as officers and gentlemen is to negate the treaty and to provide Germany with an army that's highly mobile, versatile, singularly proficient, and protected—thoroughly and indisputably—by aircraft. But it's next to impossible to create an air force, to build planes, organize them into units, supply them, and train the men who will fly and maintain them, without the Allied Control Commission's knowledge. Wouldn't you say?"

"Well, Herr General," Stachel said, coming up with the only answer that seemed to present itself, "that's supposing that you built all those planes and trained all those people within the borders of Germany."

"What do you mean by that?" von Seeckt asked quietly.

Stachel permitted himself a shrug. "What's to keep us from building our air force in South America, or someplace like that? Secretly, so to speak."

"That would require enormous sums, Stachel." Von Seeckt's tone was neutral.

"To be sure, Herr General. But the, ah, sting could be eased if we were to build our air force in a country that's somehow beholden to us—that needs our friendship, or whatever, enough to help us carry the load."

"What country would you suggest?" The general was staring directly at him now, his ice-blue eyes alert.

"I don't know, sir. I don't have many facts, what with my being out in pasture so long and knowing only what I read in the newspapers. Our allies in the war are in as bad shape as we are, I guess, and I'm not sure what other nations think of us, or are willing to do for us. I'd need more information before I could answer your question with anything that approaches good sense." Stachel hoped his confession of ignorance was not read as stupidity. The general's mention of a new air force had put an entirely new light on the interview, and he was aware now of wanting very much to measure up to the old man's standards.

The general's stern mouth softened into the slightest of smiles. "Your honesty is refreshing, Stachel. A man long removed from events can't possibly be expected to evaluate their consequences. Yet there are many who would try to back and fill and pretend to great wisdom in these areas. I'm pleased to find that you're not one of these."

"It's my nature to be frank, Herr General."

Von Seeckt sat in the swivel chair behind the polished desk. He made a little steeple with his fingers and regarded Stachel gravely. "It might interest you to learn, Stachel, that I have already taken steps to recreate an air force. The program is already well under way."

"It does indeed interest me, Herr General." Stachel thought a bit of flattery might do here. "And, while I applaud you, I'm not surprised, in view of your great repute as a problem-solver."

Von Seeckt, Stachel saw, was, as a paragon, not above pleasure over compliments. The general registered another tight little smile and waved a dismissing hand.

"There are," von Seeckt said, "eight million men of military service age in the Reich. But the treaty permits us only a token defense force—an army of a hundred thousand men, including no more than four thousand officers. Seven infantry and three cavalry divisions, three hundred artillery pieces. No tanks, no armored vehicles, no aircraft. A pitiable quantity, all in all."

"Indeed, sir."

"But there are ways, Stachel. First, we can insist on, and obtain, the very best. Do you know that almost two hundred officers applied for duty with the Truppenamt when I established it? Of those, all but twenty were eliminated by tests of their skills in military science and tactics, history, geography, political science, radio and telegraphy, languages, social graces, and the arts. And then, after attending a special school, only six of the twenty survived. Today—several years later—one of the six is serving on the staff here. One out of nearly two hundred, Stachel. Considerable odds, wouldn't you say?"

Stachel, not altogether certain what the general was getting at, said, "I certainly would agree, Herr General."

"Within the Truppenamt authorized by the treaty, I've established a Fliegerzentrale, an air force advisory group composed of a dozen key aviation officers of rank, skill, and reliability," the general continued. "This group is, naturally, secret. Its existence is not known to the Control Commission and its mission has remained, until now, primarily theoretical and strategic. But now things are different. We are approaching an active program which, in essence, parallels your own prescription for an air arm constructed—on a clandestine basis—in another country. We are preparing, under the direction of a staff of aviation specialists I call 'Sondergruppe R,' to activate a large training base in Russia."

Stachel, long inured to the unexpected and deadened to the sensational, nevertheless sat forward in his chair, reflexively astonished. "*Russia?* My god, General, why—how—why would the *Russians* want to help us build an air force? I—"

The general held up a hand. "Let me finish. Russia is not bound by the Versailles Treaty. She is a maverick nation, unmotivated by Western ideals and ethical considerations. But she shares one major problem with Germany—a problem that she must solve but can solve only with our help. That problem is Poland—a creature of the treaty and a burr under the saddle for both Germany and Russia. Poland must eventually be eliminated and the border re-established between Russia and the Reich. This can happen only via a collaboration between the Germans and the Russians.

"The Fatherland will, of course, in time have to destroy the French and possibly the English. Germany cannot survive as a nation unless the root causes of the World War are resolved in her favor, and this means the war must—at some future date—be resumed. A strong Russia, favorably disposed toward us, would serve as a strong ally in our struggle against France and England and, if she has a strong armaments industry, could serve as a source of supplementary resources —matériel, and maybe even personnel."

Stachel shifted in his chair, and the general sensed the motion as a signal for a pause.

"Do you have a question, Stachel?"

"Yes, sir. The Russians are our enemies. They hate our guts. Why would they go along with this? I mean, if they were to get strong enough, they could wipe out Poland on their own—"

"Experience, Stachel. Lenin himself has said that as much as she despises us, Russia should see Germany as a friend and benefactor in the sacred struggle against the Polish threat. Germans hate Poland, Russians fear Poland; these truths unite us, politically and militarily. For the time being, of course."

"So Sondergruppe R is ready to open for business?"

"By summer of next year. The planning is well in progress, the agreements are solid, and by June or July of 1925 there will be a complement of Fokker aircraft with replacement parts, and the necessary manpower to fly and service them." The general sounded slightly smug.

"I see. And while training Russian pilots our Sondergruppe R will also train German pilots."

"Precisely."

Stachel wondered why the general had called him in to tell him of such grandiose secrets.

"I suppose," von Seeckt said, "you're wondering why I've called you in to reveal all those secrets."

"No, sir. I assume you will explain in good time."

"Ah. Patience is also one of your virtues, eh? Patience and an ability to control your curiosity."

The words were amiable enough, Stachel thought, but there was an underlying tone of—what—sarcasm? The impression was elusive, yet it puzzled him.

"I'll admit I'd like to know more, sir."

The general's monocle was in place again, giving the left eye a malevolent glint. "I'm sure you would, Stachel. Suffice it to say that I'm having you assigned to the personnel section of Sondergruppe R. Your initial duties will be to make an inventory of pilot strength. Our fliers are scattered widely, their records out of date. You will look up, interview, and determine the present status of as many as can be found, with view toward eventual activation of those who are still competent."

"They will make up the training cadre for the Russian thing?"

"Some of them. Others will be considered for staff sections as needed."

"Very well, sir."

"I've selected you for this post because your capabilities as an aviator are a matter of wide public comprehension. You are, in other words, in a position to judge your peers."

"Thank you, Herr General." Stachel sensed the interview to be at an end, so he stood up, straightened his jacket and struggled to mask his astonishment and delight. "May I ask sir, how I'll get about? Train? Car?"

"You'll function chiefly by mail—studying service records, writing to last-known addresses, bringing things up to date via correspondence with officers or next of kin. When you must travel to follow a lead, you'll go by aircraft, of course. We still have a few," the general said ironically. "Oberst Funk, my adjutant, will prepare the necessary authorization. Meanwhile, I'll expect a good job out of you, Stachel."

"I'll do my very best, Herr General. And thank you again for the opportunity to serve the Fatherland." Stachel saluted, did a precise about-face, and marched from the room, grinning openly.

Oberst Siegfried Funk was in a very bad mood. He had just received a call from his tailor, an insufferable Jew with bad breath who had done up his new formal uniform. The man had been the only one who would accept the work on credit, and although it had been against his sensibilities to patronize a side-street shop, Funk had run out of alternatives. The folly of doing business with such a man, even in necessity, had been certified by the telephone call, however; any merchant with the temerity to call a debtor at his office in the Heeresleitung would be guaranteed to turn into a troublemaker, and Funk cast about irritably for an idea as to who might lend him enough to pay the tailor's bill and thereby remove this wart on the ass of headquarters tranquility.

He was about to call one of the ladies who adored him this week when that fellow Stachel came out of the general's office and stood before his desk.

"The general said you have an authorization for me."

"Oh, yes." Funk returned the receiver to its cradle. "Have a seat."

Stachel sat in an overstuffed chair beside the file cabinets, an expression of good cheer on his face, which Funk thought rather typical of an arrogant young snob with lots of money and connections. Who wouldn't be cheerful when he was married to a wealthy and influential lady publisher and had the likes of Baroness von Klingelhof-und-Reimer calling the general in his behalf?

Funk took an envelope from the pending tray on his desk and passed it across to Stachel. "This was signed by the general just before you came. It'll serve as your authorization until active-duty orders are written. I suggest you return to your home and get your affairs in order. The orders will be sent to you there. You are being promoted to Hauptmann, so I suggest you order your uniforms accordingly."

Stachel smiled. "Icing on the cake, eh? This gets better all the time."

Funk felt a flash of envy, which served only to intensify his rotten mood. On a better day he might have proceeded gingerly with a man of such apparent horsepower, but now he gave in to his peevishness. "Why shouldn't it?" he said heavily. "After all, the cream of society has interceded for you."

Stachel gave him a quizzical glance. "What does that mean, Colonel?"

"The Baroness, my dear Stachel. Surely you know she called."

"What the hell are you talking about, Colonel?"

"You are fortunate," Funk said, suddenly uncomfortable with the way things were going, "to have such an influential friend. Good contacts never hurt a career officer."

"I've met the Baroness only once in my life."

Shrugging, Funk glanced at his watch impatiently.

Stachel gazed at him for a long, speculative moment, then stood up and laughed aloud. "The Baroness must have something good on you fellows, eh?"

"That will be all, Stachel."

"Ta-ta, Colonel. See you in Russia, maybe?" Stachel left, still laughing.

After he was gone, Funk sat for a time, his fingers drumming on the desk. *God, what a rotten day. Rotten.*

The inner door opened and the general sauntered out.

"What do you think of Stachel, Funk?"

"He seems all right, sir," Funk said, carefully neutral.

"Do something about him."

"Sir?"

"Once he has completed his inventory of pilots, I want you to find some way to get rid of him. I don't like men who hide behind skirts."

"But the Baroness—"

"The Baroness is my concern, Funk, not yours. After enough time has passed to satisfy the Baroness that I met her request, it will be your concern to see that Stachel no longer clouds our atmosphere hereabouts. I don't care how you do it. But have him dismissed. And if any more calls come from the Baroness—or any other of that man's friends—I'm not available. Understand?"

"Of course, Herr General."

TELEPHONE TRANSCRIPT

"Hugelmeier's Delicatessen."

"I'd like to price your Sauerkraut."

"Who's calling please?"

"Laub."

"This is Sauerkraut. Twenty-three."

"Four-two-two."

"Ah, Laub. Whats on your mind?"

"I have a surveillance report."

"Anything interesting?'

"Perhaps. Chef der Heeresleiting von Seeckt has just had a caller. It could mean something."

"Well?"

"Bruno Stachel, the famous World War ace. He was in civilian clothes. His visit lasted close to a half hour. He arrived and left alone."

"All right, thank you. Establish a study on it."

"Of course."

"Sauerkraut seventeen."

"Two-two-four."

6

The orderly room was like all the others, because the army never changed. There were the board walls and the cheap yellow-varnished chairs and the faded memos on the tack-dotted bulletin board. Tinny file cabinets and desks scarred by time and use and, on the wall, a map of some territory nobody ever consulted. Windows that never seemed clean even after washing with ammonia and gun cloth; ashtrays fashioned from piston heads; a coat rack with a rain cape and Stahlhelm hanging from it; a shelf of army-regulations binders and field manuals that leaned against each other and awaited some vague time when what they had to say might be considered momentarily important. And a sergeant pecking at a typewriter, a blank-faced sergeant with a bristle haircut, bored eyes, and a snotty manner.

The sergeant examined the letter again and, without looking up, said, "'Unlimited access to aircraft,' eh? Unbelievable. But thoroughly authentic."

"Of course it is, damn it," Stachel said.

"General von Seeckt, eh?"

"That's what it says. Now roll out an airplane, give me some flying gear, and let me fly."

The blue eyes blinked and gave him a wary glance. "No offense, sir. But we have only two aircraft on this whole field, and my commander has issued strict orders that they're not to be fussed with or flown—even by official pilots of the unit—without his written authorization."

Stachel said, "Does your commander outrank General von Seeckt?"

"Well, no, sir. Of course not, sir. But—"

"Then do as you're told."

The sergeant shrugged, then reached for the field phone.

"Give me Sergeant Thom," he said into the mouthpiece. He waited, his face unhappy and his gaze indirect, until a voice crackled on the other end. He shifted in his chair and told the other man sullenly, "Ludwig here. Is Number Two ready to fly?"

Impassive, he listened to more crackling. "I don't care to hear your problems, Thom. Just answer the question."

Crackle.

"All right. Then here's what you do. Apply Class A national insignia to the wings, fuselage, and rudder. Then roll out the ship and have it ready to fly in a half hour."

Crackle-crackle-crackle.

"Well, look for the stencils, goddamnit. Class A hasn't been used since 1917, but the stencils should be stored in the loft of Hangar C. At least that's where the books show they should be."

Crackle-crackle-crackle.

"Of course the Imperial Iron Cross insignia has been

outlawed. But find the stencils, paint on the crosses with fast-drying black and white acetates, and shut the goddamn hell up."

The sergeant slammed down the phone and glared back at Stachel, openly angry and defiant.

Stachel smiled, suddenly seeing something of himself in the man. Producing a silver flask, he said mildly, "Have a drink, Sergeant. It'll cool you down."

"I'm not allowed to drink on duty," the man snapped.

"Who's going to know but you and me? There aren't more than ten people on this godforsaken patch of grass, and I outrank them all. Besides, I owe you a good snort for upsetting you so."

"You're going to get my behind in a very big vise, you know that, don't you? I mean, painting an airplane with forbidden markings and—" He shook his head in wordless dismay.

"Sergeant, relax. Simmer down. You can paint out the insignia as soon as I land. I know I'm being a pain, but if you treat me right I'll make it worth your while. I could even manage a promotion, maybe. Perhaps even a transfer out of this pest hole."

The man's blue eyes lost some of their heat, and, after a moment of speculative hesitation, he reached for the flask. He took two enormous gulps, then held it out to Stachel.

"No thanks, Sergeant. I don't drink. Finish it."

The sergeant up-ended the flask and drained it of brandy. He exhaled noisily, blinked twice, and rubbed his lips with the back of a freckle hand. "Hoo. That's first-class stuff. Why, in the name of my Aunt Hilda's piles, do you want to fly an airplane with Iron Crosses splashed all over it? I mean—"

"It's a personal matter, Sergeant. Do you have a map of Berlin?"

The sergeant began to rummage in a desk drawer. "I think so. Yes. Here. It's an old one but it shows the streets and landmarks."

Stachel spread the chart across the desk. "Where's the General Staff headquarters?"

"You mean *the* General Staff?"

"That's right. Where all the most important brass hats hang out."

The sergeant bent over the map, his lips compressed. Poking with a forefinger, he said, "See here? This building on the south bank of the Spree at the bend—the one shaped like a trapezoid?"

"At the northeastern corner of the Tiergarten?"

"Mm-hm. This circle here is Königplatz. The General Staff Building is just to the upper left of that."

"Good. What are these?"

"The oval west of the Tiergarten is the Hippodrom, next to the Technical High School. From there, running east to Unter den Linden, through the Tiergarten is the old Pferdebahn. Here, running south from Unter den Linden, is Wilhelmstrasse, where the War Ministry and the various embassies are located."

"Mind if I borrow the map? I'll return it when I land."

"Help yourself. I'm not going anywhere." The sergeant gave the flask an affectionate kiss, then handed it back.

Stachel tightened the cap and returned the flask to his overcoat pocket. "Now," he said. "Where do I find a flying suit?"

The airplane was an eight-year-old Albatros C-3, a two-seat general-purpose observation craft that had been the workhorse of the Western Front. The machine guns had been removed, and its fabric had been patched in many places, and the covers were missing from the undercarriage wheels, whose wire spokes and thin tires increased the suggestion of antiquity.

Stachel, bundled into winter flight coveralls and fur-lined boots, buckled the helmet under his chin and winked at the mechanic, who stood in melancholy silence and watched him with the special wariness the enlisted man shows for a strange officer.

"Not much of a ship, is it," Stachel said.

"It's Germany's best, sir," the man said noncommittally.

"Is it ready to fly?"

"As ready as it ever will be."

"Anything I should watch out for?"

"Its engine tends to run hot. It will be nose-heavy without someone in the rear cockpit, and it's sluggish in left turns. Otherwise it does fairly well for the old bedspring it is. The pilots tell me it's honest, more or less."

"Well, honesty's the best policy."

Stachel walked around the airplane, slowly, tugging at the bracing wires, checking the elevator and rudder hinges, and stooping briefly to examine the elastic-cord wrapping on the tail skid. For all the machine's dowdiness, it excited him, and he relished its textures and smells and sheens. It wasn't much, to be sure, but it was an airplane, and it was his to fly, and the aliveness was in him, tingling.

"So," he said finally, "let's see what's upstairs, eh?"

He placed a boot in the fuselage stirrup and, pulling himself up, stepped onto the wing root and swung awkwardly into the front cockpit. Settling into the bucket seat, he fastened the belt toggle on his chest and lowered his goggles, adjusting their fit against his cheekbones.

There was one of the late-model mixture controls adjacent to the throttle, and he set the handle on full-rich. He worked the wobble pump vigorously for a moment or two to bring up the fuel tank pressure and then, making sure the magnetos were off, he glanced down at the mechanic and nodded.

The man pulled the propeller through, and the engine made soft sucking noises.

With the switch on, the engine caught on the first pull, and the propeller dissolved into a mahogany-hued blur, beating the blue smoke that belched from the exhaust and flattening the grass. He waited, watching the temperature gauge and listening to the deep rumbling. The sweet smell of oil and burned gasoline filled the wind, and, still waiting, he breathed deeply of it.

When the engine was warm enough, he nodded at the mechanic again, signaling that the wheel chocks were to be removed. The man yanked on the lines and then ran to the left lower wing tip, where he leaned on the forward strut and served as the pivot as Stachel turned the machine into the wind.

Opening the throttle, Stachel gave the Albatros its head.

Slowly at first, the airplane began to roll; and then, with its engine blattering and its guy wires thrumming, it bounced and teetered and grew lighter, and finally, its wheels kissing the grass tops, it lifted free and rose into the metallic April afternoon.

Oh, God, how beautiful. How wonderful to be here again.

Circling, rolling slowly, climbing, stalling, recovering, he made friends with the airplane—an artist evoking a skill after long disuse. At ease once again, confident, he directed the machine toward the city.

The sky was a startling yellow where the sun sat fat and morose over the western plain, and ahead it was a sweep of intermingling lavender and pink and blue, with dots of gold where the high clouds soared. But for all its magnificence, it was empty—an airy loneliness, chill, motionless, and devoid of life.

He was, as he'd always been, hyper-aware of his airplane. A machine that trembled and sighed and rattled and roared, that rose and fell on the restless air and carried his life in its gut. For all its motion, the machine did not live; in all that racketing metal and linen, in all that colossal vault of sky, the only source of will and emotion and conjecture were the few ounces of matter that made up his brain. Up here, in the garish hues of the gathering evening, above the mists, a tiny lump of intelligence—Godlike in its aloneness.

He thought about this, enjoying the idea.

Below, gentle rises, lazy streams, geometric patterns of woodland and meadow already offered the tinge of spring. A bland, gray-green country, dotted with houses, homes, in which generations had busied themselves with the trivia that compound into lifetimes. As he watched them pass below the swaying lower wing, eyes unblinking behind the goggles, he had a distinct sense of having missed something—lost something—very elusive and precious. He'd never had a home, as such; only some rooms in the nether quarter of a country hotel, where the cooking smells and the acid traces of manure in the cow sheds at the end of the lane were always present and insistent, and the sense of strangers murmuring in the rooms above, alien and somehow intrusive and malevolent, was the stuff of unbelonging.

That house down there—the one with the green shutters that sat beside the winding brook: Who lived behind its tidy windows, moved among its familiar things, laughed and fretted and worked and loved in its amiable shadows? How had they come to live there? What magic stroke of God's whim had brought them to make their home there—right there, at that spot among the winter-naked trees on a knoll beside a nameless stream? What cosmic good fortune would assemble a family to live in such a lovely, insulated corner of the prevailing drabness that characterized the great north-German plain?

For that matter, why was he here?

What scheme of the Universe called for him, after all the terrible years, to be huddled in this drafty box, surrounded by the bellowing and rattling and keening, a thousand meters above the approaches to Berlin? Why was he not dead, like Fabian, Mueller, Willi von Klugermann, Otto Heidemann—so many others? What galactic-scale joke needed him to go on, drinking and wenching and wasting and resenting, when so many better fellows, filled with talent and promise, had gone out, like candles? Why, six years after the end of it all, was he still prepared to do this thing he would do? What difference would it possibly make? Who would care? Who would know?

His mind told him: *You'll know.*

The city was an enormous, slate-colored smear across the horizon, an expanse of zigs and zags and lights and darks that misted the lowering afternoon with driftings from factory stacks and chimney pots. Since it was not his town, he simply flew toward what seemed to be its center, where the columned buildings and meticulous parks and broad avenues gathered on the hem of a great and meandering river.

Above the General Staff Building, he sent the Albatros into a gentle 360 turn and stared off the left lower wing tip at the gardens and plazas and promenades. A major boulevard angled off the northeast, and he assumed that this would be Unter den Linden. Completing the turn, he aligned the nose on the bend in the Spree, and then, reducing throttle, eased forward on the control column. The Königplatz, with its formal ranks of trees and gardens and somber monuments, expanded into sharper focus beyond the thrashing propeller and the singing blurs of the engine rocker arms. The dive accelerated, and he waited, watching owlishly, as the General Staff Building grew in size and detail. When it virtually filled the view ahead, when the tiny dots on the pavement began running and pointing at him and clustering in lilliputian astonishment, he restored full power and pulled the control column to his groin.

The Albatros skimmed along between the building and the river, just above the disciplined trees, the racketing of its engine seeming to freeze the tiny figures. Smiling, Stachel sent the ship into a climbing turn to the left, at the top of which he cut the throttle and booted the machine into a whispering chandelle. He took up another dive, this time to rush above the building from the west, then continuing at throttle along Unter den Linden.

Four times he ran the boulevard's length, then, lifting away for altitude, he returned at last to a circling far above the Tiergarten. He checked the fuel-level gauge, the engine temperature—which was slightly above normal, but nothing to fret about—and the oil pressure reading. The dashboard clock told him he had twenty minutes before sunset.

He had no way of knowing if the machine would take it. Nearly all of his experience had been on single-seat fighter planes, built for agility and high stresses. And the Albatros C-3, for all its solid repute among airmen, was truly nothing more than a stable photo platform and bombing rig, designed to the conservative requirements of old men with heavy braid and minds full of strategic warfare. . . . Well, so be it.

He did them all.

Not well, perhaps, because the airplane was old and sluggish and unwilling. But it was faithful, and so he'd been able to do them all.

Loops. Barrel rolls. Lazy eights. Wingovers. Immelmann turns. Even a kind of ragged falling leaf and a three-revolution deep spiral that almost became an uncontrolled tailspin.

Pulling out of this at a scant hundred meters, he flew the diameter of Königplatz, heading northwest across the formal gardens with the landing wheels barely clearing the ornamental shrubs. Then, yanking back on the control yoke, he brought the Albatros virtually up the headquarters façade, over the massive roof, and up and away and into the descending twilight.

Circling a final time and heading for the airfield on the city's southern rim, he raised his goggles, peered over the side, laughed, then shouted into the wind:

"Bruno Stachel's back, you sons of bitches!"

7

Captain John M. Duncan, assistant military attaché at the U.S. Embassy, scion of the Second Manassas Duncans and the Sioux War Duncans and the Cuban Campaign Duncans, and since 1913 the Regular Army's Duncan-in-Residence, was torn by nasty conflict. Having been conceived, born, and reared in the army, he was, on the one hand, reflex-sensitive to duty and the collateral axiom that headquarters always knows best. On the other hand, he had begun secretly to suspect that headquarters didn't know its behind from a bass bassoon, and this was heresy which gave him inordinate amounts of heartburn.

In reflective moments—which he tried to avoid as much as possible—he would see that his discomfort had begun with America's entry into what everybody had called the War to Save Democracy. For five years, man and second looey, he had been an officer of the 112th Field Artillery, finally ascending to command of Battery A. For all that time he had played a tiny role in a tiny army whose only function had been to pantomime theoretical solutions to theoretical problems, using antique weapons as if they were props on a barnyard stage. But when everything turned ugly and real, when the playtime army was asked to go out and kill Germans in the name of altruism, headquarters sent the 112th Field Artillery not to France but to Fort Sill, where it became part of the training cadre for the hayseeds and lounge lizards who came sifting in on the first draft call. He hadn't wanted to leave the 112th after all those years, but to volunteer for the Signal Corps Aviation Section was the only route out of that limbo and onto the Western Front. And so he had volunteered.

It might not have been so bad, he thought now, if HQ had assigned him to a pursuit squadron. At least there he might have faced the enemy climactically; there he might, via a kind of orgasmic rendering unto Caesar, have seized the in-house repute a professional officer needed to lift himself out of the military boondocks and back into the mainstream of promotions and coveted posts. But fate had carried through its little joke and placed him in command of the most pedestrian and colorless of all the squadrons in the Air Service's most pedestrian and colorless activity, which was the advance training of air crews in observation and adjustment of division and corps artillery fire. There had been no renown-building duels in French skies, no mounting score of fallen enemy planes. John Duncan had not plunged into battle like an eagle; he had wheeled through peaceful Texas skies, like a craven turkey buzzard, until 1924.

The world's biggest war, and he'd missed it, for God's sake.

And then this: endless days in a gray-stone German city, kissing ambassadorial behinds and pretending to study the German aircraft industry and writing meaningless memos to a faceless somebody in Washington who never wrote back.

Feeling the weight of his melancholy condition, Duncan opened the window and regarded the evening without enthusiasm.

The winter had been long, and today's warmth had been a teasing thing, a sigh drifting in from the deserts a thousand miles to the south. But by nightfall it had gone, and, feeling the chill now, he closed and locked the casement and returned to his desk, where he sat in the creaky swivel chair, took a deep breath, and prepared to resume his dictation.

Miss Loomis, the number three secretary in the embassy's clerical-force pecking order, would always rank third in any competition, anywhere. She wore an expression that suggested she might have a mouth full of alum, and, although she didn't wear spectacles, she looked as if she ought to. She did not approve of Captain John M. Duncan. But then, she didn't approve of most things.

"Where were we?" he asked.

"You were in paragraph two, where you were describing your alarm over the increasing indifference Germany seems to be showing to the aircraft-restriction clauses of the Disarmament Treaty."

"I'm not alarmed, Miss Loomis. An American officer is never alarmed."

"Very well, sir." Her gaze remained fixed on the steno pad on her lap. "The last sentence reads, 'Violations, some of them blatantly overt, have reached an alarming level.' "

"Strike out 'alarming' and make it 'significant.' "

"Very well, sir."

"Next paragraph. During the past year, the so-called civilian gliding and flying clubs have grown in size and number, and there are plans for at least ten flight schools located at points in Germany where wartime fliers will be offered refresher courses. Although, under the Paris Agreement, the Germans are permitted to train no more than six military pilots a year, an undetermined number far in excess of this figure has already been trained and added to the country's reserve forces—each man posing as a young civilian seeking his sports flying license. New paragraph.

"Moreover, under the 1922 Treaty of Rapallo, in which the Germans and the Russians re-established diplomatic relations, there is increasingly stronger evidence indicating a large-scale, mutual aircraft development and flight training program at Lipetsk, a center two hundred miles from Moscow. A reliable informant in the Truppenamt tells me that this spring—no later than May 30, 1924, that is—at least thirty to forty new Fokker aircraft of the D-Thirteen model are to be freighted to Lipetsk via ship from Stettin to Leningrad, and thence by railroad. A full cadre of aircraft maintenance and flight personnel will soon begin the training of Russian fliers, and preparations to provide parallel training for German pilots are virtually complete. Next paragraph.

"The training cadre will include about a hundred and fifty military aviators whose backgrounds include extensive experience as combat pilots on the Western and Mesopotamian fronts. The cadre, our informant tells me, will be handpicked from a roster assembled via personal interviews conducted by Oberleutnant Bruno Stachel, the notorious ace of the Great War, who today was appointed to the personnel section, Fliegerzentrale, which is part of the Truppenamt. Stachel, incidentally, did some spectacular stunt flying over Berlin this afternoon. The exhibition brought thousands of people into the streets, cheering. The uproar, in my opinion, was indicative of the German national anger over Versailles' disarmament strictures."

Duncan looked out the window again and said, "Don't forget to send a carbon to the ambassador."

"You don't have to remind me of my duties, Captain."

"Don't be so snotty, Miss Loomis. I'm not a very happy man, and you're being snotty is just a little more than I need right now." The outburst surprised him. Ordinarily, he was an even-tempered, amiable fellow, and so this little explosion of heat was something to wonder about: Was this rotten duty getting to him that much?

Miss Loomis seemed surprised, too. "I didn't mean to sound that way, Captain. Excuse me."

"Excuse me, too, Miss Loomis. It was stupid of me to blow off like that."

They sat in silence for a time, she in the attitude of the waiting secretary, he in grumpy preoccupation. In the interval he gave her a sidelong glance, and there was something about her downcast eyes, her slim and rather melancholy face, her proper legs, close together under her sensible skirt, that sent a wave of sympathy through him. She must be a very lonely woman, he thought; she must have an empty and unrewarding life in this alien and cheerless city.

Incredulously, he heard himself saying, "Are you busy this evening, Miss Loomis?"

"Busy?" She gave him a glance full of curiosity. "Why, no. That is, I must see to some laundry and—"

"Do you want to go to a party?"
"A party?"
"It's a dumb thing, really. Lori Lehmann, the film star, is being given a birthday party by Max Zirko, her producer. At the Olympia. All the flying people are being invited, because her newest picture is an airplane epic. Anyhow, I've been invited to bring a friend, and there's no reason why you shouldn't go."
"Well, Captain, I—"
"Oh, cut it out, Miss Loomis. No excuses. Just powder your nose and come along. I'll pick you up at nine. Where's your place?"
"My quarters are right here in the embassy building annex."
"Oh, sure. All right, then. Nine?"
"I'm not so sure it's a good idea for us to be seen in a social situation, Captain. There are certain conventions, and—"
He laughed, still astonished at his own irrational invitation. "Baloney. There are no rules or regulations that forbid our fraternizing, Miss Loomis. Is 'fraternizing' the word? It makes you sound like my brother or something."
She smiled a frosty smile, placed her pencil in the rings of her notebook, then arose from her chair. "I don't mean to sound ungrateful, Captain. It was nice of you to invite me, but—"
"But nothing, Loomis. You're coming. By the way—what's your first name? You do have a first name, don't you?"
"Pauline. But people call me Polly."
"My first name is John."
She blushed, nodded thoughtfully, then left the office, her notebook under her arm.
He watched her go, speculation in his gaze.

Stachel despised affairs like this, especially when he wasn't drinking.
When he entered the vestibule, the party had been under way for at least two hours, and the yammering was deafening. The hotel was ornate, with gilded cornices and silk-paneled walls, but the Victorian elegance had been eclipsed by a gallery of blown-up portraits of Lori Lehmann in her various film roles, all hanging from wires strung throughout the adjoining rooms; tobacco smoke made a heavy fog, through which girls in daring, low-cut gowns prowled and giggled and showed themselves to red-faced, jaded men.

He chose a glass of white grape juice from the serving table and then took up an observer's position in the hallway, just outside the main salon, where the crowd was the thickest and the conversation cacophonous. His plan was simply to say hello to the guest of honor, thank Zirko, the host, then return to his hotel to pack for tomorrow's 06:30 train to Munich. Sipping his juice, he let his gaze wander, hoping to spot Lehmann, who, probably, as guest of honor was in one of the nearby rooms, giving an honorable lay to one of the honorable guests. As an actress, Lehmann was superb, as a woman, she was a tramp. He had met her at one of Rudi's parties at Schloss Löwenheim, and she'd been very cordial, presumably because he'd been the only man present who hadn't tried to massage her chest. Unaccountably, he'd liked her instantly.

"Good evening, Oberleutnant Stachel," an accented voice said beside him.

She was lanky, and somewhat plain. At her elbow was a man in the uniform of an American army captain, who beamed expectantly.

"Good evening, Fräulein. I don't believe we've met."

"I'm Polly Loomis, of the American Embassy. This is Captain Duncan, my superior." Her German, for all its American inflections, was smooth and idiomatic, and he envied her easy familiarity with a tongue foreign to her.

"Delighted." He gave a half bow.

"Captain Duncan is a military aviator," Miss Loomis explained, "and he's long looked forward to meeting you. He was especially impressed with your stunting over the city today, and when he recognized you in the crowd he asked me if I'd be his interpreter in an introduction."

"I see. The captain doesn't speak German?"

"Barely a word. He makes 'danke schön' sound like a sneeze."

Stachel gave the captain a friendly appraisal. "Tell Captain Duncan it's always a pleasure to meet a fellow airmen. Perhaps we've met before, in the skies over France, eh?"

Miss Loomis translated, and Duncan laughed and, waving his drink in a minimizing gesture, answered in some of his gibberish.

"Captain Duncan says that's not likely, since he merely piloted a big old artillery-spotting barge at a Texas training field."

"Well, the soldier's duty is to serve wherever duty places him. Tell Captain Duncan that, in my eye, a flier is a flier—a member of the brotherhood."

She spoke to Duncan again. The captain responded amiably.

"The captain regrets that he can't speak German. There's much he'd like to discuss with you, flier-to-flier."

Stachel nodded. "I feel the same frustration. Tell him that the English instructor of my school days was a fat old fellow who was about as good as a teacher as I am as an opera singer."

As she interpreted, Stachel studied the woman. Her features, for all their plainness, were even and well structured, and there was an underlying heat, a kind of subtle incandescence that emanated from her, almost like a scent. He wondered if she was sleeping with the American captain. He rather doubted it, since she had the indefinable look of one who has given up on such things.

"Captain Duncan says," she told him, her face red, "that you should take your English lessons from me. I am a qualified instructor in French, German, and Spanish, and part of my duties at the embassy is to tutor key personnel in German brushups."

"I see. Why doesn't Captain Duncan avail himself of your services?"

"Because," she said, her hazel eyes showing a tiny glint of irony, "Captain Duncan already knows everything he needs to know. He's a square-shouldered, square-shooting, square-headed nincompoop."

Stachel laughed. "I hope he does not indeed speak German. You'd be out of a job tomorrow."

"Just as well," she said. "I detest the job and the people I work for."

"Oh? I thought all Americans were snug and smug and happy as—what's the phrase?—'apple pie'?"

"Only those who are making money, Oberleutnant."

"And you're not, eh?"

"You don't think I dress like this because I want to, do you?" She smiled faintly.

"Would your superiors permit you to tutor me in English? I'm being posted to Berlin."

"They have little to say about what I do with my own time."

Captain Duncan broke in with a comment.

"The captain says, 'Hey, you two—what's going on?' "

"What *is* going on, Fräulein Loomis?" Stachel said coolly.

"I think that's for you to decide," she said, her eyes level.

"If I decide to engage you as my new English tutor, where do I call you?"

"Twenty-three-null, thirty-seven. After nineteen hundred hours."

"Good. Now tell Captain Duncan that I'd like the three of us to have lunch sometime soon. We can do some hangar flying together, eh?"

Miss Loomis rattled off some more English and Duncan, his darkly handsome face lighted by alcoholic good will, nodded in elaborate understanding. He shook Stachel's hand; then, taking Miss Loomis by the elbow, led her into the crowd.

She looked back once, a dim smile on her lips.

8

It was warm, almost like a summer morning, and Kaetie had her breakfast on the terrace of her chic and expensive apartment, which comprised the ground-level corner of the Hotel Brunner. The early flowers were already blooming, pale pink and set off by the bone-white gravel of the curving paths, and the fountain at the rear of the garden in the niche formed by the brick wall, made gentle little splashing sounds. Above the graph line etched by the city's horizon the sky was a deep blue, unbroken and luminescent, and there was the smell of sunwashed leaves and warm stone.

Ordinarily, morning was her favorite time. But today, for all the pleasantness around her, she was disturbed—out of sorts. In the weeks since Bruno's mad flying stunts, she'd been preoccupied with him and what they'd been to each other and where they might be going.

Even her own publications, for God's sake, had carried mawkish stories quoting various Unter den Linden pedestrians on their personal reactions to the daring exhibition. The authorities, of course, had pretended outrage over this blatant disregard of public safety, and the military command had at once promised a thorough review of the matter. But, what with the public's extraordinary, emotional outpouring of approval and enthusiasm, nothing much had come of it. Both the government and the military needed all the help they could get these days, and it was apparent even to Kaeti—who, for all her publishing empire, was only superficially informed on such things—that Bruno's aerial tantrum had, for a time, given the restless citizenry something to enthuse over. But Berlin's amusement had proved to be her depression.

Several times she had considered calling him at the Aiglon, where, the newspapers said, he was temporarily quartered. But she knew from long experience that even the most casual circumstances could degenerate into acrimony whenever their magnetic fields were adjacent. Not that it had always been that way. In the early days, even in face of the angers and frustrations in which they'd rooted their marriage, there had been superb moments—fleeting, quicksilver splinters of time in which she had seen the true man, the intelligent, sensitive, and appealingly bemused man of wit and passion who lurked behind the bravado and the pretense and the drinking. And, in those times, she suspected that he saw her in the fundamental colors of her self, too, and there would be a meeting, a brushing, an ephemeral armistice in which their secret compulsion, one for the other, would be in conjunction.

Those moments had been enough, she would admit to herself in private anger, to keep her locked to him. For every humiliation his indifference would work on her, for every lover she would take in her determination to retaliate, for every dreary mouth of clenched-teeth toleration, there would be an insistent memory of eyes meeting, bodies closing, silent inward explosions of incomparable sharing. He was sodden, egocentric, opinionated, arbitrary, capricious, paradoxical, selfish, sharp-tongued, unforgiving, and lethal. But he had touched her somewhere in some terrible vulnerability, and she would never be able to let him go. Better to keep him a sullen prisoner than to have nothing at all.

The status quo would be preserved, by God.

Pouring herself a fresh cup of coffee, she resumed her waiting for Oberst Funk.

When he arrived the colonel proved to be all spangles and crisp gray cloth and pomaded hair. He did not wear the Blue Max, she saw, but there were the Iron Cross and many ribbons, and he smelled of leather and cologne. She did not think she would like him.

After handing the butler his cap and gloves, he gave her a

taut smile and said, "It is a pleasure to meet you, Frau Stachel."

"Be seated, won't you, Colonel?" she said, waving a hand at the chair beside the terrace railing. "Coffee?"

"Thank you, no."

She returned to her chair at the breakfast table and, after a sip from her cup, regarded him gravely. "It is nice of you to come."

"As I say, a pleasure. I must confess, however, that I'm somewhat puzzled by your—"

"Summons?"

He showed that tiny curl of the mouth again.

"Well," he said, "a German officer grows quite used to the unexpected. Besides, I've long admired your newspapers and periodicals, and it's a privilege to meet their, ah, guiding genius."

She decided that she did not like him at all. "You're probably wondering how I got your name."

"The question did cross my mind, yes."

"I asked the editor of my Berlin newspaper to determine exactly who it is who has the most authority among our flying-corps units, or whatever they're called these days. He reported that you have more authority than anybody in the entire Truppenamt." (This was not altogether true, of course. She'd asked Preml, the Klarion's military-affairs writer, who it was among all the ambitious denizens of the Reichswehr headquarters that could be considered the most ambitious. "Funk, the personal adjutant of the Chef der Heeresleitung," Preml had snorted without hesitation. "He's not only ambitious—he's predatory." She had asked Preml to provide her with a complete dossier on Oberst Funk, which had arrived three days ago, and which revealed, among other things, that the colonel was a victim of one of mankind's unhappiest contradictions: an enormous appetite for luxury and an infinitesimal bankroll. The colonel had often attempted to resolve the disparity at Berlin's glossier gaming tables, but with no apparent success.)

"I see," Oberst Funk said, warming under the hearsay compliment. "Your editor is very kind."

"Despite your lofty post, Colonel, is it possible that you've heard of my husband? Stachel? Bruno Stachel?"

The colonel smiled primly. "I don't believe, dear lady, that there is a living soul in Berlin—in all Germany, for that matter—who has not heard of him."

"Are you in charge of his unit?"

"I am not directly in charge of any line organization, madam, but I do have considerable influence among them all. I am an aide to General von Seeckt, Chef der Heeresleitung, you see."

"Good. There is something I'd like you to do for me, Colonel. I want you to arrange my husband's dismissal from the service."

The colonel's flinty gaze became oblique. "I see," he said. "You realize, I'm sure, that you're asking the impossible."

"Why impossible? He got in. Now he can get out."

"It isn't all that simple, I'm afraid—"

"Tell me why."

Oberst Funk examined the nails of his right hand. "For one thing, there's no valid military reason. An officer can't be returned to civilian status on mere whim. There have to be clear-cut charges."

"Can't you bring charges against him for his stunts over the palace?"

The colonel shrugged. "You have seen the public reaction to your husband's adventure. He's too, ah, popular, so to speak. It would be somewhat awkward to dismiss, or even severely chastise, an officer who has lifted the morale—the spirits—of the German people."

"I want my husband out of the service, Colonel Funk."

"Why, madam?"

"None of your business."

"You have made it my business," Funk said coolly.

"I don't like you much, Colonel."

"A pity, to be sure."

"I had thought I'd like you, since you are a gambler at heart, and so am I."

He gave her a narrow glance. "Gambler? You've, ah, looked into my—"

"I am a very powerful—a very influential—woman, Colonel. I don't deal with people I don't know something about. Nor do I deal with the faint-hearted. It's the lions who run the world, and I refuse to associate with the lambs." She hoped she hadn't sounded too melodramatic. For all his priggishness, the man was clearly not stupid. But she was tiring of him, and so she decided to stop this silly fencing. "How much money would it take, Colonel Funk?"

"I can't be bribed, Frau Stachel," he said evenly.

"I was not implying that you could. I simply recognize, as a realist, that matters of delicacy require a great deal of time, planning, execution—all of which require money. I'm asking you to estimate the expenses. How much would it cost the army to do the paper work, or whatever, to return my husband to civilian life? If you can give me an estimate, I'll certainly not expect the hard-pressed military to pick up the cost. I'll give you the sum so that you, in your key position, can route the funds to the proper treasury."

"I see. You're speaking of reimbursement, then."

"Of cousre." She knew she had him now. His eye had revealed his appreciation of her contrivance. *Greed will find a way,* she thought bitterly.

He pretended to give the matter some careful thought, and she sat quietly, sipping coffee and waiting for him to complete his charade.

"Well," he said finally, examining his nails again, "it would be costly, certainly. Given the amount of time, personnel, the difficulty of establishing a rationale—"

She waited.

"—I'd say we're talking about the equivalent of five thousand American dollars."

"That's a considerable sum, Colonel."

"To be sure, madam."

"Where should I route this reimbursement?"

"I shall have to determine that. I'll advise you."

"Very well."

"Is there anything else, madam?"

"Not really. But I'll expect my husband home soon."

"As soon as the proper opportunity presents itself. As soon as we find the proper rationale."

"I hope you'll find it quickly."

"Patience, madam. Patience. It'll take some time. But we'll find a way."

"Correction, Colonel. You'll find a way. Your career could take a bad turn if you don't. Now you'll have to excuse me. The maid will show you out."

9

In the nineteen months of his service with Fliegerzentrale, Stachel had become increasingly aware of a rather remarkable contradiction between the government's public assertions and the facts it held secret. Over and over, the bitter charge in the press and in official releases was that, thanks to the Versailles Treaty, Germany was virtually bereft of decent aircarft. Yet in his travels, and especially since his official assignment to Sondergruppe R in April of 1924, he saw evidence to the contrary. To be sure, construction of civil aircraft, authorized by the Allied Control Commission in 1922, suffered under restrictions regarding weight, horsepower, speed, and service ceilings, while certain military machines—mainly pitiful Albatroses and Rumplers and AEGs left over from the war—were permitted to fly token border patrol and police missions. So, on the surface, things were as claimed. But behind the scenes, there were significant developments.

Von Seeckt had placed Ernst Brandenburg—a captain in the war who, as a bomber pilot, had won the Blue Max for raids over England—in charge of the Air Office of the Ministry of Transport. Brandenburg had lost a leg in a crash-landing toward war's end, but he hadn't lost his wits. He gradually centralized and amalgamated the civil aviation organizations and, with a lot of clever paper-shuffling, had managed to place the future development of civil aviation in a framework calculated to serve military needs first, passengers and mail sacks second.

Stachel hadn't been around Fliegerzentrale very long before he learned that there was a small but very efficient aircraft industry in the form of the Junkers Company at Dessau, Dornier in Friedrichshafen, and Heinkel at Warnemünde. And Lufthansa, soon to become the official government airline, was due to take over the routes set up by struggling independents flying the old open-cockpit crates. Low-keyed conversation over lunches in the Officers' Mess had it that Lufthansa, equipped with late-model airplanes and all-weather instrumentation, would be operated by military aircrews in civil airline dress. Everybody in Fliegerzentrale was jockeying for assignment to Lufthansa because he who was qualified on instruments was the one who'd get the best assignments in the air force to come. In the past few months Stachel had jockeyed as hard as anybody, of course, but Brandenburg and his key lieutenants at the ministry were opaque and noncommittal and wouldn't give anyone the slightest hint as to what the real plans were. After a time, then, Stachel felt as if he were fighting feathers (How do you jockey for position when you don't know what the position is?) and so he'd given up, assuming that if he was to get a Lufthansa assignment he'd get one, no matter who kissed whose behind.

Giving up wasn't easy, though, because it meant more of the same, and more of the same meant writing and rewriting the officer-classification reports on all the pilots he'd contracted—some two hundred of them, from fishermen working Norwegian fjords to the convalescent and fugitive Göring, in Italy to fuss in self-important anonymity on the fringes of Mussolini's Italian fascism. There were times when Stachel saw himself as a kind of errant monk, doing penance by transcribing the begats a thousand times, and it was a good day indeed when he could flee the somber headquarters building and put his "von Seeckt letter" to work at Johannisthal or some other flying field.

Like today.

At 09:30 hours his chief of section, a ramrod-type Hessian major named Kleine, had come into his office and asked him to run out to Flight Station Three and interview a reservist named Nachtigal, who had flown with the Turkish Air Force in Mesopotamia in '17 and early '18, and was now a dairyman near Lübeck. Nachtigal had written in, Kleine said, and was instructed to report to Station Three for an interview, since it was cheaper to have the man travel to Berlin on his own time than it would be to send Stachel to Lübeck. The budget was strained beyond belief, Kleine had grumped, so air trips were a thing of the past. Which was all right with Stachel, since he'd had his bellyful of hotels and trains and drafty autobuses.

Nachtigal was a small man with a button nose, a square face, and ears that stood at right angles to his head. His cheeks were ruddy like a farmer's, and his eyes, wide and guileless, were ice-pale, like a codfish's.

"I am honored," Nachtigal said, turning his hat in his hands.

"Honored?" Stachel was puzzled.

"Honored. It's a great honor to be interviewed by a famous ace."

"Are you getting smart with me?"

"Not at all, sir. By no means. I mean it sincerely. I've heard a great deal about your exploits on the Western Front. Your victories."

"That was a long time ago. This is now. And you're the subject, not I. Here. Fill out these forms. While you're working with them, I'll take a little run down to Flight Operations. All right?"

"Certainly, Herr Hauptmann."

"And don't let me hear any more of that famous-ace stuff, eh?"

"Absolutely, sir. Not another word."

The Ops officer, Randelmann, sighed when he saw Stachel. "Oh, God," he said, "von Seeckt Junior is here again. I swear, Stachel, if you show me that goddamned letter one more time, I'll break into tears."

"How about an Albatros, or AEG?"

Randelmann shook his head. "There is nothing available. Except Number Ten, and God knows not even you would want to fly that."

"What's Number Ten?"

"An LVG Trainer. With dual controls. Except that it's two hundred years old and flies like a flatiron."

"I'll take it."

"You're out of your mind."

"I won't argue that."

"Have it back in a half hour. We're having an inspection this afternoon and all equipment must be examined. Including that old wreck."

"All right. And thanks."

After dressing in flight gear, Stachel looked in on Nachtigal, who was in the examination room signing the last of the forms. The dairyman glanced up, blushed redly, and stared with great yearning at Stachel's flight suit and goggles. On a whim, Stachel said, "How'd you like to go for a hop?"

Nachtigal's blush deepened to a spectacular crimson, and he said, faltering, "That would be fine."

"There's a flying suit in that closet there. Meet me on the line in three minutes."

The lower sky was neutral in color but generally clear and still, with a band of pink separating the factory haze and the horizon. The city, a spread of grime split by a grimy river, lazed past below, looking dead and cold in the brittle light. Off the left wing tip, the open country was misty and remote, a blue expanse of cheerlessness. Stachel settled in his seat, listening to the engine and sniffing the smell of hot oil. The smokiness came down toward the climbing LVG, and then was all around, and the light faded. A fog formed on his goggles as he waited for the airplane to carry them through.

The haze below, luminous and white, formed an infinite, transparent carpet. The LVG made a tiny T-shaped shadow that raced across the gauze, and he watched this, as fascinated as he had been those years ago when seeing the effect for the first time. Impulsively, he glanced back at Nachtigal, who sat in the rear cockpit, looking grim in his helmet and goggles.

"Take her over, Nachtigal!" he shouted. "Your turn for some fun!"

Nachtigal shook his head and looked puzzled, so Stachel cut back on the throttle and the engine subsided into a series of mellow poppings.

"Your turn, chum! Show me how you did it in Mesopotamia!"

"Why?"

"You mean you need a *reason?* With all this big sky to play in?"

"I'd rather not, sir."

Stachel gave the man a long, evaluating stare. Then, turning forward again, he restored power and eased the ship into a gentle turn.

It happened, of course. Men got very rusty, not flying. But still . . .

Perhaps if he did a lazy loop the old excitement would come back to Nachtigal. Once a pilot felt the old excitement he'd be as hooked as ever, by God.

He cut the throttle again and shouted, "All right, chum, hold on! I'm going to waltz her around a bit! Then you finish the job, eh?"

Nachtigal's severe expression became further clouded by what seemed to be sad resignation, and he nodded slowly, in the manner of one who has just received terrible news from his physician.

Stachel returned to flying for flying's sake.

The LVG's nose dropped, and Stachel felt the familiar giddiness, the falling-away in the pit of his stomach, the quickness of breath. The wind and motor sounds rose in pitch, and beyond the thrashing propeller the earth came up with a deceptive slowness. He eased back on the stick waiting for the blood-rush as the airplane began its upward arcing.

The airplane did not arc upward. It achieved, then held, a shallow dive, wires humming.

He pulled harder on the control column, but it wouldn't budge. He shot a look over his shoulder at Nachtigal and shouted, "What the hell are you doing? Let go of the controls!"

Nachtigal sat numbly, his eyes glazed behind the goggles.

Stachel cut the throttle and yelled. "Let go of the controls, you stupid clodhopper!"

The man stared, unheeding.

"Let go, or we'll drive this bedspring all the way to China!"

He'd heard of men freezing on the controls, especially in basic flight training, but he'd never experienced the phenomenon, since he'd never served as an instructor. It was clear that Nachtigal was no pilot—he might never have flown before, actually. No matter what, though, the problem was to get his death grip off the control column.

Stachel peered at the floor between his legs, trying to ignore the whining of the wind, rising and insistent, and the ragged popping of the idling engine. The LVG was rigged for control from either cockpit, the stick socket in the front being synchronized with that in the rear via two actuating rods—the torque tube, for moving the ailerons, and the connector shaft, for moving the elevator rocker arm, which was located in the belly of the ship behind the rear seat. Try as he would, he couldn't get the stick to move rearward, and the ship held to its shallow descent.

He leaned forward and, pulling the cotter pin, unscrewed the stick-retaining bolt. Then he yanked the control column free of its socket, loosened his seat belt, and, half-turning, half-kneeilng, rose up and smashed Nachtigal on his helmeted head.

The man blinked and shook his head slowly from side to side. But his grip held and the dive continued.

"Let go, you bastard. You'll kill us both!"

He tried to hit the man again, if not to stun him, at least to break the hypnotic spell that seemed to have seized him. But, in the swing, the control stick hit a strut and bounced out of Stachel's hand, spinning end over end into the void.

"Damn, damn, damn!"

Since they hadn't bothered with parachutes, Stachel couldn't bail out. But he wouldn't have even if he'd been able to, he knew, since there'd be no explaining why he had left a plane that still contained a panicked passenger. Even a stupid cow-plop farmer like Nachtigal.

"You stupid cow-plop farmer!"

Stachel buckled himself tight again, and tried to think. But it was no good. The LVG was in a shallow, mushing descent with its engine at idle. There was no time for anything but to hold on and pray.

The ground came up, purple and misty. Blue-green fields. Clumps of hedge lines. Violet forests. A building. Another, An angle of road. Telephone poles. A railroad. A creek, pale in its snaking bed. More fields. Another road.

Easy. Easy . . . A touch of wheels; a screech; a bouncing, then hard rudder against a skid.

Don't skid, you old son of a bitch. Hold. Hold.

Dirt flying. A banging sound, a tearing, a terrible lurching and smashing.

A whispering of wind in grass. A dripping of oil. Then silence.

Stachel walked away from the wreck with a swollen eye and a bleeding nose. Nachtigal, whose head had struck the dashboard, had died instantly.

10

The hearing was held in the conference room of the Administration Building at Johannisthal, and it was like all other official investigations in which the facts are indisputable: pompous, precious, fastidious, and unnecessary. The presiding officer was Baron von Menzing, a reedy colonel from the Transport Ministry's Military Affairs Section, and he was flanked at the long oak table by a Major Alois Klausser and a Hauptmann Oswald Diestl, a small man with a ratty mustache and a monocle. Stachel decided they all were fatuous charlatans.

There weren't many witnesses. The first was a farmer named Koch, who told the board he had been working in his sugar-beet field when the accident occurred.

"Precisely what did you see, Herr Koch?" the colonel intoned. "In your own words, please."

"I didn't see anything at first, Your Excellency. I just heard things."

"What things?"

"A motor sound. A whistling, sort of."

"And then?"

"And then I looks up, and there's this flying machine coming down in a long slant, like. I watches it, and it hits real hard on its wheels, which break off. And then the machine bounces up in the air again, and then it turns sideways and falls on its wings, which break. And then it spins around, sort of, and slides along the ground and through my south fence, where it stops on the wagon lane in a lot of dust. I start hurrying over to the wreck and I see this aviator climb out. When I get there, I help him pull the other aviator out, who was dead. The aviator—the other, live one—tells me to go for a doctor. That's about all."

The three officers put their heads together and whispered. The colonel nodded twice, and the captain removed the monocle from his right eye, breathed on the glass, and rubbed it thoughtfully with an army-issue handkerchief. They all looked bored.

Peering out from the huddle, the colonel said, "Herr Koch, did the airplane seem to be out of control?"

"I don't know much about flying machines, so I can't rightly say. All I know is, it came down in a slow, straight slant, hit so hard it shook the ground, then began coming apart."

"I see."

There was more subdued discussion, and Stachel, seated by the window, starched and uncomfortable in his dress uniform, felt a wave of angry annoyance. The whole matter was cut and dried, but the nincompoops at the hearing table were doing their utmost to drag things out, to make their task look much more complicated and difficult than it truly was.

The colonel cleared his throat and, with a haughty nod, dismissed farmer Koch. Next he called the physician, a country sawbones who, in a remarkable economy of words, testified simply that the deceased, Karl-Heinz Nachtigal, had been dead at the scene of the crash, victim of a massive fracture of the skull's frontal bones. A county policeman was asked to confirm the location of the wreckage—there was, presumably, a question as to jurisdictions—and a frightened and worried Randelmann stated that, yes, he had granted Stachel permission to make a local flight in government aircraft D 1438.

"Hauptmann Stachel. Will you please take the stand?"

Stachel rose from his stiff-backed chair and crossed to the table, where he was sworn by the clerk and asked to identify himself.

"Bruno Stachel, captain in the Reichswehr, assigned to duty in the Fliegerzentrale, Berlin."

"Be seated, please." The colonel and his flankers eyed him in a long moment of silent assessment. Stachel was careful to return their examination, because he'd learned long ago that the best weapon against those who consider themselves your betters is a long, open stare that suggests they aren't.

"It's already been established, Stachel, that you obtained permission to fly the aircraft, LVG, model number"—the colonel leaned over the green blotter to check his notes—"D fourteen thirty-eight, on the eighteenth of October this year. Do you confirm?"

"Yes, sir. That is correct."

"And that this was a volunteer flight, not connected with your official duties at the time. Agreed?"

"Yes, sir."

"And that no specific military mission was involved."

"I disagree, sir."

The six eyes converged on him in mild astonishment in this, the first contradiction to be heard since the proceedings began. "Oh?" said the colonel, presumably for want of anything else to say.

"Involved in the flight," Stachel said, "was the maintenance of my proficiency as a military flier. To be a good military flier one must fly military airplanes as often as possible. That was the business of the flight in question."

"I see. But on what authority, Stachel?"

"I carry a letter which authorizes me to fly any uncommitted Reichswehr aircraft at any time that might not specifically hinder a specific military operation or procedure. The letter is signed by Chef der Heeresleitung and countersigned by his adjutant."

"We have seen a copy of the letter you describe, Stachel." The colonel glanced at his colleagues and motioned for another consultation. Their whispering was, with the distant clacking of a typewriter, the only sound in the room. After a time, the colonel nodded at the clerk and said, "We wish to recall Oberleutnant Randelmann."

Stachel returned to his chair by the window and watched as Randelmann, pale and anxious, took the stand.

"On the date in question, Randelmann," Colonel von Menzing said in his mincing way, "did Stachel show you his letter of authorization?"

"No, sir."

"But you had seen it before."

"Oh, yes, sir. Many times. Stachel was fond of waving it under my nose."

"But he did not wave it under your nose on this day?"

"That's correct, sir. He did not."

"Why?"

"I warned him not to. I told him I was sick of looking at it."

The colonel leaned forward. "So when was the last, most recent time you had actually read the letter, Randelmann? When was it you had last analyzed the precise language of the authorization issued in the name of Chef der Heeresleitung?"

Randelmann blushed, confused and unhappy. "I can't say, sir. The only time I recall reading the letter carefully was the first time, some months ago."

"So then you failed to note on the day of the accident that the date of the letter was April the sixteenth?"

"Well, I guess so, sir—"

Colonel von Menzing opened a file folder on the table before him and withdrew a paper. He held it before his colleagues, and they nodded judiciously. He passed the paper to Randelmann, who read it, red-faced.

"What is the document, Randelmann?" the colonel purred.

"A letter signed by Oberst Funk, an aide to Chef der Heeresleitung."

"What does the letter say? Paraphrase, if you wish."

"It's a letter that countermands Stachel's authorization."

"What is its date?"

"August eleven, this year."

"To whom is the letter directed?"

"To operations officers, all flight sections, Reichswehr."

The colonel nodded again. "And you are an operations officer of a flight section, are you not?"

"Yes, sir," Randelmann said miserably.

"But you did not read this countermand?"

"Sir, I swear, it never came into my office. I personally read and file all incoming orders and situation reports—I don't have a clerk because the budget won't permit—and I'm very conscientious in the bargain. And I can say categorically that such a countermand never came into my office."

"How can you be sure?"

"Well, frankly, sir, it would have given me much pleasure to wave it under Stachel's nose."

The colonel glanced at the clerk. "Call Feldwebel Gunther."

Gunther replaced Randelmann in the witness chair. He was a large man, with a chest like an oil drum and eyes that regarded the world as if he'd caught it in the act of shoplifting.

"Identify yourself, please."

"Alfred Gunther, Feldwebel, Ninety-Sixth Military Police Abteilung, Berlin and environs."

"Did you, Gunther, on Thursday of last week, visit the office of Oberleutnant Randelmann, operations officer, Flight Section Three?"

"I did, sir," Gunther said, bored.

"What was your mission?"

"I was authorized by this court to search for a copy of a letter, dated August eleven, this year, and signed by Oberst Funk, adjutant, Chef der Heeresleitung."

"Was Oberleutnant Randelmann present during your search?"

"He was."

"Did he see you withdraw the letter in question from his file?"

"He did, sir."

Randelmann, crimson in his confused anger, stood up and said loudly, "Somebody had to have put that letter in my file when I was out of the office—during the night—some—"

The colonel struck the table with his riding crop and barked, "Sit down, Randelmann, or I'll have you on charges!"

Stachel, his own rage gathering, shouted, "And how come I never got a copy of that countermand? I'm the officer involved—"

"Silence, both of you!" Colonel von Menzing pounded the table three times, and papers flew. "I will not tolerate these outbursts!"

There was a moment of silent shock, then the clerk scurried about to retrieve the papers, and the room returned to its electric busyness.

"Call Gefreiter Lüdke."

The gefreiter, a short man with pale eyes and a professorial air, identified himself as clerk-typist assigned to the office of Major Reinhard Kleine, personnel section, Fliegerzentrale, Berlin.

"Among your duties, Corporal," the colonel said, his voice still icy with leftover anger, "do you receive the incoming mail for Major Kleine's section?"

"I do, sir."

"And, since Hauptmann Stachel is a member of Major Kleine's section, you receive mail that pertains to him and his duties as aircrew classification interviewer?"

"Yes, sir."

"The clerk has handed you a letter, dated August eleven and signed by Oberst Funk. Do you recall ever having seen that document before this?"

Gefreiter Lüdke read slowly, his lips pursed. "Yes, sir," he said finally. "I remember this. It came in on August the twelfth. I remember stamping it with the time-and-date stamp."

Stachel sighed silently. Lüdke, he knew, couldn't remember how to find the latrine. Lüdke was not only a forgetful and lazy man, he was a liar. Unfortunately, he was not an admirer of Bruno Stachel, either, because Bruno Stachel had, at least twice, dressed him down for some little inefficiency.

"Then what did you do? With the letter, I mean."

"I took it directly to Hauptmann Stachel's office and placed it with the stack of papers already in his in box."

"Where was Hauptmann Stachel at the time?"

"In Frankfurt am Main, sir. He was on a field trip."

"Did you—or anyone else, for that matter—have cause to remove the letter from Hauptmann Stachel's in box?"

"No, sir."

"So, then, you have every reason to believe that Hauptmann Stachel received and read the letter upon his return to Berlin?"

"Yes, sir."

"That will be all, Gefreiter."

"Recall Hauptmann Stachel."

Stachel, aware now of inexorable forces closing in, sat in the chair, ready now to have the sorry business finished.

"When you went aloft in aircraft number fourteen thirty-eight, Stachel, why did you take the deceased Nachtigal with you?"

"It was on a whim. I was going to fly anyhow, I preferred to have somebody in the rear cockpit of a ship rigged for the weight of two men. And Nachtigal, reputed to be a flier trying to get back to flying, looked—well—as if he could use a bit of cheering up, so to speak."

"You say 'reputed to be a flier.' Didn't you know he wasn't a flier?"

"No. I'd given him some forms to fill out, but in the rush of things I simply took Major Kleine's word for it that Nachtigal had flown with the Turks in Mesopotamia."

"You were going to fly with a man, but made no effort to determine his qualifications?"

With a sinking feeling, Stachel said, "As I say, I assumed Major Kleine knew what he was talking about."

Colonel von Menzing's lip curled slightly; Stachel couldn't tell if it had been a smile of triumph or a mere readjustment of the mouth.

"So, then," the colonel said, "you went aloft with a man whose official forms showed him to have been an aero mechanic who had been placed on detached service with the Turkish air service from"—he consulted a note—"February, 1917, to July, 1918. Whose forms showed only that he was applying for readmission to the Reichswehr for eventual flight training."

"As I say, I didn't look at the forms."

"And, during the course of the flight, you lost control of the machine, and it crashed, killing your untrained—and no doubt bemused—passenger."

"That's the way it was, I suppose."

"Answer yes or no, Hauptmann Stachel."

"Yes."

Colonel von Menzing traded glances with the others at the table. "Any other questions, gentlemen?" When they shook their heads, he pushed back his chair, arose, and said brittlely, "We'll recess until thirteen-thirty hours."

Stachel was having a solitary coffee in the Officers' Mess when Randelmann came to his table, a steaming mug in his hands.

"Mind if I join you, Stachel?"

"I don't mind."

"What's going on in there? I mean, my God—"

"I'm being railroaded, that's what's going on. Abgekartes Spiel. The old frame-up."

"I feel so rotten," Randelmann said. "I used to snarl and snort about your von Seeckt letter, but, my God, I don't want any part of this. I hope you don't think—"

"That you're part of the frame? Hell, Randelmann, you're caught in the same squeeze. You're a victim, too."

"I—"

"You don't think for a moment that there's any future for an officer who files official communications without reading them, do you? You'll be lucky if they don't cashier you."

Randelmann groaned. "But I swear to God above—that letter was planted in my file."

"Sure. But who'll believe you? Besides, if somebody is going to all this trouble to frame me, why should they worry about framing you?"

"Oh, God. What a rotten business."

"Our sacred German officers' code of honor at work."

"But *why?* Why does somebody want to do this? I mean—"

"Who knows, Randelmann. It could be von Seeckt himself. He wasn't very happy about giving me the letter in the first place."

"But von Seeckt—a general of great honor and repute, a gentleman—he wouldn't stoop to a lousy frame-up. To lying—"

"Of course not. But I can hear him—'Oberst Funk, about that letter we gave Stachel—I'm not very happy about it. Fix it up, will you? Don't bother me with the details. Just see that it no longer applies, eh?"

"I can't imagine a top German general being so petty."

"I can't imagine anybody in this world being anything else."

When the hearing reconvened, Colonel von Menzing told Stachel that he would be dismissed from the Reichswehr, fined five hundred marks, and be required to pay for the airplane he demolished. Moreover, said the colonel in his mouth-puckered way, Stachel was fortunate that he would not be held and tried for criminal manslaughter, but, since he was a former war hero whose main dereliction had been poor judgment and inattention to official communications, he would be shown leniency.

"Hugelmeier's Delicatessen."
"I'd like to price your Sauerkraut."
"Who's calling, please?"
"Laub."
"This is Sauerkraut. Eleven."
"Six-seven-seven."
"What's the word, Laub?"
"Stachel has been cashiered. That's all for this study now."
"Thank you. Sauerkraut sixteen."
"Seven-seven-six."

11

Once the anger and shock had subsided, Stachel spent most of the following two weeks in the State Library, where he rummaged through stacks of texts. When he felt ready at last, he went directly to the Bürgerbräukeller in Haidhausen, where Bormann and the other Nazis were said to hang out, but nothing much was going on there. A handful of thoughtful men, sitting in lonely separation, sipped from mugs of beer and stared at what was left of their lives, while in a corner of the barnlike hall, round and pink-faced and scrubbed, a gaggle of waitresses gossiped in subdued tones. Three old men in Lederhosen and Alpine vests were reading newspapers, and some youngsters—probably university students—argued softly about soccer. The place smelled of sauerkraut and tobacco and sweaty wool.

Stachel sat at a table beside one of the posts and ordered eine Halbe, which he did not drink but kept at his elbow as protective camouflage while he surveyed the scene and waited for something to happen.

It didn't take long.

"Ah," a voice said behind him. "Our famous war ace pauses for a beer."

"Hello, Bormann. You must have been hiding in the woodwork."

Bormann came around the table and took a chair. "We keep a very close eye on the clientele. The lookout has orders to flash the office whenever a detective or a Communist spy might wander in."

"Which one did I look like?"

Bormann smirked. "You shouldn't be so modest. Everybody in Germany must know your face by now. Even our lookout, a wretched fellow with good eyes and bad teeth. He's one of your admirers, it seems, and was quite thrilled to report your arrival."

"Maybe I should grow a beard or something."

"Please don't. The Führer likes clean-cut Nordic types. He says only rabbis wear beards." Bormann's tone was easy and familiar, and he gave Stachel an amiable inspection. "How's everything in Berlin? Have they gotten over your much publicized aerial highjinks yet?"

"That's what I came to see you about."

"Oh?" Bormann gave him an amused wink. "You mean you didn't simply come in for a spot of beer? You actually came to look me up?"

"I've been thinking over your proposition. Your suggestion that I go into politics."

Bormann's smile tightened. "I see. Well, that was quite a few months ago. Göring was very disappointed that you didn't join our movement at the first opportunity. The captain puts great stock in spontaneity—enthusiasm. And he was sad when he learned that you were so, well, lukewarm. . . ."

"I was lukewarm because I couldn't see anything in it for me."

"Ah-ha. The ancient question of incentive, eh? Politics is a two-way thoroughfare—that sort of thing."

"Something like that."

Bormann opened his cheap serge coat and scratched his belly reflectively. His small pig's eyes were wary. "So, then, I'm to assume that you are now willing to join the Nazi party if you can have something in return. Is that it?"

"I'm not so sure I want to be active in your party. But I'll give it a good word here and there among my rich friends. Which is what you said you and Göring wanted in the first place."

"And what is it you expect in return?" Bormann asked carefully.

"Reinstatement to my duties in Fliegerzentrale."

Bormann's eyes showed amusement. "Ah," he said. "The incentive."

Leaning forward and resting his elbows on the table, he regarded Stachel with an expression that hinted of an inner anger. "Tell me about it," he said.

Stachel went over the whole business, being careful to keep his own anger from showing. These Nazis were reputed to be volatile, unpredictable types, quick to take offense, and he felt that a posture of even-tempered naïveté on his part would accomplish more than would his natural urge to kick a hole in the Truppenamt walls.

Bormann looked up from his note-taking. "You *were* rather stupid to take Nachtigal up without checking his papers."

" 'Stupid' is the word. I have no excuse."

"Let me see," Bormann said slowly, staring at his scribbling again. "Presiding was Colonel von Menzing, assisted by a Major Klausser and a Captain von Zeumer." He pursed his lips and continued to read. Then: "Do you know Oberst Funk's first name?"

"No. All I know is that he's von Seeckt's aide."

"How about your superior, this, ah, Major Kleine? What do you think of him?"

"He's all right. A bit pompous, I'd say. But, all in all, a good sort. And a fairly good administrator."

"You don't think he was in on this little exercise to railroad you?"

"I doubt it. He's not the type. Too honest."

"But you do suspect Gefreiter Lüdke?"

"Gefreiter Lüdke is a piece of dung."

Bormann made a final note, concluding with an emphatic period. Then he placed the pad in his pocket, pushed away from the table, and stood up. "Wait for me here, Stachel."

Stachel nodded and watched him cross the hall and disappear through a door in one of the far corners. Ten minutes passed, and he was wondering whether to order supper when Bormann reappeared in the doorway, beckoning.

Bormann took his elbow and guided him through the door and down a dimly lit hallway. "You have another admirer, Stachel," he said. "The Führer would like to meet you."

The room was no more than a cube of whitewashed space at the end of the corridor near the kitchen. The cooking smells were heavy, and Stachel thought of his boyhood room at the rear of the hotel in Schwalbe. Unaccountably, irrationally, he was suddenly homesick.

"Mein Führer, may I present Hauptmann Bruno Stachel," Bormann murmured unctuously.

The man was thin, with a patch of mustache and a head of black hair. He sat in an overstuffed chair, surrounded by a small hill of rumpled newspapers, and there was a large atlas open on his lap. His skin was sallow, and his eyes were large and luminous and set in heavily seamed folds. He did not offer his hand.

"How do you do," Stachel said, noting that the man seemed larger than the press photos made him out to be. He was about to add some inanity implying that he'd been looking forward to this moment, but that wouldn't be true, and instinct warned that this man would be quick to see the lie and to dismiss him as a faker. Oddly, he found himself wanting to avoid that possibility; normally he cared very little what other men thought of him, but now he felt that the glowing eyes could see everything in him and about him, and it became strangely important that he pass muster.

"You are taller than I thought you'd be." The voice was deep and throaty—a soft hoarseness that suggested great weariness. "You fliers are always so compelling. So filled with a kind of presence. What is it about the sky that works such magic on you men, Stachel?"

Stachel hesitated, wondering if the man were baiting him. But he could see no humor in the marblelike eyes, and so he said earnestly, "there's something very spiritual about flying, Herr Hitler. I suppose it eventually shows in a man's face."

"Mm. Perhaps. You have a rather marvelous presence, Stachel. You have more of it than any man I've met recently."

"Even Göring?" Stachel smiled again to show he was not one to dote on compliments.

"Especially Göring," Hitler said with the same lack of humor. "There was a time when Göring was quite a fellow, but marriage and wounds and addictions are making him ponderous and heavy-handed. I value his comradeship, but his charisma has diminished appreciably, I'm afraid."

Not knowing what else to say, Stachel said, "Time works strange effects on men."

"Sit down, Stachel." Hitler nodded at a wicker chair under the room's single high window. "I must tell you how pleased I was with your now famous flying exhibition over Berlin. The German people need such inspiration. And the Iron Crosses on the machine were a splendid, defiant touch."

"Well," he said smoothly, "I want only to serve Germany. There's so much to do, and I'd like to help do it—"

"All good Germans want to serve Germany," Hitler said, his brows lowered meaningfully.

"Many are called but few are chosen, eh?" Stachel said, feeling a bit silly.

"There will be a day soon when all will be called," Hitler said, his gaze averted. "Germans will be known by where they stand on the principles of national socialism."

"I'm sure," Stachel said, working to maintain his air of polite interest. It was very difficult to see this man as a Führer; with his tacky vest and worn shirt, his stringy necktie and high-button shoes, he suggested somebody's uncle dozing over the newspapers after a heavy dinner.

Almost as if he could hear the thought, Hitler's eyes came slowly about to settle a pensive stare on Stachel's forehead. "It will not always be like this, Stachel."

"Nothing remains the same, I suppose," Stachel parried.

Hitler closed the atlas and placed it on the heap of newspapers beside his chair, his gaze never wavering. Then he sat forward slightly, his fists clenching and unclenching, his pale cheeks showing spots of color. "Nationalist autocracy is fundamental to Germany's survival. Either we have a dictatorship of the proletariat, as the Communists champion, or we'll have a dictatorship of the state, as I specify. I propose to prevail. I shall prevail. And there is a bedrock reason why I shall prevail. Do you know what that is?"

Stachel shifted in his chair, feeling peculiarly uneasy. "I can't say that I do."

"The reason transcends mere politics, Stachel. The reason lies in the very center of the human soul. To find the reason—appreciate it—you must first look for the core of the German national discontent. And once that is explored, you will have found the key to the absolute control of not only the Fatherland but also the entire civilized world. The Russians mouth a lot of garbage about revolutionary socialism, the eventual collapse of capitalism, the workers' revolution in which the system is to be entirely possessed by the peasant, and the ultimate upheaval in which the entire world will be under a centralist, socialist ownership of wealth and property. But the Russians and their collectivism will fail, Stachel. They will fail because they can't see the woods for the trees—they are so busy prescribing methods and standards, the nuts and bolts and machinery of revolution, that they are missing the single fault of human nature which, when exploited properly, can bring the exploiter an absolute domination of society. I see the fault, and I propose to exploit it."

Hitler paused, his eyes glassy, his jaw muscles working. There was a film of sweat on his forehead. Stachel waited, recognizing that anything but an expression of rapt attention would be considered blasphemy. This man was obviously a crackpot of the first order, but—what was the saying? Beggars can't be choosers?

"What is the characteristic most common to all human beings, Stachel?" Hitler rasped, obviously expecting no answer. "What is the fault all men share in abundance? It is the overriding need to blame someone else for the prevailing unhappiness. A man will go to any length to avoid self-evaluation, self-criticism, self-accusation. A man will, rather, leap at once to any conclusion that shows the cause of his unhappiness and discontent to be an external injustice, an alien evil of which he is the innocent victim. Take the case of Jesus Christ, for example. Christ's followers, for all their tenacity over the past nineteen hundred years, are destined to fail—to wither away on some future vine. Why? Because if, as they claim, the Nazarene was indeed the Son of God, if Jesus Christ was actually God in the flesh, man will have to change—in attitudes outlook, habits, beliefs, everything. And man fears change. He'd rather hold fast to a familiar evil than try to adapt to an unfamiliar good. It's much easier, more comforting, to say, No, the man of Galilee was a faker, a ridiculous sentimentalist with an overblown ego, than it is to say, Yes, he was right—the cause of my discontent is in me, myself, and I must change my basic nature if I'm ever to be happy at all. Christianity—like communism—carries the seeds of its own failure. Men will reject both because they ask men to change—to sublimate their natural greed, covetousness, envy, their desire to acquire, own, control, profit, dominate their peers.

"Men, on the other hand, will flock to me—they will fall at my feet as slaves, and they will glory in their enslavement. Why? Because I won't ask them to change. I shall *agree* with them. I shall demonstrate to them that they themselves are obviously innocent of any transgressions, any wrong-doing. I shall then point out to them the real culprits, the outsiders, the external evil ones, who have caused all their unhappiness. And then, having named the enemy, I'll play to the individual's natural lusts for revenge, dominance, supremacy; I'll feed his yearning to acquire and hold; I'll assure him that he's perfect the way he is, and any suggestion that he change is an outrageous absurdity. So doing, I'll have triggered the fatal self-righteousness, the unseeing smugness, that invariably culminate in a rejection of reason, debate, and compromise. I'll have begun the process that will eventually enable me to rule the world. Because human nature is the same the world over. Men are naturally rotten. To control men, all one need do is to make their rottenness socially acceptable."

Hitler sank back in his chair, his eyes closed. The room was silent except for the sound of his heavy breathing.

Stachel ventured a glance at Bormann, who sat expressionlessly on the worn divan in the opposite corner. Bormann kept his gaze fastened on Hitler, giving no sign that he felt Stachel's inspection.

After a time, Hitler asked, "What do you think of that, Stachel? What do you think of all that?"

The man was mad, of course, but a little ingratiation was indicated. "I've never heard it put better," he said, elaborately sincere. "You certainly have put your finger on things."

Hitler's heavy lids parted, revealing the agatelike eyes, clouded now with what seemed to be fatigue. "How do you stand on national socialism, Stachel?" The deep voice held a challenge.

This, of course, was the crucial test. Stachel had been expecting the question from Bormann—his reason for spending all those hours in the library; but now that the question hung in the air he felt an awkwardness, a faltering akin to the tongue-tied embarrassment of a schoolboy who hadn't thoroughly prepared his lesson.

"Well," he said, "the history of the world is pretty heavy with politicians who've claimed to have found the best way to organize society. They've all failed in the long run because they've either been quickly outdated, swamped by changing times and conditions, or they've overlooked the basic fact that people aren't capable of governing themselves. People must be led. They actually yearn to be led, because, as you say, they fear the self-analysis and open-mindedness that responsible self-government would require—"

"The United States have done quite well under such a system," Hitler broke in contentiously.

"For the time being," Stachel said evenly, feeling his confidence growing. "But the United States will eventually fail as an experiment in self-government because the process will smother under the weight of special demands. I've read American and English history, and it's pretty clear that the American kind of government works fine when all of the various elements in the country feel commonly pressed, or threatened, by a challenge to the general security or well-being. They get together and collaborate on solving the problem or meeting the challenge. But you just watch—if they ever get to the point where they don't have a common purpose, the Americans will run down. They've got to have a purpose, and they've got to have priorities. If they don't have them, they'll fall into a stalemate, in which a whole flock of bickering special-interest groups cancel each other out. And stalemate is stagnation, and stagnation is death."

"So much for the Americans. I asked you about national socialism."

"National socialism—the kind you champion, Herr Hitler—is the only logical form of government for Germany, perhaps for Europe, the world, even. It establishes an unwavering order, in which the top man names the priorities, the goals, and then rewards those who do the most to fulfill them. You encourage the individual, let him acquire things, give him status, but you relieve him of the responsibility of national planning and achievement."

There, Stachel thought. *That'll show the bastard I've studied my catechism.*

Hitler, his eyes closed again, nodded approvingly. "Well said, Stachel. You are everything Göring claims you to be."

"I'd like to join your group, Herr Hitler. Hearing your comments has made me understand all the more fully why it is we need you to lead Germany out of the wilderness."

"Very well. See to it, will you, Bormann?"

"Of course, Mein Führer."

"And see to it that Hauptmann Stachel is restored to the Fleigerzentrale post. At once."

"To be sure, Mein Führer."

12

Oberst Funk read the message three times, unbelieving. Then, heavy with a sense of impending calamity, he arose from his desk and crossed to the inner door, pausing to rap politely on the enameled paneling.

"Come in," the general's voice called.

"Excuse the interruption, Herr General, but I thought you ought to see this." He held out the message form.

Von Seeckt readjusted his monocle and reached for the paper. Reading, he turned in his large swivel chair and held the paper at an angle that gave it additional light from the window. "God," he said finally, as if to himself.

"That makes the fourth," Funk said quietly.

"It's got to be coincidence," the general said.

Oberst Funk shook his head slowly. "All respect, sir, but I don't think so. Coincidence doesn't reach that far. One, two perhaps. But four?"

Von Seeckt placed the form on the desk at his elbow and sat quietly, contemplating the courtyard beyond the window. "But what is there to go on, Funk? What evidence do you have that points to anything but coincidence?"

"I have no evidence, of course, Herr General. If I did, I'd move on it. But intuition—an inner certainty—tells me that it's a plot. A scheme of retribution."

"On whose part? That Stachel fellow?" The general snorted. "He's a tinsel bumpkin. A parvenu. He doesn't have the subtlety or tenacity to conceive and carry on a vendetta."

"He's a very dangerous man. He has killed many times."

"In war, Funk. In war. There's a difference between honorable combat and assassination. I should think you'd know that."

"I do, Herr General. But—"

"But nothing, Funk. You're an old maid, seeing rapists under the bed. Relax. It's coincidence, nothing more."

Funk, his deference to rank sinking in the rising tide of anxiety, began to count on his fingers: "The first was Gefreiter Lüdke, found hanging from a shower head in a Lichterfelde barracks latrine. The second was Captain von Zeumer, shot to death in his apartment while his wife sat sewing in the next room. The third was Major Klausser, who fell—or was pushed—from a window in the Truppenamt on Wilhelmstrasse. The fourth, this one"—he pointed to the message form on the polished walnut desk—"is Colonel, the Baron von Menzing, bludgeoned to death on a bridle path in the Tiergarten. Two obvious homicides, two possibles. Coincidence, Herr General? I don't think so."

The general turned in his chair again, facing Funk and letting the monocle drop on its cord. His face was flushed with barely contained exasperation. "That will do, Funk. I've heard enough of this balderdash. Now get out of my office and let me get some work done."

"Hello?"
"Frau Stachel?"
"Yes."
"Oberst Funk here."
"Oh. What is it, Colonel?"
"I wonder if I might meet with you this evening."
"I'm afraid not. I have an engagement."
"It's most important, madam. It has to do with your husband."
"I see. Can't you discuss it now?"
"I'd rather it be where we might be assured of complete privacy. The matter is touchy, as I say, and it would be better if we're not seen together."
"All right. Do you know where the Café Lisette is?"
"The place with the red awnings on Leopoldstrasse?"
"That's the one. I'll be in my Mercedes in the cul-de-sac down the block, where the trees and the gazebo are."
"I know the place."
"At twenty-two-thirty. Right?"
"Right. I'll see you there, madam."

A gentle rain was falling, and the night was rich with the smell of damp leaves and coal smoke. The streetlights, wearing misty coronas, made silvery patterns on the wet streets, and above, in the gloom beyond the housetops, low clouds hung, sullen and promising soggy days ahead. The big old houses behind the trees showed few lights, and the quiet was broken only occasionally by cars moving on the boulevard to the east. It was a chill, melancholy time in a backwater residential section, and she huddled in her coat, wondering who lived in the hushed places around her, and why. She considered having a cigarette, but she'd been smoking entirely too much lately and so she settled deeper into the car seat and continued her stoic waiting, feeling a touch of martyrdom.

As usual, her mind wandered to Bruno, and there was the inevitable sense of guilt. She had expected to feel considerably more triumphant over his dismissal from the army, but he had gone directly off to Munich without seeing her and she had earned nothing more than remorse for her shabby tricks and schoolgirl scheming. In moments of merciless self-candor, she would admit that she'd hoped his dismissal would bring him crawling back to her—drunk, perhaps, but nonetheless chastened and malleable. But all that had been achieved was still another wordless separation, and now she was back to the same old treadmill—filling empty days with pretended activity, lonely nights with inane parties and flirtations and occasional mindless rutting.

In an odd departure, her thoughts went to the idea of God. She remembered her childhood, in which her mother had patiently taught her Bible verses and told pretty little stories of sweet Jesus, and assured her God loved her, and if she followed the Golden Rule and lived by the Ten Commandments she would be happy and pure and acceptable to the Father in Heaven, and let us pray, shall we, dear? But God and sweet Jesus had died with her mother, and her father, a remote and difficult man who believed in nothing but business and the future of Germany, had gone his remote and difficult way to the arms and bed of a widow lady in Stuttgart who had squandered his fortune and left him a pitiful hulk in an Augsburg nursing home. She had no way of knowing if her father had believed in God, but if he had, he'd been swindled, and if he hadn't, he'd gotten exactly what he deserved.

A cab pulled to the curb in front of the shuttered Café Lisette and led out a tall man in a military raincoat who, after paying the driver and watching the car drive off, stood in lonely silhouette. After a moment, he turned and came toward the Mercedes, his heels making clicking sounds on the streaming sidewalk.

Through the side window he said softly, "Frau Stachel?"

She leaned across the seat and opened the passenger door for him. "Get in, Oberst Funk. Before you drown."

He sank onto the leather beside her, a huge and dripping hulk. He stared at her in the dim light, unsmiling. "Thank you for coming," he said. "I know it's an inconvenience, but it's most important to me."

"What's on your mind, Colonel?"

His hand slid into his greatcoat and, after fumbling a moment, he withdrew an envelope, which he placed on the seat between them. "I'm returning the money you gave me, Frau Stachel. All but five hundred dollars, which I used, unfortunately, to pay some badly overdue bills. I'll return that sum to you as I earn it."

She glanced at the envelope, then at him. Quietly sarcastic, she said, "You're returning the Reichswehr's money? I thought it was to be spent on the expenses of my husband's separation from the military."

"Let's not play games, madam. I'm returning your money. Moreover, I implore you to take a message to your husband. It's most urgent that he be made aware that I'm doing everything I can to reinstate him in his former job and at his full rank. You must tell him that."

"Colonel, I've gone to a lot of trouble and expense to get my husband free of the military. I'm not about—"

"I beg you, Frau Stachel," Funk broke in. "It's a matter of the greatest urgency. Of life or death. You must let Hauptmann Stachel know that I, personally, am conducting a tireless campaign to achieve his return to full military duty. You must tell him that I'm outraged over the shabby treatment he received at the hands of the hearing board. You must do this."

"I rarely see my husband these days, Colonel. Besides, how would I explain to him my rather special knowledge of what you're doing to, ah, work in his behalf?"

"You must make up something. Tell him we met at a party, and I confided in you—told you of my outrage, and my efforts to help him. You'll think of something."

"Well, Colonel," she began, breaking off the answer when she saw the faint motion beyond the streaming window beside him. She sought to warn him, but the words wouldn't come, bemused as she was by the magical inward folding of the glass, the kaleidoscopic patterns of color as the teeming shards and splinters roiled in on the incandescent, thundering flash. She was aware, in the time-lapse photography of her paralyzed mind, of Oberst Funk's head collapsing in a dreadful red mist, and then she saw the second beautiful ball of fire, rolling at her from the black tube, swirling out in an exquisite billowing that enveloped her, lifted her, up and away and beyond, into a brilliant light of indescribable beauty.

TELEPHONE TRANSCRIPT

"Hugelmeier's Delicatessen."

"I'd like to price your Sauerkraut."

"Who's calling, please?"

"Laub."

"This is Sauerkraut. Twenty-seven."

"Eight-five-five."

"You have a report, Laub?"

"Yes. A rather significant offshoot of the Stachel study.

General von Seeckt has handed the defense minister his resignation and has been replaced as Chef der Heeresleitung by Oberst General Wilhelm Heye."

"Good God. What happened?"

"I don't know. It just happened. There are no details."

"That's fantastic. Von Seeckt isn't a quitter."

"He is now, my dear Sauerkraut."

"Anything else?"

"One thing. Von Seeckt's final act in office was to sign an order returning our friend, Stachel, to full duty. As I get it, he'll be asistant chief, Sondergruppe VS, Fliegerzentrale, Berliner Truppenamt."

"That's all for this study?"

"That's all."

"Thank you. Sauerkraut twelve."

"Five-five-eight."

13

It had begun to rain again, and a restless wind whispered in the city's canyons. Setting his cap more firmly and turning up the collar of his greatcoat, Stachel made for the cab stand. As he approached the corner, a car eased alongside, its tires hissing on the wet pavement.

"Hop in, Stachel. We'll take you home."

He peered through the gloom at the man who held open the car's rear door. "Who is it?" he said.

"Bormann. Get in. It's cold out there."

Stachel climbed into the car and sank onto the mohair seat. He sat silently as Bormann gave the driver the address.

"Now then," Bormann said pleasantly after the car was in motion, "how are things with you, Herr Hauptmann?"

"I've been wanting to talk to you, Bormann."

"I suspected as much. That's why I'm here."

"How about that fellow there?" Stachel said, nodding at the driver.

"Fredo?" Bormann's face, half light and half shadow in the flickerings of passing lights, registered a smile. "Fredo's as safe as a mother's lap, Stachel. I hold no secrets from Fredo."

"As you wish. But I'm going to do some plain talking."

"Talk away, Herr Hauptmann."

Stachel watched the passing city for a time—the great buildings with their darkened windows and chalky façades, the lacy lights, the trees stirring uneasily in the night wind. He felt a sadness.

"Why my wife, Bormann?"

"Beg pardon?"

"Why was my wife killed?"

"What's your guess?"

"Come on, you bastard—don't give me your city-slicker politician doubletalk. Just tell me straight out. Why was Kaeti shot, along with that fathead, Funk?"

"Perhaps they were having an affair."

"That's what the police suggested. But you and I know better, don't we."

"The police?"

"I was questioned for almost three days. They suspected that I shot my wife and her lover in what they called 'jealous rage.' But I had an excellent alibi they couldn't break. I was having dinner with none other than the Baroness von Klingelhof-und-Reimer, who, as we both know, enjoys an impeccable reputation." Stachel's sarcasm was alloyed with clenched anger. "The time of Kaeti's and Funk's death was set at the very time I was digging into my quiche Lorraine, according to the Baroness's impeccable butler, who was serving all six of us at the table."

"I'm glad of that," Bormann said easily.

"So why was she killed?"

Bormann readjusted himself on the seat and sighed. "In all honesty, Stachel, she happened to be in the wrong place at the wrong time. Why she was there, no one knows. But she was. And, because Fredo was concerned that she might have seen his face, he had to remove her. She was simply an innocent victim of war, like a mother or a child who dies in an air raid."

"My God, Bormann—what kind of people are you?"

Bormann gave him a careful glance. "As I say, Stachel, we are in a war. There are no uniformed armies, no battle fronts, no bands playing and troops marching. But there is a war raging, and you and I and Fredo—Göring, Hess, Röhm, all of us—are soldiers. We are fighting for Germany's survival. We are fighting to rid Germany of a cancer that is killing her. To save Germany, many will eventually have to die—some of them innocently, as Frau Stachel did. I'm sorry that your wife got caught in the cross fire. I really am. But that's what happened to her."

"You admit killing all those people, just to get me reinstated at Fliegerzentrale?"

"Do you, Stachel, admit killing all those Englishmen and Frenchmen and Americans whose airplanes fell to your machine guns?"

"Those men were fighting back, trying to kill me."

"Killing is killing, Stachel. Funk, the others—they were trying to destroy you. We did not want you destroyed. You can be a very helpful soldier in our war."

Stachel fell silent, angry still, but unable to find solid ground for further argument.

"What was all that money doing in Kaeti's car?" he asked eventually. "The police said there was a small fortune. American dollars."

"I haven't the foggiest idea. Funk was a notorious gambler and was dangerously in debt. But what that specific money was about will, no doubt, remain forever a mystery."

Stachel thought about that for a time. Then he leaned forward in the seat and asked Fredo, "Did my wife say anything at all?"

The driver shrugged, keeping his eyes on the road ahead. "Not to me, she didn't. She simply looked through the window as I came alongside the car, and she reached out, as if to warn the man. I shot him first. Then her."

"She just sat there and took it?"

"I'd say so. Yes. She just sat there and, well, sort of smiled."

"Smiled?"

"As if she was remembering something pleasant, I guess you'd say. It was just an impression I got."

Stachel sat, frozen by the enormity. There were insistent pictures of little things, unrelated, but linked by the fact of intimacies shared, even if unwillingly and belligerently. Her comb on the dressing table; the way her eyes crinkled at the corners when she gazed across her beloved lake; the puffiness of her lips when she cried; her little yipping sounds in exalted moments in the dark; the way her hand would caress fine fabrics.

The inexplicable pain was very intense, and he couldn't be certain if he were mourning Kaeti or himself.

"Sorry, Stachel," Fredo said. "It wasn't personal, or anything. It was war, like Bormann said."

14

He worked very hard at his duties during the following two weeks, trying earnestly to smother his anger under a blanket of preoccupation. But, as he'd expected all along, it proved to be wasted effort, and on a blustery Sunday night he found himself parking his car in the same rotten little alley behind the same rotten little hotel in which he and the Baroness had entered their peculiar relationship four years earlier.

The same man was on the desk, too, and Stachel, his ski jacket buttoned tight against the bitter, snow-laced wind, watched him through the window for a time. Shortly before midnight, the man yawned, scratched his bottom with claw-like hands, and came around the reception counter to push through the door that led to the kitchen.

Stachel let himself into the lobby, going carefully so as to keep the bell above the door from jingling, then moved silently to the desk. Leaning and squinting in the dim light, he was able to make out the names on the mail slots. After lifting the house key from its peg, he crossed to the stairway and went to the upper hall, a dingy tunnel that smelled of tobacco and dust. He paused for a moment at the door at the far end, then, unlocking it, stepped through and closed it gently behind him. The room was in darkness, so he flicked on the wall switch.

Fredo sat up in the bed, blinking. "What the hell's the idea?" he snarled.

"Get up and put on some clothes," Stachel said.

"What for? I—you—what the hell you doing here, Stachel? I just got to sleep—"

Stachel was aware of the rising surge of his blood. His mind, in the capriciousness that derives from stress, went to the long-ago day over the Scarpe River Sector, when he'd stared across an interval of sky at the first man—an Englishman—who sought to kill him. There Bruno Stachel had learned how easy it could be to pull on the cloak of an avenging God.

Oppressed by the sense of all the final judgments he'd since pronounced, he told this man, the newest among the legion who'd offended him, "I'm taking you to the police."

The man in the bed looked at him, his face sagging with surprise. "The police? Whatever for?"

"For the murder of my wife."

"Surely you're joking. I told you it was an accident. An accident of war, as Bormann says—"

Stachel shook his head. "It's really theft, but the law labels it murder. And I want you to pay for it under the law."

Fredo's astonishment melted, to become wry amusement. He plumped the pillow behind him and rested back against the headboard, his mouth curled in a grin. "You are an amazing fellow, Stachel. Do you honestly expect me to climb out of my warm bed on a cold night like this and toddle down to police headquarters simply because you say I should?" He laughed, his recent sleep heavy in the sound. "My God, man, I wouldn't do that even if you were a cop."

"Come on, Fredo. Get up."

"The way I hear it, you didn't get along too well with the missus anyhow. I probably did you a favor."

"I once had a bicycle. When I was a boy. I hated it, because it didn't work very well. I was about to give it to the Orphans' Home in Wiesbaden. But a kid from down the road stole it one night. I beat the hell out of him and took him to the constable. Nobody steals from me, even if they steal something I don't want."

Fredo grinned, his features sardonic in the chalky glare of the ceiling light. "You mean you're going to beat me up and then haul me off to the cops for stealing your wife?"

"No. Good sense says you will get dressed and walk to the police station with me, quietly and peaceably."

Fredo laughed aloud again, then threw back a corner of the blanket, a flicker of motion that revealed the muzzle of the tubular silencer on the pistol he had slipped from under his pillow. He fired, and there was a vicious, snickering sound and a hot turbulence in the air beside Stachel's head.

The muffled snapping of the Beretta in Stachel's jacket

pocket provided an instantaneous echo. Four of the six shots found Fredo, and he rolled slowly from the bed, taking a tangle of sheets and blankets with him. He gasped heavily twice, then raised on an elbow to point his pistol at Stachel; but his eyes, oddly thoughtful, showed a sudden indirection, and he fell back on the grimy carpet.

"I never judged you to have good sense, Fredo," Stachel said in a low voice. "Nothing personal, of course."

The lobby was still deserted, so Stachel went to the desk, hung the house key on its peg, and, after pausing for a moment to listen to the muted laughter coming from the kitchen, eased out the front door and returned to his car.

It was snowing heavily by the time he reached his quarters.

From the Münchener Tageblatt:

The body of Alfredo Laumann, an unemployed brickmason, was found today in his room at the Hotel Regal.

Police say Laumann had been shot four times in what presumably had been a fight with an unknown visitor. A pistol, clutched in the victim's hand, had been fired at least once.

There are no suspects, although the hotel's owner, Hans Wohlheim, continues to be questioned.

15

The spring of 1927 seemed to have come with dramatic suddenness; the cold and the wind-driven, gritty snows had disappeared in a green explosion, whose fallout left soft breezes and whispering leaves and smoky blue skies. At least, that's how it appeared to Stachel, who had, during the dregs of winter, immersed himself in the business of being a staff officer. His world had become an enclave whose perimeters reached no further than his work, his apartment, his field manuals, his inspection tours, and, of course, his lessons in English and his deep studies of the United States—its history, its peoples, its government, folkways, mores, industry, educational systems, and military lore and potential. There was little interest in America at the General Staff level, but Fliegerzentrale felt a need for a watch on U.S. air potential, and Stachel had been given the job. Much of this had been guided by Dr. Ludwig von Schramm, the eminent and eccentric specialist in North American affairs on loan from Heidelberg, who demanded five hours a day, six days a week, if, as he put it, "This uneducated bumpkin in the soldier suit is to have the slightest glimmer as to what is going on west of Montauk Point."

One bright afternoon in May, Stachel was called to the office of the assistant chief, Truppenamt Intelligence Section, a post held by a Major von Brandt, a cadaverous man with thin hair and watery blue eyes who always sucked on peppermint cough lozenges. Stachel didn't like him much because he looked like his Uncle Heinrich, the church sexton.

"Sit down, Stachel. Pleasant day, isn't it," von Brandt said without conviction. "Cigar?"

"No thanks."

The major sank back in his swivel chair and folded his hands before his face in a parody of prayer. Regarding Stachel from eyes that seemed to weep, he said in his reedy voice, "I understand you are making remarkable strides in your job. You are rapidly becoming our resident expert on the United States."

"That's my assignment, Major."

"Mm. Of course." Von Brandt closed his eyes, as if resting them, and shifted the lozenge to the other side of his mouth. "When are you leaving for your Russian inspection trip?"

"July first. That's the planned departure. I'll be at Lipetsk for ten days and return before the end of July. The schedule is loose because the ship and train connections are unpredictable. The Russians operate their railroads on whim, I understand."

Von Brandt nodded. "Your trip is for familiarization only, correct?"

"Yes. My request for assignment to the training cadre at Lipetsk was turned down."

"What will you do when you return to Berlin?"

"Resume my economic and military assessment of the

United States, I suppose. I've received no other instructions."

"I see." The major turned in his chair to watch a pigeon that strutted on the windowsill. The bird seemed pleased with the golden sunlight, puffing its chest and looking about importantly. "As our resident expert on the United States, what do you know about the American Embassy and its people?"

Stachel thought about that for a moment, remembering the party for Lori Lehmann. "Nothing much. I've met only two of the people who work there—a military attaché and one of his female assistants. His name is Duncan. He's a captain in the air service. She's a stenographer or some kind of clerk, I think, who tutors languages as an additional duty. Her name is Loomis. She's a cold fish and makes no bones about disliking her work. She doesn't like Duncan, either."

"Where did you meet these people?"

"At a party. It was one of those god-awful film-colony brawls. Lori Lehmann and Max Zirko had something to do with it." Stachel gave him a thoughtful stare. "Why do you ask?"

"We have reason to believe that there's a leak in Truppenamt. Somebody is giving German military information to the U.S. Embassy. We'd like to find the leak and plug it."

"I daresay."

"Perhaps we can enlist your help."

"How, Major?"

Von Brandt reached for one of the cigars in the leather-faced box on his desk. He held it up to the light, like a chemist examining a sample, then he bit off its end and set it aglow with the flame from a benzine lighter. Once he'd sucked up a satisfactory cloud, he squinted through the smoke and said, "You say this Duncan fellow is a flier?"

"That's what he says. He wears those silver wings the American pilots wear."

"Why don't you cultivate his friendship?"

"That would be somewhat difficult, Major. He doesn't speak German."

"I thought you fliers had a language all your own," von Brandt said, smiling dryly. "Why don't you take him flying?"

Stachel felt interest stirring. "That would be fine with me. But toward what end?"

"Toward two ends, actually. First, of course, we'd like to determine if this Captain Duncan, as the military attaché and therefore the likeliest one to receive and process intelligence leaking from this headquarters, is indeed running a spy in our midst. Secondly, we would like to ingratiate ourselves with the embassy—with Duncan, particularly—because we might want eventually to send you on a, shall we say, a goodwill tour of the U.S.A."

"A tour? What for?" Stachel felt a true excitement now.

The major examined the tip of his cigar. "The Americans, we are learning, are remarkably naïve. They seem honestly to believe that if they deal openly and honestly and altruistically with other nations, those other nations will respond in kind. The opposite holds true as well. By that I mean, if a nation deals in a seemingly candid and friendly way with America, the Americans virtually fall all over themselves to respond similarly." He returned the cigar to his mouth and puffed contentedly for a moment.

"It's one of the more astonishing traits of an astonishing people," Stachel said. "The more I study them the more I disbelieve them. So who responds to whom in our little scheme, Major?"

Von Brandt smiled and said, "I see you're with me. What we'd like to do is for you to permit Captain Duncan to enjoy some of the privileges we've planned for our French friends—visit some of our aircraft plants, a few flying fields, a barracks or two. We'd like also to have you invite him to fly some of our airplanes."

"I see. So that, on my good-will tour—assuming that I'm invited to make one—the Americans will reciprocate. Is that it?"

"Mm. Quite so."

Stachel was skeptical. "What good will it do to have Duncan putter around in one of our old crates and for me to do the same with one of theirs? I can tell you all you want to know about their Jennies and DeHavillands and Thomas-Morses without leaving this office. I've memorized their specifications and flight characteristics."

"Well," the major said softly, "we're interested in their new, first-line craft. The ones whose specifications and flight characteristics are still confidential."

"So how will we do that? How will reciprocity be set up, when all we have as first-line aircraft are the Fokker D-Thirteens?"

"We are going to trick the Americans," von Brandt, purred. "As we plan to trick the French, the English."

"Oh?"

"We are going to permit Captain Duncan to ride along

with you in our newest Operational two-seat fighter bomber."

"And, pray tell, what in the hell would that be?" Stachel said with undisguised sarcasm.

Von Brandt placed his cigar in an ashtray and leaned forward to give Stachel an amused wink. "Ernst Heinkel, a promising young designer in Warnemünde, has produced an experimental airplane of rather peculiar capabilities. It is a low-wing monoplane built to accommodate an experimental engine developed by Professor Junkers. Udet has flown the machine and pronounces it a perfect fright."

"This is the machine I'm supposed to demonstrate to Duncan?"

"Exactly."

"But it's only a prototype, and not a very good one at that—"

Von Brandt shook his head knowingly. "Not so. Captain Duncan will be led to believe that we already have three full squadrons operational, with more to come as the Aircraft Restrictions clauses of the Control Commission Blue Book are eased."

"He won't swallow that. Not if he's running an agent among us."

"That's why we must plug the leak quickly. Then, once we've dried up his source of inside information, we'll give him a ride in our new Heinkel Bullet, and, as he flies low over the military airfield at Johannisthal, he will see a long line of them parked before the hangars. They will, of course, be mock-ups."

Stachel nodded. "So, hopefully, I—or some other German officer, at least—will someday receive a ride in America's best. Is that it?"

Von Brandt waved an apologetic hand. "It's the best plan we have, Stachel. It isn't much, but it's the best we have."

"The idea's to convince the Americans that our best plane is a stinker. Right?"

"Mm. And in their complacent superiority, they'll let us try their best."

"Any suggestions on what to look for? As far as the leak's concerned, I mean."

"Just keep your eyes and ears open. Report to me any peculiarities, discords, contradictions, in what Duncan says and does—as soon as possible. Otherwise send me a weekly memo summarizing your contacts with him. There may be discords you don't hear, eh?" Von Brandt's little smile was not reflected in his eyes. His eyes, drooping and liquid, never smiled. "I want your memos handwritten and hand-delivered. Everybody in this headquarters is suspect."

"Except you and me, eh?"

"No. You and I are also suspect. But I'm watching you, Stachel. If you're the spy, I'll catch you."

"Is there anyone watching you, Major?"

"I sincerely hope so, Stachel. Otherwise my faith in the system would be severely shaken."

They both smiled at this.

At precisely 19:30 hours, he picked up the telephone in his apartment, consulted his address book, and, when the operator came on the line, asked her to ring twenty-three, null, thirty-seven.

"Hello?"

"Fräulein Loomis?"

"Yes."

"Bruno Stachel here."

There was a pause on the other end, and he imagined her trying to deal with the surprise she had to be feeling.

"Well. It's been a while, hasn't it, Captain."

"Have you been well?"

"Yes."

"I've been thinking about you a lot lately."

"How so?"

"It's my wretched English instructor. He's impossible. I'm getting nowhere."

"So?"

"I wonder if you might consider taking me on as a student, or whatever you tutors call a client."

There was another pause, and then: "My fees are rather high, Captain. You might not want to pay so much."

"How high?"

"Three dollars an hour. American."

"Well, that is pretty stiff. But I'm sure it's worth it. I must learn English to qualify for a position that will be opening soon. Idiomatic, conversational English."

"When do you want to start?"

"This evening, if it's possible."

"Well, I don't know—"

"Please. I have so little time, Fräulein Loomis."

He could hear her breathing, and the sound was peculiarly sensuous. "All right," she said after a time, "but you'll have to give me an hour to get ready."

"Certainly. Do I just come to the embassy annex and ask for you?"

"I'm not at the annex. I'm at number ten Hügel Strasse. Second floor."

"Oh? I assumed you lived at the embassy."

"I do. But I have a girl friend who travels a lot. She lets me use her apartment when she's away and I'm bored with the embassy bunch."

"How handy."

"Yes, isn't it."

"I'll see you in an hour."

"Very well."

He hung up and clicked the receiver fork three times. The operator came back on and he gave her the Baroness's number.

"Darling, where are you? We're already on our second cocktail. And Rudi is already banging on the piano. I'd like you to get here before he passes out."

"I'm going to have to beg off tonight, chum. Business."

She made a little sound. "Can't you come later? After the business is taken care of?"

"I doubt it. I'm dead on my feet as it is."

"I miss you terribly."

"I'll call you. We'll take a day and drive to Bad Linck. We'll share a tub and I'll personally give you a massage. Like we did on Easter."

"Make it tomorrow. I can't wait."

"Soon, chum. Have a good time this evening. And don't let the piano lid fall on Rudi's dingus. That's what he does his thinking with."

She laughed and said, "You're impossible."

"I'll say."

He rang off and went into the bedroom to change.

16

The whole idea was asinine, of course—a silly little exercise out of a cops and robbers story. Stachel's natural cynicism had received many calls to duty during his years at Fliegerzentrale, what with the pomp and petty intrigues and elaborate bureaucratic scheming on all sides. A great smothering cloud of complacency was settling over the Truppenamt, and each day he recognized anew how valuable von Seeckt had been as an energizing influence; the Heeresleitung, under the monocled Prussian, had been tight, alert, snappy with a kind of urgency that was felt at all levels of command, but now that he was gone, dilettantism and intermural politics had begun to assert themselves. The idea, these days, apparently, was to build your own little empire, drawing a perimeter of influence around you and then manning it with old cronies who played to your sense of what was good or rewarding. And now here was von Brandt, dreaming up penny-dreadful plots against the dizzy Americans—not so much in an honest effort to influence a potential ally in the struggle against the Communists but more to give himself something sufficiently dramatic in tone to warrant a higher budget and larger fiefdom.

But there was a promise of flying in the mix, and von Brandt could wear devil's horns for all Stachel cared—so long as von Brandt's machinations produced an airplane and the wherewithal to operate it. He'd kiss von Brandt's behind at the Brandenburger Tor at high noon if it meant a chance to do some real flying.

Besides, the Loomis woman might indeed be able to help him with his English.

She placed three bottles on the silver tray, the one her Aunt Ruth had given her the Christmas before her mother died, and then carried the tray to the sideboard. He would probably drink the cognac—Germans rarely liked American bootleg—but she'd provided a quart each of bourbon and gin against the possibility he might be one of the exceptions.

Checking the time, then giving herself a final inspection in the foyer mirror, she recognized the irony. There had been a time when the mere sight of a whiskey bottle would be enough to immobilize her with anxiety. That had been in Chicago, when she was a girl, and they were living in a cheap house on the South Side, and her father worked as a machinist in a tool factory, when he wasn't falling-down-sick drunk. Which was almost all the time, in his final years. She would come home from school, blue from the wind and cold, and he would be there on the sofa, eyes like slits, and reeking; she would go about fixing supper, pretending she didn't see him there, sucking on his bourbon and watching her silently. And then, finally, there was no longer a job at the tool factory, and she had to quit tenth grade to play piano and sell sheet music in a five-and-ten so that the rent would be paid and there'd be, at least, breakfast and supper for them all and noontime milk and graham crackers for Donnie at school.

She went to the Victrola and wound it, so that she wouldn't have to fuss with the dumb thing at maybe a crucial moment. Her glance fell on the stack of brown and blue records, and on the top was "Peg O' My Heart," which had been a raging success in sheet-music sales after its introduction in 1913 and was playing the night of her sixteenth birthday when George Hector had bought her virginity for five dollars, the son of a bitch.

One thing about George, though: He'd taught her how to make a fast and easy dollar. George told her one night that, if she'd let him be her manager, he could get her a lot of dates—one for every night in the week for a take-home of as much as ten dollars a night. And she was really tempted, because fifty to seventy a week was a king's wage, and she had plans to get her diploma and go on to a normal school and become a teacher in some nice little tree-shaded town in the South, where the winters were warm and people called you "ma'am." There was no way she could make this all happen on what she was earning legitimately, but it was also very unlikely that she could keep her reputation if she went into professional dating, no matter how selective or infrequent. And reputation was everything. A decent working girl had a difficult row to hoe as it was; a girl who was discovered to have screwed for money might just as well go off a bridge, if she ever had any hopes of teaching school or getting married, or whatever.

She'd found the solution rather by accident.

George held a smoker one night at his apartment and had asked her if she'd give him a hand in the kitchen while the boys played cards and, later, watched a picture show. She'd peeked at the film, a very grainy, jerky, poorly lit thing that told a story of how a poor servant girl had got to marry a millionaire by sneaking into his study one midnight and servicing him in every conceivable way, and in some ways that stretched imagination. Actually, she never really felt much while men were working on her, but the film showed her how a woman presumably should act and react, and it occurred to her that maybe this was the way she could land her own millionaire: just act like the woman in the picture show.

It had almost worked.

Reginald Albertson, the department-store tycoon, had come in one day to buy his wife a copy of "Ja-Da," the newest song hit, and since he was rich and well-known, there had been a lot of fuss. Mr. Bleeker, the store manager, and his creepy assistant, Fred Stitzinger, had come down to the music department and fluttered around and looked on with beaming approval as she played the tune for Mr. Albertson. While they were all standing around in a little knot afterward, the rich man had coyly patted her on the rump. She realized in an instant that this was her chance to test her theory, and so, just as sneakily, she'd returned his caress, precisely where he'd be sure to notice it the most.

She wanted to smile, even now, after all this time. His eyes had looked like two fried eggs, he was so surprised, and, once he'd recovered, he darned near fell all over himself being nice to her. Within several weeks, he'd placed her in a secretarial school, with the understanding that she'd become his personal administrative assistant as soon as she graduated. He'd kept his word, too, and she'd traveled all over the world with the family, taking his dictation, arranging his schedules, reading to the ailing Mrs. Albertson. Nights, and on lazy afternoons, she'd imitate the girl in the motion picture, and Reginald Albertson became a new man, glorying in the golden sunlight of the Spanish coast, blooming in the cool green hills of France, and, in 1921, when Germany and America had made their official peace, exalting in his commission from the State Department to advise the Reich's Minister of Trade on how

Deutschland might once again become über alles in der drygoods-Welt.

When Albertson died, the family had returned to Chicago, and, with nothing better to do, she had remained in Berlin to take a job at the embassy, offered by the ambassador himself, who had innocently believed Mr. Albertson's enthusiastic tributes to "Miss Loomis's astonishing secretarial capabilities."

That had been a year ago. Albertson, the dirty rat, hadn't even mentioned her in his will, and so she had once again been entirely dependent on her own earning capacity, which—as a reformed, straight-shooting, severely chaste secretary—hadn't been so goddamn great. Now, though, the new arrangement with Georges Doubet, doing special duty for the Allied Control Commission, was bringing in enough extra to brighten her horizon considerably.

There was a tapping on the door, and she let him in.

Stachel's gaze ran up and down her figure. "You look fine in a short dress," he said.

She hung up his things. Over her shoulder she said, "The flapper style, Herr Hauptmann. I don't dare wear it outside these walls, with Berlin and the diplomatic corps as conservative as they are."

"You should wear it everywhere."

She nodded toward the sitting room. "Take a seat. Would you like a drink before the lesson begins?"

"No thanks. I don't drink." He said this absently, as if deep in thought. He settled into an overstuffed chair by the window, and his eyes roamed. "Nice place your friend has."

"Isn't it."

She came across the room and sat on the divan, facing him across the coffee table and giving him a serious gaze.

"Was I supposed to bring a textbook or anything?" he asked.

"No," she said. "We'll just talk."

"Where did you learn your German, Fräulein Loomis?"

"In Germany. I was personal secretary to Reginald Albertson for nine years—five of them here in Berlin. For some reason, I have a very good ear for language. I learn rapidly." She paused. "Why are you staring at me, Herr Hauptmann?"

"I can't get used to the difference. The way you looked at Lori's party, the way you look now."

She examined the palm of her right hand, her eyes dark in the soft lamplight. "The embassy—Captain Duncan, especially—expects me to be crisp, efficient, ladylike, and, unfortunately, drab."

"Why? I've heard America and the Americans are lighthearted, devil-may-care. Twenty-three skiddoo, and so on."

"Not official America. Official America is every bit as stuffy as official Germany. Only, where you fellows wear helmets and boots, our fellows wear derbies and spats."

Stachel smiled, feeling that she expected him to. Then, not knowing what else to say, he said slowly, *"What o'clock leaves the train toward New York?"*

She glanced at him and returned his smile. "Ah. So you want to try your English. All right. First of all, one says it this way. *'What time does the train leave for New York?'* "

"That doesn't seem to come together right. I—"

"In English, please, Herr Hauptmann."

"That comes not so good—"

"No. The train. Ask me about the train again."

She listened to him, watching with deadpan amusement as his Germanic tongue, throat, and lips agonized over the unfamiliar sounds and constructions. She insisted that all German be dropped, and if they were to talk at all it would have to be in English, and he tried manfully to stay within the restrictions. She would correct him, careful not to discourage him and trying casually to lead him away from the schoolbook prattling about trains and theater tickets and farmers visiting the city and into a more realistic conversational atmosphere. At the half-hour mark he finally rebelled.

"Oh, hell," he said, shaking his head and waving his hands in surrender. "I can't go any more of this. Let's get back to German."

"Very well, Herr Hauptmann. I might say, though, that you're really not half bad. Your pronounciation is quite good, you seem to be mastering your TH's, and your mimicry with new words, new usages, is, well, impressive."

"Good. But my endurance is low. I admit it, Fräulein."

She placed a cigarette in a sequined holder and lit it, taking a long, deep breath of smoke. "What is that medal you're wearing at your throat?"

"This? It's the Pour le Merite. Commonly known as the Blue Max."

"It means you are a hero?"

He smiled dimly. "That's what people think it means. Actually I won it for an action I don't even remember."

"You were wounded and out of your mind?"

"No. I was drunk."

"Oh?"

"In all truth, the Blue Max is awarded for meritorious service over a protracted period of time, rather than for a single action, as your Congressional Medal is awarded. But, since I can think of nothing meritorious I did over any specific period, and since I was awarded the medal after an incident I can't remember to this day, I don't feel particularly heroic."

"But you consider the medal important enough to wear."

"Of course. It makes me socially acceptable, wherever I go. I wanted the medal very much back in my war days. It symbolized something for me. I was a hick, and the Blue Max would make me as good as anybody else, you see. I was awkward, unsure of myself, defensive, thin-skinned, lonely, frightened, unhappy, and filled with a sense of my unimportance in the scheme of things. But alcohol and the Blue Max made me instantly as good as—even better than—anybody in the whole world."

She took another drag at her cigarette to hide her very real astonishment at the man's frankness. "How do you feel about it nowadays?" she asked carefully.

"I'm still all those things. And I'm still wearing my Blue Max. But I was a boy then. I'm a man now. I deal with my hickdom a little more effectively—a little more realistically—these days."

"That's why you don't drink?"

"Can you think of a better reason?"

She sat silently for a time, smoking slowly and staring at him, thinking. He seemed to be aware of her need to do this, and so he waited, impassive and polite, returning her stare with faintly amused eyes. He was incredibly attractive, she thought; too Teutonic, perhaps, what with his straight-backed squareness, but animal-like and taut, like some kind of cat ready to claw your ass off. She decided to make her move.

"Let's talk business now, shall we, Herr Hauptmann?"

"Business?"

"I want to work for you."

He regarded her with unblinking eyes. "I'm not sure I understand, Fräulein Loomis."

"I'm offering to spy on American activities for you. To report to you regularly on what goes on at the embassy."

"Oh?"

"I will tell you anything you want to know, do anything you want me to do."

"I see. And for all this, you expect—what, Fräulein Loomis?"

"A thousand American dollars a month. A fully furnished apartment. Open accounts at the best boutiques. A full larder every week."

She saw him trying to adjust to what must have been, for him, an astonishing turn of events. She waited.

"Well," he said finally, his gaze unwavering, "you have a very high price tag. I'm not sure my superiors would consider your services worth that kind of expense."

She shrugged. "I'm willing to bet that they will. After all, they will be getting absolutely reliable information, straight from the embassy's most secret files."

He nodded reasonably. "Naturally, I'll convey your offer to the appropriate people." After a brief pause, he said, "What makes you willing to, ah, indulge in treason against your people? My people will want to know."

She considered the question, then decided to answer it in his own terms. "I don't owe my people anything," she said solemnly. "You say you were a hick? Well, I was worse than that, Herr Hauptmann. I was a girl. You were lonely, frightened, unhappy—filled with a sense of unimportance? You should've seen it from where I sat. I very nearly starved to death on the raw edge of a slum in those beautiful United States; I was beaten by a drunken father, paid a fraction of what a man would get for the same work, and crapped on by just about everybody in those noble United States. Until I got wise. Until I finally saw that money was the great equalizer. And so I decided that I'd do anything for money. And I did. And I still do. Money's more important to me than anything. And I'll do anything I have to—even if I have to sleep with Field Marshal von Hindenburg himself."

Stachel laughed. "Now that would take some doing, I'm afraid. Do you have any idea how old the field marshal is?"

"What difference does that make?" she said, smiling herself now.

"Well," Stachel said, rising from his chair, "they say money is the cleanest incentive there is. And since money is your single motive in all this, the matter's considerably simplified. I'll tell my people I think they ought to hire you. I'll tell you what they say when I have my next lesson."

"You're leaving already?"

"It's late. And I've a lot to do tomorrow."

"Don't you want to take advantage of my obvious vulnerability?"

"No. Fräulein," he said, touching her chin with the back of his hand, "I think I'll keep things on a straight business basis."

"Don't patronize me, Hauptmann. Don't give me that superiority crap."

"How could I, Fräulein Loomis? It's as you say—I see a great deal of myself in you. And it saddens me. It really does."

"I only want your money. I don't want your pity."

"I'm sorry, Fräulein," he said gently, "but you'll be getting them both. Good night."

17

The meeting had been under way since lunch, and most of it had been dominated by a colonel of engineers who droned on about airfield construction and the proper drainage of runway and taxi areas.

Everyone was hard put to keep awake, what with the man's monotone and the sounds of spring coming through the open casements, and Stachel found that it helped to glance around the big table, first clockwise, then the other way, looking at noses. The general's nose was thin and long; von Diemer, the colonel in charge of Services and Supplies, had a nose shaped like an electric light bulb; Schneider, chief of Air Intelligence—and, as such, von Brandt's boss—sported a nose that made him look like one of those Greek statues; Oberst Eberlein, Personnel chief, had a nose like a carrot; Kleine, Eberlein's assistant, had a nose like a radish; Oberst Siemering, Plans and Training chief, was fitted with a snowplow; and Riemann, like Stachel a Hauptmann and assigned to Research, Foreign Potentials, resembled an anteater.

The engineering colonel paused to consult some notes, and during the lull the general stirred, cleared his throat. "How are things at Lipetsk, Oberst Siemering?"

"Proceeding on schedule, Herr General. The ten fighter-pilot candidates, selected from the commercial flight school at Schleissheim, have already reported for training. Our cadre there now numbers two hundred and ten."

"Our instructors are continuing to train Russian pilots?"

"Yes, sir. However, now we are ready for the program that will also train German pilots. Incognito, of course."

The general glanced at von Diemer. "You are still figuring on a thousand first-line aircraft by fiscal 1930?"

"Yes, Herr General."

"The D-Thirteen Fokkers continue to work well in Russia?"

"Yes, sir," von Diemer said. "They've been adapted for ground-support operations—bomb racks, smoke-screen apparatus, and the like—and attrition has been very low. We've lost only two aircraft, one in a landing accident, the other in a wind storm, but none through mechanical failure. This, I'm sure, is because the airplane is an extremely durable machine and because the Russian maintenance crews are, happily, quite capable."

The general nodded with apparent satisfaction. "Good. Good." He made a note and, while scribbling, asked, "Tell me, Schneider, did the recent disclosure of the Lipetsk operation in the Reichstag cause us any real trouble?"

"No, Herr General. There was surprisingly little reaction to Deputy Scheidemann's speech denouncing the Reichswehr. The Social Democrats were incensed, of course, over our secret reciprocation with the Russians, and they continue to call for a thorough shakeup in the Truppenamt."

"Any foreign reaction?"

"No, Herr General. A few editorials here and there—one in the *Manchester Guardian*—but nothing to worry about."

"Speaking of foreigners," the general said, "I'm wondering about the status of the American military aviation effort. Any pearls of wisdom, Stachel?"

"Nothing much new since the last meeting, Herr General. The U.S. Navy will soon fly its new Curtiss fighter, a model designated as the F Seven-C, which is the latest in the series of Hawk types developed by Curtiss in the past three years."

"This is the same airplane used by the American Army?"

"Essentially, sir. Curtiss received an order for fifteen of these aircraft in 1925—models designated P-One by the army. And the navy ordered eleven of them under the designation F Six-C."

"Fifteen. Eleven. The Americans aren't exactly enthusiastic airplane buyers, are they?"

"No, sir. The American military budgets are at virtual starvation levels."

"Well, we don't have very much to brag about ourselves."

"No, sir."

"Where is the Curtiss factory located, Stachel?"

"Buffalo, New York, sir. That's a city beside one of the large inland lakes along the American border with Canada."

The general regarded Schneider. "We'll want to get a look at that factory sooner or later, Schneider. You have plans toward that end, I assume."

"Yes, Herr General. We were hoping to arrange a visit for Stachel."

"Very well. But don't tarry too long. Try to make it soon."

"Certainly, sir."

Stachel noticed with considerable interest that neither Schneider nor von Brandt made mention of the effort to put a cork in the headquarters leak. It was one of the larger problems facing Truppenamt and Fliegerzentrale, yet no one dared to discuss it openly at a regular staff meeting. *Fear and suspicion are running deep indeed,* he thought.

The evening was spectacular, with a rosiness superimposed on the high blue and the breeze soft and scented with baking bread and twilight fires and lilacs damp with the coming night. Stachel breathed deeply, savoring the city's essence and wishing nameless wishes.

Von Brandt was gaunt and withdrawn, kicking stones as he walked and silent with thoughts known only to himself and God. Stachel was in no mood for conversation himself, wearied as he was by the endless meeting and its hours of superficialities and posturings, and so he simply matched the major's stride and kept his own peace. The Baroness would be waiting for him at Stigelmeir's, where she kept a private dining room, and so it was only a short walk through the park to a cabstand and eventual escape from the gray and altogether oppressive headquarters ambience. It was a rotten assignment for a flying man.

But it was the only assignment he had.

To break the gloom, he said, "You've been very silent today, Major. You barely said a word in the meeting."

"Nobody asked me to speak. I am the shadow cast by our good Colonel Schneider, to paraphrase the old saying."

"I have the feeling something's bothering you."

"Oh, I'm bothered by many things, Stachel. The pitiful condition of our nation. The pitiful condition of our army and air force. The pitiful condition of my hemorrhoids."

"Well," Stachel said lightly, "inflation's under control at last, the General Staff is rising again, and the doctors have plenty of Novocaine. So why are you unhappy?"

Major von Brandt was not given to levity in any form, so there was no answering smile. Even so, Stachel thought, the major seemed uncommonly dour. Angry, almost.

"It simply irritates me beyond words," the major said finally, "to see the indifference, the serene obliviousness to what's really going on."

"What do you mean, Major? I don't follow you—"

"They sit there, all smug and polished and cool around their big table, and they refuse to recognize the monstrous thing that's growing out of Munich."

"You mean the Nazi thing?"

"The General Staff today—like Seeckt before them—refuses to abandon their political detachment. They sit there in all their braid and medals and tidy haircuts and act as if they are an island, a pocket of immunity and indifference, and that the growing strength of that gross person, Hitler, has nothing to do with them. They play soldier, and the Fatherland crumbles."

Stachel felt a gathering uneasiness. "What would you have them do, Major?"

"I would have them be men first. Husbands, fathers, Citizens. Then soldiers. But they pretend that being a soldier is the end-all and be-all of existence—that, once they've entered the holy cloister of the General Staff, they have no further responsibilities to their family, to their countrymen, or even to themselves. They satisfy themselves with developing military strategies, accomplishing military aims, that are the fulfillment of the policies handed to them by politicians. Without even once examining the policies, or the political origins of those policies, in light of sociology or the national interest."

Stachel sniffed. "If you ask me, there's a lot of politics in the General Staff. There's always a lot of pushing and shoving, jockeying for position—"

"That's purely internal, Stachel. The General Staff is a

small but very powerful trade union, originally designed as an elite group of super-competent craftsmen who could counsel the politicians on when and how to apply the tool of extreme violence. But the elite have built their own bureaucracy, and now the pushing and shoving you see is merely General A trying to get one-up on General B, Colonel C trying to elbow aside Colonel D. Meanwhile, the main event—the political fire storm raging out of Munich—goes unattended."

"A lot of people think Hitler has much to offer," Stachel said, feeling oddly defensive. "He must be saying something to somebody—"

Von Brandt gave Stachel a sidelong glance, full of bleak anger. "I'd expect you to say that, of course."

"What do you mean by that, Major?"

"Oh, hell, Stachel. I know all about your relationship with the Nazis. I am, after all, a professional information gatherer. You, and officers like you, are the cancer that will kill Germany."

Stachel, aware of his own developing anger, said, "Easy, Major. Don't let those hemorrhoids blow out on you."

"I'm serious, Stachel. I despise what the Nazis stand for. I therefore despise you."

"Well, now. That cuts out all the guesswork, doesn't it."

Von Brandt said nothing, but his pace quickened.

"Besides, what makes you so sure I'm a Nazi?" Stachel said.

The major sounded a soft, sneering sound. "Pigs that wallow together get dirty together. I know for a fact that you spent nearly half an hour with Hitler himself. I know for a fact that you are on excellent terms with Göring and Bormann."

"What are you going to do about all this? After all, we're supposed to be working together," Stachel said dryly.

Von Brandt gave him a sidelong glance, full of contempt. "I have arranged—with the co-operation of your ingratiating superior, Major Kleine—your transfer to the 417th Service Batallion. It should be forthcoming soon."

"You've assigned me to a bunch of plumbers and window washers?"

"The request is already en route to Personnel."

"You bastard, you're kicking me out of the air force because you don't like my *politics?*"

Von Brandt sauntered off, and Stachel watched after him, motionless and blank-faced.

18

The dinner at Stigelmeier's proved to be anything but quiet. The Baroness was in one of her ebullient moods, and that called for a crowd and music. Stachel put in his appearance, but the drinking and noise were intolerable, so he pleaded a duty assignment and left before soup. She had not been pleased, yet she made a show of understanding, in the manner of a vexed mother who understood not at all.

The denunciation by von Brandt had scored heavily, and Stachel, for months convinced that he'd built a solid equity in the business of being sober and responsible, now felt shaken and cut loose from his tie to respectability. After leaving the restaurant he walked slowly along the boulevard, stopping occasionally to peer into shop windows. The traffic was already thinning, despite the early hour, and the sunset's afterglow, a great swash of crimson in the purple night, gave the sky a melancholy, doomsday cast that made him feel his solitude anew.

He was not aware of having made the decision. He simply hired a cab and told the driver to take him to Mosler Platz 17, recognizing the foolishness of trying to recapture the mellow exaltation of a single evening a decade before. He had taken her to dinner at the request of her husband, and, in the fleeting encounter, had discovered how broad and inflexible the wifely virtues of loyalty and selflessness could be. Frau Heidemann was by every measure a decent woman and, since decency had been for him a quality in short supply, she'd remained in his mind ever since.

Inside, there was a smell of ancient cooking and disinfectant. He went up the narrow stairway, squinting at the name cards on the dimly lit doors and trying not to be further depressed. The dark-brown walls and linoleum floors and stair treads that creaked and the squalling of a baby somewhere above were the things of despair, and he knew that if he were compelled to live in such a place he'd most surely die.

Her name was on an oaken door at the top of the stairs: OFFIZIERWITWE HEIDEMANN. There was no bell, so he knocked and waited. After a time he knocked again, and there was the sound of slippered feet and a rustling in the room beyond the door.

The knob turned, the door opened a crack, and from the darkness inside she asked, "Who is it?"

"Frau Elfi Heidemann?"

"Yes. Who—"

"Bruno Stachel."

"Who?"

"Stachel. I flew with your husband. In France."

"Oh, yes. What do you want?"

"I'd like to see you. Talk with you."

"Why?"

"I've never forgotten our dinner together that night."

"That's no reason."

"It is for me."

She held the door back for him to enter, and in the gloom he could see that she was frowning with puzzlement. She was wearing a bathrobe and soft yellow mules, and her hair was damp. "How did you find me?" she said.

"I looked up your address in the Reichwehr's next-of-kin-files. I've known where you live for some time now. This is the first I've had the nerve to call on you."

She closed the door behind him and said, "Nerve?"

"I never visited you to offer my condolences when your husband died. And I'm ashamed of myself."

Taking his cap, she motioned him toward what seemed to be a parlor—a small room with a divan, a floor lamp, some book shelves, and a faded imitation oriental carpet. It was all scrupulously clean, for all its dowdiness, and the curtains at the window were crisp and snowy. He sat in the only chair, an overstuffed thing with lumpy springs, and traded stares with her.

"It's been a long time," she said. "And Otto and I were never much for the rituals people apply to births and deaths."

She was older, of course, with lines appearing at the corners of her eyes. But she was still very good-looking, her eyes clear and green, her skin smooth.

"I'm not the most diplomatic man in the world, either," he said.

"I know. I remember."

Somehow it pleased him that she remembered something about him—anything at all. But he had a feeling that she did not want him here. She sat on the edge of the divan, the robe held correctly about her, her attitude silent, absorbed, as if his presence were a kind of embarrassment.

"I know it's rude of me to call unexpectedly like this, Frau Heidemann, but I've been thinking about you a lot lately, and—"

"Why?"

There it was, he thought. That directness of manner he remembered. That unwillingness to temporize, to play the devious little games society liked to euphemize as courtesy. Where most proper matrons would have parried his claim with proper little noises and proper little smiles, she'd fixed him with a cool stare and challenged him outright to justify an intrusion made on patently preposterous grounds.

"Because," he said, determined to give her measure for measure, "I am up to my eyebrows in the hypocrisy and deception and posturizing that go with an assignment in the Truppenamt. I am surrounded by charlatans, and I'm sinking into the swamp of two centuries of aristocratic cow shit. Of all the people I know in this city, you are the only one I can think of who can be expected say what she thinks. I need to talk to somebody like you."

She folded her hands in her lap and considered him gravely. "You still have a foul mouth, I see."

"I'm a foul man."

She shrugged, a small motion of a shoulder. "Only a person who's unsure of himself uses foul language."

"That's me, all right. Nobody's more unsure of himself than I am."

"Do you want a cup of coffee?"

"No thanks."

"I'm sorry about your wife. It was a dreadful thing."

"You read about it, then?"

"It must have been very difficult for you."

"Yes. My wife didn't like me much. But I miss her."

"I understand."

They became silent for a time, as if listening to the sounds of the traffic coming through the open window. One of the curtains stirred in the evening breeze, and there was the smell of pork frying on some distant stove and the "a-ooga" of a car.

"What are you doing these days?" he asked eventually.

"I'm a nurse."

"Are you working at it?"

"I'm a counselor in the outpatient clinic of the Staatsnervenheilanstalt. The years have been full."

"Why haven't you remarried?"

She shrugged again, showing a remote, tight little smile. "I suppose it's just that I couldn't go through all that again. I loved Otto in my way, and he responded in his way, and there were some good times, actually. Along with the bad times. But I'd only begun to deal with marriage on a sensible basis when he was killed. I never had a chance to be the wife he deserved."

"I tried to keep him from flying that airplane, you know."

"Yes," she said, "I know. They told me later."

"He was a stubborn fellow."

"Indeed he was."

"He was crazy about you."

"I know."

"He went to a lot of trouble to get me appointed squadron commander. He wanted to get back home to you so much he actually set me up as his replacement."

"I suspected as much," she said, her green eyes averted.

"A professional officer has to be really crazy about his wife to go to that kind of trouble. Especially in wartime."

"Perhaps it's just as well that he was killed. He would have died of shame eventually. Otto was a fine officer. With a terrible, cancerous homesickness. But once at home, he'd have died of shame."

"I suppose so. A man can't have it both ways."

Stachel sat quietly in the shadows, considering the change that had come to Frau Heidemann. She was wearing her hair shorter now, of course, and there was a kind of somberness that gave her the severity of a spinster who had been stung by life and was determined never to be vulnerable again. She had shown this same quality when he'd met her on that night in 1918, to be sure, but at that time there had been a trace of pliability, as if her face, recently awash in tears, had only begun to set up in starch. Now she seemed flinty and brittle, and her reception of him was devoid of encouragement or warmth, and he knew that she was placing him on notice that nothing dare be made of their moment of meeting and sharing all those years ago.

She broke the silence. "What is it that you would like to talk about, Hauptmann Stachel?"

"I'm not sure."

"Let's put it this way. What do you think I know—or might have experienced—that could be helpful to you?"

He thought about that, his eyes downcast. "I can't say exactly. I think it has something to do with the way you handled your drinking. I mean, you told me flat out that night how you'd been able to stop drinking by learning how to look yourself in the eye."

"You find it difficult to look yourself in the eye?"

"Sometimes."

"Why?"

"I have a great talent for wanting to do one thing and ending up doing something else. I'd like very much to be—well—a good person. You know—inside. And so I'll promise myself that I'll do such and so, but I'll do just the opposite. Then I feel shame. And so it's not very comfortable. Looking myself in the eye, that is."

She glanced at him with a new curiosity. "That's biblical, you know."

"Biblical?"

"Paul, in his letter to the Romans. He said, 'I don't understand myself at all, for I really want to do what is right, but I can't. I do what I don't want to do—what I hate. When I want to do good, I don't; and when I try not to do wrong, I do it anyway.' "

Stachel nodded. "That says it, all right."

"So you see, Herr Stachel—you are not alone. Everybody—even Paul, the prototypal Christian powerhouse—has the same problem you have."

"Well, I don't go much for that biblical nonsense. It's all just mythology and mumbo-jumbo."

"Then you'll never understand your problem. And you'll always have trouble looking yourself in the eye."

"You believe in that God stuff?"

"Well," she murmured, "I have a Lutheran friend who has an answer to that. It's an old saying, but it's become my private property—my compass bearing. 'I'd rather live as if there were a God, and then find out there isn't one, than live as if there isn't a God and then find out there is one.' "

Stachel, embarrassed by Frau Heidermann's religious sentimentalism, recognized that he'd been a fool to come here. *One can never go back* was another old saying, his mind told him, and his memory of this woman had betrayed him into believing he might.

He consulted his watch, then stood up. "I'm glad that you're working out your life, Frau Heidemann." He gave her a small smile. "I wish I could claim the same for myself."

"I wish you could, too," she said. "You will, if you remember one thing. Two things, actually. First, remember that the world doesn't make you unhappy; you make yourself unhappy. And second, no one can make you be what you don't want to be. Remember those two things, Hauptmann Stachel, and you'll stop losing and start winning. You'll find the answer to whatever brought you here this evening. You'll find the answers to questions you can't even ask."

"Thanks for the advice, Frau Heidemann. I appreciate it." He retrieved his cap from the small table near the door and, giving the officer's bow, said formally, "I hope I might have the pleasure of seeing you again some day soon."

She held the door open for him, her face expressionless. "I think not, Herr Hauptmann."

"Oh?"

"I still have a long way to go. I still have a lot of forgetting to do. I'm trying to build a new way of living. I'm trying to be honest with myself, and with other people. I've begun, at last, to feel truly alive, worthwhile. That's very precious to me."

"I hope you don't consider me a threat."

"Frankly, Hauptmann Stachel, you frighten me to death."

"Why?"

"Because I see in you everything I used to be."

He stood in the open doorway for a time, thinking about this. Then he put on his cap and left.

He'd hoped she would tell him why he shouldn't call Bormann about the von Brandt matter. But there was no way he could comfortably have worked the question into all her prattle about God. The simple fact was, he'd lost control of the conversation.

19

Captain Duncan was having a quiet drink at Ziggi's, a chic café on the Briennerstrasse, with his old friend Major Doubet, a deputy chief of the French representation of the Allied Control Commission. Doubet, all Gallic and philosophical, had been rambling on in his accented English about the decline of his commission's effectiveness as a brake on the resurrection of German air power, but Duncan's attention was only superficial. Doubet could be as upset as he cared to be over the bogus corporation in Warnemünde that was a cover for the training of naval aircrews; Duncan simply couldn't work up any interest in such things, what with his preoccupation with Polly Loomis.

"You are not listening to me, my friend."

"Sorry, Doubet. I've got something on my mind."

"Ah. A lady, perhaps?"

Duncan gave his friend a wry smile. "How did you know?"

"That expression you are wearing is only seen on men who are thinking about women."

"Do you know anything about women, Doubet?"

"I? You forget I'm married, eh? Men who are married know the least about women."

"Do French women make good wives?"

"Why? Are you planning to marry a French woman?"

"Heck, no. I just wonder, that's all."

Doubet held his glass of wine to the sunlight and examined it with pursed lips. He always pursed his lips when he was about to be profound. "Well," he said. "You could certainly do worse. I'm French, of course, and biased. But I've lived many years in other countries—quite a few of them in England and America—and I can only say that there is no woman anywhere capable of warmer or more generous friendships than a French woman. No woman can give a man a deeper, more discreet and lasting loyalty."

Duncan smiled. "You sound like you've had a bunch of women."

"I've had my share," Doubet said amiably. "But, as you can see, I'm partial to the Frenchwoman. She is a bit of the snob. She's naturally simple and unpretentious. She's competent, intelligent, diplomatic. Someone once said that if you were to give a Frenchwoman some mental and moral independence and the kind of liberal education you find in England you'd have perfect womanhood."

"One thing about Polly—she's sure perfect in design. God, what a shape."

"Ah. The lady's name is Polly."

Duncan drained his glass. Placing it on the table with a contented sigh, he said, "I didn't think she was much, at first. I took her to a party one night—a kind of afterthought thing—and she looked like somebody's aunt. But a few weeks later I stopped by this little apartment she shares with a girl friend. She wasn't expecting me. And, wow, she was all gussied up in a flapper thing, and it was like she was another person. I mean, she was oh-you-kid."

"And now you're thinking of marrying her?"

Duncan blushed. "Well, no. Not really. I mean, I'm thinking about politics. My family is pretty well known back home—insurance and real estate. And now that my military career seems to be on a dead-end street, I've got to start thinking about my future. I come from a dinky farm state that has only one at-large congressman. Two senators, of course. I want to run for Congress, and then I want to be one of the senators."

"I'm not sure I understand these things," Doubet said, motioning to the waiter for a refill.

"A man with the backing of a certain four rich and influential people in my state can knock off the congressman's job pretty easy. Two or three terms in the House to prove to these four people that he's reliable, then on to the Senate. Keep your nose clean, give the yahoos some vaudeville, and you can stay in the Senate for a lifetime. Top salary, expense account, prestige, power. Who could ask for more?"

"Why wouldn't Polly be welcome in all this?"

"Polly's too prim and proper. She wants to be a schoolmarm in a town with elm trees. She's a plain-Jane, and she won't even let me hold her hand, for cripes sake."

Doubet sipped at his fresh wine. "What you're saying is that an American politician needs a wife with glamour—sex appeal, and so on, is that it?"

"That's right. And there isn't a single thing about Polly that would interest a rich old election manipulator. I don't think she knows much about men, actually. She's too wholesome."

Doubet sighed. "As I say, you Americans confuse me. It would seem to me that wholesomeness would be a welcome quality in a politician's wife."

Duncan thought about that for a considerable time. "Maybe," he said finally. "But Polly wouldn't last a minute among all those wolves."

"Who is this Polly? I mean, how do you know her—"

"She's a secretary at the embassy. She also served occasionally as an interpreter and translator. That sort of thing."

"I see. And, as such, she's a commoner, eh?"

"Well, we don't have class distinctions in the States, but—"

"Every society has class distinctions," Doubet broke in. "The United States are worst of all, because Americans refuse to admit their class distinctions. They pretend they don't exist."

"Well, what I mean is—"

"What you mean, my dear Duncan, is that you feel superior to Polly."

"Hell, no. I don't mean that at all. I think it's probably the other way around. She's exceptionally proper. She's very intelligent. She has very high moral values—even worries about us being seen together in a social situation, me being her boss, and all. She's quality, in a dependable, correct kind of way, and I always feel a little like an ill-mannered rube when she's around. It's because she's so, well, decent and sensitive that I'm afraid American politics would chew her up."

Doubet sighed and rolled his eyes in the French manner. "I can't follow your reasoning, Duncan. It would be my pleasure to have such a woman at my side when entering the jungle of my own country's politics. It would be reassuring to have someone I could count on, as your idiom has it. Moreover, it seems to me that considerable glamour could be attached to such a woman—a woman who has served her nation at a high level in foreign areas, a woman who is conversant with international dealings, even a little intrigue, eh?"

Duncan smiled defensively and fell silent, pretending interest in his wine glass.

Doubet ordered lunch and they ate slowly, making a quiet ritual of the process.

20

The Baroness had acquired a new Mercedes sports coupe and asked Stachel to go for a spin. She drove badly, overcontrolling on curves and braking too late and too abruptly at intersections. But it was a beautiful day, with a velvet-blue sky and puff clouds, and the breeze was out of the south, and warm, and so he was alternately stabbed with various little alarms and soothed by the fragrant springtime. She took them on the highway that led southwest through Sedlitz and Lichterfelde and then on to Potsdam, where they crossed the Lange Brücke over the Havel. After driving through the heart of the city and its wooded hills, she skidded to a dusty halt on a promontory overlooking the sparkling blue sweep of the Heilige See.

"There," she breathed in the blessed silence, "you have had a ride in my darling new car."

"So I have. But I respectfully request that I be allowed to drive your darling new car on the way back, lest we break our darling necks."

She made a little face. "You don't like the way I drive?"

"That's the understatement of the year."

She laughed and it was a pleasant sound in the bright afternoon. "I love Sundays," she enthused. "They're so fat-bellied and sleepy-eyed. So snoozy and sensuous. Why don't you make love to me? Right here. On the car seat, in the sunlight and breeze."

"It's against the law."

She laughed again. "You're so unromantic."

"And you're a dirty-minded old bawd."

"It's true. I won't deny it."

"Good. I'm crazy about dirty-minded old bawds. Especially when they have new Mercedes sports cars."

She kissed the end of his nose. "You only love me for my money."

He had not intended to mention the matter until dinner, but it seemed that now was as good a time as any. "Odd, that you should mention money, chum. I was about to bring it up myself."

She looked up at him. "Oh?"

"Mm. I need a loan."

"I see." The amusement in her eyes began to fade. "You want me to lend you money?"

"I've never asked you before, as you know. When Kaeti died, her estate went to her Aunt Jutta in Dresden, which means that I've been living on my army pay."

"Darling," she said brightly, gathering herself, "you know that all you have to do to get anything from me is to ask."

"I don't like to borrow from my—" He hesitated.

"Mistress?" she put in with slightly elaborate helpfulness.

"Friends. I don't like to borrow from anybody. Especially my friends."

"Nonsense. What are friends for, after all." She turned away to gaze at the lake. "How much do you need?"

"Ten thousand American dollars."

She glanced at him quickly, something indefinable in her eyes. "Hoo," she said. "That's a handsome sum."

"Indeed it is."

"Does it have to be in American dollars? I mean, wouldn't the equivalent in German currency do as well?"

"No."

"I see. Well, it'll take a day or two."

"I'll need it by tomorrow evening. Timing's important."

"Oh? You're buying something that won't be available after tomorrow evening?"

He took her chin in his hand and turned her face to him. "Easy, chum. No questions, eh? I mean, I have something I must do, and I simply can't talk about it right now."

"Of course," she said with a forced smile. "I didn't mean for a moment to pry into your affairs. You know me better than that."

"You're all right, chum. I owe you a lot more than money."

"Such as what, chum?"

"I've told you—gratitude. For your willingness to accept me for what I am. For your unwillingness to meddle, to try and change me."

She sighed and, pushing away, sat erect to open the door beside her. He thought he saw something like regret in her expression.

"Well, then," she said, suddenly cheery, "we'll have to be getting back to Berlin if I'm to call my business manager and get things under way." Handing him the ignition key, she said, "Here you are, darling. Don't break our darling necks."

They said very little on the return drive.

Stachel, feeling a regret of his own, sensed that their relationship had somehow been forever altered. And it was sad. Oh, well. What the hell. Flying was the only thing that really mattered.

21

Headquarters was buzzing Monday over the weekend's non-stop flight of the American, Lindbergh, from New York to Paris. Stachel had been in his office for no more than ten minutes when Major Kleine came in to announce that the general was waiting to see them.

"What about?" Stachel found it difficult to look at Kleine, knowing as he did that the major was collaborating with von Brandt to have him transferred.

"What else?" Kleine snorted. "Lindbergh, of course."

Stachel's irritability broke through his efforts to keep cool. "Doesn't the general want your buddy, von Brandt, to come along, too?" he said acidly.

"Von Brandt?" Kleine's eyebrows went up, and his face reddened. "Whatever for?"

"He seems to be very close to you these days."

"What are you talking about, Stachel?"

"Never mind. Let's not keep the general waiting, eh?"

They strode down the long corridor, their boots making echoing sounds on the marble floor. Kleine made small talk about the beautiful day, but Stachel, still working to contain his anger, remained silent.

The general returned their salute and motioned them to chairs.

"What," the general said in his grating way, "do we know about this Lindbergh fellow and his machine?"

Because of his rank and office, it was up to Kleine to answer. "Nothing of any consequence, sir. But we'll be working on it."

"What do you mean, 'of consequence'? What does that mean?"

"Well, sir, simply that technical data are, well, not very, ah, complete. We know only that the man is a former airmail pilot and that he flew a machine built by the Ryan Company, I believe."

The general snorted. "I know that much from the newspapers. I want to know more. Much more. Especially about the airplane's engine. Germany has no airplane, extant or on the drawing boards, that could come anywhere near the American achievement. Certainly no aircraft power plant that could operate more than thirty hours without faltering. In fact, engines are going to be our biggest problem if we hope to mass-produce high-performance military airplanes."

"Yes, sir. Quite so, sir."

The general glowered. "How long will it take you to give me details on the Lindbergh engine, Kleine? The minister is waiting. I hadn't even removed my cap this morning before he was on my telephone."

"Well, Herr General, I'll put Stachel on it at once, of course—"

The general gave Stachel a cold glance. "This is a priority matter, Stachel. I want you to drop everything else and get me some hard information by tomorrow afternoon."

"I have it for you now, sir."

The general's flinty eyes narrowed. "You what?"

Stachel took a paper from his tunic pocket, unfolded it, and said, "According to my notes, the Lindbergh machine is a special adaptation of a stock model M One mail plane produced by the Ryan Aircraft Company—a semicantilever-type monoplane. It's powered by a nine-cylinder Wright Whirlwind radial engine of the J Series—J-Five, to be exact

—which develops two hundred and twenty-three horsepower at eighteen hundred r.p.m. The engine originated in an experimental contract granted by the U.S. Bureau of Aeronautics. The first model, produced by the Lawrence Company, was fitted to certain U.S. Navy aircraft about four years ago. The J-One model was sophisticated by the Wright Company after its merger with Lawrence. The Americans seem to have licked the problem of fuel distribution in radial engines with an enclosed valve gear and a three-barrel carburetor. I have rather complete data, Herr General—bore, stroke, displacement, compression ratio, overall dimensions—including the engine's weight, complete with propeller hub, flange and bolts, carburetor and two magnetos, high-tension wiring and synchronizer drives. I also have a rundown on the accessories, such as magneto types, plugs, and so on. I'll have them all typed and delivered to you within the hour."

There was a long pause, during which the general examined Stachel with undisguised interest. The clock on the mantel ticked loudly.

"Well, now," the general said. "I am pleased. Very pleased."

Stachel said nothing, listening to the clock and trying not to be aware of Kleine's ruby embarrassment.

"You have the makings of a real intelligence officer, Stachel."

"Thank you, Herr General."

"You have a complete description of this engine? I mean, truly complete?"

"Yes, sir. Even to starting procedures, maintenance schedules, and so on."

"Excellent. Excellent. The minister will be most happy." The general raised a questioning brow. "Where did you get this information, Stachel?"

"From one of the manufacturer's employees, sir."

"Excellent, Excellent." The general smiled openly. "You are dismissed, gentlemen. And remember, Stachel—within the hour."

Kleine said nothing until they had returned to the echoing corridor. Then he cleared his throat and, without looking at Stachel, said, "You realize that you've humiliated me, don't you?"

"I suppose I have."

"You've probably ruined me."

"Yes."

"Why didn't you tell me you had the data on that engine?"

"You didn't ask me."

"But you could have said something. You could have kept me from making such an ass of myself—"

"Why? What do I owe you, Major Kleine?"

The major gave him a sidelong glance and offered no answer. They both understood that there was no answer.

When they reached the end of the corridor and prepared to enter their separate offices, Kleine hesitated and turned to regard Stachel with despairing eyes.

"Tell me one thing, will you, Stachel? Where did you learn so much about the American engine? Who was your informant? I've seen no field agents' reports—"

"I don't think I'll answer that question, Major."

"Why not, for God's sake? I'm still your boss."

"I don't think you will be for long, sir."

Kleine's thick features reddened again, and he blinked slowly, twice. Then he turned wordlessly and disappeared into his office.

Stachel watched after him with a mixture of contempt and pity.

The truth was, he'd read about the Wright J-5 Whirlwind in a sales brochure and a maintenance manual distributed by the manufacturer, the Wright Aeronautical Corporation of Paterson, New Jersey. He'd sent directly for the material last fall, and it was now resting on a shelf in the Technical Library, no more than five or ten meters from Major Kleine's office. It was there for anyone to read.

But nobody had read it. Nobody ever read the stuff in any headquarters library. Nobody but ambitious young officers like Bruno Stachel.

22

The day had been wretched. She had been assigned to work on a batch of correspondence—much of it highly technical—in which the embassy sought to unravel trade complications rooted in Germany's monopoly of patents and technology in various fields. Manufacturers of textiles, and businesses that depended on dye stuffs, medicines, seeds, and what were called "organic chemicals" had suffered heavily in the German wartime prohibition against the export of goods to America, and now they were trying to recoup. And the German owners of patents seized in 1918 by the Alien Property Custodian in Washington were suing for retrievals —even for damages. But Americans who had purchased the rights were equally angry: German owners had been very tricky—sometimes revealing all but the essential element in a formula, or adding a few ingredients which, when the formula was tried, proved to be ruinous to processes and equipment. It was an ungodly mess, and she would be glad to see once again her routine mountain of gripes and entreaties from discombobulated tourists.

She drew a hot bath and soaked for a half hour, trying to think of nice things. What she wouldn't give to climb on a train at the Hauptbahnhof and rush through the night to the Italian coast, where she could run naked on the sand and drink wine with some dark-eyed, curly-haired paisan who would knock her down in the surf and ride her until her ears rang.

She was in very bad humor when she dried herself and wrapped her tired body in a robe and went to the sitting room for a slug of rye. She felt like a bug in a Mason jar, and there was nothing she wouldn't do to find a way out of it.

The bell rang. Pulling the robe tighter, she went to the door.

"Hauptmann Stachel?"

"Good evening, Miss Loomis."

"There's no lesson scheduled for this evening. Besides, it's only six."

"I'm sorry to intrude, but I'll not be long."

"What's up?" She took his cap and waved him toward the sitting room. "Are we at war again?"

"Not yet, Miss Loomis." He settled in the overstuffed chair and regarded her thoughtfully.

"All right," she said, selecting a cigarette from a small glass tray on the side table, "what's on your mind?"

"My supervision has decided to accept your offer."

"At my price?" She lit the cigarette and sank onto the sofa.

"Well, my supervision would like first to test the arrangement."

"How?"

"We'd like you to deliver a package. If you take the package to a certain place at a certain time and place it in the hands of a certain gentleman, you will be paid a thousand American dollars."

She blew a stream of smoke at the ceiling. "That's all I do? Just deliver a package?"

"That's correct."

"And if I do it as instructed, I'll be paid a thousand?"

"If you perform well, we'll have another job for you. A job that pays four thousand."

She raised a brow. "Aha. What package, and to whom? When?"

Stachel withdrew an envelope from his pocket and leaned forward to hand it to her. It bore no address, she saw.

"We want you to deliver this at noon tomorrow to a German officer who will be seated at the corner table, under the awning and beside the entrance, at the Cafe Heinrich on Loperstrasse."

"He has no name, this officer?"

"It's not important, for your purposes. He'll be the only officer at the only table beside the entrance."

"All right. But I'd like to amend the terms."

He gave her face a wary inspection. "Oh? How so?"

"I'll deliver your package as instructed. But the price is twelve hundred and a bit of socializing."

"I'm not a whore, Miss Loomis."

"That's nonsense. We're all whores. Everybody in the world whores for something. Every man who has ever worked for a boss he can't stand is a whore, whining and complaining and making excuses, and all the time taking the dirty rat's money. Every woman who has ever stayed with a husband she doesn't love is a whore—trading her body and services for economic security, or for status, or for the biggest rationalization of all—the so-called good of the kids. Don't give me that prim stuff, Hauptmann Stachel. Anybody who's ever done something he doesn't want to do simply to get some money, or some advantage, or some distinction, is a whore."

"Well—"

"Tell me honestly now, Herr Hauptmann. What do you want most? What's the most important thing in your life?"

"Flying."

"Do you like flying enough to screw for it?"

"I've already done much worse, Miss Loomis."

"See? So take off your clothes."

At some point she said, "I'm cold. Let's get under the blankets."

They did, and it was soft and warm there, and they dozed.

"What time is it?" she murmured eventually.

"Nineteen-fifteen."

"You mean a quarter after *seven?* My God, my date will be here in forty-five minutes."

"Think you'll make it?"

She rolled over and touched her nose to his.

"You're a magnificent adventure, Miss Loomis. You are an absolute artisan. I won't forget you. Ever."

He was lying, of course, saying only what a gentleman would say.

Miss Loomis, languid and radiating damp heat beside him in the bedroom twilight, was an experience to carry in a corner of his mind for a long time, certainly. Yet now, at this moment, he felt only abysmal unfulfillment, the understanding that he'd had the best and it was not enough. He should have been dozing in silent triumph, aglow with the sense of his manhood, but instead there was indescribable remorse and a terrible yearning for, of all people, Frau Heidemann. Against his closed eyelids he could see the span of his life, and it was an endless reel of failures and disappointments and lapses of faith and judgment, and the greatest failure of all was this last. This evening, as in all those years past, he had exchanged vile treason against himself for—what?

But Miss Loomis had been faking, too. For all of her heat, he'd known that she really had not been craving him. She communicated something subtle, elusive, and he'd finally identified it: Miss Loomis hadn't wanted him—she only wanted to want him.

He sighed, and she must have read something in it because she raised up on an elbow and gazed into his eyes.

"What's the problem, Your Excellency?"

"I was just thinking of how the world is full of play-actors."

She kissed his chin and said, "We all keep doing things we shouldn't be doing. We all try to bull our way through. It's pride. False pride. We've all got it. Pride is a plague that will wipe us all out. The whole damned world."

"A philosopher, she is."

"Well, I'm serious. We all create little visions of ourselves—how we look, how special we are, what great things we're going to do someday. But the trouble is, when the squeeze is on and we come face to face with reality, we keep on pretending—even to the point of ruin. Hell, even nations fight wars because they'd rather die with their illusions than live with their truths."

"What's your illusion, Miss Loomis?"

"That I'm a diamond in the rough, waiting to be discovered by some darling man."

"And what's the truth?"

"I'm a seedy nobody nobody wants."

"Self-pity, Miss Loomis?"

"Hell, no. Like everybody else, like all the nations, I live with my illusions, ignore my truth. Why should I pity myself?"

She yawned, and then, remembering, she grabbed his wrist and peered at his watch. "Good God, seven-thirty. I've got to run now, pal."

She bounded out of the bed and went to the bathroom, where she turned on the taps and shouted over the rushing, "Leave the package on the table! With my twelve hundred!"

When she came out to dress, Stachel had gone.

She hid the envelope and the money under her lingerie in

the dresser drawer. Then, just as she was putting the finishing touches to her rouge, the bell sounded.

She opened the door and said gravely, "Good evening, John."

"Hi, Polly. Ready for a little hell-raising?"

"Please. That sounds so tacky."

Duncan grinned sheepishly and said, "You really ought to unbend a little. I respect your being so proper and all, but, you need to relax."

"John, to me, propriety is everything."

23

Oberst Schneider, chief of Desk IV, as Air Intelligence was now called, rubbed his Grecian-statue nose and regarded Stachel with eyes like wet stones. He was fresh and crisp in his uniform, his face pink from its recent morning's shave, and he smelled of talcum powder and bay rum.

"What is it, Stachel?" Schneider said from his big chair beside the windows. "I'm expected in the general's office in five minutes, and I can give you three."

Stachel nodded pleasantly and glanced at his watch. "Certainly, sir. I don't think I'll need more than that."

"So?"

"So I have found the headquarters leak."

Oberst Schneider's eyes widened slightly, and the monocle dropped on its string to glisten against the breast of his immaculate tunic. "Aha. Have you, now."

"Yes, sir."

"Have you told Major von Brandt?"

"No, sir."

"Well, why not, Stachel? He is your supervisor, after all."

"Major von Brandt is the leak, sir."

Schneider's eyes went even wider. "You can't be serious."

"I'm afraid I am, Colonel."

"You have evidence? I mean, hard certifiable evidence?"

Stachel nodded with great seriousness.

"Well, then let me see it, man."

"I'd rather have you catch him red-handed, sir. I'd like you, personally, to arrest him in the act of treason."

Oberst Schneider returned the monocle to his right eye and gave Stachel's face a moment of silent study. Then he coughed gently and said, "Would you explain that, please, Hauptmann Stachel?"

"As you know, Colonel," Stachel began, choosing his words carefully, "I have been asked to exploit certain contacts with the American Embassy, and in the course of doing so I determined that an important link in the U.S. intelligence apparatus is a woman—a secretary named Pauline—called Polly—Loomis. Under the guise of taking English lessons from this woman—one of her cover duties at the embassy is language tutoring, and she takes certain well-paying students after hours with the knowledge and permission of her superiors—I have developed a good relationship with her. Good enough, I might add, to lull her into a sense of ease and trust. And—"

Oberst Schneider leaned forward. "You mean you have seduced this—Pauline Loomis?"

"In a manner of speaking, sir. In any event, she is unwary in my presence. And I have learned, from piecing things together, that she has been seeing Major von Brandt and has been paying him for the information—the confidential military information he deals with as your assistant—which he delivers to her on a regular basis."

The colonel shook his head, dumfounded. "This is incredible. I mean, von Brandt, of all people— He's so, so *keen*—"

Stachel nodded again, pretending elaborate sorrow. "I understand how you feel, sir. I, too, was terribly disappointed, shocked, to learn that a colleague who seemed so hardworking, so dedicated, is in fact a spy for the Americans. Tragic. Tragic."

"His father will be devastated. I've known his father for years. Served together at Verdun. Was with him when he lost his leg at Soissons."

"Yes, sir. It's the family that always suffers in cases like this."

Stachel forced himself to concentrate on a single thought:

It's von Brandt or me. It's von Brandt or me. He knew that, if he didn't, he would most certainly retch. It was easier to kill a man than it was to frame him. To kill his reputation. His honor.

Well, to hell with the bastard.

It's von Brandt or me.

Oberst Schneider consulted his watch, suddenly all business. "I must not keep the general waiting. Stachel. What do you purpose?"

"The Loomis woman tells me that she is scheduled to deliver von Brandt's latest payment tomorrow at noon at the Café Heinrich on Loperstrasse."

"I know the place."

"She will be delivering a plain envelope in which there will be five thousand American dollars."

"Von Brandt doesn't come cheap, does he," Oberst Schneider said sarcastically.

"No, sir, he does not."

"So? What else, Stachel?"

"I think it would be quite fitting for you, as chief of Air Intelligence, to witness the transfer of funds from Loomis to Brandt. And then personally to arrest the traitor, confiscate the funds, and hold him for prosecution."

"And the Loomis woman?"

"I urge you to leave her out of it, Colonel. She's a valuable source of information for us, and it would be a shame to lose her services for the mere satisfaction of having her declared persona non grata and expelled."

"So what's the plan, then?"

God in heaven, Stachel thought, exasperated. *Doesn't this nincompoop have any imagination at all? If this is our chief of intelligence, God help us....*

"Well, sir, I suggest that you station a party of men in hiding around the Café Heinrich, to be certain that von Brandt won't make it if he decides to run. I also think it would be a good idea to have at least two cameramen on hand, to snap pictures of the actual transfer of funds. Then, once the photographs have been made and Miss Loomis has left the scene, you can step from your own hiding place and make the arrest."

"I see. Capital. Capital." Oberst Schneider looked pleased.

"And it might also do no harm to have the photographer catch you as you actually arrest the culprit. It won't hurt to have the military trial judges seeing photographic evidence of your personal efficiency and élan, will it, Colonel, eh?" He managed to smile and wink.

"Quite so, Stachel." The colonel beamed. "That's capital, that is."

"Would you like me to make the necessary arrangements, sir?"

"Yes, yes. Of course. By all means."

"Very good, sir. All you'll have to do is show up at the Café Heinrich tomorrow at noon, when you'll make the arrest. I'll have troops and photographers on hand."

"Capital, Stachel. Good thinking. Now I really must report to the general." Oberst Schneider pushed back from his desk, stood up, and smoothed his hair with a faultlessly manicured hand. Then he made for the door, and as he prepared to leave he paused and glanced back at Stachel.

"Should I tell the general about all this?"

"I wouldn't, sir. Not yet. I'd show him the pictures first."

"Ah. Yes. Quite so." He thought for a moment. "Stachel?"

"Sir?"

"I'll need a replacement for von Brandt as my assistant."

"Yes, sir."

"Would you like the job?"

"I'd much prefer to visit Lipetsk, sir. I have the trip all scheduled, as you know."

"Of course, I mean after you return. I'll hold the post open for you."

"That's very nice of you, Herr Oberst. Thank you, sir."

"Thank *you,* Stachel."

Schneider glanced at his watch again, rolled his eyes in pretended shock at his tardiness, and hurried off to see the general.

Stachel went directly to the second floor and down the chill corridor to the door marked Air Intelligence—Operations. Von Brandt was at his desk, chewing a pencil and staring out the window into the inner courtyard.

"You're late," von Brandt said without turning in his chair.

Stachel sat at his own desk, which was on the opposite side of the small room. He lifted a packet of correspondence from the in box and riffled through it with elaborate disinterest. After a time he broke the silence. "What are you going to do about the Duncan contact?"

Von Brandt glanced across at him, his sad eyes indifferent. "Do? What am I supposed to do?"

"Well, after all, he's a potential source of considerable information from the U.S. Embassy. When I leave, he'll be left dangling. You really ought to put somebody on him."

"Have you made any progress with him?"

"Only tangential. I'm taking English lessons from his girl friend. The Loomis woman. She promises to be a better source than Duncan himself, as a matter of fact."

"How so?"

"Duncan is an ass. He's a silly, idealistic fellow. A true Victorian, full of romantic nonsense about duty, honor, country. She's smart, observant. Cynical. Ambitious. She's also privy to a broad spectrum of sensitive material, being a ranking stenographer."

Von Brandt took his pipe from an ashtray, peered into the bowl, then began to scrape it with a penknife. He was deep in thought, and Stachel feigned busyness with the incoming mail.

Von Brandt began to pack his pipe with tobacco from a ceramic urn on his desk. Without looking at Stachel, he said, "Have you established her as an agent yet?"

"Not yet. I'm right on the verge. She's expressed a willingness, and I've told her that if she delivers us a first-class secret as proof of her good intentions and capabilities, I'd arrange regular payments for her."

"How much does she want?"

"A thousand dollars. U.S., a month. An expense account."

"Good God. That's robbery."

"She could be worth it."

"Did she say when she was going to deliver her first-class secret?"

Stachel nodded, concentrating on making his face show indifference. "Mm. Tomorrow. Noon. Café Heinrich."

"To whom? You?"

"Mm."

There was another silence, broken only by the soft sounds of von Brandt's sucking his pipe into life. A cloud, gray and smelly, drifted across the room.

"Maybe it would be a good idea if I were to keep the rendezvous," von Brandt said around the pipe stem.

"Loomis doesn't know you. She wouldn't turn a secret over to you. Only to me."

"Well, she would if you were to vouch for me."

"Vouch for you? Hell, she'd run like a deer if I showed up at the Heinrich with anybody else."

"No. I mean you could call her. Tell her you're being transferred and that I'm replacing you as her German contact. As her money-bearer."

Stachel pretended to think about that. Then he said, "No. I don't think that would work."

"Look, Stachel," von Brandt said dryly, "don't try to suggest that you're indispensable as Loomis's control. I won't fall for it. You're going to be transferred, and that's that."

"Nobody can handle Loomis except me. I've worked very hard to cultivate her. She's edgy. If she'll turncoat on her people, it'll be for me and me only. I'm the only one she trusts."

"That's nonsense."

"You'll see. Transfer me, and Loomis dries up."

"Oh no, Stachel. *You'll* see. Set it up."

"What do you mean?"

"I mean call Loomis. Right now. Tell her about me. Tell her that you've been assigned new duties and that I've been appointed as your successor. Tell her to bring me the secret tomorrow, as planned."

"I don't think that's a good idea, Major—"

"I don't care what you think, you Nazi clod. Now pick up the phone and call her."

"I can't call her at her office. I'll have to drop by her place this evening, after hours. It'll take a bit of handling, a little diplomacy, so to speak."

"Well, then, do it. What's the arrangement tomorrow?"

Stachel shrugged. "I'm to be seated at the table beside the café entrance. Under the awning. At precisely noon. She will simply walk up to my table, hand me an envelope, and then walk on down the street."

"Any conversation?"

"None. Just a transfer of an envelope."

"All right. Tell her that if the secret qualifies her, I'll be in touch with her. I'll be her paymaster."

Stachel held up his hands and sighed a sigh of surrender. "All right, Major, all right. I'll set it up this evening."

TELEPHONE TRANSCRIPT

Hugelmeier's Delicatessen."

"I'd like to price your Sauerkraut."

"Who's calling, please?"

"Laub."

"This is Sauerkraut. Twenty."

"Four-three-three."

"What's up, Laub?"

"Status report, Stachel study. Major Ernst von Brandt was arrested this date at twelve-forty hours. He was picked up at the Café Heinrich on Loperstrasse and placed in the rear of a Mercedes staff car. Onlookers heard him complain bitterly about a frame-up.

"So then what happened?"

"The car moved off, followed by another car bearing two men with cameras. There were sounds of a truck in the alley to the rear, and residents of the area reported that the truck carried off a dozen men dressed in identical, army-type raincoats. Three hours later, Major von Brandt's body was found in a detention room at headquarters. The official army report says he took his own life in a fit of remorse over his illegal trafficking in government secrets. But there are those who say this is untrue; they say he was executed by his guards."

"He wasn't in your chain, was he?'

"No. But I'd been watching him. He showed negative symptoms. Nothing actionable, though."

"Speaking of your chain, is it still intact?"

"Yes. And expanding. I have good links as far away as Bavaria now. We're preparing to establish a lot of new studies."

"Does the von Brandt furor imply any problems?"

"No."

"Good. How about you? Need anything?"

"No. My cover's too good."

"All right, then. All for this study?"

"Yes."

"Sauerkraut. Eighteen."

"Three-three-four."

24

Two days before his departure for Lipetsk, Stachel was given a complete physical examination, and upon his return to headquarters, Feldwebel Raumann met him at the door to tell him that General von Lemmerhof wanted to see him. Curious, and touched by foreboding, Stachel went directly to the general's office, taking a moment in the anteroom to run a comb through his hair.

"Hauptmann Stachel reporting as ordered, Herr General."

"Yes-yes, Stachel," the general said, answering the salute with an idle wave of his hand. "Sit down, please."

Stachel sat in the indicated chair and tried to look cool, yet pleasant and attentive. This was what this general liked to see in his men—an attitude of calm and amiable alertness—and Stachel had worked hard to master the pose.

The general arose from his chair and stood by the french doors overlooking the balcony and the river beyond. He clasped his hands behind him, and his boots glittered like mirrors as he rocked back and forth on his heels. Squinting at the sunlit distant view, he said, "I want you to postpone your inspection of the Lipetsk facility, Stachel."

Stachel felt a sinking, and he understood now the source of his earlier misgivings: premonition. "I'm sorry to hear that, sir," he said, struggling to hide his disappointment.

"I realize that you must be quite disappointed."

"I'm sure the general has excellent reasons," Stachel managed.

"I do indeed."

Stachel waited without further comment while the general continued his contemplative rocking.

"The reason," the general said at last, "is that we want you to concentrate on the exploitation of the American air attaché. There are rumors that he might soon be returned to the United States, and to let him get away from us before we, ah, maximize his value to us would be, of course, regrettable."

Again Stachel kept silent.

"Supplementary investigations reveal that Captain Duncan, despite his relative obscurity in the military service and his reputation for naïveté, has political aspirations which could, thanks to his family background, be realized within a few years. It could benefit us to have a friend—someone amicably disposed toward the Fatherland and its military professionals—well placed in the American political structure, wouldn't you say?"

Stachel, still dealing with his bursted bubble, said, "I wouldn't count too heavily on such an advantage, sir. Duncan is from a minor state, predominantly agricultural, whose influence at the national level—in the Congress in Washington—is less than significant. Even if he were to win a seat in the American Senate, he would be a long time acquiring the political muscle that could be meaningful to us. He's an egg that will be very hard to make into a juicy chicken, so to speak."

The general glanced at him. "Have you begun your development of him?"

"No, sir. There've been many priorities. But I've called him on the phone to try out my English, and he's called me twice, but nothing more."

"How are you coming with your English, by the way?"

"Miss Loomis, who, as you know, is my tutor, expresses considerable satisfaction with my progress. She says I'm one of the fastest learners she's come across in some time. Duncan, too, for all his provincialisms and for all my, what he calls, 'Dutch accent,' thinks I'm doing well."

"Good. Good. English is a rotten little language. So illogical in construction. Disorderly. Never could deal with it myself."

"May I ask a question, Herr General?"

"Of course."

"It's not altogether clear to me—my place in the organizational structure, that is. My new assignment has been to Air Intelligence as assistant to Oberst Schneider. But with the priority you have placed on the Duncan development it would seem that the many details I expected to handle for Oberst Schneider will not get the maximum attention they deserve—"

The general nodded and smiled, looking, Stachel thought irrelevantly, like a benign turtle. "Quite so, Stachel. Quite so. That's why you are being promoted to Major and being given a new title—Chief, Special Projects. On the organization chart you will replace Major Kleine, who, thanks to his ineptitude in the Lindbergh matter, is leaving us for other duties."

"I see."

"We are having an office fitted out for you in the Richter Building, which is close enough to Wilhelmstrasse to be convenient but sufficiently removed from our forbiddingly massive headquarters"—the general's voice hinted sarcasm—"to permit our Captain Duncan an easy and comfortable access to his friend Major Bruno Stachel."

Stachel allowed himself a small smile. "Which compels me to make another point, Herr General. We are counting on Captain Duncan's friendship, but it could very well be that he won't, ah, like me. That is to say, I have considerable talent for alienating people, and—"

The general laughed outright at this. "Oh, I know, Stachel. I know. In our investigations of your background it became quite clear that you are not likely to win any awards for your sunny disposition. In fact, if there was anything that could be said to be common to all the reports we received on you it was the fact that you are a surly, arbitrary, willful, and ruthless fellow who drinks too much at the wrong times."

"Correction, Herr General—I don't drink at all, now."

"We know that also. And we expect it will continue that way."

"I do, too."

It was depressing and irritating to have the surprise of his new status shot suddenly through by the understanding that this man and his faceless minions had been rummaging so thoroughly in his past. Such investigations were standard operating procedure, of course—he had supervised hundreds of them himself in the past year or so—but the knowledge that strangers had been checking on his personal habits, his associations, his attitudes, was to have the sense of having been violated. He wondered how much they really knew about him. *Perhaps,* he thought in a fleeting irony, *they'll let me in on the secret—I sure as hell don't know about myself.*

His mind jumped to Elfi Heidemann and her smug prescription for mental composure—"The world doesn't make you unhappy, you make yourself unhappy; no one can make you what you don't want to be"—and his depression deepened. The world was rotten and the only way to survive was to beat it at its own games. The very fact that he was sitting here was due to the fickleness of destiny, the vagaries of chance, or whatever the literati like to call plain old spit-in-the-wind luck. He had wanted only to return to military flying, and yet, thanks to pure circumstance, he had been stuck in a dim corner of Berlin and told to study up on the Americans. In the past four months, he'd flown four times—each a half hour's turn in a primitive trainer merely to keep his pilot's badge current. No one can make you what you don't want to be, indeed. Elfi Heidemann was a Pollyanna birdbrain. To hell with her.

The general returned to his chair and checked his appointment book. Without looking up, he said, "Oberst von Diemer will give you the keys to your new office, Stachel. He has also been instructed to provide you with an airplane."

Stachel was unable to resist an impulse to lean forward in his seat. "Airplane? I don't follow you, Herr General."

"We're assigning an airplane to you. For your personal use in the, ah, cultivation of our Yankee friend. Oberst Schneider advises me that the best way to seal a friendship between aviators is to permit them to fly together."

Stachel, finding it difficult to believe this incredible twist of fortune, blurted, "Oberst Schneider is a very astute and sensitive officer, sir—"

"Oberst Schneider is an ass, Stachel. Like that idiot Kleine, whom, incidentally, I've transferred to the Supply School in Mannheim. But the war minister's sister is Oberst Schneider's wife—a fact that makes Oberst Schneider a politically acceptable ass. We would be much better off to have you as chief of Air Intelligence, Stachel. We don't need an ass in charge of intelligence; we need an ambitious scoundrel—a role you fit admirably."

"I don't know what to say, Herr General."

"Oh, yes you do, Stachel. You know exactly what to say. But, as an ambitious scoundrel, you will not say it. Eh? Ha-ha." The general winked.

"Well, sir, I'll admit that I'll be forever indebted to Oberst Schneider for his recommendation."

"Quatsch! You owe Schneider nothing, since Schneider has

trouble finding his own dingus. We know that you, and you alone, tracked down and exposed that wretch von Brandt—despite Schneider's claim to have been the mastermind behind your every move. And Schneider's 'recommendation' regarding the airplane was forthcoming only when I suggested he make it."

"I see. Then I have you to thank for my airplane, Herr General."

"Of course. And the promotion. And the ten-day leave that you've been granted, effective the first of the month."

"Good God, General—you overwhelm me."

"You're a good man, Stachel. But I expect certain consideration in return."

Stachel felt his native suspiciousness stirring. "Oh?"

"Yes. I overwhelm you with good things, not only because you are a competent officer worthy of them, but also because I expect something in return."

"What would that be, Herr General?"

A smile ghosted across the general's dry lips, and he winked again. "I understand you are on familiar terms with Herr Hitler."

Stachel, wary, said, "I've met the man."

"Good," the general said. "Between you and me, I consider Herr Hitler to represent Germany's future. I want you to tell him that. I want you to tell him that, unlike so many of our general officers, I applaud his efforts. But I want you to tell him this in the utmost confidence."

"I venture to say, Herr General, that the Fuhrer will be delighted to know he can count on you."

"Good. Good. Now you really must excuse me, Stachel. It's a dreadfully busy day I have ahead."

Stachel arose briskly, clicked his heels, and made directly for the door, his heart pounding.

On the stairs leading to his floor, he slapped his leg and laughed aloud.

25

"Take a memo, please, Miss Loomis."

"Yes, Major Duncan."

"Don't we sound businesslike, Polly? Just like in the movies, eh?"

"Careful, Major. I think we should keep things businesslike in the office."

"Sure. So take this memo, then. To the Chief Attaché, from Assistant Attaché for Air, et cetera, et cetera:

"Re our source of information in the German air staff headquarters. New arrangements must be made somehow, since our informant, Major Adalbert Kleine, has been transferred to Mannheim. He will be in charge of the housekeeping company at the Supply Officers School in that city. The transfer effectively removes Kleine from the headquarters mainstream which effectively plugs the leak we've enjoyed these many weeks. And—"

"You used 'effectively' twice in the same sentence."

"So what?"

"It's bad composition."

"All right, fix it up, then. I'll see you at dinner. O.K.?"

"I can't tonight. I'm scheduled to do some manuscript typing for Major Doubet."

"The Frenchman is still at his memoirs, eh?"

"Mm."

"What kind of memoirs can a guy on the Allied Control Commission write, for God's sake? It must be as dry as sand."

"Well, I can use the money. Ann's being transferred Stateside, and I'll be taking over her apartment full-time. Besides, I'd type the Moscow phone book backwards if it brought in more money."

"Yeah. Well. You've got to save tomorrow night for me. We're invited to cocktails at the Press Club."

"Very well."

"Meantime, put the Kleine memo on the front burner. The loss of Kleine cuts off our water, and Washington won't be too happy about it."

"Bruno?"

"Yes, Miss Loomis?"

"Are you asleep?"

"Deeply."

"Want to talk a little business?"

"I always talk business when I'm lying in bed with a nude woman in my arms."

"It's about Major Kleine. Your boss."

"What about him?"

"He's been giving information to my boss, Major Duncan."

"Oh?"

"Our people are upset, now that Kleine has been transferred. As Major Duncan said in a pompous memo I typed for him today, 'the leak at German air headquarters has been effectively plugged.' Now our people are scrambling to find a replacement."

"Let me know if they find one, eh?"

"Sure. Now go to sleep, I can't spend the whole night gabbing with you."

"Sorry. I didn't mean to keep you up."

But he didn't go to sleep for some time, since he remained on the rim of outright, hilarious laughter.

26

The airplane was atrocious.

He hated it from the moment it had begun its takeoff roll.

The landing wheels were too close together, a condition that caused the ship to yaw and bounce, and the right wing had a rotten tendency to drop. And then, once they were airborne, there was a sluggishness in the climb.

"Beautiful day, eh, Dutch?" Duncan's nasal inflections were metallic in the headphones.

" 'Beautiful' is the word," Stachel said. "You have right."

"You *are* right. My God, when're you going to get that straight, you dumb squarehead?"

"I don't know. It is one of the awkward usages I can't seem to master."

"You do so damned good on so much of it, I can't see why you flub the little things."

"Be still, Duncan. I'm flying my aircraft."

"You can't talk and fly at the same time? You, the big German ace?"

"The cemeteries are filled with fliers who better than they flew talked."

Stachel leveled off at a thousand meters and began to feel out the other characteristics of the airplane. Duncan hummed a tune and seemed to be very pleased with himself and the world in general. In Stachel's rearview mirror the American was grotesque in his flying suit and helmet, and he appeared to be much impressed with the instruments confronting him in his rear cockpit.

"My God," Duncan said finally, "how does anybody keep track of all these things?"

Stachel had been wondering that himself, until he realized that many of the gadgets and dials were window dressing, placed in the machine simply to impress his passenger. *Jesus,* he thought acidly, *if we spent as much time and money on real hardware as we have on bedazzling the idiot in the back seat, we'd have some first-class airplanes.*

"It is the modern science, my friend. Germany is much advanced in the modern science."

"Don't put so many 'the's' in your sentences, Dutch."

"Why do you so often name me Dutch?"

"Nothing personal. It's a kind of nickname we use for Germans."

"What do you name Dutchmen?"

"Dutch."

"Americans are a very confusing people."

"I'll say. Never could understand them myself."

"You want to fly, Duncan?"

"You're giving me the plane?"

"Show me the—what do you call it? Exhibition?"

"Hold your hat, Dutch. Daddy's gonna take you for a Ferris-wheel ride. Hoop-de-doo-da."

Duncan was good.

He took command of the airplane with firmness, and in the opening maneuver—a slow roll—the machine responded with surprising crispness. Following through with an inside loop, he said, "This sumbish isn't the hottest thing going, is it?"

"What do you mean?"

"You have to kick it in the ass to get it moving. Reminds me of a horse I had in the old artillery days."

"It's Germany's best, Duncan."

"Then you guys have got a beeg problem. Hang on. I'm going to see if it'll stand on its hind legs."

The blue-green platter of the earth fell behind the rudder as Duncan eased the ship into a straining, nose-high altitude without adding power. It stalled almost at once, dropping its nose with sickening suddenness and rolling into a lurching, incredibly tight spin.

"Shee-it," Duncan snorted. "This thing ain't got no manners at all."

Stachel, ignoring the blur of whirling earth ahead, studied the movements of the stick and rudder pedals as Duncan countered the spin. At the end of the second revolution, the controls were set precisely for an authoritative pull-out, but the airplane required nearly another full turn before the hellish wrenching ceased.

Diving out, then recovering his lost altitude, Duncan sighed and said, "Yessir-ee. A beeg, beeg problem."

Stachel said, "Perhaps one day we two a pretended combat have could."

"Lordie, Dutch. Put your words in order, will you? If you fly like you talk, I can take you with a box kite."

"How should I say it?"

"Maybe we can have a mock dogfight someday, eh?"

"Mabye we can have a mock dogfight someday, eh?"

"That's the way, buddy."

"Well? What do you say?"

"Sure. You rassle up the planes and we'll raise some hell Just tell me when. Meanwhile, let me goose this old lady and listen to her squeal."

Stachel sat back in his bucket seat, satisfied that Duncan

knew what he was doing. It was a beautiful day, cloudless, with the earth delineated in engraver's strokes below, and he gave himself over to his enjoyment of the airplane's mad twistings and howlings.

It was a wretched airplane. But Duncan was doing good things with it.

After landing, they went to the International Officers Club for lunch. Duncan had his usual number of drinks and fell into a long and fatuous debate with Doubet. Stachel, who had only a nodding acquaintance with the Frenchman, tried to project interest in the discussion but eventually surrendered to boredom and began reading a newspaper.

Several times he caught Doubet studying him.

Maybe, he thought in a moment of private whimsy, Doubet was a fairy considering him as a possible target.

Lord, what a world.

27

The new office was elegant. It was on the second floor of a large half-timber building that had served as an inn during the Middle Ages and had been renovated and divided into office suites in the time of Bismarck. Plumbing came with the turn of the century (according to the porter), and electric lights during the Kaiser's war. Stachel's suite had a large room whose diamond-paned casements overlooked the street and a small park beyond. There were low-slung oaken ceiling beams, a tile corner oven, and a wall of bookshelves in the main room, and in the center, facing the windows, an antique desk flanked by some really quite comfortable chairs.

One of his first visitors was Major General, the Baron Ludwig von und zu Lemmerhof, chief of Aviation Services.

The porter, with Stachel supervising in shirt sleeves, had just finished filling the shelves with reference books when the general sauntered in, slapping an immaculate field-gray thigh with his black leather gloves and smiling a distant, unhappy smile. Stachel dismissed the porter and fussed awkwardly for a moment at the business of pulling on his tunic.

"Sorry, sir," he said. "Won't you be seated, please?"

The general examined the room with noncommital eyes, then sat tentatively on one of the chairs. Stachel tried very hard to disguise his surprise at having such an important person simply pop in like an old pal.

"Relax, Stachel. I was on my way to my quarters, and, since I had to pass this way, I thought I might take a moment to inspect your new digs."

"I'm honored, sir," Stachel said without enthusiasm.

"Are you happy with your office?"

"Oh, yes, sir. Very much."

The general opened a silver cigar case and selected a long Havana. He removed the end with a clipper, also silver, and then bent to the flaring match Stachel held out for him. "Did you have a pleasant leave, Stachel?"

"Yes, Herr General."

"Sit down, sit down. Your standing there, all stiff like a cadet at drill, makes me uneasy. I expect you to burst into a marching song or something."

"Sorry, sir. I'm just a little—"

"Surprised to see me?"

"Well—"

"I assure you, my boy, I don't make a practice of dropping in on subordinates. But you're not just any subordinate, are you?"

"I don't follow you, sir."

The general held up the cigar and examined its forming ash. "Have you been able to inform Herr Hitler of my interest in him and his, ah, political movement?"

Caught by surprise, Stachel improvised. "Only indirectly, sir."

Von Lemmerhof gave Stachel a quick glance—a mere flicker of those gray eyes. Then he said, "What does that mean?"

Stachel, seated in a chair beside the windows, leaned forward in a manner that fell just short of confidentiality. "I've been in touch with him through one of his key men. While he appreciates your interest, Herr General, he has, well, reservations. Not just about you, but all General Staff officers."

"He doesn't trust us?"

"He trusts you—spoke quite warmly of you, according to my friend—but there are some of your peers he seems to have trouble with."

General von Lemmerhof nodded thoughtfully, his face wan and thick in the light of the deepening evening. "There aren't many of them I trust, either," he murmured, as if reminding himself of something.

"I'm sure that if I handle matters correctly there should be a meeting in the near future. The time and place will, of course, be selected by Herr Hitler."

"Arrogant chap, isn't he," the general said mildly.

"He doesn't want to appear abrupt, Herr General. Especially with you. But his schedules are unbelievably complicated."

"Oh, I'm not offended, Stachel," the general said, shrugging a shoulder. "Nor am I in a hurry. All in due time, as the saying goes."

"You're very understanding, Herr General. I'm certain that Herr Hitler would appreciate your patience."

The general tapped his cigar so that the ash fell into the brass tray on the desk. "How are you coming with your American studies?"

"Quite well, sir," Stachel said carefully.

"I cannot overemphasize the importance I place on your work in that area. The Americans and their aerial potential must remain one of our government's primary concerns."

"Well," Stachel parried, "I'm confident that there are many of our people studying many aspects of the American potential. Including their airpower."

Von Lemmerhof sighed. "Not so, Stachel. You're the only one, I'm afraid. The army, the navy, the diplomatic corps, the intelligence service, the economic analysis people, the banks, the commercial institutions, even our educators are examining the American scene with much ado and considerable jealous rivalry. But I've yet to see a report on military air potential. And even if I had, I doubt that I'd base a military judgment on it. German bureaucracy is so infernally full of wishful thinking. We see the world, not as it is, but as we wish it were. That's why I want my own air intelligence. I'll listen to the others, naturally, but I'll depend only on myself. On you, as an extension of myself."

Stachel displayed a suitably earnest expression. "I'm honored, sir. You can be certain that I'll give you nothing but tested fact."

"Oh, I'm certain of that, all right." The general smiled in his oblique way. "What do you think of the Americans, by the way? Really, I mean. As a people."

Strange, Stachel thought, how that question seemed always to surface in any conversation that so much as touched on the Americans. There appeared to be a great curiosity about the United States, and, because he had been assigned by due authority to make an official study, it was in the German nature to assume that he was now, in turn, an unimpeachable authority on the entire complex matter. In the German mind, the local postman was the postal service; the policeman on the corner was the legal system; the parish priest was Rome; Bruno Stachel was the U.S. Air Force. Pardon me, Herr Briefträger, how long will it take for this package to reach Istanbul? Excuse me, Herr Polizist, what is the crime rate in Augsburg? Tell me, Herr Pfarrer, what is on God's mind today? By the way, Hauptmann Stachel, what are the Americans like, and what makes them do what they do?"

"What strikes me most about them, sir, is the many contradictions. In philosophies. In government. In values. In almost everything. Just when you think you have a basic understanding of one of their characteristics, something will prove to be contrary—exceptional. They make much of individualism, the right of every man to express his specialness; but in the same breath they'll claim that all men are equal. They say there should be freedom of religion, yet their Protestants sneer at Catholics, the Catholics snarl at the Protestants, and they all kick the Jews around. They claim the right to say what they want, anywhere and at any time, but they tar and feather editors, hang witches, ban books and plays, jail writers who write about sex. They damned near destroyed themselves in an internal war to free their black slaves, and yet they continue to treat the black man as a slave. They preach brotherly love and altruism but pound the living hell out of anybody who gets in their way. They are, Herr General, the craziest bunch of bastards I've ever come across—in books or otherwise."

Von Lemmerhof smiled again. "Do you think Germany could defeat them, Stachel?"

"You mean militarily, sir?"

"Militarily."

"The Americans have a lot of potential, no doubt about that, and they gave us a lot of trouble in 1918. But we were tired old men, and they were children on an outing. Given a fair match, army for army, national will against national will, the Americans wouldn't have a prayer."

"You mean that, Stachel?"

"Of course, Herr General. The Americans are like children. They want to play at everything. Even war. Even survival."

"Well, I wish I were as positive as you are."

"The American is a materialistic brat, Herr General. We'll subdue him next time."

Von Lemmerhof stood up and took his cap from the table. Appearing to be deep in thought again, he extinguished his cigar with little jabbings in the brass ashtray. His face, creased and pale, suggested a weary uneasiness. "If you're right, Stachel—and there's no reason to suppose you're not—we'll have to be a lot more ready than we are now."

"To be sure, Herr General."

"We're going to need direction. New will. Exuberance."

"Indeed, sir."

"We are still tired old men, Stachel."

"A new generation is coming along."

"Ah. You mean the Nazis, then."

"Yes, sir."

At the door, the general placed his cap carefully on his boxy head and adjusted his tunic. "I agree with you, Stachel. Hitler and the Nazis will bring a new day. I hope I'm still in the army when that day comes."

"I, personally, will see to that, sir. I guarantee my friend, Adolf Hitler, will not permit a talent and intelligence as great as yours to go wasted. You will, Herr General, be in the van of the New Germany."

"Ah. So. Well, then." The general waited for Stachel to open the door, nodded briefly, then sauntered to the stairway. Without glancing back, he said, "Good evening, Stachel."

"Good evening, sir."

He went into the lavatory and freshened up. Dabbing at his face with a towel, he leaned forward to examine himself in the mirror.

"Stachel," he said aloud, "you are full of more manure than a Bavarian bull."

Laughing, he turned off the lights and went out to dinner.

28

The Baroness sat in the limousine at the end of the flight line and watched the airplane make a circuit of the field, its surfaces flashing like signal mirrors when they caught the low-lying sun. The machine went into its final turn and sank in a whispering glide to within a few feet of the turf, where it flared out and dropped neatly to the grass. It rolled for a long time and then, wings teetering, came back toward the hangars with its engine rumbling and snorting and its propeller whipping up plumes of spray from the puddles that dotted the field. Stachel's helmeted head bobbed from side to side in the cockpit as he nursed the silver biplane into a parking berth. The engine bellowed once more, then subsided into a soft ticking that concluded with a gasp and a convulsive jerking of the prop. Stachel raised his goggles, rubbed his eyes and sat for a time, seeming to be deep in thought. Eventually he swung out of the cockpit and dropped to the ground, hands at his throat as he loosened the helmet straps.

She left the car and met him halfway. "Hello," she said. "Welcome to beautiful Bavaria."

He took her hand, and they stood for a time in the twilight, trading smiles. "Nice of you to meet me," he said.

"How was your flight? From Berlin to Munich in one day. Remarkable."

"Not so remarkable. I got lost north of Regensburg and I had to follow the railroad to Munich."

She laughed easily. "You? Lost? The great aviation ace?"

"We all have our bad days."

He helped her into the car, then leaning through the door after her, said, "Do you mind waiting while I see to my ship?"

She took up the speaking tube and told the driver, "Stop

the motor, Alois." Then, running a forefinger over the fabric of his flight coveralls, she said. "You look darling in your little playsuit, Bruno. But I don't want to wait too long to get it off you."

"You're a sex maniac, Baroness."

"Lucky for you, eh?"

He grinned, squeezed her knee, and returned to the airplane, where he stood among a small knot of machanics and gave them low-voiced instructions.

She watched his every move, simultaneously adoring him and hating her inability to do anything about him. After so long it was time for an end to this affair, but instead of cutting him off without ceremony, as she had all the others before him, there was this hesitation. It confused her and worried her and left her peculiarly off balance. She had hoped that his act of borrowing money from her would provide the impetus she needed to break things off. When he was away, when the entire length of the nation was between them, she could fabricate all kinds of methods by which she could gracefully end the matter; but one look at him sauntering across an airfield, golden in the evening sunlight, and she'd be steaming and breathing hard in the wreckage of all her careful constructions. *Damn him.*

The city, lavender and gold in the descending night, was oddly hushed. As they moved through the murky streets, she could see the strollers, seeming aimless and silent and forlorn. These were bad times, and the colors and textures and movements of the land were chorded to suit the melancholy refrain of lostness.

"You're quiet," he said.

"I'm taking in the evening. The city's quiet, too. Have you noticed?"

"Mm. That stillness you hear is the sound of depression and poverty."

"It's terrible. So many out of work. Aimless. Poor. It's grotesque, and it frightens me."

Stachel nodded slowly. "Ah, yes. I suppose you're worried, at that. You're down to your last twenty billion, I hear."

"It's nothing to laugh about."

"Who's laughing?"

"Well, you seemed to be making a joke of it."

"Sorry. I was only trying to cheer you up. It seems to me that you don't have too much to worry about."

She sighed. "Well, it still troubles me. The Communists are trying very hard to destroy us. They should be deported to Russia, or something."

"You're beginning to sound like one of those Nazis," he said, laughing and poking her in the ribs with a playful finger.

She tried to return the mood, but she found she simply couldn't break the sense of foreboding. "Well, that Hitler fellow certainly seems to agree with me. He never ceases to preach against the Marxists and the Jews. He says the Reds are a threat to private property and the Jews are gobbling it all up. He says Germany won't be a safe or healthy place to live until both the Reds and the Jews are stopped in their tracks."

Stachel shrugged. "Maybe so. I've met the man, and he says some sensible things. But he also says some dumb things. Like all of us do."

Startled, she felt an electric excitement—sudden and intense. "Really?" she said, turning to gaze into his face. "You've actually met—talked with Adolf Hitler?"

"Sure. What's so great about that?"

"My *God,* Bruno! He's the biggest thing in Germany these days! He's going to be a very, very important man. Soon. Very soon."

"Well, so am I. And I don't see you wetting your drawers over that."

She giggled, enjoying the destruction of her depression. "My God, here you are on speaking terms with a fantastic celebrity and you *joke* about it."

"Hitler may be a celebrity, but he's hardly fantastic. He's a drab fellow, all gray and watery in the eyes and always has a frog in his throat and can't say good morning without making it sound like a speech."

"Marvelous. Will you introduce him to *me?*"

"Why?"

"Because he *excites* me. He wants to preserve my title, my fortune, my *property*. He's the only one in Germany who seems to understand me and my class."

"Don't kid yourself, chum. He's a politician. He says what fits the occasion. Any occasion."

"I command you to introduce us at the very soonest."

"As ordered, Your Royal Highness. But, meanwhile, let's change the subject. I'm on leave, and I didn't fly five hundred kilometers just to talk about national socialism."

"What did you fly five hundred kilometers to do?"

"Wait until I climb out of my playsuit. Then you'll see."

She laughed, openly and fully, glorying in the release from gloom and the sense of new adventures at hand.

He said, "By the way, all this talk of your fortune brings up a subject. I was going to deal with it after our fun and games, but it might as well be now."

"So?"

"So," he said, producing an envelope and placing it on her lap, "here's four thousand of the ten I owe you. The rest will be returned to you before the end of the year, I hope."

"You're welcome to keep it you know."

"I know."

"I'll give you anything you want, darling."

"I know that, too. And I thank you. But I want us to stay friends. I don't want money and gifts to come between us."

She nestled her head against his shoulder and sighed, full of pleasure and warmth and a nameless something akin to gratitude and relief.

29

On the third day of his leave, Stachel called the Munich number Bormann had given him. There were two rings at the other end, then the phone lifted and Bormann's voice came on the line.

"Hello."

"Stachel here."

"Ah. I'd heard you were in town. What can I do for you?"

"I'd like to see Hitler."

There was a moment's silence. Then: "He's very busy these days."

"So am I."

"What would you like to see him about?"

"I'd rather not say."
"Then forget it."
"You decide who the man sees, Bormann?"
"Not exactly. But he won't see anybody unless he knows in advance what it's about." Bormann sounded annoyed.
"Then tell him I want to discuss recruitment."
"You've recruited some new members?"
"I said I want to talk to Hitler about it, not you."
There was another pause, after which Bormann said coolly, "Let me tell you something, Stachel. You might have ingratiated yourself with the Führer, and you may have Göring in your debt, but you don't impress me. I find you disrespectful, arrogant. You treat me as if I were dirt, and I resent it."
"Dear me. I may weep."
"I tolerate you only because the Führer says I must."
"That's a pretty good reason, eh, Bormann?"
"I make a prediction, Major Stachel—you won't last long."
"I tremble, Bormann, I tremble. Meanwhile, where do I see Hitler?"
"Come to the Klingelhaus tonight. There's a social for some of the UFA film people. The Führer will attend."
"Remember, I want to see him in private. I don't want a gallery."
"You will see him precisely where he says you will see him. He specifies, Stachel. We conform."
"You're a very tiresome fellow, Bormann. You know that, don't you?"

There was an explosion of clatter and piano music when the door opened, and Stachel stood near the entrance, peering through the smoke and alcohol fumes for a face he recognized. The man called Himmler was holding court at the end of the bar, but Himmler was someone he could do without. Two UFA film stars, Erik Hahn and Georg Lindl, traded little witticisms for a clutch of worshiping, painted girls, but he knew them from their motion pictures and therefore he knew them not at all. He watched the actors for a moment, struck by their ordinariness; on the screen they were giants of grace and magnetism, and here they were only loud and beefy men, red-faced and with sweat beading their foreheads.
Hitler was nowhere to be seen, which, of course, didn't surprise him.
On the theory that if you don't know them you might as well drink with them, he headed for the bar, edging around a

circle of women giggling over a story, replete with obscenities, being told by a tall redhead with sequins in her hair. A short man with eyeglasses and a checkered suit spilled some of his drink, and Stachel felt the splash on his shoe. And a waiter asked him if he was the gentleman who had placed the call to Düsseldorf, while Konrad Busch, the character actor, nudged his elbow and asked him for a cigarette. He made the bar finally and ordered a grape juice.

"Pardon me, sir," another waiter, this one a fatty with talcumed cheeks, crooned in his ear. "The Führer would like you to join him."

"Where is he?"

"Just follow me, sir."

They went through an archway, then a heavy door, and then down a softly lit corridor whose deep carpeting and textured walls assured a reverent silence. At the end of this, the waiter tapped discreetly on another door, which was opened by a huge man in a brown uniform that featured a swastika armband and a pistol belt. Half-bowing, he held the door open for Stachel to pass through. It was a large room, elegant and without any of the fussiness of the others, and mellow with the glow of lamps. Candles flickered on a faultlessly set table by a large window that framed the Old Town against the moonlit wall of the distant Alps. Hitler sat in an easy chair, a forgotten book on his lap, gazing out at the city lights. After a moment he glanced over his shoulder, nodded, and said in that husky voice, "Good evening, Major Stachel."

"Good evening, Herr Hitler."

"Forgive me for not greeting you out there. But I can't stand that crowd."

"Then why do you have them around?"

"To subjugate them. I have to control these people. Since they are from the film colony, where everything is predicated on image, I give them what they want more than anything else: the chance to tell others that they hobnob with the truly great—the truly respectable."

"With them out there and you in here, I wouldn't say there's much hobnobbing."

"I greet them, I trade platitudes with them, then I leave. They have seen me at party's beginning, when their alcohol has not yet established amnesia. The next morning they remember only that they were here, that I was among them. For months afterward they will boast among all who will listen that they're old comrades of the Führer. As time goes by, they'll actually believe this, and then forever I'll control them."

"But where does the respectability come in?" Stachel asked blandly.

Hitler waved at a chair and said, "Sit down, Major."

Once Stachel was settled, the Führer explained conspiratorially, "You must understand these people. The emotionally balanced adult is one who gives equal weights to his natural instincts for material possessions, for sex, for social approval. But should one of these instincts become excessive, balance is lost and the individual lurches around and around like some grotesque eccentric wheel. Those oafs in the other room long ago sated their drives for wealth and orgasm. But in the process they stifled their natural need for social acceptability. So now, in a kind of mad reaction, this long-subdued instinct is the most powerful one, and they are now lurching around, emotionally unbalanced."

"You mean"—Stachel smiled—"that all the lurching I saw in the other room isn't due entirely to alcohol?"

Hitler did not return the smile. "The people in there have a lot of material possessions and, God knows, a surfeit of sex. But they don't have an ounce of respectability. It's the exploitation of their consequent eccentric wobbling that enables me to control them."

The man is loony, Stachel thought. *A real case.*

"Bormann tells me, Major Stachel, that you have an inordinate fondness for alcohol yourself."

Stachel considered the tone of this flat statement and decided that it contained neither challenge nor accusation. It had been a cool mention of established fact, as if Hitler had noted that the sun rises in the east.

"I did at one time, Herr Hitler. But I decided that it was more trouble than it was worth. So I stopped drinking."

"They say a drunkard never really stops."

"Then they—who ever the hell 'they' are—don't know what they're talking about."

"What enabled you to stop?"

"I realized I wanted not to drink more than I wanted to drink."

"I despise alcohol, you know."

"So do I."

"I have only contempt for drunkards."

"So do I."

"I'm putting you on notice, Stachel. I like you. I'm impressed with your wartime accomplishments. I'm happy to have you among my supporters. I have good plans for your future. But there is a price you must pay. Sobriety. Abstinence. The slightest sign of drunkenness, and you're finished. Understand?"

Stachel studied Hitler, dropping any pretense of politeness: the agatelike eyes, with their drooping lids and ever-present moistness; the pale skin, hinting of inner decay; the somewhat sunken frame, suggesting years of dissipation and neglect. He looked directly at these things, and after a time understood that Adolf Hitler, for all his claims to superiority, was really Bruno Stachel's inferior in a single significant sense.

"Go easy, Herr Hitler. You need me more than I need you."

Hitler gave him a glance that was full of sudden heat. But when he spoke his voice was under control. "You are being dangerously presumptuous, Major."

"And so are you. I don't appreciate anybody lecturing me on my drinking. Or on any aspect of my private life, for that matter."

"I warn you, Major—"

"Warn me of what? That I'll be drummed out of the Nazi party? That I'll be shot for not kissing your foot? Not likely, Herr Hitler."

The pallid face had spots of red showing now, and there was a deep anger crease between the metallic eyes.

"You make much of respectability," Stachel said. "But you and your party need it more than anybody. You and creeps like your stoolpigeon, Bormann, are not really going anywhere until, and unless, you have the enthusiastic support of the Fatherland's wealthy and influential people—the nation's opinion leaders, the moneylenders. To attract them, you'll have to do more than say the right things—you'll have to have go-betweens, salesmen, so to speak, who will induce these upperclass people to support you with money and good words. And it'll take a lot of selling, Herr Hitler, what with the thugs, the perverts, the drug addicts, the Bormanns who've rallied around you. It'll take a lot of continuous selling on the part of people like me—who admire you, support you, are willing to fight for you, but who also have excellent connections among those of the upper crust who still have doubts about you. You know this. I know this. I'll survive without you, my friend, but you'll go nowhere without the likes of me."

Hitler leaned forward in his chair, his fists knotted. "Just what," he asked huskily in suppressed fury, "have you done for me, Major Stachel? Name one significant thing you've done to warrant this contemptible, supercilious attitude of yours."

Stachel held up a hand and smiled disarmingly. "Please, Herr Hitler. I'm truly on your side. And I think I have an answer to your question."

"You are being quite insulting, Stachel—"

"Perhaps. But I want you to understand that I'm not one of your obsequious, genuflecting toadies."

Hitler remained silent for what seemed a full minute, his glassy eyes glaring straight into Stachel's. Then, in the quiet, there was a small movement at the corner of the gashlike mouth, and the movement became the ghost of a smile.

"You are insufferable, Stachel."

"Indeed I am."

"But I like you. I get very tired of all the bowing and scraping—the oily and ambitious hangers-on. And I do need you."

Stachel winked. "Let me tell you about my recruit."

"Who is that?"

"Major General, the Baron, Ludwig von und zu Lemmerhof, chief of Aviation Services in the Reichswehr in Berlin."

Hitler blinked. "You have induced Lemmerhof to join us?"

"Only after considerable selling on my part."

"Can he be trusted? He's the archetypal Junker—"

"I can assure you, Herr Hitler, that I've persuaded him that you represent Germany's future. He now agrees to help you in any way he can, and he's authorized me to assure you of his undying fealty."

"Good God. What a coup."

"Indeed. But there's more."

"More?"

"I think I've been successful in my attempts to recruit Anna-Marie Elsbet Karlotte, the Baroness von Klingelhof-und-Reimer. It has not been easy, but I think I might have turned the trick."

"Good God."

"She represents one of Germany's greatest fortunes. You

can imagine, Herr Hitler, what it could mean to the party to have the Baroness as a source of funds."

"It would guarantee our solvency, of course."

"But she's very wary of politics and politicians. She is especially wary of national socialism, because she's heard so many lurid tales of the beerhalls and the brawlings and the killings—that sort of thing. And I needn't remind you that she's an extremely proper lady who sets the tone for the highest social circles. A good word or two from her, and additional millions would pour in from those who hang on her slightest gesture."

"Do you think it would help if I went to see her?"

Stachel shook his head slowly. "In my opinion, that would not be wise. You might give the impression that you were coming to her, hat in hand. I'd much rather see her come to you."

Hitler made an irritable gesture. "How do we do that, if she's so high-nosed about my ruffian reputation?"

"You misunderstood me. It's some of your party people she doesn't like. She's intrigued by you, personally. I've told her a lot about you—about the compelling human being behind all the headlines."

"So what are you getting at, Stachel?"

Stachel manufactured a sincere smile. "I suggest, Herr Hitler, that I arrange a meeting on neutral ground. You could meet in my private office, say. You could slip in without fanfare, and you'd not risk the appearance of obsequiousness, which almost always falls to someone—especially a politician—who pays visits to the very rich. The Baroness, on the other hand, could avoid the press attention—the notoriety—that would most certainly be generated if she were to visit you. You can meet in quiet surroundings and size each other up."

"Your office is this private?"

"It was General von Lemmerhof's idea. Since I'm in military intelligence, he felt I should have a place for confidential meetings."

Hitler thought for a moment. "How about von Lemmerhof? Might I have a meeting with him there, too?"

"Let me see what I can do."

"Any day will be all right with me."

Stachel shook his head again. "No, Herr Hitler, I think you ought to let the Baroness set the date."

"Why? damn it, Stachel—"

"So that you might find it inconvenient. After you've

rejected two of her alternative dates, set your own. The harder you are to see, the more she'll want to see you."

Hitler gave him another long appraisal, then laughed, a small explosion so unexpected it caused him to start.

"All right, Stachel, all right. God, but you're a sly rascal."

They laughed together.

TELEPHONE TRANSCRIPT

"Hugelmeier's Delicatessen."

"I'd like to price your Sauerkraut."

"Who's calling, please?"

"Laub."

"This is Sauerkraut. Twenty-nine."

"Eight-two-four."

"Hello, Laub. Report, please?"

"Adolf Hitler visited Stachel's office today. He arrived at thirteen-thirty hours. At thirteen-forty hours, the Baroness von Reimer entered the office. She left at fourteen-ten hours, three minutes before General von Lemmerhof arrived. The general was there for fifteen minutes, all told."

"Was Stachel there?"

"I must assume so. I didn't see him, but it was, after all, his office."

"That's all this report?"

"That's all."

"Sauerkraut eighteen."

"Two-three-seven."

30

By 1931, Hitler had moved out of the beerhalls and was presiding at great party rallies in key cities. Everyone was listening to him these days, because the faltering economic recovery that characterized the latter twenties had collapsed, leaving Germany in a state of abject stagnation, and the people were simultaneously crying for relief and calling down the wrath of God on the Communist traitors and Zionist plotters who had caused it all.

The Führer had directed that Stachel and the Baroness be given the best of seats for the party convention in the Luitpold Hall outside Nuremberg. They'd driven up from Munich in her Mercedes, and, after luncheon at the villa of the von Lohmanns, lifelong friends of her family, they had gone directly to their hotel to rest and freshen up for the evening's excitement.

And that was the word for it, Stachel thought, watching the pageantry.

There had to be thirty thousand people in the hall, he guessed. Multi-colored banners formed a restless sea, bands pounded and blared, and there were legions in brown uniforms chanting a gigantic chorus of slogans, and Klieg lights sent crisscrossing beams of glare about the thundering cavern. He'd heard about how dramatic these events were, but the fact was far more powerful than the word of it. There was a fever, a high-tension electricity, a superheated atmosphere, an indescribable kind of religious fervor to the whole thing. The faces were shining, the arms were waving, the throats were full of hosannas, and over all was the spirit of all things being possible.

The Baroness, next to him, put her arm in his and, leaning close, said over the din, "My God. Have you ever seen such a thing? It's utterly fantastic."

"Now you see what those Roman emperors were doing with their circuses, eh?" The cliché was all he could summon by way of answer.

"Fantastic."

The band suddenly stopped playing, and a hush—wilder, more eerie even than the roaring—settled over the throng like a palpable mist. There was an interval, expectant, taut, and then the band struck up the "Badenweiler Marsch," a springy tune that had become the entrance signature when Hitler made formal appearances.

"There he is," the Baroness hissed in his ear.

At the rear of the auditorium there was a stirring, and then Hitler appeared in the center aisle, alone, to stride slowly toward the great stage, solemn and pale in the chalky light. Behind him, marching in measure with his pace, came Hess, Göring, Himmler, Goebbels, and a platoon of sycophants, and around them thirty thousand hands were raised in the Nazi salute.

"Am I supposed to put my hand up, too, Bruno?"

"Only if you want to get out of this place alive."

As Hitler and his escort reached the stage, an enormous symphony orchestra in the pit sounded Beethoven's "Egmont Overture," and the searchlights, filtered in various colors now, played back and forth across the dais and the party officials and military officers gathered on the tiers behind the podium. When the music ended. Hess intoned a list of names, of charter-member Nazis who had been killed in one street brawl or another and who were now canonized by the party. There followed a speech of welcome by some gauleiter from somewhere, and then Hitler came forward and began a speech heavy with high-sounding catch phrases and sarcastic references to the Weimar Republic and laced with acid denunciations of Jews and Bolsheviks and Marxists and liberals and effete intellectuals.

"I tell you," Hitler rumbled, "one energetic man is worth more than a thousand intellectual babblers—who are the useless waste product of our nation!" And the crowds cheered and applauded wildly, and somewhere the "Sieg heils" were taken up in a kind of voodoo chant.

Now there's a statement for the baboons to chew on, Stachel sniffed, listening to the incredible roar. He remembered the old school days and Epictetus, the Greek stoic, who proclaimed that "the end of man is an action, not a thought," and he saw that Hitler was playing to his own touchstone philosophy, which held that humans—academicians and oafs alike—would rather follow unquestioningly than think for themselves. Looking at the crowd around him, he found instant confirmation: within arm's reach there were well-dressed men, stylish women, calloused farmers, baby-faced soldiers, all aglow and dewy with adoration of the rasp-voiced mesmerizer at the lectern. Not one of them gave evidence that he might have seen the absurdity of the claim; not a single soul seemed to understand that Hitler was proclaiming himself the messiah of the misbegotten and maladjusted and that, as such, he would lead the way to his Father's Home, Which Art in Hell.

Stachel, in a flicker of private honesty, recognized that he had been a charlatan long enough to know another when he saw one. So it was no great feat to see that the hard center of the Hitler movement was composed of neurotics and malcontents who brought to their politics Satan-size shares of hatreds, frustrations, ambitions, greeds, and plain malevolence. Hitler, as their leader, was the biggest fraud of all, but—since Bruno Stachel was just such a man himself—it was unlikely that good old Bruno would ever truly fall under the Führer's spell. Only those who view themselves as paragons are seduceable by evil, Stachel reminded himself. Evil men like Bruno Stachel are not vulnerable to evil, in the same sense that a drowning man is not vulnerable to rain.

So all these Bürgers in their starched white collars and monocles, their carefully-barbered aura of respectability, would happily join with the lushes and the drug addicts and the whoremasters and crackpots and perverts and felons: Their self-righteousness had been sapped by self-doubts, and now the Nazis were offering a self-justification. But Bruno Stachel would never belong to the Nazis—he would use them, by God. Especially that egotistical bastard at the microphone. Especially that one.

Stachel and the Baroness shook hands with presiding functionaries in the receiving line and then drifted into the main current of the gala, a lavalike flow of humanity through the hotel banquet hall and its adjoining rooms. Hitler was nowhere to be seen, which was no surprise to Stachel, since the Führer was death on tobacco and the smoke already hung in a stinging cloud that virtually obscured the far end of the throng. Conversation was impossible, what with all the shouting and laughter; which was all right with Stachel, inasmuch as he had nothing to say anyhow.

They were at the buffet when Rudi came out of the crowd to beam at them and to click his heels and give the Hitler salute. He was crisp and natty in a brown SA uniform.

"Rudi!" the Baroness said, her eyes wide. "My God, what have you done—enlist in the army or something?"

"Don't be ridiculous, Mutti," Rudi chortled. "I am now in the service of the Führer. Am I not absolutely gorgeous?"

"My God," she said, shaking her head.

"Bruno—I ask you. Am I not gorgeous?"

"You look like a garage attendant."

"Careful, old boy, or I'll have you denounced as a Jew," Rudi said in an elaborate imitation of a Prussian general.

"It'll never stick. All I have to do is wave my dingus."

"Bruno!" the Baroness said in mock reproval. "You shouldn't be so obscene in a social gathering like this."

"Obscene? Your little boy's the one who's being obscene. What's more obscene than bullying Jews because they're Jews?"

"Hold on, old boy—the Führer has made it clear that Germany's problems today have been brought about by the Zionists."

"That's Quatsch, Rudi. Some of our best people are Jews. I owe my life to a Jew. I would have burned to a crisp in a wrecked airplane if a Jew hadn't hauled me out at the risk of his own life."

Rudi shrugged, already tired of the subject. "All right, all right. You're a real pain when you defend the downtrodden."

"Defend the downtrodden? When in hell have I ever defended the downtrodden?"

"Will you two please stop and be sociable?" the Baroness put in, laughing. "Every time you two get together I always end up serving as referee."

"Sorry, Mutti. But Bruno's a frustrated clergyman, I suspect. He always looks for an underdog to stand up for."

The Baroness sought to be diplomatic. "I don't think that the Führer is really so disapproving of the Jews. I don't think he's really against anybody's religion."

"Well, think again, Mutti." Rudi was making himself a huge belegtes Brot, smearing great gobs of mayonnaise over the slab of pumpernickel. "I had a long talk with Ernst Röhn the other day, and he says that the Führer will never rest until the last Jew is gone and all the churches in Germany serve the Fatherland and God instead of some outside power."

"Outside power?"

"Sure. The Jews are all Communists, and they do whatever Moscow tells them to do. Ernst says we Nazis don't intend to have a foreign power ruling in the Fatherland, like Moscow. And what do you think the Vatican is? It's a foreign power telling thirty million Germans that their primary loyalty is to the Pope and his henchmen in the Catholic hierarchy. Why should we let a despot in Rome give us orders any more than we should jump through hoops for a Bolshevist in Moscow? Either the Catholics stop listening to the Pope or we'll turn off their water."

Stachel selected an olive from a large tray. "We? You and Ernst Röhm are we?"

"He personally enrolled me in the SA."

"The word is that he's a fairy."

Rudi blushed. "That's sheer nonsense. He's a very masculine kind of fellow."

"It means nothing to me. I'm just saying what the gossip is."

"You're inferring that I'm a homosexual, too?"

"I know better than that."

"You should. You've personally watched me bed at least four women—Natali, Loni, Gerta—"

"Rudi! After all, I am your mother."

"Hell, as my Mutti, you know that I'm one of the busiest wenchers in Germany. I never made a secret of it."

"How did we get into this kind of talk? Bruno, tell Rudi to stop talking that way."

"Stop talking that way."

"Oh, go to hell, Bruno. You can't call me a fairy and get away with it."

"I didn't call you a fairy. I merely said that Röhm's supposed to be one. Hell, I don't care how somebody takes his pleasure. To each his own, I say. But homosexuals aren't very popular in Germany, my boy, and you could make a lot of problems for yourself by hanging too close to a man like Röhm."

"He's a fine, decent man. A soldier."

"For God's sake," the Baroness said, her good humor clouding over. "Let's change the subject, shall we?"

"I'm for that," Stachel said.

They fell silent, making a business of rummaging through the lavish spread of food.

"Excuse me, Major Stachel," a voice said behind him.

It was an SS man, a wiry fellow with bushy eyebrows and a fawning smile.

"Well?"

"The Führer wonders if you'd be kind enough to escort Baroness von Klingelhof to his suite."

He glanced at her. "Are you ready for another dose, chum?"

Her face was radiant. "Oh, my God, yes."

"Can I come, too?" Rudi asked the man.

"The invitation is for only the Baroness and Major Stachel."

"Sieg heil."

31

The hospital had become full and solemn with whispering and struggle, and when her tour was done she dozed on the homebound trolley, drifting in and out of nightmare reprises of the day's lonely defeats. Even so, she was dully awake by the time the car rounded the curve into Blumenstrasse, and, stepping into the fog at her corner, she realized she was hungry. Making her way through the misty night, she took a mind's-eye inventory of her tiny pantry. There was a heel of black bread, a wedge of cheese, two onions, and the section of liverwurst she'd been saving since Tuesday. Two small apples and a half liter of milk. An egg and a tin of tea. It would have to last her until Monday, when she would be paid.

I must find a way to make more money, she thought, numb and dispirited. *I must eat better, if I'm to last, and I need a new coat and my shoes should be half-soled. I am alive, but not much, and I hate this city and this world, and I want to cry all the time but I dare not, because to cry would be to surrender, and die. If only I weren't so tired. It wouldn't be so bad if only I weren't so tired.*

At the door, she stood in the darkness, fumbling with the key and feeling the night chill.

"Frau Heidemann?"

The voice seemed to be almost at her feet, and when she recovered from the surprise, she saw that the man was huddled on the steps, his head sagging in the shadows.

"Who is it?" she heard herself say.

The man coughed, a hard sound, full of pain. "Forgive me for frightening you," he rasped, "but I need help, and I didn't have anywhere to go."

"Who are you?"

"My name is Ziegel. I knew your husband. I was ground

technical officer of his squadron at the front in '18." His voice was throaty, as if he spoke through a liquid. "Please—will you help me inside?"

She opened the door and let some of the light from the hallway fall on him. His face was swollen, and there seemed to be a lot of blood. "My God," she said, "what happened to you? You're—"

"Please. I need to lie down and get warm. I'm so cold."

She caught him under the arms and somehow heaved him to a kind of moving crouch. He wasn't a large man, but his bulk, all limp and staggering, was virtually impossible to control, as fatigued as she was.

"I'll try not to pass out," he said in that awful voice. "You won't be able to handle things at all if I pass out."

"Stop talking. I'll manage. Just do what you can."

She pressed him into the vestibule, watching his feet with concern, because if he stumbled she would no longer be able to support him, and he'd fall, and the whole mad struggle would have to be repeated. They were on the lower stairway, weaving, when she was aware of the partially open doors in the hall beside them.

"Please," she called out, "will one of you help us?"

The doors closed, quickly, with the metallic sounds of bolts being thrown. She thought she might have seen the face of Frau Lockermann in the shadows near the kitchen, and the idea horrified her. Frau Lockermann, who, with her chubby cheeks and animated blue eyes, looked anything but the typical landlady, was nonetheless precisely that. She was (she would tell all newcomers to her lodgings) the widow of a sergeant major in the Kaiser's cavalry, who had fallen for the Fatherland in the first skirmish of the war against the Czar. She seemed to take particular pleasure in the irony of having lost her man before the war's first month was out, positively blushing with pride when tongues would cluck in elaborate sympathy. While there was no formal rule against it the unspoken understanding was that women lodgers must not receive men in their rooms; the only violation of this tacit law had ended with Fraülein Vogel's middle-of-the-night ejection from 2-A the December before last, when she and Herr Wolff, the haberdasher, had met secretly, drunk too much Yuletide grog, and fallen down a flight of stairs without either of them having a stich on.

In evicting Fraülein Vogel, Frau Lockermann seemed to have personified outraged decency, and there were subsequent times when, in dreams, the landlady would appear to point scornfully at the private sins of Elfi Heidemann, those dark, unacknowledged, libidinous fantasies that would inevitably rise from the dreary swamps of enforced celibacy. And so she would go to considerable lengths to pay obeisance to Frau Lockermann—even to the point of having dropped by the day after to explain Hauptmann Stachel's courtesy call as a member of Otto's wartime command. Fortunately, Frau Lockermann was enough of an army widow to be familiar with such niceties, and so her own past experience, coupled with the brevity of Stachel's visit to full uniform, had saved the day. Frau Heidemann knew that she did not in any way fear Frau Lockermann as a person, but the loss of her apartment would be a calamity of crushing dimensions and was to be avoided at all costs.

This situation, however, was a different kettle of fish.

This man—Ziegel, was it?—was injured and in need of help, and she was, after all, a nurse. Frau Lockermann and her niceties would simply have to wait.

She got him to her flat, finally, and he sank onto the bed with a groan. A quick examination showed her that he'd been severely beaten about the head, and, opening his shirt and running her fingertips over his lower chest, she was fairly sure that, under the black bruises, there were fractured ribs. The blood was from a ragged laceration under his right eye and a split lower lip. His nose appeared to be broken as well.

"Can you talk?"

"I think so," he said.

"Who did this to you?"

"Two Nazis."

"Why?"

"I'm a Jew. They caught me on a bench in the park down the street."

"Do you know who they are?"

"Of course. I've known them for years. Long before they were Nazis. We've always been—antagonistic, so to say."

"Shall I call the police?"

He managed a crooked smile. "They are the police, Frau Heidemann."

"My God. Policemen did this to you? Because you're a Jew?"

"These are modern times."

"Hold still. This will sting."

He groaned again. "You're right. It did."

"We ought to get you to a hospital," she said.

"That's very funny, Frau Heidemann."

"Why?"

"It's the first place the police would look for me."

She paused in her work to give him a long, searching stare. "You mean," she said eventually, "you're hiding from the police?"

"I fought back for a time. The way they hoped I would. Then I pretended unconsciousness. They left me lying on the grass when they went to get their car. I rolled down an embankment and was able to hide in some bushes until after dark, when I made my way here."

"Why here? Don't you have friends?"

"I came here because it was close by, for one thing. For another thing, I knew you'd help me."

"How did you know that?"

"I feel I know you as well as I know anybody in this world. Your husband used to talk about you all the time. He was crazy about you. He bragged about you."

"My husband liked to delude himself. I was nothing to brag about."

"You mean your drinking? Hell, he even bragged about that. He was very proud of how you licked the habit."

"Otto talked too much. He always did."

"Maybe. But he was crazy about you, all right."

"Sit up. I've got to get this bandage around you."

"Jesus von Christ. You're killing me."

"Sit up. Easy. There. That's the way. You live in this neighborhood?"

"I'm a traveling salesman. I sell locomotive stokers. I have to live some place. I picked this neighborhood."

"Why? And how did you know I was here?"

"I've kept tabs on you."

"Why?"

"Curious, I guess. I had to see if you were as great as your old man said you were."

"You've been spying on me?"

"Hardly. But I've watched you on occasion. On trolleys. In the park. At the delicatessen. That kind of thing."

"Didn't you have anything better to do?"

"Not really. I'm a bachelor. No living relatives. And Otto sort of made you my family, so to speak."

"I don't think I like being watched by a man I never heard of."

"You could do worse. You could be watched by those sweethearts who gave me my new color scheme."

"How come you never introduced yourself? Why, if you had a curiosity about me, didn't you speak up?"

"Because women never like me. I didn't want to be sniffed at again."

"That cut should have stitches. And that lip needs help."

"Just let me rest for an hour, then I'll be on my way."

"All right. But I'll have to go to the apothecary's down the street. That lip of yours needs a salve."

"Don't bother. It'll mend."

"Lie back and be still. If anybody knocks, ignore it."

"Frau Heidemann.'

"What is it?"

"Thank you. I'm very grateful for your help."

"Any friend of my husband is a friend of mine, as the saying goes." Unaccountably, she felt a new and undefinable fear.

Frau Lockermann was waiting at the foot of the stairs. Her face, pale in the glow of the solitary hallway lamp, was devoid of expression, yet her eyes held a level gaze that reflected an awareness, a special knowledge of all the evil and woe of all the years of all history. As a woman—as a landlady—Frau Lockermann had seen everything there ever was, and her unmoving dark stare spoke of accusation and weary indignation over this, still another betrayal and disillusionment.

"You have a man in your rooms, Frau Heidemann?"

"Well, yes—"

"A drunken man?"

"No. An injured man."

"I see," Frau Lockermann said, making it unmistakably clear that she didn't see at all. But in her gaze was every sort of suspicion and condemnation, and Elfi Heidemann knew, at that moment, that her home—such as it was, with its mean little parlor, its combination bedroom and wardrobe, its bleak bath cubicle of stained porcelain and ancient disinfectant, its tin kitchen—hung in the balance. She stood accused before the bar of German bourgeois propriety, and denials, explanations, even pleadings for understanding, would serve only to guarantee her banishment to the streets.

Oh God, oh God, why do you forsake me so?

If only she weren't so weary and hungry and frightened, maybe she'd have thought of something. But in her mind, in her benumbed mind, only one move suggested itself.

She crossed in front of Frau Lockermann to pick up the telephone on the vestibule table. Eyes averted, so as to avoid the thinly veiled accusation in the landlady's stare, she asked the operator to get her the police. She gave the sergeant who answered her name, address, and telephone number, as he requested. Then:

"I want to report a fugitive. His name is Ziegel. He is injured. I gave him first aid, but now he's preparing to flee again."

"What is his crime, madam?"

"I'm not sure. Resisting arrest, I believe."

"Where is he now?"

"I've got him locked in my flat."

"Very well. Our men should be there shortly."

She returned the receiver to its hook and then, suddenly sick and full of despair, passed along the hall to the lavatory under the stairs, where she would spend her nausea.

As she went, she heard Frau Lockermann's voice, oily with approval and virtue: "Well done, Frau Heidemann. You are a good citizen, and I'm proud to have you in my home."

32

The general, Stachel sensed, was in a mood. He had spent the morning inspecting the facilities and station troops at the various airfields near the city, with Stachel trailing a respectful military pace behind, making notes and looking earnest. And, while von Lemmerhof's expression retained its usual inscrutability, his continual slapping of his thigh with his gloves was clear evidence of irritability barely contained. The symptom had become familiar to Stachel over the weeks, and it always foretold a stormy day or two for the headquarters staff. Yet in the car, returning to the city, the general's aloofness and taciturnity seemed to ease off; he was still no life of the party by any means, but his anger appeared to have abated and once, when spotting an enormously fat farm wife waddling gooselike among her roadside flock of geese, he even smiled. After a time, he coughed and sighed.

"Bombers are the basic problem," von Lemmerhof said, as if to himself. "We'll need bombers, and nobody has really done anything about it yet."

"Quite right, sir."

"If we only had the proper engines. We fuss and fiddle with grander and grander aircraft designs, but nobody takes the trouble to develop engines that will make them fly."

"We could always buy the Pratt and Whitney Company and move it to Berlin," Stachel said dryly.

The general shrugged. "I'd even settle for that."

All of this was familiar territory for Stachel, since one of the general's favorite complaints was the lack of engines, and hardly a day passed without his making some bitter comment or another. It was now a kind of headquarters joke. Whenever anything went wrong, or was displeasing, or had some negative implication, somebody was most certain to grump, "Well, things would be different if only I'd had the right engine." Augi Riegelschmidt, the headquarters company adjutant, had, in fact, started the fad one lunchtime, when he'd convulsed the staff mess with a story of his latest romantic misadventure, involving a young lady of certain cavernous dimensions who'd been exasperated with his inability to gratify her. In a perfect imitation of von Lemmerhof, he'd uttered the now-famous line, and he was currently viewed as the Reichswehr's reigning wag. Either the general, who had been on a field tour at the time, had never heard of the incident, or he was a good sport of the first order, because he continued to treat Augi with the same cool correctness he displayed in all his official relationships.

"I think we can expect great things from Professor Junkers," Stachel said, hoping to feed the general's apparently improving spirits. "His Jumo engine seems to have done pretty well on the G.Thirty-eight passenger transport. Lufthansa is very enthusiastic about it. It has a Germany-to-North Africa round-trip capability."

"Are you trying to cheer me up, Stachel?"

"The thought had occurred to me, sir."

The general gave him a sidelong glance, and Stachel could sense the amusement behind the gray eyes.

"By the way, General, I have something that should cheer you up even more."

"Well, for God's sake tell me, then. I need all the cheering up I can get."

"The Baroness von Reimer has asked me to ask you to set aside the evening of the fifteenth."

"Oh? For what purpose?" The gray eyes showed guarded interest.

"She's having a party. You'll get a written invitation, of course. But she puts great importance on your being there, and that's why she's commissioned me as her messenger. She wants to maximize her chances that you'll attend."

"My God, Stachel, but you're sickening when you're being so polite."

Stachel grinned. "It's not one of my customary roles, to be sure."

"Sickening."

"Very well, General. I'll put it this way: Lotte wants you to come so that Herr Hitler's friends will be impressed with the quality of her friends. She's using you to put on the dog, so to speak."

Von Lemmerhof raised an eyebrow, his interest showing openly now. "Hitler will be there?"

"Mm. The party's being held in his honor."

"Dress?"

"Yes, sir. Full uniform. Medals and things."

The general turned his boxy head to regard the passing scene. The bright day had dulled, and there was a promise of rain, and the tidy houses and manicured suburban gardens looked oddly crestfallen in the gray light. The driver had taken them the shorter way through side streets and the park, probably because he suspected it to be the general's favorite route. Von Lemmerhof was a crusty prune, but the enlisted ranks seemed fond of him and would often do little extra things to make his day go better.

"I recognize," the general said quietly, "that my developing friendship with Hitler can be traced to your sponsorship, Stachel. And I'm grateful for it."

"Well, General, that isn't exactly the case," Stachel said truthfully enough. "Hitler would have been sure to look you up sooner or later."

"Perhaps. But you've speeded things along, and I appreciate it. You know how concerned I am about the Fatherland. I think Hitler can help. I think I can help Hitler."

"I'm sure of that, Herr General."

"Now don't start that disgusting politeness again, Stachel.

My day's been difficult enough without having to endure your playing the courtier."

They traded smiles.

When he returned to his office, Stachel found a small pile of correspondence stacked neatly on his blotter. Feldwebel Ruger had been very efficient these past few days, since he was planning to ask for a three-day furlough and was trying to build up a reservoir of good will. Stachel had been a soldier long enough to recognize the symptoms.

He was studying the Plans and Training Section's summary of achievements at Lipetsk, now in the final stages of deactivation, when the intercom buzzer sounded.

"What is it, Ruger?"

"There's a lady downstairs here, sir. Wants to see you."

"A lady? What lady?"

"Frau Heidemann. She says her husband flew with you in France."

"Show her up here at once. Quickly Ruger."

He pushed back his chair, stood up, and went to the small mirror in the lavatory to wash the day from his face and smooth his hair. He had just returned to his desk when Ruger held the door open for her.

"Frau Heidemann," Stachel said, trying to keep his very real surprise from showing. He dismissed Ruger with an eyebrow and, after she'd taken a seat, sank into his swivel chair.

"I know I'm intruding, Major Stachel. I should have made an appointment. But I don't have a phone, and—"

"No need to apologize. I'm glad you came. What can I do for you?"

She wasn't well, he could see. Her eyes, usually clear and cool and green, seemed shadowed somehow, and her cheeks were pale, and she'd lost weight. She had obviously worn her best for the visit, but her dress was out of fashion and faded, which gave her an overall wilted look, like a flower too long in a vase.

"I need help on a certain matter, and I really didn't know where else to turn," she said in what sounded like a rehearsed speech. "You are an important man in the military, and you seem to have been, well, fond of my late husband, and because of these facts I've presumed to call on you like this."

He was tempted to tell her to stop putting on all the

precious formality, but the unnamable thing in her eyes—was it worry, or fright, or, maybe, guilt?—made him go carefully. She was like a nervous deer at the rim of a clearing, and he feared he might spook her by bashing about heedlessly in the thickets of her sensitivities. His curiosity simply outweighed his abiding dislike of etiquette's little shams, and so he said nothing.

"My problem is," she went on, "that there is someone who has been arrested. I'd like to try to help him if I can."

He contemplated her again with new care. "You said him. Is this man a relative? Or—" The question, which he saw would be a presumptuous invasion of her privacy, hung unasked in the quiet room.

"I don't even know him," she said with a distracted air. "I mean, he lives in my neighborhood, and he once served with my husband's squadron in France, and he'd been injured and had come to my door for help. He seems to have known where I live, and that I'm a nurse . . ." Her voice fell away, and he wondered where all her previous assurance, her faint air of superiority, had gone. He remembered her for her aura of independence, her serene, level-eyed confidence that all would be well if she simply remained true to truth, to life as it was, to herself as she was. Now, with the blue circles under her eyes, the fingers toying nervously with a button on her jacket, with the odd furtiveness about her, she was a hare hiding from hounds. So much for Christian fortitude, he thought tartly.

"If he served with your husband, I might know him. What's the man's name?"

"Ziegel. He said he was a technical officer, or something. I don't know any more than that. Except he said he's now a traveling salesman, having something to do with locomotives."

Stachel's mind went back to that day long ago. The Fokker had barely gotten him back to the field, its engine laboring fiercely, its wings trembling. The undercarriage had caught on a hedgerow in the landing, and there'd been a smash-up, and Ziegel had risked his own neck to cut him free of the burning wreckage. He knew Ziegel, all right. A dark, brooding Bavarian Jew with an appreciation of the droll, the caustic. A sardonic fellow, to whom Stachel just happened to owe his life.

"I know Ziegel," he said. "What's his problem?"

"I'm not sure, Herr Major. When I found him at my doorstep he was bleeding rather heavily, and I managed to get him to my flat, and I bandaged him up. He told me he'd been attacked by the police."

"Why?"

"He said it was because he's a Jew. He said he and the policemen in question had never gotten along very well. You know how things are these days, Herr Major."

"Frau Heidemann, would you please do me a favor and stop calling me 'Herr Major'?"

She lowered her eyes, and her hand fluttered at the button again. "Excuse me, but this is all so official and all—"

"I am still Bruno Stachel," he said testily. "A war comrade of your late husband. A man who took you to dinner one evening. A man who is grateful to you for understanding and advice."

She sat motionlessly in her chair, staring at him and offering no further comment. After a moment of silent, mutual inspection he said, "Now just what is it you want me to do about Ziegel?"

"Well," she said, hunching a shoulder, "I want to find him if I can. Try to pay his fine, or somehow get him released."

"Why?"

The cloudiness in her eyes deepened. "I feel I owe it to him. He's in custody because of me."

"Because of you? How could that be?"

"My landlady has very severe rules against female lodgers having men in their rooms. She knew I'd taken Herr Ziegel to my flat, and I was afraid she would evict me. To prove to her that Ziegel was nothing to me—was exactly what I claimed him to be, an injured passerby—I used her phone to call the police. To turn him in as a fugitive."

"I see. And now you feel guilty about it."

"I'm terribly ashamed. I went against everything I've ever believed in. For the sake of a rotten little apartment of rooms." Her voice had a peculiar huskiness, and he could feel her misery.

"And you want me to find Ziegel and to tell you where he is. Is that all?"

She gave him one of the direct looks he remembered so well, and she seemed to be gathering strength from the fact of her confession. "That's all," she said, a firmness in her tone.

"Have you asked the police about it?"

"Of course. But they won't tell me anything."

"And so you've come to me to cut through the red tape."

"Yes."

"What makes you think I'd do anything for a Jew? You

realize that Jews are in very bad, ah, repute these days. And it'll get worse. Especially for those who try to help them."

"I don't care. And I suspect you don't care, either. You've always impressed me as a man who's very much unafraid of convention, of bureaucracy. I'm sure that if there's anybody in Germany who can find out where Herr Ziegel is, who can do something to help him, it's you."

"Why should I risk my neck to help you, a holier-than-thou who forgot her religion, her ethics, at the first squeeze?"

She stared at him unblinkingly. "Major Stachel, you have no idea how many times I've asked myself the same question. And if you think you can insult me, forget it. I've already called myself far worse names than you could possibly manufacture."

There was a silent interval, and then she stood and gathered herself to leave. "I'm sorry, Major Stachel. I should have known better. Thank you for your time."

He arose and escorted her to the door, where he took her elbow and turned her to his full gaze.

"I'll find Ziegel for you. But only on one condition."

"Condition? What condition?"

"That you stop at once all this groveling. That you stand up and look the world in the eye the way you used to."

"That's easy for you to say, Herr Major, with all your power and affluence. You don't know what it's like out there."

"Now you are being presumptuous, Frau Heidemann. You haven't the foggiest notion of who I am, where I've been, what I've seen. Who are you to judge me?"

He closed the door behind her and returned to his desk, feeling a terrible, indefinable anger.

33

The refurbishing of the summer villa on Berlin's Wannsee was completed exactly a week before the party, so the

Baroness had been able to leave her suite at the Olympia and take up residence while supervising the final arrangements. The villa was one of several she kept (the others were at St. Johann for skiing, Cannes for sunning, and Wicklow for the mere Irish hell of it) and she'd never really spent much time here. Looking around now, Stachel could wonder why. It was incredibly scenic, with distant views and shaded lawns and impeccable gardens with gazebos overlooking the shimmering lake. The house itself was cordial, for all its noble dimensions, and in this particular twilight it seemed to be aglow with an anticipation of its own. Even so, he'd had a bad moment or two when, having arrived early as the Baroness had requested, he had been shown to the piazza; the place reminded him instantly of Sonnenstrahl, and there was an aching memory of Kaeti, golden in the last rays of a long-ago Oberbayern sundown. He hadn't thought much about her in recent years, but now it was as if she'd never left and would be strolling out of the evening shadows, smiling that pensive smile, her arms full of flowers. The sense of her presence was very strong, and he stood filled with an awful regret over her dislike of him and the unhappiness it had caused her. The fact was, he knew, nobody liked him much, and the recollection of Kaeti reminded him of how truly alone and lonely he was. The Baroness was cooling in the sunset of their affair; Elfi Heidemann saw him as a mere pompous bureaucrat; there was no one, and the realization of it was like a wound.

A gypsy band was playing subtle, insistent music under the arbor near the carriage house, and there was a swarm of chattering diners around the buffet, which had been set up on long tables on the lawn. Japanese lanterns and flickering torches put a flattering glow on the sea of bare shoulders and starched shirt fronts, and the night was soft and fragrant and sensuous. All in all, Stachel decided, Lotte had designed a first-class party, and he knew that she had scored a lot of points for herself by naming Hitler as the guest of honor. The Nazis, it was said, never forgot either a transgression or a favor, and it seemed to him that an event of this size, in a setting like this, to salute the party's spiritual leader was a favor of considerable uniqueness and magnitude.

Hitler, as Stachel had expected he might, arrived with his official retinue. He was wearing a dark-blue suit and a maroon four-in-hand tie, and still managed to look more formal than anyone, including Göring with his tentlike tuxedo and kaleidoscopic array of medals and ribbons. The Führer had come through the main hall at the point of his wedge of toadies, nodding right and left to the ripple of applause and appearing to be somewhat ill at ease. He had taken the Baroness's hand and brushed it with his lips in the Viennese manner, and Stachel had to marvel at how the man could make such a dated and intrinsically silly gesture seem dramatic and important. Hitler was full of little surprises.

The Baroness had led the official party to the terrace, where Hitler declined champagne in favor of fruit juice. Göring, like a square-rigged schooner under full sail, descended on the buffet, where he set about heaping a plate between long draughts of wine. Goebbels, a ratlike little man with a limp, began to hold court in a circle of foreign press dignitaries that formed near the fountain; Hess and Bormann stood awkwardly to one side, trying unsuccessfully to look as if they were happy to be here; Röhm and Himmler chatted in a corner, waving champagne glasses to punctuate a conversation that seemed to have none of the deep animosity the two were said to have for each other. The lesser lights—Lutz of Hannover, Heydrich, Kruger, Sepp Dietrich, Daluege, Ley, Wagner, Weber—clung together, a knot of pioneers in an alien wilderness, wary, sniffing the air.

"It looks as if they're choosing up sides for a soccer brawl, doesn't it," Rawl said at his elbow. "Nazis versus the Swells."

"Oh, hullo, Rudi. I was wondering where you were."

"Look at Mutti. She's positively radiant. And she doesn't seem to worry at all that the guests are about as compatible as cats and dogs."

"She certainly seems to be taken with Hitler, all right."

"The word is that he's a real ladies' man."

"I've heard just the opposite."

"You mean that gossip about his having only one ball? About how he tolerates Röhm because he's a fairy himself?"

Stachel shrugged. "Not exactly, no. I mean the more heady stuff—about how he's dedicated to his work, all wrapped up in his mission to save Germany, and doesn't have time for women."

"You always were an idealist, Bruno. I prefer to dwell on the vision of Hitler and Röhm making love together. Isn't that one of the funniest pictures yet?" Rudi, already half tight, laughed uproariously. "Can you imagine climbing in bed with that ridiculous mustache? Yecks."

"Easy, Rudy—that ridiculous mustache might hear you. And then you'd end up with not even one ball."

"Haven't you heard? Hitler likes me."

"He likes your mother's money. That's why he likes you."

Rudi drained his champagne glass and beamed at a passing film starlet. "Your place at one, right?"

The girl, a lacquered blonde with a stunning smile, winked over her shoulder and said, "Make it two. He'll have left by then."

"My God, Rudi," Stachel said, "don't you ever stop?"

"Of course not."

"Who's that man with Himmler and Röhm? The one in the evening suit that doesn't fit?"

Rudi glanced across the piazza. "Ah. That's Diels. Rudolf Diels. He's chief of the infamous Department One-A of the Prussian State Police, and as such specializes in ferreting out Communists. He's been a career policeman all along. He's not a Nazi. He's a satrap. But smart, they tell me, and full of official secrets. He's said to be a protégé of Göring, who plans big things for him when Hitler takes over the government one day soon."

"Diels is not a Nazi?"

"Mm. He's an out-an-out cop. Indifferent to politicians."

"Then why is he here?"

Rudi laughed again. "Touché! Good old Bruno—always there with the needle when balloons fly. The fact is, though, Diels is probably wondering the same thing. Mutti invited him because I asked her to, and I asked her to because *I'm* a politician. I drew up the guest list because I want to kiss as many asses as possible, so as to speed my climb to the top of whatever German national government evolves from all this push and shove that's going on these days."

"As a politician, Rudi, you'd make a fine cowherd. Why don't you stick to drinking and wenching?"

"Oh, I will, I will. I give you my solemn promise."

The Baroness, having promised the Führer a campaign fund of substantial size, had left him at the peak of his astonishment and delight. She'd long ago learned the trick of pleasing a man and then withdrawing at once to allow him to exult, and her last glance at Hitler before she'd gone on to the buffet showed him talking animatedly with General von Lemmerhof, himself all flushed with carefully controlled pleasure at being so close to one so identified with Germany's salvation.

The party seemed to be going well, she decided, and after a brief side consultation with the wine steward, who wanted permission to open another cellar, she made a hostess's circuit of the guests, pausing long enough at strategic points to register her interest but not so long as to diffuse whatever forces had been at work there. She had a moment of concern when, at the sill of the terrace, she realized that the garden music of the gypsies was clashing with the dance orchestra in the main salon; but then she dismissed the matter, assuming that alcohol would serve to mute the problem for any overly discriminating ears.

"Ho, there! Baroness! Come here, goddamnit!"

The voice was too loud, even for a free-spirited evening like this, and she turned with a flare of annoyance to see who was calling. It was that man Lutze, the Gauleiter from Hannover, or Bremen, or wherever. He was beefy, red, rumpled, and tipsy, leaning on a table among a small circle of ladies from the von Klawssens and von Richters of Saxony, each of whom seemed pale with embarrassment.

"What's going on here?" she asked with forced amiability. "They say boisterousness is a sure sign that a party's a success."

The women tried bravely to match her mood, but their smiles were strained, and she decided that she would somehow have to steer Lutze away to a less sensitive area. If dealt with correctly, these women could unleash considerable resources in the cause of the Führer, and she wanted nothing to preclude that possibility—especially a drunken bastard who wore a pretied bow and oxfords with his dinner jacket. Even as she evaluated the situation, she could wonder at the bizarre paradox that could permit her to think in a day laborer's language and, at the same time, be offended when a day laborer in tails used the language aloud. Where was the sense in a contradiction like that? How could she be amused at her own foul mouth and annoyed by someone else's? Cooled by this fleeting puzzlement, she was able to smile when Lutze confided loudly, "I was just about to show these hens a little trick. You want to see my little trick?"

"It all depends, Herr Lutze. There are tricks, and there are tricks."

"This one always gets a laugh. It's one of Hitler's favorites. He has me pull this one when there are too many old biddies cluttering up the scene and he wants to get down to man-talk, or when a room is filled with pompous farts who think they're better than anybody else. Watch."

Lutze's fingers went to his left eye and, with a practiced jab, removed the eyeball and dropped it into his champagne. After stirring the drink with a lumpy forefinger, he gulped it down, glass eye and all. He opened his mouth to show the frozen-faced ladies that he'd swallowed the eye, then pretended after a moment to belch it up and into his empty wine glass. Roaring with laughter, he scooped up the eye and returned it to its socket.

"There you are! Hilarious, eh?"

"Herr Lutze," the Baroness said evenly, "I'm here to deliver a message. Herr Hitler has asked for you."

"Oh? Where is the skinny bastard? Talking politics, I suppose."

"Will you ladies excuse us, please?"

There was a mortified nodding of heads and a compressing of lips, and then she had the man by an elbow and was steering him through the crowd. Near the side entrance to the house, at an ell in the hedge bordering the porte-cochere, she turned him to the light and hissed, "Listen, you suet-faced son-of-a-bitching bastard—I'll give you just one minute to get that lardy ass of yours into a car and off my property."

"What the hell you so upset about, Baroness? I was just having some fun."

"Those women have enough money between them to put Adolf Hitler in the presidency tomorrow morning at eight o'clock. You might just have seen to it that they won't give him a Pfennig. You and your disgusting little tricks. Don't you have a sense of what's right, what's proper? How can we hope to put Adolf Hitler in power when clods like you smear him with your barnyard dung?"

"Don't get so high-nosed about me, lady. I was helping 'Dolf when he was still peddling postcards. Who in hell are you to lecture me on Hitler?"

"Do you want me to call a few of my men? Or will you leave now on your own?"

"Oh, I'll leave. But you've made a bad mistake, lady. You'll see who knows 'Dolf."

"Out!"

34

They had gathered in the small library at the far end of the west wing, toward the lake. Stachel knew it to be one of her favorite rooms, with a fireplace, many books, a studio piano, and aromatic plants. She'd hoped that the three men would respond to the atmosphere there, but they were uneasy, Stachel sensed, and not too happy with her for mixing business with a party evening. She went ahead anyway, coming directly to the point.

"The subject is money, gentlemen," she said, perching on a corner of the piano bench and regarding them with frank friendliness. "I've asked you here to solicit your financial support of Adolf Hitler."

The Graf von Zeumer huffed on his monocle and rubbed it with a linen handkerchief. He was a small, gray man, and in the big leather chair he seemed much like a scholarly and pensive elf. The Baroness had told Stachel that he was anything but, having been hated and feared as an oppressive employer by virtually every coal worker in the Ruhr. "You surprise me, Lotte," he said, examining the lens. "Your sponsorship of Hitler, and those incredible thugs swilling your champagne out there, is simply extraordinary. And now you want us to do the same? Absurd."

It would not be an easy session, Stachel saw, maintaining a discreet observer's role from his chair in the corner. She'd asked him to be there, just to give her courage, but he could see already that she would make mincemeat of these old buggers. Von Stolz, the shipyard magnate, had married von Zeumer's daughter, and he was therefore inclined to defer to his father-in-law. Von Berthold, fat and bald and perspiring, deferred to them both, since he was a spineless imbecile with no more than his millions to recommend him. All three,

Stachel knew, resented Lotte, first for being a woman, and then for being richer than any of them.

She apparently decided to concentrate on von Zeumer, recognizing that to persuade him was to persuade the others.

"You do," she said coolly, "want to see Germany rehabilitated, I suppose."

"We're not politicians, Lotte. We're businessmen. As such, we disdain political activity. I should think you'd know that."

"Besides," von Stolz put in, "Fritz Thyssen and the steel people seem to have been pumping quite a bit of money into the Hitler thing. Certainly their contributions are enough—"

She nodded reasonably, a motion Stachel recognized as her way of disguising her gathering annoyance. "Fritz has done a lot, of course," she said. "But Hitler needs more, Otto, if he's to be successful in November's parliamentary elections."

Von Zeumer placed the monocle in his left eye and gave her a glance full of challenge. "I tell you, Lotte, Hitler will not rise to power in Germany by democratic means. He simply can't control enough votes to win the presidency or to demand appointment as chancellor. He is, for all his undeniable mystique, a grubby little man who is, as Hindenburg says so perceptively, barely suited to be postmaster. He's just not our kind, after all."

Von Berthold stirred in his chair and raised a finger of interruption. "Ah," he said in his reedy way, "but our kind is on the way out, Kurt. The days of aristocracy and rule by the educated titled class died with the Kaiser's escape to Holland. We will have a dictatorship, either of the left or right. It behooves us business people to see that it turns right. Communism is entirely inimical to business."

There was a silence, during which Zeumer and Stolz stared at their fat friend as if he had just returned from the moon. Stachel felt a surprised amusement. Perhaps there was hope for Putzi von Berthold after all.

Von Zeumer cleared his throat. "Well, Putzi, there's something in that, to be sure. But my point is that we should see Hitler as a kind of propaganda vehicle, a rallying point for the anger and resentment and vengefulness that boil in the people today, the generator of enthusiasm for the causes you and I and the rest of German industry deem beneficial. But the actual management of the process—the running of the nation—we should put in the hands of someone who is, well, not quite so seedy and mercurial."

"I certainly subscribe to that," von Stolz said pompously. "Did you see how he was dressed this evening? Depressing. Depressing."

"And," von Zeumer said, fixing the Baroness with his pale stare, "Dr. Hugenberg is himself increasingly disenchanted with this man Hitler. Look how Hitler has used him in the past two years: Hitler cuddled up to Alfred in the plebiscite against the Americans' so-called liberalized formula for the payment of German reparations, but as soon as Alfred's party lost, Hitler shifted his stance and dropped Alfred like a hot pan. The man has the loyalty of a mirror."

Putzi von Berthold sighed. "Well," he said, "Alfred Hugenberg isn't exactly a paragon himself, I'd say. He doesn't exactly inspire a great fire in my chest, for all his nationalistic drum-beating. He has the largest newspaper in the Fatherland—next to the von Klugermann's, of course—and he dominates the film business and heads up the largest conservative political organization we have. He is very definitely one of us. But to bring Germany back, I, frankly, would prefer Hitler over Alfred. Hitler is, as I see it, a shifty, ruthless, opportunistic gangster, and that's precisely what the Fatherland needs at its head if it is to survive in a world full of gangster governments."

Stachel couldn't restrain a smile. Putzi very definitely had more to him than generally supposed.

"You see?" the Baroness said, looking at Zeumer. "Putzi may have been harsh on Herr Hitler's character, but he's saying what so many of us feel. I, for one, am thoroughly charmed by the Führer. He's a man with many cares, woes, tragedies, and discouragements in his life. And so he presents a very intense façade to the world. But behind his remoteness is a man of great warmth and sincerity. He cares about Germany. He cares about us."

Von Zeumer shrugged. "Perhaps, Lotte. Perhaps. But what does he want of us? And what does he promise us in return?"

"You, Kurt, have a powerful voice in the Bergbauliche Verein and the Verband der deutschen Eisen-Industrie. As I understand it, these two associations have developed a political fund of rather enormous proportions. The Führer would like you to sponsor the release of these funds to the Nazi cause."

"Emil Kirdorf administers that fund, Lotte."

"I'm aware of that. But Emil is a great admirer of yours. He listens to your every word."

"My point is, Lotte, that Emil seems already to be heavily disposed toward Hitler. He's attended a Nuremberg party rally and he's come away with considerable enthusiasm for the Nazis."

"But, Kurt, you old dear—he must be encouraged, directed. He is, after all, well into his eighties, and you are his obvious strength. His successor."

"And a very worthy one he'll be, I'll tell you," von Stolz assured them all in his son-in-law's way.

"Assuming I engineer such support," von Zeumer said, "what else does Hitler expect of us?"

"Personal contributions, of course. The more the better, but any amount would be most appreciated. I myself have presented him with a rather sizable fund."

Putzi yawned, patting his damp little mouth with a pudgy hand. "He's got one from me, Lotte, dearest. I'll instruct my people to set it up on Monday. Since you seem to be the Führer's personal advocate, I'll have the details sent to you, eh?"

"Good. And I thank you, you sweet thing. I know that Herr Hitler will be forever grateful to you. And, contrary to the gloomy assessment of our dear old Kurt, Herr Hitler is capable of vast and unshakeable loyalties and gratitudes."

Von Stolz glanced at von Zeumer, waiting his cue.

"You haven't answered my question," von Zeumer murmured. "What does Herr Hitler promise us?"

The Baroness said, "He promises you, first, a strong conservative, nationalistic central government with a set of carefully drawn priorities. From that base he can assure you a climate entirely favorable to business."

"There are rumors that he plans to nationalize all heavy industry—perhaps all business activity."

"He has personally assured me, gentlemen, that he plans no such thing. On the contrary—he proposes to give the Fatherland's industrialists carte blanche, since he can't realize Germany's international political and economic goals without a strong domestic industrial foundation. And he recognizes that the free-enterprise technique—lubricated by a governmental policy that looks benignly on cartels and other competition-minimizing devices—is the fastest and most efficient supplier of such a foundation."

"In effect, then, he's saying that if we provide him money he'll leave us alone."

"Exactly."

There was another interval in which the only sounds were

those of the partying on the distant lawn. Von Zeumer adjusted the fit of his monocle, then stood up and considered the Baroness with the trace of a smile on his lips.

"I didn't realize, Lotte, that you had this affinity for politics. I knew you were astute, of course, but this—this activism—is a new facet to your personality."

"It excites me, Kurt. I feel useful for the first time in ages."

"You have spent some time with Hitler, then?"

"As much as he'll permit me. He's a powerful teacher, and"—she laughed—"he says I'm a fast learner."

The other two men arose from their chairs and beamed at her. "I don't usually care for women who busy themselves in a man's world," Putzi chuckled, "but you, dear Lotte, are a delightful exception."

"Hear, hear," von Stolz crooned.

"I'm assuming, then, gentlemen, that the Führer can count on you."

Von Zeumer nodded, his monocle glinting in the lamplight. "I think that's a safe assumption, Lotte. Tell your friend Hitler that I'll do what I can with the association political fund—via Kirdorf, of course. And there will be a credit line for him at my bank, effective Monday."

The Baroness glanced at Stachel. "Bruno, would you please escort the gentlemen to the refreshment table? I'll join you later."

Stachel could barely contain an urge to guffaw. "I'd be delighted, my dear Baroness."

When they had left, she sank into the leather chair and kicked off her pumps. She sighed and smiled when the cloakroom door opened wide and he came out of the shadows.

"How did I do?" she asked.

"Very well indeed," Hitler said quietly.

"Von Zeumer had me worried for a time."

"Von Zeumer had better watch his manners. I won't forget his remarks about me."

"Oh, Kurt's all right. He doesn't like anybody much. He's never liked me at all. But I don't take it personally. And neither should you. That's just his way."

"We'll see."

"You look tired. Terribly tired."

"Weariness is the price of any holy mission."

"Can I put you up for the night?"

"No. My car's waiting."

"I'll lead you to it. We don't want anybody seeing you. They all think you left an hour ago."

"It's good of you, Baroness."

"My friends call me Lotte."

He took her hand and gave her one of his intense stares. "I'll not call you Lotte. You are indeed my friend, and I'll always be grateful to you for your devotion. But our friendship must remain a formal one, since any personal relationship between us would be sure to deepen. You are a most admirable woman, dear Baroness, and I could very easily become your slave. But Germany awaits me, and to become your lover would distract me, dissipate my strengths and concentration. Now—will you escort me to my car, please?"

35

The police building was severe, and it smelled unpleasantly of disinfectant and unwashed humanity. There was an air of hostility and melancholy about the place, and the tall windows, with their steel bars and time-etched panes, cast a gray light that gave the duty sergeant a corpse-like color.

"What can I do for you, Herr Major?" The man's eyes traveled slowly, almost insolently, over Stachel's uniform, pausing briefly to examine the Blue Max at his throat.

"I want to speak privately with the officer in charge."

"We have several officers in charge of several areas of activity, Herr Major," the man drawled, seeming about to yawn.

Stachel decided to wake him up a bit. "I've already discussed the matter with Herr Diels, and he suggests that I see the ranking officer on duty. Surely you do have a ranking officer on duty, don't you, you pot-bellied ass?"

The sergeant's little eyes widened a millimeter. "Herr Diels? You mean, ah, *our* Herr Diels?"

Stachel continued the attack. Drawing himself up and

slapping his left hand with his gloves, in the manner of an irritated field marshal, he snapped, "A brilliant surmise, Sergeant. With keenness like that you should go far in police work. Now see me to your presiding officer. At once."

"Excuse me, sir," the man said, wavering, "but I'll have to see if Herr Kratzer is available. Excuse me, please."

The sergeant pushed back from his desk, stood up, brushed the wrinkles from his uniform, and disappeared through a door marked Entrance Forbidden Except to Authorized Personnel. Waiting, maintaining his pose of Prussian arrogance, Stachel watched the sad and silent traffic in the reception hall and its tributary corridors.

The sergeant came back to usher him into an unmarked office in an elbow of a corridor beyond the forbidden entrance. There was a medium-sized desk, a metal file cabinet, a picture of Hindenburg on the wall, a hanging calendar, and a single window overlooking an inner courtyard. The chairs were all hard and uninviting, and the smell of old sweat was particularly strong.

"Sit down, Herr Major. Herr Kratzer will be with you in a moment." The man bowed slightly, then left the room, closing the door behind him with a polite click.

In precisely five minutes the door opened to admit a small man wearing a blue serge suit and a massive watch chain across his vest. He was bald, except for a gray fringe above the ears, and a pince-nez sat on his stubby nose.

"You wanted to see me, Major Stachel?"

"You know who I am, then."

"Of course. There are few Germans who don't."

"You are Herr Kratzer?"

"Yes." The man motioned to a chair, then sat behind the desk, his eyes watchful behind his glasses. "Take a seat, Herr Major. How can I serve you?"

Stachel sat on one of the hard chairs and took the small notepad and silver pencil from his tunic pocket. As if consulting notes, he said crisply, "The subject is a man named Ziegel. Bernhardt Isaac Ziegel, last known address Schmittstrasse Eight, Berlin. Said to be a traveling salesman for a locomotive supply concern. Our records show that he served on the Western Front in 1917–18 as a ground technical officer for several units of the Imperial Flying Corps."

"What is your specific interest in this man?"

"I'd rather not say, Herr Kratzer."

"Then I'm afraid I can't help you."

"This is a matter of national urgency."

"I have only your word for that."

"You doubt my word as a German officer?"

"Of course not. But the ways of bureaucracy are many and specific, Major Stachel, and I happen to be deeply involved in one of the most specific of all. Police work, and its demands on those who direct it, are altogether unforgiving of deviations from the prescribed, the norm. In this case, the official requirement is for a request for custody of a prisoner, written in full on military letterhead and spelling out in detail the nature of the suspicions against the prisoner. Without such a document, you are wasting my time. And your own, of course."

Stachel's annoyance deepened. "I must have custody."

"Sorry, Major."

"May I at least see the prisoner?"

"Sorry, Major. Only an attorney may see the prisoner."

"Where is he being held?"

"I'm not certain. Here, I would imagine."

"You mean you don't know? Or won't say?"

Kratzer hunched his shoulder again. "Such questions are academic, wouldn't you say?"

"Why are you being so difficult? Seriously. I'd like to know."

"It's quite simple, Herr Major. I don't like you Nazis."

"Oh? What makes you think I'm a Nazi?"

"It's common knowledge. You are widely known as a friend of that man and his henchmen. And I will not deliver Ziegel to you, since he's a Jew, and you probably plan to kill him."

Odd, Stachel thought, where you find courage. This little son of a bitch was probably fifty-five years old and had an ulcer and a fat wife and a gloomy little walk-up apartment in a gloomy little part of the city. He would be retired with a letter of commendation and a modest pension and an eternity of empty days and nights. He had nothing to gain and a life's work to ruin by resisting the political tides. It would have been very easy for him to hand over Ziegel without a fuss, and it would, certainly, have been very wise as well. But he was one of those rare ones, a hero without a cause, a fighter for an inner principle he probably couldn't describe or, perhaps, even recognize in himself.

Uncomfortable, Stachel knew there was no choice. It was Ziegel or Kratzer. It was Ziegel he owed. "You realize, I'm sure, Herr Kratzer, that the police organization—particularly here in Prussia—is rather extensively infested with Nazis? Policemen who believe in Hitler and support him?"

"I regret to say that's true."

"And you realize that if the Nazis really wanted to kill Ziegel they could do so at any moment—wherever he may be, in whatever police station he might be held?"

Kratzer nodded silently.

Stachel, depressed beyond words, said nothing for a moment. There had been something in the man's softly spoken defiance that had touched his memory, taking him back some fifteen years to a field in France. It had been a raw day in early November, the morning of his last victory. Fittingly, the other man had been a Frenchman, flying one of those silly little Nieuports with the flimsy wings and the rasping little motor that spewed castor oil and it had been just the two of them, high above Fismes in the cold blue. He'd shot the Frenchman's airplane to rags, but still it didn't fall, and still the man kept coming at him, his single machine gun tapping a futile, thin staccato. When at last the Nieuport sank to a wispy collapse in the great wide field, he had been unable to resist the need to look his enemy in the face. The man had been so utterly defiant, so unwilling to concede another piece of France to a German gun, it seemed that he must actually *be* France, and it was fundamentally important to peer into his eyes. He'd landed the Fokker and taxied to a halt beside the wreck and the Frenchman, huddled in his shattered cockpit, bleeding beyond repair and staring through a glaze, had aimed a service pistol at him. But the man died, the unfired pistol dropping from his oil-smeared glove, and Stachel had stood beside him for what seemed to be a very long time.

"Very well, Herr Kratzer," Stachel said, putting away the notebook and pencil and rising to leave, "I'm sorry that your political persuasions have muddied your professional perceptions. I really am. You could have made things quite simple for all of us—you, Ziegel, me—but like so many Germans these days you're living off your angers instead of your brains. Too bad, really,"

"Good day, Major." Kratzer stood up and bowed stiffly in the old manner.

"I'll get Ziegel, you know."

"I know."

"And you won't have proved a thing."

"I'll have proved something to myself."

"Good day, Herr Kratzer."

He returned to his office and dialed Bormann's Berlin number.

"What is it, Stachel?" Bormann said testily. "I'm due to leave for Garmisch in twenty minutes."

"I want a hand with something."

"So?"

"There's a police superintendent at the Praesidium. Man named Kratzner. He has something I want, but he won't deliver it because I'm a Nazi."

"What is it you want?"

"I'd rather not say."

"All right. But what would you have me do?"

"I want Kratzer to be told that he'll be demoted, transferred to East Prussia, and denied a pension. Unless he recalls my conversation with him that is. He'll know what it's about."

"I'll look into it."

"I don't want Kratzer hurt."

"I abhor violence, Stachel. Despite what you might think."

"No crime waves. Just a message delivered by whoever Kratzer reports to."

"Give me a day or two."

"I'll be waiting. Meanwhile, have a good trip."

TELEPHONE TRANSCRIPT

"Hugelmeiers Delicatessen."

"I'd like to price your Sauerkraut."

"Who's calling, please?"

"Laub."

"This is Sauerkraut. Twenty-four."

"Six-one-one."

"Hello, Laub. What goes one?"

"Stachel visited the municipal police today. In the interest of the Jew, Ziegler. At the request of Frau Heidemann. There's nothing else on this study."

"Sauerkraut twenty-two."

"One-one-six."

36

For reasons he couldn't grasp, Stachel's depression persisted, and that evening, instead of working on his month-end report, due the next Thursday, he went on the town. No drinking—merely a cruise of the city's hot spots to see who was doing what with (or to) whom. Watching the revelers, he could marvel over his prevailing disinterest in alcohol. Through some magical process he had somewhere in time, begun to stop thinking of alcohol as a friend and to recognize that he had changed—a deep, fundamental change in outlook and values. He knew he couldn't fully describe the outlook yet, or name the values, but they had been altered, contrary to popular wisdom, which cautioned that people never really change and once a stinker, always a stinker.

Wandering through the tobacco smoke and the shrillness and the tootling and thumping of the American-style jazz bands he thought again of all the years since he'd reported to the Jasta on the rim of that miserable little clutch of buildings called Beauvin. He remembered the terrible vulnerability, the lonely nights, the deadly days. The striving. The blind and insistent need to obliterate his dislike of himself in the frenzy of combat and the anesthesia of drink. But for all the memories there was much he couldn't remember. Too full of self-hatred to live, too full of self-love to die, he'd induced his own amnesia and perhaps it was for the best. It had to be for the best, damn it.

Those years were gone, and tomorrow wasn't here yet.

He was about to leave the Klein Blume, where a platoon of American tourists sat in the blue light and slavered over the simulated copulation of the bored and heavily powdered adolescents on the penny-size stage, when someone called his name.

"Welcome to Indiana-on-the-Spree" John Duncan said,

waving a glass and beaming. "Isn't that funny? These fat bastards are on a spree, and that's what the river's called—the Spree."

"It isn't pronounced 'Spree,'" Stachel said over the orchestra's groaning. "It's pronounced 'Spray.'"

"O.K., so the Kiwanians from Indiana are on a spray."

"Are you with these people?"

"God, no. Not me. I just dropped in to watch the screwing. Or the pretended screwing. Or whatever those kids are doing."

"Well, it is nice to see you. But I am leaving."

"I'll go with you. Where-to?"

"I was going to my quarters."

"Have a nightcap with me. Come on. There's a quiet little place on the Konigstrasse. Which is on your way, Red Baron."

Duncan was drunk, of course, but not offensively so which meant he was talkative and magnanimous, explaining brightly how Americans in their natural habitat were not nearly so hedonistic and should not be judged by their manners in foreign fleshpots. "Would you believe," he said confidentially, "that most of those people watching that show are probably church deacons or scoutmasters or members of the Ladies Altar Guild or whatever? They are most likely very strait-laced at home, and they'd cluck and roll their eyes and say sorrowful, resigned things if they so much as saw a dirty word chalked on the sidewalk. But when they leave their towns they get disassociated, or disoriented, or dissomething, and they run around after hours like high schoolers with bulging pants, looking for thrills—safe ones of course, that Momma or the Boss won't know about, ever. And when they come to Europe, wow! Even Momma catches the fever and goes along to blush and giggle when Pops takes in a horny show."

Stachel, not sure he'd followed all this, said nothing, choosing instead to nod thoughtfully, as if considering a great verity.

"But, what the hell," Duncan said expansively, "you Krauts aren't anything to write home about, either. You are two people all in one, way I see it. You can be really peachy—nice to old folks, kids, strangers, and you whomp up all kinds of great stuff in science, fine arts, music—all that cultural shit. Then at the same goddamn time you can be boxing kids' ears till they bleed, pushing old ladies out of trolley seats, castrating Jews in the street, and knocking the living pee out of France and Belgium and all those other godforsaken, asshole places that seem to displease you for one reason or another. And the real trouble is, nobody ever knows which side of you is going to be showing today, know what I mean? I mean, what's Fritzie going to be today, fellas—Beethoven or Bismarck? What's he going to dish up—music or mayhem? Eh? Ha-ha."

Duncan broke off long enough to signal the waiter for another Schnapps, which he called "potato whiskey," and which, he assured Stachel solemnly, was one of the great achievements of Deutsches Kultur, ranking right alongside Diesel engines and cuckoo clocks. Then he resumed, giddy again, yet benign—"You're ham-handed politicians, too. Lordy, but you're really something to watch, you Jerries. Like, I was in Tegernsee this week, talking to a bunch of your Lufthansa people about their buying some of our aircraft engines, or whatever. There was a lot of pushing and shoving —all pesudo-genteel, you understand—between Erhard Milch, the Lufthansa big cheese, and the big shots from Junkers, who are building a transport that Lufthansa wants three motors on and Professor Junkers insists should have one motor. Milch's going to win hands down, though, my dear Red Baron. Göring has already offered him the job of state secretary for the new air ministry he—Göring—is going to set up as soon as Unca Dolf cons Hindenburg into making him chancellor. And there's got to be something to it, the way all those squareheads were kissing Milch's ass, I'll tell you. When he burped everybody ran for a napkin, believe you me."

Stachel held up a hand. "Duncan, my friend, would you do me a service, please? Would you be so kind as to speak English? I understand most of what you're saying, but much of it simply must be Tibetan."

"Aw hell, pal, I ain't saying anything important anyhow."

"Very well. Then I go to my quarters. Good night."

"O.K. I think I'll stay for a nightcap."

"You had your nightcap an hour ago."

"That was last night's nightcap. This is tonight's. It's already tomorrow, so I'm having the nightcap for tomorrow's tonight."

Stachel stood up and settled his cap on his head. "Tell me, Duncan—why are you celebrating so fiercely? I should think you'd be with Miss Loomis, your fiancée."

"She's working for Doubet again. Typing his memoirs."

"And you're drinking away your loneliness?"
"Naw. I'm celebrating. Senator Rasmussen died yesterday and the governor has appointed me to fill his unexpired term."
"You are now a United States senator?"
"I will be, soon as I resign my commission, get home, and get sworn in. Got any babies you want kissed?"

37

The wind began to stir toward dawn, and the sky promised rain. The car, a Horch cabroilet, had been arranged by Elfi, who assured Stachel that Klaus, the driver, was an old friend who could be trusted. As if to put a seal on her claim, she'd come along to sit in the back seat and support Ziegel's head on her shoulder and tuck blankets around him.

"This will be a rotten morning for flying, Stachel," Ziegel croaked.

"Don't talk. Just rest. You let me worry about the flying."

They had driven west to Charlottenburg and then southwest through the Spandauer Heide-und-Forst to the Wannsee, where Stachel had parked his airplane. The Baroness's meadow at Wannsee was private, and there would have been too much attention given at Johannisthal to two men and a woman wrestling a battered Jew into the front cockpit of an FW trainer. No that there was anything particular to hide, but he'd learned long ago that, in today's Germany, the smaller the audience the easier the breathing.

Something of the same must have been on Elfi's mind. Out of the darkness behind him she said, "Does the Baroness von Reimer know you're taking Herr Ziegel to Schloss Löwenheim?"

"Not yet."

"Don't you think you'd better tell her?"

"You and Ziegel are a pair, all right. Always fretting. Let me handle this, will you?"

"Well, a woman should know who's in her household."

"The Baroness has a hundred people running her estate at Schloss Löwenheim. She's got maids and gardeners she's never laid eyes on. One more presence is not about to be felt."

"All the same, she should know."

Ziegel said, "Why are you people doing this for me?"

"For God's sake, will you two just shut up? I'm in charge here, and I don't need all your dumb questions. It never fails to baffle me, how you can try to help somebody and they'll sit around and pick at you wanting guarantees and explanations."

They all fell silent, rocking in the dawn light as the car negotiated the bumpy road. Rain began to spatter the windshield, and in the distance, over the sound of the grinding motor, Stachel thought he could hear thunder. Somewhere in the interval, Klaus, a bland and oddly shapeless man, began to whistle "A Mighty Fortress Is Our God."

One of Frau Elfi Heidemann's religious-crank friends, no doubt.

The others sat quietly while he consulted the chart and established his course. He would fly by pilotage from Wannsee on a heading that would take him parallel to the railroad to Leipzig, and then over Chemnitz to Hof to Nürnberg. From there it was southwest, between Augsburg and Munich to the castle, below Kempten. If the weather permitted visibility all the way, he could pick up fuel at Bayreuth, some three hundred kilometers southwest of Berlin.

Despite the gusts and rain spittle, he took his time checking over the airplane, especially the engine. After inspecting the propeller hub nuts and cotter pins, he checked the spark plugs for cleanliness and the ignition wire connections. Then he cleaned the air maze on the carburetor intake housing, the fuel and oil strainers, the sump drain cock, and tested the cylinder base flange nuts and engine mounting bolts for tightness. He even shot some machine oil into the magneto-bearing access holes and removed the rocker-box covers and gave the rocker arm and push-rod assemblies a careful going-over. Finally he walked around the ship, testing the rigging-wire tension, the turnbuckles, the elevator and rudder hinges, the fabric sheen, the struts in their sockets, and the air in the tires. Fortunately, he'd had the fuel and oil tanks topped by the Wannsee estate chauffeur immediately upon landing the past Saturday.

With Klaus's help, he was able to get Ziegel into the front cockpit without too much fuss. Ziegel was still under the sedation Frau Heidemann had given him at her flat, and so handling him was a bit tricky. The two plainclothesmen had delivered Ziegel to Stachel's quarters the previous midnight, and it had required a number of phone calls to set up the trip. One of the most difficult parts had been to get Ziegel out of his blood-soaked filthy clothes and into some military fatigues. He was now nodding in his seat, his face almost obscured by Elfi Heidemann's knit ski cap and tatty fur coat.

"All right," Stachel told her, buckling his helmet under his chin, "you and Klaus go back to Berlin. I'll let you know how Ziegel's doing from time to time."

She nodded somberly giving him a direct and thoughtful examination. "You know how much I appreciate this, don't you?"

"I guess so. But I'm not doing it for you. I'm doing it for me. I owe Ziegel one."

"I hope you have a safe journey"

"I do, too. The weather's making up."

"Hurry, then."

They were airborne at sunrise.

He kept the climb even—not too shallow, not too steep—and over the roofs of the mansion house he made an easy turn to the left and picked up his heading. The engine bellowed steadily and sent back the sweetish smell of full-rich exhaust, and below the goggles the rain tingled on his cheeks. Leveling off, he let his eyes roam about the airplane, checking again, catching little snapshots: the fabric drumming on the lower wing; the wheels, caked with mud still turning slowly; the propeller's dim disk against the dirty-gray sky; the rigging wires vibrating like cello strings. The things of flying. The awarenesses. The feeling. The knowing. The exaltation. All the sensations—together and separate, tangible and subjective—that ensnared the souls of idiots like Bruno Stachel

He held the machine at five hundred meters, high enough to take care of emergencies but low enough to let him see ground detail. The broad earth rolled by below, with its farms and roads and villages and little trains chuffing. He liked railroads. Railroads were the airman's friend. They always led somewhere, and at the somewhere there would almost always be a sign on the depot that would tell him where he was. And when he flew low along the tracks to spot the sign there would be people down there—in the streets, in gardens—who would look up, their faces flashing dots in the splinter of time he'd be above them. And for that tiny moment he could forget he was anxious and lost, and feel sorry for those poor earthbound clods who would grub away their lives, never to know the godlike feeling.

His eye would occasionally fall on the wool-topped head of Ziegel, and it impressed him anew, the absurdity of transporting one obscure, bunged-up Jew from Prussia to Bavaria, just as if he were some kind of potentate, when all over the nation thousands of Jews—millions, maybe—were enduring 1932 in abject fear of what seemed to be coming. That it was coming was hardly in doubt. Hitler's direct challenge to Hindenburg had been bold—arrogant and cocksure—because the old man was the very personification of Germany and probably couldn't be beaten in straight election by any opponent, Jesus Christ included. But it had been absolutely astonishing, the fact that Hitler had amassed eleven million votes to Hindenburg's eighteen. By all rights, he shouldn't have expected to get eleven thousand votes, but here he was, now on the brink of a November runoff against Herr Deutschland Himself.

Hindenburg hadn't helped his own cause by forcing Chancellor Brüning to resign. Brüning had been one of Hindenburg's most enthusiastic supporters, and now he'd been replaced by that fop von Papen, a limp-wristed aristocrat with a headful of hydrogen, when in times like these the Fatherland needed a hardworking peasant with cast-iron guts. It would be a frigid day in Hades before Papen put together a government. Meanwhile, Hitler was standing by, and the chances looked much in favor of his forcing Hindenburg to do something about him after the November thing. And, with Hitler in, Göring would be in (the bastard) and he and Milch would be running the air force and coolies like Bruno Stachel would be remade in the Führer image.

It wasn't only Ziegel who had problems.

He'd been able to skirt the bad weather all the way to Nordlingen, but south of there, roughly over the Danube, hellish black clouds filled with sleet had closed in, and the FW had bobbed around like a toy on a string. He'd been forced to fly with his wheels kissing the treetops on the final leg, and when he at last found the castle, virtually invisible in the storm swirling about its hilltop, he had gone straight in without circling first, expecting trouble and eventually getting it.

There was a line of ornamental poplars that formed an L on two sides of the meadow at the base of the hill, and the wind was coming directly from the northeast. Which meant that he had to land over the trees, a factor that required a delicate, last-minute side-slip if he was to avoid running out of field on the roll-out.

He came in, the propeller ticka-tacking and the rigging wires hissing, the wings teetering in the buffeting wind. He thought he felt the landing gear tremble as it tore through the flimsy top branches, but then he'd accomplished his slip and the plane was down, wheels first, bouncing. Correcting quickly at the apex of the high bounding, he let the FW fall back to earth in a proper three-point altitude. But it was stubborn. It bounced three more times, once alarmingly, before it permitted him to resume command. By the time the machine stopped rolling it was no more than a meter from the far fence.

He cleared the engine with a flippers-up blast, then turned off the fuel and let it run dry to a halt.

The silence was wonderful.

He pushed up his goggles and said, "Are you alive, Ziegel?"

"No."

"What's that voice I hear? It sounds like yours."

"I'm speaking from Beyond. Through a medium."

"Well, hold on. I see Alois coming with the car."

"I don't know who Alois is, but I hope he has a liter or two of Schnapps with him."

"Alois is the Baroness's head chauffeur. You'll be working with him in the garage after you're mended. You'll like Alois. He hates Hitler and loves Schnapps."

"I say let's run Alois for president."

38

Ex-Inspector Kratzer placed the last of his lawbooks in the packing box and stood in the geometric center of the floor, examining the barren office with weary neutrality. So many years, so many problems—a few of them solved—and now an end to it, and a sense of wasted time and failure.

There was a tapping at the door.

"Come in. It's unlocked."

It was Laub, who, as usual, seemed out of place in this stained and melancholy building. Laub for all his ingenuous appearance, was one of the old ones—a detective wise in the way of the streets. He wore a neat suit, conservatively cut, and always seemed cheerily shaved and barbered. He was among Kratzer's favorites.

"So, then," Laub said with uncharacteristic dourness, "you are truly leaving us."

"I'm afraid so, my dear Laub. All things end."

"Do you need anything?"

"No. Thank you, but no."

"Are you all right?"

"I think so. You arrived just in time. I was on the brink of a massive attack of self-pity."

Laub's lean face attempted a reassuring smile. "I don't think you'll mind it in Langendorf. After all, you'll be chief of police there. Run things your own way, without always having to look over your shoulder at the minister and his toadies."

"Langendorf is a miserable, provincial town in a miserable, provincial corner of nowhere, my friend. It's just barely inside Prussia."

"Well," Laub said, seeking the silver lining, "at least you're not out of a job. Which is more than a lot of our former comrades can say in these days of palace politics."

Kratzer grimaced. "Believe me—a job as a policeman in the town of Langendorf is to be out of a job. Have you ever been there?"

"No."

"It's a crossroads, and all the rotten little buildings make a lumpy X around it. It sits out on a plain, and there's hardly a tree to break the horizon. Two trains a week pass over the spur line that connects its sugar-beet processing plant with the outside world. There is a bus to Schwerin, but only on Wednesdays. It's hotter than hell's attic in the summer and an absolute Siberia in winter."

"No wonder you were feeling self-pity."

"Mm."

Laub sighed, his good-natured eyes downcast. "Well, I'm not one to consider you finished. Not August Kratzer. You'll make plenty out of that job. Langendorf will have the best police force in the Reich."

"You are very kind, my dear Laub. But there's only one accomplishment I look forward to. I will do my job, of course. But my greatest pleasure will be eventually to even the score—somehow—with a certain Nazi swine."

"That Stachel fellow?"

"That Stachel fellow."

Laub said, "I have only the vaguest notion of what he did to you, of course."

"That's just as well. When it comes to Nazis, what you don't know can't cause you problems."

"I'm not afraid of them," Laub said stoutly.

"I am, Laub. I am terrified of them. They will destroy Germany. Even if, as they promise, they make Germany the most powerful and wealthy nation in the world, they will destroy the Germany I love."

Laub spread his hands in a gesture of bafflement. "What I don't understand is why you are so bitterly opposed to those fellows. They're only politicians. What does a Prussian policeman have to do with politicians, after all? Police work knows no politics."

"I can only answer with an ancient cliché, Laub. 'If I have to explain, you'd never understand.' "

"But you've deliberately thrown away your career. You've—" Laub faltered, obviously realizing that his protest was in direct contradiction to his earlier brave assurances.

Kratzer smiled. "Don't worry, Laub, my old friend. I now have a mission with which to fill the rest of my life."

"Mission?"

"If there's nothing else I do, Laub, I'll someday put that Stachel swine in his proper place in hell."

39

She was thinking of her father, of all people. Maybe it was the snow hissing at the windows; it was a sound that used to fill the nights in Chicago, when she'd lie in her narrow bed under the skylight in the dark-brown back room and the wind would come from Lake Michigan to hum around the panes, seething with winter. Her father would sit up until the wee hours, making unintelligible noises in the front room, clinking glasses and mumbling Irish ditties and, sometimes, sobbing. Sad, unfulfilled man. A lifetime of factories and trolleys and a lunch box on his arm, of grimy brick walls and lonely streets, of long nights—solitary, and womanless, and drunk beyond redemption. Why would God, if there was a God, point to Thomas Mulveney Loomis, a generally kindly fellow with black hair and very blue eyes and a winsome grin and a sort of sweetness about him, and say this fellow I condemn to a life of missed opportunity and lonely, sodden weeping? What whim causes the Creator of All Things to permit the Thomas M. Loomises of the world to die in DT's, unappreciated, unhappy, instead of granting them long lives of brilliant accomplishment as butcher, baker, candlestick-maker, or president of General Goddamn Motors? Why, for that matter had the Creator created these lousy winters? Or pain? Death? Anger? Vengeance? Greed? Meanness? Poison ivy? VD? Corsets? Any God who knew his business wouldn't invent a mosquito, by God. . . .

"What are you thinking" Stachel asked.

"Of how much I'm going to miss you."

"Come, Miss Loomis—you are soon to be Frau Senator. You'll miss nothing."

"Maybe. But I've really acquired a taste for you. Like sausage. For years I couldn't stand sausage. Then, all of a sudden, one day I couldn't get enough of it."

"Why do you Americans persist in thinking of Germans in terms of sausages?" His voice was muffled by the heavy feather quilt.

"I don't think of you as a German anymore. I can actually look at you, all shiny in your black boots and leather belt and medals and things, and I see a clean-cut little boy who needs the end of his nose kissed."

"Little boy? My God, woman—I'm thirty-three years old. And feel eighty right now, if the truth were known."

She laughed and turned in the bed and circled him with her arms. He was warm and smooth and they lay quietly for a time, listening to the storm together. She wondered how many other women had seen that boyishness in him. Not only was he clean and sexy but he was also the most masculine goddamn thing she'd ever laid her eyes on. Germany—especially Berlin—had become an enormous, uncaring bordello, unbelievably ready to abandon, seemingly overnight, the Victorian pruderies and to pick up, cherish, the zany and promiscuous ways of the U.S. It was only a couple of years ago when she'd hesitated to appear in public in a flapper skirt for fear she would offend the starchy Bürgers and their pasty, remote, and servile Frauen. In 1932 she could probably walk down Unter den Linden bare-assed and with a bunch of bananas on her head, and be dismissed by the passing crowds as just one more of those loony kids you see around these days. As for Stachel, a fellow as well set up as he could expect to screw himself cross-eyed; every little Gretchen from every little hamlet was ready to open up for a Pfennig or two nowadays, and most of them would give it away if the target looked like Herr Major Bruno Stachel, deputy to the Chief of Air Staff for Intelligence and Swordsman First Class.

"Bruno?"

"Mm?"

"How many lovers do you have?"

"Four hundred and seventeen thousand, not counting weekends."

"I'm serious."

"Why would you want to know something like that?"

"I'm doing a survey for *Women's Home Companion.*"

"That's the trouble with you Americans—you do something you enjoy, like gambling or fornicating or drinking Coca-Cola, and, because your enjoyment makes you feel guilty, you develop all kinds of statistics either to rationalize or justify or explain away the activity."

"I don't feel guilty about fornicating. I'm going to fornicate until I'm ninety-five, myself."

"Really? With whom? Certainly not Senator Duncan."

"Don't sell the senator short."

"He flies an airplane pretty well. I'll give him that."

"You two have been flying a lot lately. He said he'll miss that. He said you and he still owe each other a dogfight."

"We've been too busy these days. And planes are hard to come by. The ones we have operational are committed to official duties. Fun-flying is taboo."

"Do you like the blue dress I wore tonight?"

"It's very nice. Why?"

"I want you to like me. The way I look."

"Why, for God's sake? You're betrothed. You and your husband-to-be are leaving for the United States the day after tomorrow."

"Are you angry about that?"

"Why should I be angry?"

"I've told you all along that I'd be staying here until John gets established in Washington."

"It makes no difference to me. A woman should be with her husband."

"I thought you might at least miss me. And if not for my soft, warm body, then at least for the information I bring you."

Stachel yawned. "I rather thought you would miss my soft, warm money, eh?"

She chuckled again, snuggling against him. It was not so much the money she would be missing, she knew, although it was a wonderful comfort to be sure. No, her real loss would be the excitement, the keen-edge thrill of walking the high wire above the abyss of discovery and punishment. She could readily identify with the kleptomaniac. "I love your money, Bruno, dear. But I like what comes with it even more."

"You're a peculiar woman, Miss Loomis."

"Why do you always call me Miss Loomis? Why not Polly?"

"I don't want our relationship to become too personal."

"Now who's being peculiar? You've just laid me twice."

"There was nothing personal in that."

"Oh." She laughed openly, a pleasant sound in the darkness. "I *am* going to miss you."

"Would you like to continue spying for me after you're established in Washington?"

"No. I don't think so. I've thought about it, but I decided against it. It's one thing to meet you in a beer garden or to bounce around on a mattress, but it's altogether another thing to operate radios or send letters in invisible ink. Our arrangement here has been fun. Spying in Washington could become work—a real bore."

Stachel held up an arm, and the radium dial of his watch glowed. "I'd better be going" he said. "Busy morning ahead."

"Why not leave from here?"

"I need fresh underwear."

"Oh."

As he dressed, he asked, "What are the Americans saying about Hitler these days?"

"They're wondering why he doesn't play his trump card. He obviously wants to be chancellor so bad he can taste it, but the Old Gentleman, Paul Super-Kraut von Hindenburg, won't hear of it. So why, all the memos fluster, doesn't Hitler play his ace of trumps?"

She sensed his gathering curiosity.

"Trump?" he said, somewhat too casually. "What in hell are you talking about, Miss Loomis?"

"Some intelligence chief you are."

"Stop being coy. What are you talking about?"

"Well, the way I get it Avery Hines, the first assistant political affairs analyst, has picked up a heavy rumor that President von Hindenburg has been profiting at public expense. His hand in the cash box, so to speak."

Stachel snorted. "Really, Miss Loomis. You don't mean that the embassy people would give credence to anything that ridiculous. Von Hindenburg personifies Germany. He's the one constant—the rock—to which the German people have secured themselves in all this hellish time. The mark might inflate out of sight, and the army might dwindle into campfire clubs, and the unemployment might reach disastrous levels, but von Hindenburg never changes. To accuse him of petty thievery is as if you were to accuse, well, Abraham Lincoln of owning a slave ship."

"Even so," she said, "Hines says his source is unimpeachable."

"Just what is von Hindenburg said to have done?"

"Oh, I don't know all the ins and outs, naturally. I've just typed some highly classified internal memos, and I've heard some discussions. But the gist of the thing seems to be the Eastern Aid Fund—that subsidy established five, six years ago to help the big land-owning Junkers of the eastern provinces hold on to their estates. The word has it that President von Hindenburg has secretly made a profit of more than six hundred thousand marks on this cute little piece of legislation. Not only that, but he's turned over his estate to his son, Oskar, without paying a Pfennig in death duties or conveyance fees."

"I don't believe that."

"Why? When you come right down to it, I mean. After all, it's a rare politician who can pass up an easy kill."

"But von Hindenburg isn't a politician. He's the Old Gentleman. The German father image. One step down from God."

"Take it from me, Bruno, dear—von Hindenburg puts on his pants one leg at a time. If there's anything I've learned in my disreputable life it's the fact that with little men there are little greeds, with big men there are big greeds. Von Hindenburg is a big man all right, but he's a man. An ambitious, proud, arrogant Junker général. So if somebody says he's sneaking a bit here and there, don't ask me to be surprised."

He fell silent, and she listened to the storm. After a time, he kissed her cheek and let himself out with no further acknowledgment of the fact that in the following day's dawn she'd be sailing from Bremen, dropping from his life forever.

As she drifted into sleep, it occurred to her that they'd spoken only German the entire evening. Ah, well. Sieg Heil, Polly.

40

Elfi turned off the radio, lost in loneliness. There was nothing these days but jabber. Jabber about politics, the Fuhrer, the delight of the German workers with the economic revolution now unfolding to their glory and advantage. About the Fatherland's intelligentsia, and how they were flocking to the Savior of Greater Germany. About enlightened Communists who were embracing the Nazi movement because "German socialism is directed by Germans; international socialism is an instrument of the Jews." About the Church and its benignity toward the Führer and his unequivocal opposition to the Red nihilists. Jabber, jabber, jabber—all in the idiom of righteousness. *We are good because we are right; they are bad because they are wrong. If they don't agree with us, they must be destroyed. Those who think as we do are good and right. The world must think as we do or die.*

She went into the tiny kitchen and poured a cup of broth, overwhelmed with the understanding of how sad it is to be always right. She stood, sipping, and listened to the silence. Outside, evening was assembling, and at the top of the window, where the twilight was deepest, there were the first summer stars, high and brittle and remote. They, too, were always right aways exact, sad and terrible in their immutability.

Like Elfi Heidemann.

How many years had she spent similarly beyond change? A thousand? Since confirmation? Since her school days? Since Otto? How long ago was that? And before she was born: had she, even then, as the shadow of some idea of God's, been unvaryingly and inflexibly right? She thought of her father, of her mother, of her brother, of her school-day love affairs, of Otto, of her great disillusionment and lonely despair and drinking and its abject aftermath and they all ran together —a wild confluence of memories, flung like paint onto the canvas of Elfi Heidemann's tiresome correctness. Her mind had wandered far among these things in recent days.

Strange, how an encounter—a random, tangential brushing of personalities—could slam one against the wall of self. A Ziegel drifts through your day and says some words, and the careful construction of self-protective rectitude wobbles and teeters and begins to collapse, and you see the self you are. And then a Stachel, for no discernible reason other than his liking for you, goes out of his way—dares great personal damage—to help you deal with the gathering disaster.

What do you do, now that this strange, arrogant, self-enamored, know-it-all in the soldier suit lifts you out of your shame, dusts you off, and sets you on the road again?

You stand in your stupid little kitchen, sipping broth and looking at the dying afternoon, watching your mind roam through the debris of a wasted lifetime, that's what you do.

The doorbell rang, and it startled her.

She untied her apron and hung it carefully on its hook

beside the pantry door, then went to the foyer, smoothing her skirt and patting her hair. It was Klaus.

"So downcast you look," he said smiling.

"Come in, come in. Would you like a cup of broth?"

"No thanks. It's too close to supper. Are you all right?"

"I suppose." She waved him to the chair. "What's up?"

"Well," he said amiably, "I wanted to see how you like your new flat, for one thing. To give you a little report, for another."

"The flat is habitable. That's about all I can say for it. Except of course, that it's a lot better than trying to endure Frau Lockermann's prying eyes. And, as for your little report, my dear Klaus, I'm not sure I want to hear it."

"Why? It's about your friend Ziegel."

"He's not my friend. I mean, he's just someone who—"

Klaus laughed. "You'll have to admit that you went to considerable trouble to get him out of a jam."

"Because I got him into it, that's why."

"Well, for your information, my dear, the word is that he's recovered nicely and is earning his keep in the garage at Schloss Löwensheim. We are supporting him until we can find a way to get him out of Germany."

"By 'we' I suppose you mean the church people."

"Who else?"

"You are going to get in trouble—all of you."

"Somebody has to do it."

"The Nazis are virtually in power now. They control almost everything."

"That's precisely why they must be resisted."

"You'll get yourselves killed. Or worse. I'm sure Pastor Lentz has warned you all about this."

"Pastor Lentz is one of our keenest workers."

"I wish you hadn't told me that."

"You can't stay on the fence forever, my dear Elfi. You must choose to resist the madmen. You must choose the gospel over their madness. Not to reject them is to be one of them."

She sighed, making a helpless gesture. "It's all so confusing."

"What's so confusing? The Nazis are determined to make the Protestant Church an instrument of their propaganda and political action. As German Protestants, we have a tradition of co-operation between church and state, but Hitler's stooge, the Reichsbischof Mueller, has gained control of the church illegally and has abandoned the scriptures and the reformational confessional in favor of Nazi racial doctrines. We are now two churches—Hitler's and Christ's. For you as a Christian, there is no choice but tireless resistance to those who refute the holy word."

She went to the kitchen and rinsed her cup in the tiny sink. Her anxiety and doubt were heavy, remembering as she did her weakness and panic and the single-minded concern for self-preservation she'd felt the night Ziegel had appeared at her door. "I'm sorry, Klaus," she said, "but I've learned that I'm not up to confronting lions in the Colosseum. I'm a sniveling coward who failed her first test. You and the others would do well to keep me out of your movement. I can be nothing but a threat to your safety."

Klaus stood up, turning his hat in his hand. "Well," he said, smiling faintly, "you've already committed yourself. By helping Ziegel, you became one of us, like it or not."

She felt a stir of annoyance, resenting this arbitrary judgment. "So then, I take it, our pure Aryan Nazi first-class, Major Bruno Stachel, is also one of you. He flew Ziegel to Bavaria, so that makes the Nazi Stachel into the anti-Nazi Stachel."

"Perhaps not. But there's one thing you can count on—Stachel is most unlikely to make table conversation of the fact that he aided a Jew. He will remain a docile, neutral fellow in this matter, I assure you."

"I can't imagine Bruno Stachel being docile in any matter."

Klaus stubbed out his barely smoked cigarette in an ashtray, and then went to the door. "Well, my dear, I'm off. I'm glad you're resettled. And I'll keep you informed on Ziegel's situation."

"Don't you understand, Klaus? I don't want to be kept informed on Ziegel's situation. Or anything else you dear, brave, stupid people are doing. I'm a nurse. I'm not a religious philosopher—a Christian zealot. I don't even go to church regularly. So leave me alone. Leave me to my nursing."

"Souls need nursing, too, Elfi."

"Let the Jews take care of Ziegel," she snapped, her anger swelling.

"How, Elfi? *How?* Every Jew in Germany is a potential Ziegel. They all need help. Our help."

"Why should I get killed helping Jews?"

"Christ was a Jew. He got killed to help you."

"Oh, leave me alone, Klaus. Please. Leave me alone."

He put on his hat and, after opening the door, took her hand and patted it gently. "All right, Elfi, dear. But remember —you've already done the hard part. Ziegel is alive because of you. You are committed."

She said nothing, and he left, his footsteps strangely loud in the drab hallway.

Night came, and she sat by an open window, watching the street and seeing none of it in her preoccupation with the world and its unreasonable ways. Somewhere in the silence she tried to think of God, and it was very difficult, because she couldn't envision a God of love, as Pastor Lentz called him, in a universe so thoroughly steeped in hate. She had always, she knew, had a limited concept of God—an image formed by, restricted by, her own human experience. If God loved the way she loved, no wonder the world was a stinking bog, eh?

She thought suddenly of Stachel, and of the lofty, smug, and preciously correct little sermon with which she'd dismissed him when he'd come calling all those months ago. How supercilious she must have sounded. How resentful he must have felt. And now, with his special knowledge of her cowardice and lack of faith, how contemptuous must be his private view of her.

She owed Bruno Stachel an enormous debt of apology. He had shown more godliness in the depths of his godlessness than she had been able to muster from her lifetime of catechism. She was a hypocrite.

She put on her cardigan and went to the telephone kiosk on the corner and called Klaus.

"Hello?"

"Elfi here."

"Oh. Well, now. What can I do for you, my dear?"

"The question is, what can I do for you?"

"I don't—"

"I'm with you, Klaus. If I can help in any way, let me know."

"Good."

"I'm a rotten Christian."

"So am I."

"I don't want to be."

"Neither do I."

"I don't know the first thing about God."

"Yes, you do, Elfi. You've proved it. Amply."

"I don't understand—"

" 'For I was hungry, and you gave me to eat; I was thirsty, and you gave me to drink; I was a stranger, and you took me into your homes; I was naked, and you covered me; I was sick, and you visited me; I was in prison, and you came to see me . . . I tell you the plain truth, inasmuch as you did this to one of these least brethren of mine, you did it to me.' "

"Oh."

"We've a desperately big job ahead, Elfi."

"All right. Count me in."

41

There were tens of thousands of them. They had been marching since nightfall, waving torches and singing. The crashing of boots in military cadence, faces exalted in the demonic light. The thundering of drums, the metallic anger of cymbals and brass, the blood-red banners with their spider-like cross.

From the Tiergarten, through the great ugly gate, then south on the Wilhelmstrasse, past the frowning, monumental buildings of state and warfare and law to the bitter January heart of the enormous city.

Rank upon rank. The Sturm Abteilung, all brown and hoarse and ecstatic; the Schütz Staffel, dark and arrogant and triumphant. The hangers-on: ruby-faced and drunk and weeping.

Heil. Sieg Heil. Heil Hitler. Für unser Führer, ein dreifaches Sieg heil: heil, heil, heil. Die Fahne hoch, in Reihen fest geschlossen.

Nothing will stand in our way. Heute gehört uns Deutschland, morgen die ganze Welt.

Heil Hitler.

There are no limits on our capabilities and potential. We shall prevail everywhere, always.

Deutschland, Deutschland über alles.

At the Kaiserhof, Hitler, his eyes brimming, took the hands of his friends, who had waited at the hotel through the long day and evening.

"We've done it," he said huskily. "The Thousand-Year Reich has begun."

42

The Gasthof had been painted recently, he saw. The shutters were a crisp black, and the sign on the facade had been freshened with an authoritative crimson. Already the window boxes were overflowing with geraniums, sparkling and new-looking after the rain just past.

He instructed the driver to wait in the Bierstube, feeling suddenly self-conscious under the village's scrutiny. He'd lived in Bad Schwalbe long enough to know that no arrival went unnoticed, especially that of a spit-and-polish colonel on a Sunday afternoon, and although the square was now deserted he knew that many eyes were watching from the shadows behind the casements all around.

"Hello, Emma."

The round woman behind the reception desk turned, her bright blue eyes widening with surprise. "So. The prodigal son."

"It's been a long time."

She was torn, he could see, between her natural ebullience and the need to maintain the composure of a proper innkeeper's aide. Nature won out, and she came around the corner to take his hands and beam up at him. "Bruno. You're beautiful. Your uniform is gorgeous."

"You look fine, too."

"We've been reading about you in the newspapers." Her manner made it clear that she was, despite an emotional need to do so, unable to approve of this. Emma, who had been hired as a chambermaid when he was in knee britches, knew just about all there was to know about him. But the reverse was true, too, and of all the things he knew about her, from her illegitimate daughter in Idstein to the brandy she kept in her wardrobe, the most useful to him was her transparency. Since there wasn't an ounce of originality in her, the opinions of the elder Stachels were hers, and so he could read now on the dial of her broad Hessian face that his notoriety had not set well with his parents.

"Your father has gone to the city. He won't be back until evening."

"Where's Mama?"

"Resting. Her eyes haven't been too good these days, you know. It tires her out, not being able to see good."

She was in her sewing corner in the oriel that overlooked the distant meadows and blue, misty hills. Silvery sunlight came through the medieval panes to cast a checkered pattern on the sheet she'd been mending, and she sat back in her chair, eyes closed against the weariness of years. At the sound of him in the doorway, she turned her head, peering.

"Bruno?"

"Yes, Mama. I came to visit you."

She held out her arms and he crossed the polished plank floor to lean over her and kiss her brow lightly. "I'm so glad to see you," she murmured, a choking in her voice.

"Emma says your eyes have been bothering you."

"Quatsch! Emma always talks too much and says too little. I'm fine. Fine."

He pulled up a stool and sat beside her chair, holding her thin hands and returning her smile for a long, wordless moment. Her age was wearing heavily on her now, he saw, and he felt a wave of something akin to sorrow—a mourning of years wasted and words unsaid and tendernesses withheld.

"You're looking splendid, son."

"I'm glad, Mama."

"There was a time when I worried terribly over you—your health."

"I know."

"All the drinking—"

"I know, Mama. It's finished now."

"You were so young. So—intense. I guess that's the word. And now you look splendid. Calm."

He cleared his throat. "How is Papa?"

An indirection came into her smoky gray eyes, and he

knew it for the anxiety it was. "He's all right," she said softly. "He still works very hard to hold things together."

"He won't accept anything from me. I've sent him money. But he always returns it."

"Your father is a very prideful man."

"He's also stupid to turn down help," he said, smiling.

She sighed, a small sound in the quiet afternoon. "There is nothing stupid about your father, Bruno. He's simply prideful. As you've always been."

"I've never turned down help from my own flesh and blood."

"It's the Nazi thing, Bruno. He's so terribly against them, you know. And when all the newspapers showed that picture of that preposterous fellow Göring congratulating you on your promotion to Oberstleutnant—well, he was very disappointed."

Stachel felt another smile forming. "Mama, Mama—you always were the diplomat. Disappointed? What a quaint understatement for what must surely have been Papa's roaring outrage."

"He was very upset."

"Most fathers would be very much the opposite if their sons had been snapped with someone so famous and important."

"Your father is not like anyone else. You know that. He suspects virtually all politicians. But he hates the Nazis. He says they will destroy the Fatherland. And he's, well, mortified over your having joined them."

Stachel gazed out at the hills, the feeling of sorrow and loss heavy in him. The rain had passed on to pile enormous blue and white clouds over the eastern horizon, and even here, in this tranquil corner redolent of soap and spices and clean linen, he could smell the moisture and the deep-green freshness of the forests and grassy slopes where he'd spent that splinter of time called boyhood.

"I'm sorry Papa dislikes me so."

"He loves you, son. It's because he loves you that he's so—upset. So disappointed."

"What's love, Mama? I don't really understand that word."

She sat silently for a time, watching with him the restless, far-off clouds. Then she sighed again and said, "There are as many definitions of love as there are people, I suppose. But to me, it's a giving—a selfless concern for the well-being of someone other than the self. I suppose you don't know what the word means because you've never learned truly to give of yourself."

"You've always said that I'm a generous fellow, Mama—"

She made a tiny motion with her hand. "I don't mean that kind of giving, Bruno, dear. Of course you're generous. The very fact that you've tried to send us money from your soldier's pay is certainly testimony to that. I'm speaking of a different kind of giving—the understanding that living our lives purely for ourselves is unfulfilling, empty, meaningless, and that living our lives to bring about the happiness and fulfillment of someone else is the route to our own happiness and fulfillment. It's the single area of human existence in which the more we give away the more we get back. To love is to gain by losing."

He thought about that, searching for a practical translation of the abstract language. "It sounds very difficult," he said.

"Of course it is. But yet it isn't. To love, one must first be loved. Your father and I love you. And beyond that, God loves you. So you've had the experience of being loved. Now it's up to you to pass it along, give a similar experience to someone else—at least one other person—if you are to complete the circuit and let love's electricity light up your own world."

"Well, if Papa loves me as you say, then why does he begrudge me my success?"

"Success? Where is the success in hate? The Nazis personify hatred, greed—the very opposite of love. Your father and I want you to be truly happy. We know that you'll never find happiness in a fellowship built on the despair of others."

They fell silent again. Somewhere in the interval she said, "You must be hungry. Let's go to the kitchen and I'll give you some cold pork. There's potato salad, too—"

"I've had lunch, Mama. I ate at the airfield in Wiesbaden."

"Some hot chocolate then. I could use some myself." She arose from her chair, old and uncertain, pausing to give him a loving examination. "Your Blue Max—you're not wearing it."

"I wear it only at ceremonies now. I've been uncomfortable with it lately. I suppose it reminds me of times I'd rather forget."

Her gaze turned away. "I don't understand such things. All I know is that the Blue Max once meant something very special. And now it doesn't. Germany once meant something very special. And now it doesn't."

"It's on its way to unprecedented greatness."

She shook her head slowly. "No, Bruno. It's not."

"Mama, do me a favor. Be careful where you say things like that, eh?"

"Why? Is your Führer afraid of criticism?"

"You know how things are today."

"Your father and I are not ones to keep silent in the face of unfairness, stupidity, or crime. And your Führer is an unfair, stupid criminal."

"My God, Mama. I don't mind you saying it to me. In the privacy of your own home. But, for God's sake—"

"Come on, let's go get that chocolate."

They spent the remainder of the afternoon nibbling cheese, sipping chocolate, and discussing relatives, friends, food prices, weather, music, cinema—an infinitude of trivia. They carefully avoided politics. And he felt alone, as usual.

TELEPHONE TRANSCRIPT

"Laub speaking."

"This is regarding your inquiry as to restaurant supplies of sauerkraut."

"Oh. Yes. You are Herr Hugelmeier, of the delicatessen?"

"I'm calling for him."

"Ten-ten-ten."

"Which study are you calling about?"

"The Stachel study. There's a change in management. Sauerkraut is changing to Schnitzel. Same procedures. But deal with Schnitzel."

"Very well."

"This is all for this study. Schnitzel. Forty-one."

"Ten-ten-ten."

43

The first eighteen months of the Thousand-Year Reich had been given primarily to the process of organization, which meant a seemingly interminable series of seemingly interminable meetings for those who labored in the vineyards of professional government. The worst offender was Göring. As Reichs Air Commissioner, as Minister of the Interior for Prussia, as Minister without Portfolio, and as an idolizer of the Führer, Göring would have appeared to most observers to have plenty to keep him occupied. But Stachel, now serving as the Intelligence Section's liaison to Göring's staff, knew the truth: Göring was becoming an indolent, self-indulgent clod who, having delegated virtually all chores to subordinates, called meetings to salve his own boredom and harass the bureaucracy. Worse still, Göring relished increasingly romantic recollections of his miraculous rescue from the policeman's club all those years ago, and so he had smothered Stachel under all kinds of favoritism—the most arduous of which was the standing requirement that he attend any meeting involving Göring himself. Since he had no duties there, nor any contributions to make, Stachel developed the very real suspicion that Fat Hermann was using him as a kind of good-luck charm, like a rabbit's foot or a lady's garter.

Today's session was especially irritating. He'd planned to go flying in the new Heinkel 51, a biplane that had been ordered in quantity to serve as the new fighter-of-the-line. But the phone had rung just as he was leaving his desk and the prospect of a pleasant hour or two aloft had dissolved into four hours of tedium.

Milch, as chief of Air Production, had opened the meeting with a long explanation, full of false modesty, as to how he had, since the beginning of 1933 until now, doubled the number of aircraft-construction plants and increased the ranks of skilled aviation workers from 4,000 to more than 20,000. The aim was to produce more than 4,000 in twenty-one months, he said. "What kind of aircraft?" Göring knew, but he'd asked anyhow, since Göring was said to dislike Milch intensely and enjoyed humiliating him.

"Well, sir," Milch said in his pedantic way, "they won't all be combat machines of course. Some forty percent will be training planes, and"—he consulted some notes—"there will be eight hundred and twenty-two bombers and two hundred and forty-five fighters. The rest will be reconnaissance aircraft."

"That's a hell of a lot of bombers," Göring said blandly.

"Well, sir, about half of them will be JU-Fifty-two transports, actually. They'll be fitted out with two defensive machine guns and three thousand three hundred pounds of bombs."

Göring sneered. "JU-Fifty-two's? God's blood, man—they'd never make it to any target. They don't move much faster than an ox cart."

Obviously groping for a way to deal with this sarcasm, Milch was saved by a comment from von Kolberg, a major general from the Air Force General Staff. "The Fifty-two's are only a stop-gap measure, Herr Commissioner. They will be replaced as soon as the new Dorniers and Heinkels come on the line."

"All right," Göring sighed. "I've heard enough of these statistics. Sit down, Milch, and we'll get on to the substance of this meeting, which is organization of air intelligence. Are you going to give it to us, Kolberg? Or who?"

"Yes, sir," Kolberg said, standing to take position beside a chalk board placed on the sunny side of the room. "The air chief of staff has asked me to thank you for this opportunity to explain air intelligence and to offer his regrets that illness has kept him from attending—"

"Oh, shit on that, Kolberg," Göring snapped. "Get on with it, will you?"

Von Kolberg's esthete's face reddened, and he made a thing of checking his notes. The others at the table pretended interest in the ceiling, or their nails, or the ends of their pencils.

"The plan," Kolberg said, drawing some rectangles on the board, "is to refine the intelligence-gathering function of the air service, so as to co-ordinate it better with those functions of the army and navy. With—"

"And the Gestapo," Göring broke in. "The best intelligence service going is my Gestapo."

"Well, ah, yes, sir. Of course."

"Himmler may be interior minister and head of the Security Service, but the Gestapo is my creation. I've taken the old Prussian political police and made it into something really worthwhile. Don't you forget that."

"To be sure, sir."

"Well, don't stand there like a cow plop. Say what you have to say, for Christ's sake."

"Yes, sir," von Kolberg said, thoroughly miserable now. Stachel, watching from his chair in the corner near the door, could only pity the poor fellow.

"The long-term plan, as authorized by the Führer," Kolberg managed, "is to establish the air service as a separate branch of the Wehrmacht. The high commands of the branches will be known as Oberkommando des Heeres, or OKH, for the army; Oberkommando der Kriegsmarine, or OKM, for the navy; and Oberkommando der Luftwaffe, or OKL, for the air service. Reichsminister Göring will, of course, be OKL, in addition to his responsibility for civil aviation and—"

"For all aviation, Kolberg. Anything that flies in Germany is mine. Don't anybody forget that."

"Yes, sir."

There was another awkward pause, and then Kolberg gathered himself for a long dissertation on long- and short-range air reconnaissance, photo groups, air fleets and air divisions, technical intelligence, and foreign air-force evaluations. Miraculously, Göring chose not to interrupt again, and there was discernible relief among those in the room.

"This is all pretty far down the line," Stachel heard Kolberg say at last, and from the man's tone it was clear that he'd reached the end of his commentary. Stachel yearned to stretch and yawn, but only Göring, OKL-to-be, felt free to do that.

"All right," Göring said, rubbing his eyes, "let's end this before my ass turns to stone. Any questions?"

There were none, naturally, since no one at the table was so naïve or stupid as to admit to anything less than a thorough grasp of all things in heaven and earth and between.

"You're all dismissed. Except you, Stachel. I want to talk to you."

There was a scraping of chairs and much rattling of papers as the others left the room. Stachel stood, waiting quietly with briefcase in hand, until Göring looked up from some notes.

"So then, old comrade, you heard all that Quatsch?"

"Except the parts where I was sleeping."

"God, that Kolberg drone could put an insomniac owl to sleep. I'd transfer him to Sewer-line Maintenance if the bastard weren't so smart."

"Well, we can't all be great orators like the Führer."

Göring's eyes narrowed. "Are you getting fresh, Stachel?"

"Come on, Captain. Where's your sense of humor?"

"I can tolerate your familiar ways with me. After all, I do owe you my life. But I'll not tolerate even the slightest smart-aleck remark about our Führer."

"You owe me nothing, Captain."

"Bormann is especially peeved these days. I don't mind telling you he doesn't like you much. And I might warn you—he makes a vicious enemy."

"To hell with Bormann."

"God, Stachel, you're impossible, but I trust you."

"Why?"

"I don't know. But I do."

"Then why don't you get me off this silly assignment and transfer me to a squadron? I'm not doing anything around here. I study the Americans. I follow you around like a puppy. I write reports. I sleep in meetings. I'm bored out of my frigging boots. Let me go."

"I want you to stay in intelligence. I want you to be as expert on American aircraft as you can get. I want you to become my personal agent."

"What the hell does that mean?"

"I'm going to promote you to Oberst. And, while you will remain in your present duties, I want you secretly to serve me as my eyes and ears in those corners of the Luftwaffe that might escape my attention."

"You mean you want me to be a spy for the management?"

"Well—"

"Forget it. I'm no Bormann."

"There's great latitude. No requirement to keep regular office hours. Lots of flying. No reports to write."

"What is it about you Nazis—always wanting to spy on people, sniff around, sneak looks?"

Göring belched, covering the sound with little pats of his pudgy hand. "Oh, calm down, Stachel. I'm a flier, too. I'd much rather be upstairs, wringing out a ship, than to be sitting here arguing with a prima donna like you. I need a man I can trust telling me frankly—without embellishment—what's really going on behind the reports I get. You know as well as I do that the German military travels on ten percent brains, thirty percent guts, and sixty percent cow shit. You heard that porky little satrap Milch rattling off all his numbers and quotas and goals—well, I must know how much of that is cow shit."

Stachel said, "I'm no engineer, accountant, factory manager. How would I know cow shit from pink pearls?"

"You let me worry about that. You just look around, get a sense of what's going on, listen to what the people are saying, and give me your own impressions of what's going on in the air service. Or anywhere else, for that matter."

Stachel stood quietly for a time, thinking about this, his anger subsiding. Göring had just presented him with what amounted to a free ticket to anywhere. Passage would be guaranteed by the Reichsminister himself. Achtung! Cow shit verboten!

"Well?" Göring said.

"Do I still get my personal airplane?"

"The best. Talk to Ernst Heinkel or Willi Messerschmitt. They'll fix you up."

Stachel hunched a shoulder. "Don't you think you're trusting me a little too much? Hell, I could become a holy terror around the shop. And a lazy conniver to boot."

Göring gave him one of his cat's grins. "If I thought that to be true, Stachel, I'd never give you the job. As Bormann says, you're a pain in the ass, but you're a diligent pain in the ass."

"Even so, pal, I can be as sneaky as any of you."

"That's not quite true, Stachel, old comrade. I'm the sneakiest of all. And I'll be watching you. You can fool everybody else, but you can't fool me. Eh?"

44

It was Saturday, the last day in June, and it wasn't even noon and already the heat was oppressive. The sun, pale and coinlike in the gauzy sky, beat down with unremitting intensity, and out on the steaming lawns insects whirred. The lake was polished steel, unmoving in the breathless day, and the boats sat white and dead atop their reflections, sails furled.

They were in the purple shadow of the awning, thinking private thoughts and staring at the distant view. The Baroness sighed and shifted in her wicker chair.

"Damn, but it's hot," she said to no one in particular.

Rudi, who was nursing a hangover, tried to be nice, even so. "Would you like more iced coffee?"

"No thanks. I'm awash as it is."

"How about you, Bruno? What can old Rudi do for you?"

"He can shut up," Stachel said, closing his eyes against the glare.

"Oo. You're certainly in a mood, I must say. What's the matter? Menstruation?"

"A bad week. Climaxed yesterday afternoon by a four-hour meeting called by my beloved chief, Hermann the Fat."

The Baroness clucked her tongue. "You'd better ease off on talk like that, Bruno, dear. Hermann's new Gestapo has big ears, they tell me."

"I hope they aren't as big as Hermann's ass," Rudi said, chuckling. "God, what a tub of lard he's turning into, eh?"

"He's not my favorite person," Stachel said, "fat or skinny."

"Did he say anything about the SA in your meeting?" Rudi's question was idle in tone—too idle, and therefore showing that he was especially interested in an answer. Stachel, in a flare of intuition, thought he knew why.

"No he didn't, as a matter of fact. The whole thing was devoted to a talk by a pedantic fellow named von Kolberg, from the air force chief of staff's office. Göring was playing soldier, and we all had to humor him."

Rudi took a magazine from the wrought-iron table and began to leaf through it, trying to appear nonchalant. "There's an atmosphere around Berlin these days," he said testily. "Something's going on here, and damned if I can get a line on it. For every rumor there are three others. But one thing's certain—Göring figures in it somewhere."

"Sure. Göring figures in everything these days."

"It really is absurd, you know," the Baroness put in languidly. "Hermann's actually a rather inferior fellow, and I'll never understand how he managed to be promoted from captain to general in a single leap. It's simply unbelievable."

"Not," Rudi said, "when you realize that he's been buying dear, dying Paul von Hindenburg, who, as president, has the power to promote him."

"I just don't believe that von Hindenburg has been corrupt," Stachel said.

"Nor do I," said the Baroness in a surge of supportive patriotism. "Paul is a decent man, above petty graft."

"Petty?" Rudi snorted. "Göring personally gave Hindenburg—or, his son, that is—Langenau, the big estate owned by the government and its state forest of Reussenwald as a so-called gift of national gratitude for services rendered in the World War, and manure like that. Four days later, Göring is promoted to general. You call that coincidence? You call that petty? I'm no political philosopher, no intellectual like dear Bruno there, but even I see through that."

"Watch who you're calling an intellectual. That's a rotten thing to say about anybody, let alone about the man who drinks your iced coffee of a Saturday morning."

"You're an intellectual, you dumb ass. All you do is sit around and stare at people and think things about them. And I resent your thinking things about me."

"I don't think anything about you at all. Unless it's how silly you look in that swimming suit."

The Baroness protested, "I think Rudi looks darling in his swimming suit. He has darling legs. Come now, Bruno, admit it."

"That's right, Bruno, you bastard. Admit it."

"I think you have darling legs. You are absolutely the most darling-legged fellow I've ever known."

"They've got hair on them, though." Rudi made a face.

"Well, it's blond hair. Which is reassuring in these days of Aryan ascendancy."

"Do you think if I show them to Ernst Röhm I might get promoted from SA trooper to field marshal?"

They all laughed together then.

"Speaking of which," the Baroness said, "there's all kinds of talk about Röhm. The Führer is said to be displeased by some of the statements he's made recently."

Stachel yawned. "What do you expect? Röhm and his SA—with the special exception of our darling-legged Rudi—are riffraff. They were very helpful to Hitler in the beginning, in the street-brawl days, but now that he's in power the bully-boy stuff is suddenly more a liability than an asset. You've seen it yourself, Lotte. You saw that oaf Lutze, no more than two meters from this very spot, taking out his glass eye and talking like a farmhand in front of the upper crust. Well, you multiply that by all the members of the SA, by the glass-eye equivalents they've been springing on all of Germany's decent folk in these past few months, and you can see why Hitler's started to chew his mustache. Hitler needs class now—especially with Röhm and his people splashing the country with the uncouth stuff. And when Röhm starts shooting off his mouth, criticizing Hitler for abandoning the old ways of revolution, Hitler's got a leadership problem. He's not displeased. He's purple-faced furious."

"How do you know?" Rudi challenged. "Have you seen him lately?"

"No. But I've seen him enough to know that he doesn't like problems. He doesn't like blabbermouth fairies criticizing him in public speeches."

The Baroness, as usual, sought to change the subject. "How was your visit with your parents, Bruno? You said very little about it when you came back."

How, indeed, had his visit been? He'd asked himself the question in various ways and at various times, and the answer still eluded him. Only one aspect of the interlude was clear, and that itself was diffused by even larger, more unanswerable questions. He'd left Bad Schwalbe with the understanding, grounded in his mother's monologue, that all the failures of his past and all the restlessness and frustration of the present were rooted in his inability to think beyond his inner pain. His problem was like a blister on a heel: the spiritual and emotional abrasions in his life made it impossible for him to think or feel beyond the hurt itself. His mother had made a theologian's plea for the art of loving; yet how could one so preoccupied with the blister on his soul find the much-touted rewards of loving—of focusing his mind on the fulfillment and happiness of others? It might perhaps be possible to concentrate on the needs of others when the mind was unblurred by pain; but with the kinds of agonies he'd suffered—loneliness, anxiety, inadequacy, inferiority, frustration—it had been possible to search only for anesthesia. Physical action, alcohol, ruthless competitiveness, wenching: these were things of the single-minded self and left no room for his mother's kind of love. Yet he knew with a dreadful certainty that his mother's case was unimpeachable. If ever he was to find relief on this earth, if ever he was to experience the ultimate anesthesia, it would not be in external agents but in the abstraction of what his mother called love.

"I didn't see my father," he said. "He was away on business. My mother's all right. Her eyes bother her, but she manages."

"That's good. I'd like to meet them sometime."

"No you wouldn't, chum. They're old and unbending. They wouldn't be able to handle you, and so you'd think them strange and stuffy."

"When they really aren't, eh?"

"Something like that."

"Fah," Rudi said over his magazine. "You and your parents are snobs. You think your poverty makes you superior to us rotten little rich clods."

The Baroness was about to speak when Leopold, the friar-bald butler, materialized in the shadows and cleared his throat, "Excuse me, madam, but there are two gentlemen calling."

"They want to see me?"

"No, madam. They—"

His words were interrupted by the appearance of two men in dark suits who came under the awning with the easy movements of cats on a fence.

One of them, a short fellow wearing a celluloid collar and a sweaty upper lip, regarded Rudi amiably and said, "Are you SA Trooper Rudolph von Reimer?"

Rudi, puzzled, asked, "What can I do for you?"

Glancing at the Baroness, the man said, "Lutze sends his regards." Then he and his friend produced Mauser automatics and fired three shots each through Rudi's magazine.

The Baroness screamed, and the shorter man barked, "Don't move, any of you. This is state business."

Transfixed, Stachel watched as the two turned and strode off toward the east gate.

Rudi folded the magazine slowly, and Stachel could see great smears of blood across his midsection.

The Baroness was on her knees beside Rudi's chair, holding him to her in a terrible silence.

"They hurt me, Mutti," Rudi said faintly. "Kiss it, and make it go away."

"Yes, darling."

Rudi died there, in the summer shadows.

45

Senator John M. Duncan had the clear impression that his life was out of control. The idea formed as he was seated at his desk in the Senate Office Building, signing mail by the light of the fading afternoon. He had put his name to a letter assuring a jobless Olsonville carpenter that he would indeed give the most careful consideration to John L. Lewis's labor-law proposals and was about to initial a statement—drafted by Alex Logan, his administrative assistant—urging President Roosevelt to go easy on his usurpation of congressional prerogatives. In that tiny interval, his mind went blank, returning to a semblance of function a full two minutes later, when he found himself at the window, staring at the gathering twilight and feeling vaguely nauseated.

The interoffice phone purred, and he crossed to pick it up. "Yes?"

"The German Embassy is calling," Miss Malone announced.

"The German *Embassy?* What the hell do they want?"

"They didn't say, Senator." Miss Malone's voice sounded strained.

He lifted the outside phone. "Hello?"

He heard a click and then a cool, amiable man's voice come on. "Ah, Senator Duncan. General Friedrich von Boetticher here. Military and air attaché. I have the ambassador's permission to call you direct on a matter that may please you."

"Hi, General. Always glad to get word on something that'll please me. Ha-ha. What's on your mind?"

"As you may know, your government has authorized certain of our people to visit and confer with various members of American industry, and so on. Educational, purely educational."

"Yes," Duncan lied heartily. "I've heard a lot about it. Good idea, too. Can never do too much educating between countries, eh?"

"One of the gentlemen scheduled to visit with the Curtiss Aircraft people in Buffalo is an old friend of yours. Oberst Bruno Stachel."

"Stachel? No kidding. He's coming here? When?"

"He will arrive in New York next Tuesday, then entrain for Washington and conferences with the ambassador. He is expected in Buffalo the following Monday."

"Well, I'll be damned. Good old Stachel—"

"Oberst Stachel has asked me to ask you if you would be available, merely on a social basis, at any time during his stay here in Washington. He says you have enjoyed many hours together during your tour as attaché in Berlin."

"You bet your life, General. Stachel is an old pal of mine.

And you tell him I'd be very put out indeed if he'd come here without looking me up. Have him call whenever he arrives and I'll set aside everything else. You tell him that, hear?"

"Very good, sir. It is most kind of you. And the ambassador appreciates your permitting us to approach you on this matter in an informal manner."

Duncan hung up, returned to the window, and said aloud, "Shit-oh-dear. This is all I need." Struggling against the nausea, he buzzed Alex Logan and told him to come in.

Logan's eyes were close together, a fact that always disturbed the Senator because it made Logan look shifty. Logan was no more shifty than anybody else in this lousy town, but it would be necessary some day soon to fire Logan and replace him with somebody who presented a cross between Lewis Stone and James Cagney. It was a shame, too. Logan was smart and loyal and hard-working. But he just plain-old looked wrong.

"What's between Tuesday and the following Monday, Alex?"

Logan took out his little black book, pursed his lips, and regarded the future recorded there. "Tuesday and Wednesday, there're subcommittee hearings on the agricultural subsidy bill; Tuesday's a hearing on water power; Wednesday and Thursday, there's markup on the tax-reform bill; Friday's a tentative vote on the National Labor Relations Board being pushed by Senator Wagner. Then on Monday you have a speech at the Legion dinner in Wilmington. I also have alerts on visits by the Eastern Star ladies, Albert Trogman of the Grange, the Klineburg High School band members and their principal; lunches with Alessandro and Murphy of the national committee, Mrs. Cathcart of the DAR, the ministers from the Methodist conference, Allen Maxwell of the banking lobby, and Sam Goodman of the *Randlersville Gazette*, who wants a feature on how senators handle their mail. Tuesday a dinner party at the Willard for the chairman of Apex Industries, in town for the labor hearings. Wednesday, cocktail party, Mrs. Llewellyn at her Georgetown place. Thursday, ribbon-cutting at the new International Relief headquarters, followed by dinner dance. Saturday, picnic and softball at the VFW do in Silver Spring. Sunday, address the men of the Presbyterian conclave in Baltimore."

"Jesus."

"Slow week, eh, Senator?" Logan ventured a smile.

"Cancel that Wilmington thing. I'll make it up to the congressman from Delaware some other way. Reschedule all the lunches but the ministers' and Sam Goodman's. Regrets for the Llewellyn thing and the ribbon-cutting."

"How about the VFW?"

"Are you out of your mind? Fool with the VFW? Shee-it, man."

Logan made notes. "Anything else, Senator?"

"Beat it, Alex. I got to call my wife."

This was the part he didn't like. He sank into the big leather desk chair and stared at the phone, his tired mind seeking a reasonably neutral approach. She answered on the third ring.

"Hi, honey," he said, using his happy-husband inflection. "Having a good day?"

"The day's almost over."

"Well, what you been up to. Anything exciting?"

"If you really believe that bridge with the Ladies of St. Jude is exciting."

"I appreciate your taking that on, sweetie. It was real important that we be represented there. I owe Mrs. McCarthy, and she'd have had a fit if you hadn't shown up."

"What's on your mind?"

"Good news. Something really exciting. Bruno Stachel's coming to town."

There was a silence.

"You there, honey?"

"Yes. I'm here."

"Stachel's a colonel now. He's going to visit the Curtiss airplane people in Buffalo and he's popping by to see us."

"When's he coming?"

"I thought maybe we could take him to dinner Wednesday night. The country club. He can meet some of our people."

"No. Dinner here at the house. We can't talk in that madness at the club."

"Swell. Anything you say."

"Will you be home this evening?"

"No. I got one of those stupid Rotary things. I'll change here at the office. See you around midnight."

She rang off with no further comment, and he sat for a time, listening to the homebound traffic on the street outside.

"What's with the phone call?" Harry said. "You look upset."

"It was my husband."

"My God, is he coming home?"

"Don't be ridiculous. He never comes home."

"I'm not very good at grabbing my pants and dropping out windows bare-assed."

"You could walk out the front door bare-assed, right when my husband was coming up the walk, and he would nod, smile, and say, 'Nice to see you.' Then he'd give you Handshake Number Three-A and shove a cigar in your mouth."

Harry laughed softly and, throwing back the sheets, sat up to light a cigarette. "You really sound like him when you talk like that."

"I thought you didn't know him."

"Not personally. But I've heard him plenty. At committee hearings. On the Floor. And he visited our agency one day last November, gave a little speech. He's a character."

"John's all right. Dull. Predictable. Conscientious. Honest. That's what's tearing him up on that Senate job. He's too honest."

"That's a tough rap for a politician, all right."

"Funny thing is, most politicians are basically honest. The problem is that people put them in impossible positions, press them into conflicting situations where hypocrisy of some form is the only way out. Then, when people see the politician being a hypocrite to please them, they aren't pleased—they get sore and say, 'What do you expect? All politicians are phonies, crooks.' "

"Well, I'm still glad your husband's a senator. It gives me a chance to squeeze in between the Ladies of St. Jude and dinner with the secretary."

"You like me, huh?"

"You're the best." He pinched her knee and winked. Then, giving her a steady gaze, he said, "You still look upset."

"Not upset. Not really. I'm trying to deal with a big surprise. John called to tell me some news and I'm still trying to deal with it."

"I hope it's a happy surprise."

"I do, too."

46

Dinner had not gone well.

John Duncan had become a flushed and garrulous back-slapper, full of himself and unable to sustain anything beyond the most superficial conversation. He'd made a great business of mixing cocktails and chattering about the best recipes for martinis, and he'd pontificated on ocean travel, asking Stachel how the voyage had been and then failing to wait for an answer.

Even through the meal itself, a really quite decent roast of beef and an array of vegetables prepared in the bizarre American fashion, the senator had gone on, rambling and not thoroughly cogent, about the gathering struggle between Roosevelt and the Supreme Court, the turbulent labor scene and the surge of unions, the NRA, the Depression, the rotten influence of Hollywood, the Red threat, the Ku Klux Klan, and someone in the South called Huey Long.

Through it all, his wife—Stachel persisted in thinking of her as Miss Loomis—would attempt to interject questions: How were things in Germany today, what did he think of America at first sight, didn't he feel uncomfortable in the Washington heat with that high-collar uniform, would he have a chance to do some sightseeing. But then Duncan would break in again, off and running with a discourse on tourist traps, the coming boon of air travel, or why the Germans were wasting their time, fooling with Zeppelins. She and Stachel eventually subsided into mere monosyllabic response to the senator's soliloquy. Even so, Stachel noted, she seemed up on current affairs and presented, all in all, the picture of a proper matron living on the rim of evolving history. He decided that she was enormously likable still, and he wondered how it was for her, being the wife of an ingratiating windbag. A crashing bore, probably.

Fortunately the senator had had to excuse himself after coffee, pleading "an absolute commitment" to attend an unforeseen meeting involving an important visitor with the unlikely name of Big-Bob something from Duncan's home state. When he'd gone finally, after another spate of pseudo-hearty assurances that they'd fly together again some day "real soon," Stachel felt genuine relief.

Settled on a divan in what she called "the living room," Stachel looked about him and said, "I like your home. It's very pleasant."

"Thanks. It'll do. It might have been grander, but we have to keep two houses—one here, another back home—and so the money gets sort of tight now and then."

"John seems to be happy with his work. And you? Are you happy?"

"Let's use German. I need the practice. I miss the old days in Berlin."

"How so?"

"They were intense, exciting days. My life now is so—well, routine. Stodgy. I'm a woman who thrives on excitement. Risk."

There was an awkward pause. Then she lit a cigarette, and said idly, "The Baroness—is she well?"

"Not really. She had a rather terrible experience."

She gave him a glance full of curiosity. "What happened?"

"Rudi. He was a member of the Brown Shirts—the SA. He was shot during the so-called Röhm purge. He died in his mother's arms. At her home. On a sunny summer morning."

"Oh, God."

"Yes."

"Why didn't you tell me before this?"

"It didn't seem to be appropriate when your husband was here. I sensed that he wouldn't appreciate talk of such gloomy things."

"Well—" she faltered, and it occurred to him that this was the first time he'd seen her less than serenely sure of herself. The passage of years does indeed work strange wonders, he thought in private irony. "I'd like to know about it," she said.

"It was a question of legitimacy," Stachel said. "When Hitler seized power last year, he was careful not to violate the idea of legality—openly, that is. And all through, he's tried to keep big business, the bankers, industry, on his side, so he's gone very slowly on radical government experiments. But his efforts to tone things down, keep everything legal and inoffensive to the German middle class, have irritated some of the more radical types, especially those old-timers who weren't fit or smart enough for the plums the Nazi takeover was making available. This bunch began to form an opposition, with Röhm and the SA as the nucleus. Röhm began to shoot off his mouth, and it got bad enough to compel Hitler to choose between loyalty to all the old boys who'd been left out in the cold and his need for continuing legitimacy. He chose legitimacy, and so Röhm and his key supporters had to be shut up." He paused.

She sat quietly, absorbing all this. Then she said, "The Baroness's son was a key Röhm supporter?"

"Hardly. He was only a trooper. But he was a von Reimer, and his mother had alienated some Nazi big shots—Göring, Lutze. And when the purge began, Göring and Himmler and Lutze and the others used it as the excuse to settle a lot of personal scores. Rudi—dumb, unthreatening, fun-loving, apolitical Rudi—represented somebody's decision to put the Baroness in her place."

"Jesus-to-Jesus."

"Yes."

"What did the Baroness do?"

"She went to visit Hitler. She called him all kinds of names."

"You saw this?"

"I was with her."

"And Hitler had her shot, too, I suppose," she said sarcastically.

"Hitler is a very unpredictable fellow. He seemed to be as dismayed as anybody. He told the Baroness that Rudi's death was an inexcusable excess and that the two men who had shot him had themselves been executed. He told her he was sorry and that he'd ordered a full-scale military funeral for Rudi."

"What did she do then?"

"She went directly to her castle in Bavaria and has seen no one since."

"Not even you?"

"Especially me."

"Why?"

"I am a Nazi."

"Are you? Really?"

"Everybody who holds a job of any importance has to be a member of the party."

"That's no answer."

"It's the only one I have."

"What kind of dirty son of a bitch are you?"

"I'm a German officer."

"Why don't you leave Germany? Why do you take part in that unbelievable horseshit?"

"Why don't you leave the United States?"

"What the hell does that mean?"

"You've got millions of people unemployed, starving. You've got troops beating up war veterans who march on Washington for a bonus to keep them alive. You've got police beating up workers who strike for a decent wage. You've got people who kill Negroes because they're black. You've got rules against letting Jews in certain hotels and restaurants and suburbs. You've got Chinese and Japanese and Italians and Irishmen—even Germans—rotting in ghettos because they are what they are. Why do you take part in that unbelievable horseshit, Mrs. Senator Duncan?"

"That's different."

"How?"

"Here it isn't government policy, goddamnit."

"Don't be so sanctimonious. Who needs policy when human nature does the job? When you explain why you don't leave the United States, I'll leave Germany. Until then, I'll stay there and try to work within the system, to make the system better."

"Don't you feel *anything* about Rudi? He was your buddy, after all. And his mother was—is—your mistress. I—" She broke off, her face a study in baffled rage.

"There are no words for what I feel."

"Do you want to make love to me?"

"No."

"Why?"

"Because I am a different man from the man you knew. I am a different man from the man I knew."

"Why aren't you wearing your Blue Max on that fancy uniform?"

"For the same reason."

"I'm still attracted to you. You know that, don't you?"

"No you aren't, Mrs. Senator Duncan. You're attracted to excitement, adventure."

"You're the only man who's ever made a dent on me."

"I'm sorry for you."

"Don't pity me, you bastard."

"I didn't say I pity you. I said I'm sorry. That I'm the best you've had, that is."

"I didn't say you were the best. I said you're the only one who ever made an impression on me."

"Whatever." He shrugged. "It's still a bleak thought."

"Get out of here."

"All right."

"No. Don't. Stay. Please. Make love to me."

"No, dear Miss Loomis. It's time for you really to be Mrs. Senator Duncan. The old times are gone."

"Not for me they aren't."

"Good night, Mrs. Senator Duncan."

47

Stachel had taken what the embassy people called "the sleeper" from Washington to Buffalo. He'd always had the airman's fondness for railroad tracks as navigation aids but only distaste for trains, since they were slow, confining, and boring. But the dislike was brought to outrage when he found that U.S. railroads expected their patrons to sleep on rock-hard beds suspended from the ceiling and encapsulated in funereal curtains. So he wasn't in the best of moods when he stepped from the taxi at the airport and entered the Curtiss Aircraft Company field office.

There was quite a delegation waiting, and he could see that the Curtiss people were giving him the visiting-potentate treatment. They were all young—pink-faced, scrubbed, keen, and anxious to impress "the famous German ace," as Anson Whitlow, the superintendent, introduced him. He felt somewhat ostentatious in his uniform, what with all the rolled-up shirt sleeves and loosened neckties he saw around him, but von Boetticher had prescribed military formality in view of the Führer's desire to "show the sword everywhere," and so he stood there, stiff and pompous and looking to be the very kind of brass hat he himself detested.

They all went into the hangar, Whitlow and he leading, the young engineers trailing anxiously, as if the visiting German were a Hun planning to ravage the village virgin.

"There it is," Whitlow said exultingly, waving his arm at the biplane, which was suspended from a chain hoist, its tires just clearing the concrete. "A beauty, eh?"

Stachel nodded politely, unable to show enthusiasm. "It's a handsome machine," he said. "But it looks very much like the F Two-C."

There was a stilted pause as the inevitable embarrassment made its rounds and was absorbed. Then Whitlow said, "We've beefed up the tail area considerably. I don't think there'll be any more trouble."

Stachel's mood hadn't improved, so he prodded the sore. "Udet was very nearly killed last month at Rechlin. He was demonstrating the F Two-C for our authorities and the tail fell off."

"Well, we certainly heard about that, indeed we did, sir. Ernst had arranged to purchase an F Two-C of the export version during his, ah, barnstorming tour of the States last year. And—"

"You mean your export versions are always inferior to your domestic versions?"

"Well, no, of course not. But, ah, the F Two-C Udet was flying was closer to the, ah, prototype than the one you see here. We've made modifications, improvements."

"This represents, then, the best fighter-bomber of the American miliary forces?"

"Well, we certainly like to think so, don't we, boys?" He glanced around at the circle of young technicians and there was a sycophantic bobbing of heads.

"If it is the best, why are you willing to export it?"

There was another awkward interval, in which Whitlow obviously was hard-pressed to find a diplomatic answer. To his credit, he decided on honesty. "The truth is, Colonel Stachel, that the U.S. military forces are on an extremely limited budget. They aren't buying many planes these days, operating under what we call the Coolidge Theory."

He knew the answer, but he feigned curiosity, still getting even with the Americans for his miserable train ride. "Coolidge Theory?"

"President Coolidge, when he was in the White House, figured that, since there was never to be another war, the air service needed only one plane, and each pilot could take his turn flying it. It's not really precisely that bad, of course, but our government has seemed to follow that general philosophy ever since, and so we manufacturers sell our planes where we can. Nobody in Washington cares, apparently, because there's no rule against exporting what in more normal times would be considered national defense secrets."

Stachel nodded gravely. "Well, Mr. Whitlow, your country's loss is the world's gain, I'd say."

Whitlow smiled uncertainly. "Ah. Yes. Well, then—shall we have her rolled out for you, Colonel?"

"I'd like that very much, Mr. Whitlow."

He sat in the cockpit while the earnest young engineers explained everything to him. There were a lot of instruments, something for everything, but he would be flying contact on a clear day and with no true engineering studies to accomplish, so he concentrated on the location of the basics—altimeter, airspeed indicator, tachometer, turn indicator, engine heat, oil pressure, fuel level, compass. The radio and various testing and recording devices he considered, then dismissed. Then the chief engineer patted him on the shoulder and wished him bon voyage, and he taxied downwind to the run-up apron at the far end of the field.

He remained there for a time, listening to the engine's rumbling and running his eye over the dials. Everything was government-hued: olive this, olive that, with little signs and labels that cautioned him to do this and don't do that. He tried to ignore them, too, but he was a compulsive sign reader and didn't make another move until he'd read them all. Finished at last, he gave the safety belt and parachute harness another check, waggled the control surfaces one more time, lowered the goggles over his eyes, then turned the ship into the wind and gave it full throttle.

The machine took off smoothly, fast. When its shadow began to fall away, he retracted the gear and set the trim tabs for a long climb, keeping his eye on the trembling needles on the dash. He became absorbed in the little fussings that went with flying, and when he ventured a glance over the side, the great steaming arcs of Niagara Falls were already below and falling astern. He did not want to fly over Canada, so he turned due east along the shore of Lake Ontario and began to acquaint himself with the airplane's character. He rocked it and yanked it and felt out its stall tendencies. He watched the ailerons, the rudder, the elevators, the wings themselves, as he rolled and turned and climbed and eased into shallow dives. It was a nice machine, all shiny in the sunlight and honest in its dealings, but it wasn't anything to swoon over when compared to the airplanes coming out of the laboratories of Heinkel and that much-maligned young iconoclast, Willi Messerschmitt. The Americans were still in the open-cockpit biplane era, and that made them stupid indeed.

He'd flown no more than twenty minutes when it was clear that the machine offered nothing the Germans hadn't already mastered and left behind as obsolescent. Even so, it was a beautiful day, and any airplane—like any decent horse—needed a decent workout.

At ten thousand feet on the dial, he did two snap rolls, first to the right, then to the left. His mood lifting, he smiled to himself and began to put the machine through its paces. After another five minutes of loops, Immelmann turns, chandelles and barrel rolls, he reset the trim tab and took the Curtiss to eighteen thousand feet. It was cold up there, and the lake was a great, metallic platter off the port wings, shimmering faintly in the distant sunglare.

He checked: High pitch? Rich mixture? Gear tight in its wells? Stabilizer rolled? Rudder tab adjusted? Breathing deeply in the thin air, he went slowly, deliberately, in making certain the machine was ready.

He heard his own voice: "All right. You're supposed to be a dive bomber. Let's see you dive."

Easing back on the throttle, he rolled the ship on its back, then guided it into a vertical plunge, feeling the awful, momentary, elevator-like dropping in his stomach.

The great slab of earth was directly ahead, remote and inscrutable, beyond the flickering propeller blades. In the corner of his eye, he saw the airspeed needle race around its dial, and he was aware of the brutish roaring and howling, so loud it seemed eventually to be soundless. The altimeter wound downward at an insane rate: fifteen, twelve, eleven, ten thousand feet. The airspeed indicator was hard against the stop and no longer moving. The ship trembled at terminal velocity, its rigging wires screaming at peak pitch and holding.

At eight thousand feet, he began his recovery, coaxing back the control stick. A red dimness began to creep over his vision as the stupendous inertia worked against his body, tearing, savage. It was sheer labor to breathe, and there seemed to be a great fist closing about his head. He raised the goggles, hoping to speed the clearing of his sight, when there was a sudden lurch and a terrible, exploding sound, and his head snapped forward against the dash panel. Dully, heavy with pain and a dim, faraway alarm, he sat back in his seat, clawing the goggles over his wind-sealed eyes.

When he could see again, the earth was whirling in sweeping, lopsided circles directly ahead. The upper and right lower wings were gone, and the remaining wing section, badly bent was whipping the wreck in a gigantic, eccentric spin.

He unbuckled the safety belt and somehow stood on his seat pad, and then he was out and away, tumbling, breathless, incapable of thought. There was no time, no space, no dimension, even that of sensation, except for a sliver of awareness that told him his parachute had opened.

After the nothingness, there was a stunning clarity—sudden, beautiful. He was drifting under a tent of billowing white in a sky of brilliant blue, and far off, twisting and moaning in its solitary descent, the shattered airplane glittered in the summer glare.

He watched it plummet into an orchard, dissolving in a fountain of dust and debris. It did not burn.

He came down in a field of corn, and, after collapsing the chute and working free of its harness, he sprawled in the shadows of the stalks and leaves, which whispered dryly in the lazy breeze and told him how good it was to be alive.

"Are you all right, mister?"

He opened an eye and saw a young woman with a stubby nose and a broad-brimmed straw hat peering at him from behind a row of corn.

"Yes. I think so."

"I saw the whole thing."

"Then you must tell me about it. Because I certainly didn't."

"You talk funny."

"I'm a German."

"From Germany?"

"Mm."

"You flew all the way over here?"

"No. I'd explain it to you, but my head hurts too much."

"You need a doctor?"

"Probably."

"Come on. Let me give you a hand. The house isn't far."

The farmhouse was a rambling structure that presided over a sweep of croplands and orchards from a maple-shaded hill. He sat in a rocker on what the girl called "the front porch," sipping lemonade.

"When do you think they'll come?" she said.

"It depends on how the roads are between here and Rawsonville."

"They're pretty good, far as Coley's Corners. Then they're dirt. From the airport where your friends are landing Pop'll make good time, far as Coley's Corners."

"They're not my friends. They are the Curtiss Airplane people. It was their machine. They are probably most displeased."

"Well," the girl said, her brown eyes amused, "you'll have to admit that you were pretty rough with it. Wow. Such goings-on."

"You saw it all?"

"Bet your life I did. I was whitewashing a fence for Pop and I heard your motor, way up. Then I saw you, a little silver dot, and you came down, lickety-split, and roaring like I never heard. Then, blooey, pieces of silver started to string out behind you, and next thing I knew, there was this big crash over in Gilley's apple orchard and you came down in the field no more'n fifty yards from where I was. Do parachutes always make that funny hissing sound?"

"I don't know, Miss Williams. It was my first time."

"Alice. Call me Alice."

"I appreciate your help, Alice. Yours and your father's. It's very kind of him to permit me the use of your telephone, then to meet the Curtiss people. I could have accompanied him."

"No sir-ee. They had to come and look at the wreck anyhow. Best you waited for them here so Doc Davis could look you over."

Stachel gave her a small smile. "You will be married to Dr. Davis?"

"Why do you ask that?" she said, instantly red and disconcerted.

"He was looking more at you than at me. And I was the pale and trembling victim, not you. You are unquestionably in good health."

"Do you always wear that fancy soldier suit under your coveralls?"

"You're changing the subject, Alice," he said.

"Are you one of those Nazis?"

He felt his smile tightening. "What do you know of such things?"

"It's in all the papers. Hitler and the Nazis. What they're doing over there. Killing people. Taking property. Land."

"You mustn't believe everything you read in the periodicals. They tend to feed on their own prejudices. All Germans aren't Nazis., Alice Williams."

"I'm not asking about all Germans. Are you a Nazi?"

"I don't know."

"How can you not know something like that?"

"I'm going to change the subject now." He nodded toward the road, where, on the far horizon, an approaching car sent up a plume of dust. "That will be your father with my angry friends from Curtiss, eh?"

MEMORANDUM

FROM: German Embassy
The Military and Air Attaché
Washington, D.C.

23 August 1943

TO: Attachegruppe
Berlin

SUBJECT: Destruction of U.S. Secret Device

Last September, as you recall, Ernst Udet, on a tour of the U.S., was personally invited by the pioneer American aviator, Glenn L. Curtiss, to fly the new F2-C Hawk, developed by the Curtiss Co. as a dive bomber for the U.S. Navy. Udet was so impressed with the machine he recommended that the Air Ministry purchase a pair for tests at our Rechlin center. With business bad, and with no objections from the U.S. government, Curtiss authorized the sale.

Although one of the aircraft was destroyed last month when Udet demonstrated it for the Luftwaffe General Staff, the Air Ministry believes that the American theory of dive-bombing is a good one and has initiated studies aimed at producing German machines better suited to the technique.

Meanwhile, Oberst Bruno Stachel, presently touring the States, was last week invited by Curtiss officials to test the new, improved version of the F2-C Hawk. This airplane, too, disintegrated when Stachel attempted to dive it, and the Curtiss people were, of course, mortified—apologizing profusely for the structural failure of the machine and seeming to be very solicitous of Stachel.

However, the most significant aspect of the incident has just surfaced: the machine Stachel crashed was (we have discovered via informants in the American military) carrying a secret, experimental device that aims bombs by radio signal. Our informants tell us that the U.S. War Department is outraged, since destruction of the device at this stage has severely delayed the weapon's development. Moreover, U.S. military authorities are said to be privately convinced that Stachel knew about the device and, under orders from the Reichskanzlei, Berlin, deliberately caused the plane to crash. We've questioned Stachel in the matter, but he says he has no knowledge of any such device and feels our informants are making up stories simply to mislead us or convince us they are worth more than we pay them. We cannot agree with this assessment, since our informants are most carefully selected and reliable.

It is my personal view that, if Stachel was indeed following secret orders from the Führer, it was an audacious, inspired idea worthy of the greatest admiration and acclaim. In fact, it is hard to imagine anyone but the Führer being the source of such bold, far-reaching sagacity.

Heil Hitler!

Von Boetticher

Von Boetticher
General

VIA CODED CABLE Berlin
4 Sept. 34

Personal to von Boetticher

Re the radio bomb-aiming device turned up by Stachel: Could we get more information on the —technology, capabilities, state of the product, delivery dates, etc.—if we were to put one of our agents on the job over there?

Patzig
Abwehr

VIA CODED CABLE Washington
5 Sept. 34

Personal to Patzig

Absolutely not. I forbid—and the Führer concurs in this—the establishment of any formal embassy espionage machinery in the United States. The Americans are so open, so guileless, so ready to share everything they know, the placing of spies here is not only unnecessary—it could severely damage my relationships with naïve, ingratiating American sources.

Von Boetticher
Attaché

48

The house had been one of Polly's ideas, and as Senator Duncan drove up the birch-lined driveway he studied it in detached resentment. Fieldstone, with white-painted frame ells, all cozy and cute and expensive in its setting of old shade; a set piece of upper-income Kultur, washed with a breeze carrying the scent of hunt-club whiskey and money. He had never liked this house, since the old place in Alexandria—a comfortable clapboard bungalow on a sensible lot near the stores and a tolerable drive from the Hill when the traffic was right—had been just fine for living and working and, in the old days, loving. But Polly, arguing that his rise in influence and fame demanded certain associations, had persuaded him to buy this ladies' magazine photo prop in Greenwood Hills, the citadel of big old fortunes, parochial minds, and inbreeding. He'd known what Polly apparently did not: even if his power and money were to exceed those of the President himself, they—he and Polly—would always be, to the denizens of Greenwood Hills, John and Polly Duncan, those hicks playing Senator. Still, he'd humored her.

He parked the car in the turn-around and went into the house through the side door. The kitchen was silent, and he remembered that this was Emma's day off, so he continued on through the butler's pantry and dining room to the library, where he opened the bar cabinet and poured himself a scotch. Standing by the big window, he sipped his drink and watched the autumn leaves whirling on the lawn and tried not to feel the loneliness. The house seemed to watch, too; it shifted its weight with a gentle creak and its stomach rumbled when the far-off furnace did something. The house, like the rest of Greenwood Hills, didn't like the Duncans much, protesting their intrusion with dampness in the cellar, falling roof tiles, and outrageous cracks in the master-bedroom ceiling plaster.

As he made for the bar and a refill, he heard a car crunching in the driveway. He pulled aside one of the drapes and saw Doubet descending from a glossy Cadillac.

This was, of course, a rather astonishing development, because Doubet, being typically French, valued his own privacy and was therefore not given to violating the privacy of others. He rarely would make unannounced calls on anyone—even a close friend like U.S. Senator John M. Duncan, known throughout the length and breadth of these great United States and in the hallowed chambers of Congress as that splendid Amurrican, the distinguished gentleman from Clodhopper Valley, who was certainly not one to stand on formality, no-siree.

He went to the front door and flung it open just as the Frenchman was about to press the bell button. "Now this *is* a surprise," he said heartily, turning on a smile of welcome. "How in hell are you, Georges? And what in hell brings the French military attaché to my humble little adobe-abodey, eh?"

Doubet nodded affably and touched the brim of his homburg with the silver head of his walking stick. "Ah, so I've cornered you in your den at last. You are an elusive one, my friend."

"I was going to return your phone call tomorrow, Georges. Honest. Yesterday and today have been pluperfect hell. Here, give me your hat and cane. Want a drink?"

"Thank you, no."

They went into the library and sat in the evening light and traded amiable appraisals. Doubet was beginning to show his age, Duncan saw, but it did well by him: graying temples, lines of character around the eyes, a touch of weight, all coming together to present a sophisticated presence in the Chevalier mode.

"What's on your Gallic mind, Georges? I know you never do anything on whim. Especially dropping in on friends."

Doubet, as was his manner, came readily to the point. "How is your career going? I read the periodicals, of course, and I find your name frequently—doing this, voting that. But, as a friend—how are you really faring?"

Duncan felt his political smile, so habitual it had become reflex, transforming into the frown he carried in his heart. Of all the men he'd known in his life, Doubet was among the few with whom he could share his true feelings, and the little Frenchman's arrival at this bleak interval seemed providential. "The truth is, pal, I'm not a very happy fella."

"I thought as much."

"It's just that there's no escape from it. Everything is politics. Nobody does anything, says anything, without a political motive. Nobody thinks of anything but influence, acquisition, power. Everything is ambition, suspicion, competitiveness. I can't walk down a hall without wondering who sees me and what he thinks of me and even, for God's sake, what he thinks of my being in the hall. I get so preoccupied with second-guessing people's motives, with doing the politically right thing, with protecting my ass, I don't have time to judge the real world outside—to decide what my constituents need and want and deserve. I'm so busy being a senator I can't get the work of a senator done. Does that make sense?"

"Mm."

"I put in twenty hours a day and don't get a thing accomplished. If I worried as much about my own affairs, if I worked as hard on them as I do on just getting my phone calls handled, I'd be a goddamn trillionaire."

Doubet shrugged. "As your idiom puts it, my dear Duncan—you asked for it."

"Sure. And I'll keep working at it. I'll keep doing my damnedest, as long as I have breath."

"Why?"

"Power, that's why. I enjoy being powerful."

"So then why are you unhappy? Power has a price most pay gladly."

"Because even generals get a rest. Senators don't. I can't even sit on the pot without some yuk peering over the top of the booth and asking can I get his brother-in-law a job at the post office."

Doubet cleared his throat and gazed into the garden, his eyes half-closed. "Would you be interested in another job, Duncan? A job that pays a very high salary?"

Duncan gave him an amused look. "I'm a senator, pal. Remember?"

"Fifty thousand dollars a year, tax-free. Plus expenses. Plus a considerable number of perquisites. Beginning this fall, when your current term expires."

"My God. That's several times what I get now. What's the job?"

"I can't say until there's a definite expression of interest of your part. It's rather delicate, all in all."

"I see. You will tell me more if I indicate I'll give up my run for the Seventy-sixth Congress?"

"Not indicate—promise. If you promise to withdraw your name from the slate, you'll be hired as of November three."

Duncan thought for a time, sipping his drink. Then he put down his glass and said, "I told you I like power."

"There is power in this employment, Duncan. Of a different sort, indeed. But power nonetheless."

"It's not lobbying, is it? Serving as an agent of French interests here in the States?"

"No."

"Don't misunderstand; I don't have anything against lobbyists. But if I ever lobby, it'll have to be for American interests."

Duncan fell silent, feeling a peculiar excitement, and he thought momentarily of his old days at the Point, when a holiday was at hand. But the picture was followed closely by another: the headwaiter at the Willard, obsequious, and bowing him to a table. For some reason he wanted to laugh.

"Why me, Georges?"

"Because you have a special knowledge that happens to be most valuable to the people who are interested in you."

"It's legal, isn't it?"

"I'd have nothing to do with it if it were not."

"May I have some time to think about it?"

"Of course. Call me at my home at this hour tomorrow."

49

Dieter Laub regarded his old friend with affection. According to his reckoning, they had served on the Berlin police force together for sixteen years, which was no insignificant amount of time in these days of liberalism and change and transience. Kratzer was a good man—slow, deliberate, pragmatic—and, being older and therefore more experienced, he had been of considerable help and no little inspiration in Laub's own development as a detective.

"Why are you smiling?" Kratzer asked in his professor's voice.

Laub shifted on the hard bench and recrossed his legs, seeking unsuccessfully to establish a comfortable position. "I was thinking of how much I owe you for coming out in this miserable rain to see me off."

"Nonsense. I owe you a debt of gratitude for coming down to this godforsaken place at all. But when you do it simply to say hello and see how I'm doing, well, then, that's something special."

They resumed their amiable silence, listening to the storm and trying to ignore the sense of isolation. The depot, a primitive structure with spartan appointments, sat on the rim of the village, and, because it accommodated only two through trains daily, there was no attendant. Laub felt that he and Kratzer might very well have been the only two souls to visit this forlorn and grubby place in the past century, give or take a decade or two.

"Winter will be here soon," Kratzer observed. "And then this rotten little town really goes to sleep."

"Well, no place is much in winter."

As if to confirm the point, there was a brilliant flickering outside, followed almost immediately by a nasty clap of thunder and a lashing of rain at the shabby windows. It occurred to Laub that many of the important occasions in his life had been accompanied by thunderstorms: his entry, as a boy, into the Kaiser's army; his loss of virginity to a milk maid in the Vosges; his wounding at Ypes; his first promotion as a policeman; the death of his wife. And now this.

A switching engine from the sugar-beet factory chuffed by in the darkness, hissing and clanking and sending a trembling through the depot. Then it was gone, swallowed by the night, and Laub felt a chill of loneliness and sorrow. People were like that, he mused. They came into your life, sent a trembling through whatever foundation you might have, and then they were gone, leaving you in the eternal nighttime that surrounds the human heart. He missed his beloved Maria especially much right now, and it was hard not to be angry with her for having died so early and with such little prior notice. He should have recovered from her leaving long ago, but the pain was as intense this night as it had ever been.

The mood was probably deepened by his dislike of assignments like this. But Schnitzel had been quite specific, and there was nothing to do but to carry out his instructions, as incomprehensible as they might be. Still, it was a terrible wrench. Kratzer was an old friend, and it was always unpleasant, having to mix political necessity and friendship. It never got easier, only worse.

"I envy you, of course," Kratzer said. "I'd give anything to be returning to Berlin with you."

"Well, my dear friend, you seem to be doing astonishingly well by yourself as it is. It's amazing to me, how you did it."

"The Stachel investigation, you mean?"

"Yes. Amazing. You have so few resources, yet—" He shrugged.

"You haven't seen anything yet, Laub. My discovery of Stachel's implication in the von Brandt affair was primarily a piece of luck. I rather stumbled onto that. But it falls right in with the suspicions surrounding the deaths of his wife and that Colonel Funk, whose body was found in the car with hers. The pieces are fitting together now. I'll have Stachel in court within the week."

"I guess it was lucky, your coming across the affidavit of that corporal. What was his name?"

"Gerhardt Rupp. His deposition, made in 1918 and accusing Stachel of causing the death of Willi von Klugerman, his wife's nephew, in a plane crash, turned the trick. I'd been trying for months, Laub, months, of my own nights and weekends and holidays, and was having no success in tying Stachel directly to the death of that Jew, Ziegel, whom he kidnapped from our very headquarters. But with Rupp's deposition, I saw I had something better than the Ziegel matter. The Rupp deposition had been known to Major von Brandt, Stachel's superior in the Truppenamt. And soon thereafter von Brandt was dead. Of his own hand, rumor has it. But of Stachel's fine hand, I'd say. Whenever Stachel has been threatened, there have been bodies."

Laub yawned and glanced at his watch, comparing it with the clock on the sooty station wall. "I've said it before, and I'll say it again, my dear Kratzer—I'd certainly never want to have you as my enemy. Such tenacity. Such a capacity for vengeance."

Kratzer nodded thoughtfully. "I suppose I do appear terribly single-minded in this—even vindictive. I suppose there will be those who'll claim my two-year investigation of Stachel rests in my determination to make him pay for my dismissal from the Berlin police. But it's deeper than that. Stachel broke a law. He stole a suspect from our protective custody, and the man has never been found—never seen again. Stachel must pay, if not for this specific crime, then for some other crime. Because Stachel's greatest crime is using his status as a military hero, a paragon, to betray Germany. Stachel's crime was that he became a Nazi."

Poor old Kratzer, Laub thought. He had to be getting senile. There hadn't been a bit of sense in anything he'd said. But that was exactly why Schnitzel was concerned.

"Well," Laub said, "we've been policemen long enough to know that justice takes many forms. That behind any truth is a larger truth."

Kratzer made no further comment, but sat in the wan light, polishing his pince-nez, and brooding. Later, though, he coughed and said, as if to himself, "The Nazis must be destroyed. We'll start with that swine Stachel. Swine belong in the mud."

At 21:37 hours, three minutes behind schedule, the through train's headlights showed, and its whistle piped, far away and unhappy. The storm had eased up, but a fine rain was still falling and the wind, sharp and cold, blustered in the eaves of the ancient platform.

"So, then, good-bye, Kratzer, old friend," Laub said, extending his hand in the trackside dimness.

"Good-bye, Laub. Thank you for listening to the prattlings of an old man."

"My pleasure. I never fail to learn from you."

As the train loomed, an enormous blackness that steamed and rumbled and squealed, Laub twisted the old man's arm against itself, and, using it as a lever, shoved him—almost gently—into the night.

He met the train captain as he swung to the platform. Presenting his credentials, he said briskly, "Inspector Laub, of the Berlin police. There's been an accident. A friend of mine was seeing me off, and he lost his bearings in the rain and he has, I'm afraid, fallen under your train."

50

Although he was anointed by orders assigning him to special duties under Göring, Stachel was still perplexed by his inclusion among those seated in the royal box during the 1935 Heroes Memorial Day services at the State Opera House. In fact, he could have touched Hitler himself if his chair had been a half meter to the right. And compounding the puzzle was the odd embarrassment that came with his discovery that he seemed to be the only colonel within eyesight. The main floor was a gray-green ocean of army brass, interspersed with generals and admirals from the World War and beyond; and from this sublime, the pageant went to the abjectly prosaic—a platoon of enlisted ranks arrayed on the stage, as unmoving as mannequins, under a stupendous Iron Cross insignia that hung from the curtain loft.

There was much excitement, not only in this magnificent auditorium but throughout Germany as well. The Führer, only the day before ("March 16, 1935, will live forever in the hearts of good Germans everywhere"), had announced a new law rejecting the military provisions of the Versailles Treaty, restoring universal military service as the base for a regenerated German defense force, and establishing a standing army of twelve army corps and thirty-six divisions. World news services had gone wild, of course, thanks to Goebbels's clever manipulation of Saturday's news briefings for Sunday's release schedules; and while there was dancing in the streets of Deutschland, there was consternation in London and Paris, according to intelligence reports he'd seen this morning. The new law, following on the heels of Göring's revelations to the London *Daily Mail* that he would be minister for air and head of a re-created military air force, simply acknowledged publicly what had been going on secretly in the decade since von Seeckt's ascendancy and decline.

The orchestra thundered Beethoven's "Funeral March," and brilliant stage lights played across the soldiers and the Iron Cross, and there was much emotion evident in the audience. Stachel felt the elemental force that had swept an unknown corporal from the degradation of a Viennese flophouse to the summit of power, and he sat rigidly, impassively, unwilling to concede his personal vulnerability to weepy patriotism. Even so, his heart swelled, and there was a thickness in his throat, and he loved his poor, benighted, doomed Fatherland very much.

Von Blomberg, the new minister of defense, brought the throng to its feet, cheering, when he said from the podium, "The world has been made to realize that Germany did not die of its defeat in the World War. Germany will again take the place she deserves among the nations. We pledge ourselves to a Germany which will never surrender and never again sign a treaty which cannot be fulfilled."

And Hitler, looking benignly grim, nodded approvingly as his defense chief concluded, "We want peace with equal rights and security for all. We seek no more."

During the stirring, tearful singing of "Deutschland Über Alles," Stachel saw the foreign press contingent standing in subdued isolation, deadpan and gray and curiously solemn. *We know,* he thought. *They and I . . .*

The death of the world starts here.

His plan had been to drop by his office after the parade and do some catch-up reading in the American periodical *Aviation Week,* back copies of which had formed a modest pile in his in box. (The magazine was a marvelous source of information on U.S. technical advances, and he'd occasionally been tempted to indulge his fondness for pranks by writing a letter to the editor, stating that his subscription provided him with what simply had to be the best and most inexpensive agent in the history of German espionage.) But as he stood beside his Mercedes staff car, pulling on his gloves, an SS Hauptsturmführer, huge in his black uniform and steel helmet, approached, clicked his heels, gave the stiff-armed Deutscher Gruss, and said, "Heil Hitler!"

"What's on your mind, Hauptsturmführer?"

"The Reichskanzler's compliments to Colonel Stachel."

"The Reichskanzler? You mean Hitler himself?"

The captain's eyes narrowed slightly in obvious disapproval of the colonel's cool offhandedness in face of such monumental news. "Yes, sir. The Reichskanzler requests the colonel to report to the Führerbüro in the Reichskanzlei. At his earliest convenience."

"I suppose my earliest convenience would be right now, eh, Hauptsturmführer?"

The SS officer's features clouded even more. "Indeed, sir."

"Very well," Stachel said, suddenly weary of Nazi humorlessness. "I'm practically there."

The Chancellory was an overpowering composite of marble, banners, shining boots, stern faces, sentries, and polished windows. It glistened, buzzed, whispered; telephones purred politely, secretaries pounded typewriters with proud ferocity, heels clicked on waxed floors, and everywhere there was the smell of raw power.

Stachel was led through a series of hallways and anterooms, and at each reception desk he was scrutinized by a stony-eyed SS officer whose rank elevated as the Führerbüro came closer. And at each stage the quiet became heavier, more portentous.

Eventually he was ushered into a large chamber, which, he assumed from the glistening conference table and the baronial chairs, was the cabinet room. There were soft voices and hushed, stilted laughter, and he saw that he was in the presence of the Third Reich's mightiest, from Göring and Hess to the placid Erhard Milch and his retinue.

Stachel stood in the doorway, overwhelmed by his apparent apotheosis, and was about to enter and mingle with the angels when an inner door opened and a beefy man he recognized as Schaub, Hitler's personal adjutant, stepped through to announce in organ tones, "Gentlemen, the Führer."

Heels crashed in salute, and a stillness settled. Hitler came in, crisp in sharply creased brown, his hand raised in a nonchalant Deutscher Gruss. He went to the red-leather chair at table's center—the chair whose back was higher than the others and carried the initials AH and the Hoheitsabzeichen eagle—and nodded briefly. "Be seated, gentlemen."

Stachel took a chair at the wall near the door. When everybody was settled and mutely attentive, Hitler cleared his throat. "Before we get on with the regularly scheduled meeting, the air minister has an announcement."

Göring looked about at the sycophantic faces, his eyes moving in slow arrogance. Obviously filled with a sense of his importance, he drawled, "As you know, gentlemen, the Führer last year established a national order honoring party comrades who fell on nine November, '23, in the National Socialist march against the Bavarian Government in Munich. To be eligible for the award, recipients must have taken part in the Munich Putsch and have been members of the party as of one January, '32. Because so many good people died under government guns, the medal has become known—both officially and popularly—as 'the Blood Order.' The medal is the highest nonmilitary award the Reich can give. He who wears it does so with the sure knowledge that he is among a very special elite."

Glancing across the room, Göring said, "Oberst Stachel, will you join me at the head of the table, please?"

Conscious of the sudden burning that always came to his cheeks when he became the object of stares, Stachel stood up and strode briskly across the carpeting, his bearing earnest and military as a means of disguising his astonishment.

Göring opened a fancy folder, evincing a ludicrous mixture of martiality and piousness. "Face me, Stachel, and stand at attention."

"Yes, Herr Reichsminister. As ordered."

"There. That's good." Göring held out the folder and began to read: "Reichskanzlei, Berlin, sixteen March, 1935. Subject: citation. To: all agencies, commands, and NSDAP units. Text: On nine November, 1923, when national socialism met its initial test under the withering fire of the enemies of Germany's regeneration the blood of fourteen comrades stained the streets of Munich and created a symbol of sacrifice that will endure until the end of time.

"As a lasting tribute to those who fell, and in grateful recognition of the courage and loyalty of those who survived, a special decoration—the Blood Order of the Munich Uprising—has been established in my name, effective with the advent of the Third Reich.

"In fondness, gratitude, and undying fealty, I have personally stipulated the granting of this order to Generalmajor Bruno Stachel, who was there, with his Führer, on that fateful day. May he wear it in dignity and honor forever. Sieg heil! Signed: Adolf Hitler."

Göring took a deep breath, closed the folder, and handed it to Stachel. Then, with a theatrical flourish, he produced the medal, a silver disk hung from a scarlet ribbon, and, lips pursed in the manner of a fussy tailor, affixed it to Stachel's right breast.

"It's genuine silver, Generalmajor Stachel," Göring murmured. "Engraved with your very own identification number.

You are now one of the Third Reich's holy men, so to speak. Congratulations. You may stand at ease."

Stachel made a business of looking down at the medal, which glowed softly against his uniform. He experienced a dreadful moment when he thought he might laugh outright. Controlling the impulse, he said gravely, "Thank you, sir."

There was a ripple of courteous applause and approval, and Hitler, showing a controlled smile, said, "Well, then, Stachel. I daresay you are pleased and surprised."

"Indeed I am, my Führer."

"You have done a good job. You deserve recognition, promotion."

Bormann, in his bull-necked, intrusive way, said, "Especially for the coup you pulled off in America last summer. That was rich, that was. Brilliant execution of difficult orders."

"I don't understand," Stachel said, meaning it.

"Your deliberate crashing of that airplane. The destruction of the American secret bomb-aimer. Daring plan, daring execution." Bormann's brutish face showed traces of sly sarcasm—the stuff of belligerence and challenge.

Stachel had thought that this Quatsch had been put to rest long ago, and he resented Bormann's resurrection of it at such an awkward moment. It seemed to him that Bormann was contriving to embarrass him in some way, and the sense of forces beyond his perception and control was strong.

"There was no secret device on that plane," Stachel said bluntly, aware now that Hitler and the others were watching him closely. "And the crash was pure accident."

"Oh, come now, my dear Stachel," Bormann crooned, "there's no need to pretend any longer. You're within the innermost circle. No more secrets to hide."

"By the way, Generalmajor Stachel, where did such an inspired plan have its origin?"

The question had come from the ferret-faced propaganda minister, Goebbels, and Stachel had the quick impression that Bormann and Goebbels were articulating a carefully prepared script. It was a whisper of thought, gone in a blink, but it left an afterglow that could not be extinguished or ignored. He glanced at Hitler, who regarded him coolly with noncommittal blue eyes, and it came to him that somewhere in the labyrinth of political and military ambition in which this man lived there was a special need—an unspoken demand for a burst of power that would keep Adolf Hitler's authority more precisely on course. And, at the moment, Bruno Stachel was crucial somehow; in some unfathomable way, he represented a small yet critical trump in some power play whose nature and detail he would probably never be permitted to know. The entire Nazi system hung on a slender parody of monotheism—with the one god given absolute, singular authority rooted in personal infallibility. And now the one god needed Stachel's active complicity in the travesty so as to control someone, deny someone, rebuke someone, or achieve some subtle end in the business of government.

Gazing directly into Goebbels's cynical eyes, Stachel reminded, "There is only one source of inspiration in the Reich today, Herr Minister."

He felt an immediate easing of an indefinable tension, and there was a nodding of heads and a chorus of well-said, indeed, and hear-hear.

Göring beamed at Hitler. "It was a real coup, my Führer. According to General von Boetticher in Washington, you've set back American preparedness plans immeasurably. Ingenious. Ingenious beyond words."

Hitler waved a minimizing hand. "Generalmajor Stachel deserves the credit."

"And you have given me much more than is my due, my Führer."

The watery blue eyes gave Stachel careful new appraisal, but they revealed nothing of the thoughts behind them. "Your future is bright, Generalmajor Stachel. Very bright. Meanwhile, it's back to work for me. You may leave us now."

On his ride back to the office he stared absently at the neck of his driver and tried to absorb the day's events.

He thought briefly of Hitler, and then of Polly Loomis's claim of years ago, in which she saw men and nations preferring to die with their illusions than live with their truths. She'd been right: Hitler dealt with the world, not as it was, but as he wished it could be. Hitler was a chameleon who, in trying to project the illusion of total righteousness, would inevitably lose track of himself.

Ah, well. Who was Bruno Stachel to talk? A Blue Max for an action he couldn't remember. The Blood Order for a march in which he never took part. Illusions? God!

51

The shipment went out at dawn, on schedule. They were a man and his wife, neither very old. They were to go the B-Route, which was more dangerous than the A, because it was always easier to disguise men as itinerant venders. This way, the woman would have to have a carefully drawn cover story and precision documents, and women were always more likely to come apart emotionally at moments of crisis. Especially Jewish women, since they had already been put through so much before they arrived at the castle.

"More tea?" Ziegel asked.

"No, not now."

"Has the Baroness eaten yet?"

"Not unless you took it to her."

Ziegel sighed. "Poor woman. She just sits there, day after day, staring up the valley. Did you ever get the impression that she's waiting for something special?"

"She's wallowing in self-pity, if you ask me," Elfi said. "She's not the only one who's lost a son. Who's been betrayed by those monsters in Berlin. Just ask the people who come through here."

"Well," Ziegel said in his soft, forgiving way, "we each bear our burdens with different amounts of strength, grace. One man's sorrow is another man's relief, so to say."

Elfi gave him a wry glance. "What does all that mean?"

"I don't know. I'm just trying to be profound. It's a beautiful morning, and I like to be philosophical on beautiful mornings."

She smiled and shook her head in mock resignation. "You are a strange man, Ziegel."

He did not disagree, and they sat there at the ancient, scarred table and gazed out the open casement at the incredible sweep of mountains and the deep valley, with its meandering river and little white houses dotting the meadows on its flanks. A warm breeze was stirring, and it filled the alcove with the scent of distant pines and damp grass.

Elfi loved the summer. She had never lived in Bavaria, but she knew a lot about it, having visited her Aunt Leni in Nesselwang in virtually every August of her childhood. Yet this area, with its gigantic views, its awesome amalgamation of fearsome peaks and gentle flatlands, was new to her, and it frightened her somehow. It was a place of contrasts, contradictions, paradoxes; it lured the eye with its beauty and repelled the heart with its stern immutability. Berlin, being a city, had its own kind of beauty and its own brand of changelessness, but it had a beat, a throb, a vibrancy that seemed to be missing in the silent crags and misty fields of Oberbayern. Here all was huge, still, relentless.

She had brought the man and his wife to Schloss Löwenheim in Klaus's Horch cabriolet, which developed motor trouble south of Ulm and had to be fixed at a crossroads garage. The money had come out of her own pocket, and, unless Klaus reimbursed her this week, she would be hard put to pay the rent again. Oh, well, nobody had promised her that the work would be easy. . . .

Ziegel lit his pipe for the thousandth time since breakfast. Puffing it to life and speaking all the while, he said, "Klaus says the Lisbon people are asking for more money."

"They've discovered how really desperate our clients are, I guess."

"Well, there's such a thing as pricing oneself out of the market. If the Lisbon people get too greedy our clients will have to take their business elsewhere."

"Which elsewhere? Be sensible, Ziegel. There is no elsewhere."

"I'm told that there's a group of rich Americans who are willing to subsidize Jews fleeing Germany outside quotas. They put them up in big mansions in a place called Hoboken."

"Don't believe everything you hear. Americans aren't magicians."

"Maybe not. But they seem to be the only people who give a damn about Jews."

"Oh, that's rich, that is," she said, feeling a flare of annoyance. "Just what do you think Klaus and I and all the others are doing? Denouncing Jews to the Gestapo?"

"Excuse me, Elfi," Ziegel said, putting out a hand of

apology, "that was a stupid thing for me to say. I meant the Americans, among those outside Germany, are the—"

She broke in, "I know what you meant, Ziegel. It's all right. Forget it."

"I just get weary, Elfi. Weary of going to so much trouble to smuggle a handful of pitiful, unpapered Jews out of this godforsaken country and into other countries that don't really want them any more than Hitler does. There are thousands upon thousands who would give anything to get out of Germany, and we get them out by ones and twos. It's like eating soup with a fork—"

She took his hand. "Easy, my dear Ziegel, easy. We're doing the best we can, and it's the trying that counts. If we help just one, it's worth it."

"Do you remember Herr Goldmann, the architect? He paid two hundred and fifty thousand American dollars to the Lisbon people for a visa to a Central American country. And when he got to his destination the authorities turned him over to the German Embassy for return to Germany on the next boat."

"Who told you all this?"

"Maurice. The man at our Mulhouse exit."

"Fah. Maurice always dramatizes. You can divide what he says in half, and you're still far from the facts."

"Well, then, if he's so unreliable, why is he working for our apparatus?"

"Because he has guts. Because he knows how to outwit the border patrols. Because he established, practically single-handed, the safe-house chain across France. That's why."

"I know all that, but if he talks a lot—"

"Damn it, Ziegel, you *are* in a mood today, aren't you? What's got into you? You're not usually one to whine."

He shrugged, baffled by frustration beyond articulation, and she was filled with a sudden compassion, a warmth that seemed close to love for the dark-eyed, brooding man whose hand clutched hers. He loved her, this she knew. He'd never said it in so many words, but she knew it with the certainty of a woman accustomed to years in a world where affection was unknown. Does one who is starving recognize the smell of bread?

That afternoon they were adjusting the telescope atop the northeast turret, and so they saw Klaus's truck when it was still a tiny blue dot on the chalky ribbon of the road from

Kempten. It seemed to move slowly, as if pained by the prospect of reaching the castle.

They were waiting in the cobblestoned courtyard when the truck finally pulled in. Klaus swung down from the driver's seat, yawned, stretched, and looked about as if the place were new to him.

"Ha," he said, squinting in the lowering sunglare, "there you are. How about something to eat? We're starved."

"We?" Elfi said. "There's somebody with you?"

"I've got company. This time I didn't have to ride alone with a load of potatoes and beans." He turned. "Hey, come on out."

A man climbed out of the passenger side of the cab, taking off his cap politely, and giving Elfi and Ziegel a pleasant smile. "Good day," he said in an easy baritone. "I've heard a lot about you two."

"Elfi, Ziegel—may I present my newest helper?" Klaus said heartily. "Meet Dieter Laub, who is a Lutheran minister."

52

Göring had permitted Stachel to visit "Operation Magic Fire" on a single, inflexible condition: that he not participate in combat missions. "Observe all you want to," he'd said, "but don't start trading bullets with the Communists—you're too valuable, and you know too much to risk your capture and interrogation."

Half a loaf is better than none, Stachel thought sourly. He was at three thousand meters, cruising through lacy clouds, watching the bombers below as if he were some kind of warlord peering down on his maneuvering legions, enduring the peculiar guilt that goes to him who hangs back while others dare.

But why should I care? he reminded himself. *The whole grubby show is an exercise in vicariousness.* General Franco's Nationalists were in rebellion against Spain's Republican government—Facists trying to oust Communists. Franco had originally asked Hitler for the loan of a few transport planes to ferry troops from Morocco to mainland Spain. Hitler and Göring saw the invitation as a marvelous opportunity to test the Luftwaffe under real combat conditions. But so did the Soviets, and so by now, the summer of 1937, two rather considerable air forces—one German, one Russian—were dueling in Spanish skies, ostensibly in the interest of Spaniards but really in the interest of war games with live ammunition.

Hypocrites. The world is filled with hypocrites. . . . Ah, well.

The new Messerschmitt 109 was an exceptional airplane, and he could feel it around him, alive and eager and full of tremblings, whirrings, and rumblings. It was a low-wing monoplane that would fly as high as air would reach, it seemed, and it was fast, responsive and deadly. Sitting in the brilliant sunlight, heavy with flying suit and parachute and oxygen mask, with the radio crackling in his helmet phones and the slipstream screeching outside the thick-paned canopy, he remembered the old days in France: the D-7 Fokker, and how wonderfully primitive it had been; the clattering engine, the icy wind eddying in the canvas cockpit, the smell of hot metal and oil. God, how much had changed, how much had happened. How *old* he felt. The crews of the bombers down there were downy-faced children, all enthusiasm and healthy teeth and clear eyes, and he was a thousand years old, an aviating Methuselah, compelled to watch from a quiet corner while the boys played their games in the sun.

The Heinkel 111s were letting down for their bomb run. They were ugly—swollen and round, the shape and color of dog dirt. The target, a village said to conceal the headquarters and main supply depot for a Republican brigade, looked tiny and forlorn—a scattering of porridge-hued dots on the rolling tans and greens of the Basque hills. To the north, far beyond the highlands, the terrain met the Bay of Biscay, a great sweep that blended with the distant sky and gave the illusion that the seacoast was actually the end of the world.

The village disappeared in a series of flickerings that left enormous, rising columns of smoke. The bombers wheeled majestically in a lazy turn, holding their tight formation, while the escorting 109s fanned out in protective arcs.

Out of the west, coming like wasps, four stubby monoplanes skirted the lower clouds. They were I-16s, Stachel saw, the late-model Russian fighters. Four against eighteen bombers and a squadron of Messerschmitts. The Cocos, if they attacked, were as good as dead.

They attacked.

Rolling on their backs and dropping in wide arcs, they came at the bomber formation in a high-angle, head-on approach. Stachel could hear no firing at this distance, but as the little fighters lifted away for another pass, two of the Heinkels were falling—one aflame, the other a brown T that twisted and turned until it dissolved against a hillside in a welter of fire.

The 109s struck, descending like a shower of dark arrows, and three of the I-16s went down, two burning, one a bundle of collapsed metal, spinning. The survivor, instead of running, turned inside the 109s and made for the Heinkels again, and a bomber at the trailing edge of the formation vanished in a bubble of fire and smoke.

Unbelieving, Stachel watched as the little fighter continued its pass, doggedly, unheeding of the crisscrossing tracers pouring from the bombers and the pursuing Messerschmitts. Another Heinkel fell away, limping, and the I-16 darted for a bank of cumulus drifting in from the west. The 109s circled angrily, waiting for their quarry to reappear, but Stachel guessed they would have a long wait indeed.

As he turned for home, he saw it.

The enemy monoplane was directly ahead and below, still climbing and making for another tier of clouds. It was in perfect position, a sitting duck under his nose guns, and only the slightest adjustment of his rudder would put him in an ideal angle for a long burst.

He flipped off the gun button lock, leaned forward to catch the I-16's image in his sights, and, squinting, prepared to fire.

It occurred to him then that he had nothing at all against the man out there. A Communist? What was that? A Spaniard? A Russian? An American volunteer, perhaps? What had they done to him? This wasn't his country or his fight.

The man ahead, isolated in his tiny box of metal and wires and dials, had done nothing to offend Bruno Stachel. He'd killed some Germans, certainly—youngsters with white teeth and smiling eyes. But the Germans had invited their end, coming as they had to level a drowsy village on a sunny afternoon.

The man ahead had shown great courage. And the world, with what must surely lie in its future, would need all the courageous men it could find.

Stachel re-engaged the gun lock and watched, impassive, as the monoplane continued its climb, eventually to fade from sight in the mists.

He returned to base and turned in his borrowed airplane.

After another day at Nationalist headquarters, conferring with swarthy officers in baggy uniforms who smelled of sweat and wine, he closed his notebook, climbed aboard the JU-52 personnel transport, and dozed throughout the long flight to Germany.

Once, when coursing through the night over the Taunus region, he thought of his childhood. And then he dreamed a melancholy dream, a mishmash of images involving his mother and father.

When he awoke, the sadness persisted. It was still with him when he left the plane in Berlin.

53

Polly had gone to a movie after lunch at the country club. It was one of those things in which Olivia deHavilland sighed a lot and persevered in the face of incredibly compounding difficulties. Emerging from the theater into the late afternoon sunlight, she hailed a cab and told the driver to take her to the Algernon. On the way, she positioned herself on the car seat so as to practice the deHavilland smile—that vague, winsome, long-suffering, sweet turning of the lips—in the rearview mirror. She gave up after a time, deciding that, as a smiler, she would make a great ad for heartburn tablets.

Harry was waiting at the bar, as he'd said he would be. He was tall and sandy, bluntly good-looking, and tremendously pleased with himself, as were all highly placed State Department officials. It went with the territory, she told herself in silent sarcasm: since her first day at the Berlin embassy all those years ago—a thousand years, at least—she'd been given to understand that career personnel above consular level were Ivy League prigs who thought they weewee-ed eau de cologne. And Harry proved to be no exception.

Harry said the usual things, smiling, but all the time looking around the room to see who was noticing how charming he was being. Then they went to their table in the far corner, settling in for small talk that was considerably drier than the martinis.

Somewhere in the gabble he paused, gave her an evaluating glance, and said, "You're very quiet today."

"Quiet? How can I be quiet when I'm blabbering about Amy D'Alonzo's dinner party, the deteriorating quality of the food at the country club, the difficulty in getting a maid who doesn't drink herself blind on my husband's scotch, and the dress my dry cleaner ruined?"

"Well, not that kind of quiet. I mean the other kind of quiet. You're saying a lot of things but you're really not listening to yourself. You're in a closet somewhere, thinking about something else."

She felt real surprise, since such intuitiveness had never before been apparent in Harry Taylor. Awareness of the prevailing atmosphere at a party, yes; sensitivity to political trends, true. But ability to read her thoughts, her mood-behind-the-mood? This was new. She hunched a shoulder, saying, "A friend of mine's got a problem, and it's rubbing off on me, I suppose. Sorry. I didn't know it showed."

Harry waved to a group across the room and gave them State Department Smile 64-A, as modified for murky saloons. "What friend?" he said through his long-distance sociability. "What problem?"

"It's personal."

"Personal? My God, Polly—I know that your eyelids flutter when you're having an orgasm. That's about as personal as you can get. So what's about this friend I shouldn't know?"

"It's something deep. I can't describe it because I don't understand it myself."

"You've taken another lover and don't know how to tell me?"

"Oh, come on, Harry. Who do you think I am, Hot-pants Hattie? When I cheat on my husband, it's one at a time. When I take another lover you'll have been long gone, pal."

"Don't get sore. I simply—"

She patted his hand, the one that rested on the table, and

caressed the stem of his cocktail glass. "I'm not sore, Harry. Honest. I'm just confused."

He seemed relieved, and it occurred to her that he'd been really upset over the idea that she might have another boy friend. Contrite, she decided Harry deserved an explanation.

"Back in my days with the department, when I was with the embassy in Berlin, I met this German. He and John and I became pretty good buddies. He visited us a while back and I've been sort of worried about him—"

"You mean Bruno Stachel, the great war ace?"

"Oh. You know him?"

"No. But Winchell had a mention in his column the other day. Something about Senator Duncan playing footsies with Nazi creeps, or whatever. I put two and two together."

"And came up with a new lover for me, eh?" She smiled wryly.

"Well, not exactly," Harry said, grinning uneasily. "But now that you mention it—"

"I won't kid you. Stachel and I had a few sessions back in the old days. But he's gone very proper. And that's what gets to me."

"What do you mean?"

"Something's bothering that guy real bad. He used to be a hell-for-leather sort, all cool and icy yet full of hot vinegar at the same time. Now he's just cool and icy. I can't explain it. It's just a feeling—a hunch."

Harry blew a kiss at a woman who waved good-bye from the doorway. "A high-ranking Nazi like Stachel has plenty to fret about these days. Besides, cool and icy is becoming the German national attitude. Supermen are above hot vinegar, my dear."

"That's just it, Harry—I don't think Stachel is a Nazi."

"He's sure got the credentials."

"But that's just it. He's supposed to be Mr. National Socialism, according to all the gossip. But I talked to him and he came across as a man divided. A man who is caught up in a two-way stretch. A Nazi who hates Nazism."

"How can you guess that, Polly?" Harry said skeptically.

"I don't have to guess. It's the same thing I see in my husband. John's supposed to be a hot-shot U.S. senator, the obscure politician from an obscure state who became one of the powerful men on the Hill. Well, that's baloney. John is actually a little country boy playing games. He's about as at ease being a senator as I'd be in a nunnery."

Harry finished his drink, and she could see that he was no longer aware of the people in the room; with his eyes level and indirect, he was a man deep in thought. Someone in the crowd around the piano dropped a glass, and there was a small explosion of self-conscious laughter, and with the sound his attention came back to her. "So if all this is true," he said, "why are you upset? What's it got to do with you?"

She shook her head in exasperation. "I don't know. I've asked myself the same question. And I don't come up with any answers."

"Maybe it's because you have a real case for Stachel after all," Harry said gently.

Polly looked at him appraisingly, deciding that it really didn't matter enough to continue her little self-deception. "Maybe it is, Harry. I made a real hard pass at him before he went back to Germany. But he wasn't buying. Maybe I'm a woman scorned."

"A woman scorned is angry. You're worried."

"I don't want that dumb Kraut to let his disenchantment show, at the wrong time, in the presence of the wrong people. It could get him killed, and that would be a real waste of a very rare commodity these days—a German with second thoughts."

"You are gone on him, aren't you?"

"None of your business."

"The hell it isn't. I'm your lover, remember?"

She laughed, and so did he, and she decided he was a pretty neat guy, when all was said and done. "You're O.K. Harry," she said, patting his hand again.

"So are you. I like you very much."

"You want me to get a divorce so I can marry you?"

"Hell no. I don't want to marry you. I just like to sleep with you."

"Good. Anything else would ruin our beautiful friendship."

They laughed together again.

"Know what you need, Polly? You need a job. You're just frittering away your life, playing at the housewife thing. That's a real waste, to have an old State Department hand like you sitting around on her pretty little kiester."

She looked at him. "You mean you would hire me?"

"Not at all. I don't have any openings. Besides, the only thing worse than having a wife working for you is having your girl friend working for you. No. I mean a job in the department somewhere else. A place where your experience would count. Shoot, I don't have anything to do with direct diplomacy—the embassy stuff—and that's your cup of tea."

"It's been years—"

"You could brush up in nothing flat."

"Well—"

Harry signaled the waiter for another round. "You don't have to, if you don't want to, naturally. But I just don't like to see you this way, all whim-whammy. And what good are friends if they can't help you? I can help you by nosing around, seeing if there's an opening that might suit you."

"That's nice of you, Harry, but—"

"Nice, hell. I don't want the whim-whams to wreck my love life. I'm being selfish."

She laughed. "O.K., big boy. Maybe you're right."

Harry beamed and shook hands with himself above his head, like a prizefighter. "Ah," he said, "things are looking up again."

Across the room, seated at a corner of the bar near the checkroom alcove. Doubet caught Harry's signal. He took a final sip of his wine, paid his tab, exchanged a few pleasantries with Oscar, the bartender, then sauntered into the evening to enter his waiting car.

On the way to the embassy he was deep in reminiscence. How concerned, how naïvely unsure of himself John Duncan had been those years ago when speaking of his plans to marry Polly Loomis. How sad, and droll.

Well, Frenchmen were supposed to be blasé about such things.

54

The free-floating assignment given him by the indolent Göring had proved to be a case of falling into a sty that concealed diamonds. Stachel, not one to overlook convenience or advantage, quickly learned that his special commission—enhanced by the red rosette of the Blood Order—left few doors closed to him. Unhappily, most of the doors opened on little of consequence, leading as they did to turgid bureaucracies with grand titles and feathery substance. The Luftwaffe, as an entity, was fast developing into a tactical air force, thanks to Göring's maddening indifference to the details of management, Udet's nostalgia for the World War knights-of-the-air nonsense, and Milch's even more maddening willingness to go along with them both. As von Lemmerhof had said aeons before, bombers were the key: a strategic air force built on long-range bombers would control Europe, if not the world. But an air force built on fancy racing planes and two-engine grenade droppers would be hard put to control anything for long, and Milch should have known better. Göring and Udet could be forgiven their idiocies, since their dilettantism and egotism and self-indulgence were universally recognized; but Milch—sly, ambitious, technically skilled, and pragmatic Erhard Milch—should have had his behind kicked for not standing up to Fat Hermann and demanding top priority for strategic bomber development. Somebody should do something about it.

Even the fighters weren't all that good.

Stachel had used his rank and privileges to acquire the personal use of an ME-109, the machine he'd tested in Spain, but with certain refinements. It was asserted to be the very best fighter plane in the world; and it was good, certainly, but the more he flew it the more he was convinced that if it weren't already obsolete it soon would be. There was very little he didn't know about the airplane at this point, and the sum of his knowledge was depressing: Germany was building thousands of fighters which would, by the time they were committed to operational squadrons, be inadequate to the task Hitler seemed to have in mind.

"Seemed," of course, was the functional word these days. Everything seemed to be significant but would, on careful examination, prove to be somewhat less. There was no central authority for intelligence, for instance; each branch of service had its own jerry-rigged system for collecting information on potential enemies, but the interpretation and application of the information was left to Hitler himself. Incredibly, the new Oberkommando der Wehrmacht, ostensibly the supreme command for all the armed forces, had no integrated intelligence and limped along, depending on the Führer to tell it what it was going to do after he'd chewed over data provided him by lesser commands. Nor was there any true co-ordination of intelligence among the branches, and so Stachel found it necessary to wander among them all, picking over an ungodly potpourri of reports for material that might someday be of some kind of use to him. It could not possibly have been done without his carte blanche from Göring and his Blood Order from Hitler. With these trinkets backing him, though, he'd begun to build a quite thorough understanding of Germany's military structure in general and its complex intelligence apparatus in particular.

However, the trinkets didn't seem to work their magic this day, which he'd devoted to the problem of radio intelligence as conducted by the Forschungsamt.

The agency, a creation of Göring himself, was supposed to be a function of the Air Ministry. But Stachel had discovered rather early that it was an intricate, incredibly well-camouflaged intelligence-gathering system calculated to serve Fat Hermann foremost and the Fatherland only incidentally. It was headed by a snooty blue-blood named von Hessen, who was said to be related to a chum of Göring's and who had proved to be too busy to escort Generalmajor Stachel on his tour of the radio-intercept facility on Schillerstrasse, just off the Tiergarten. The chore had fallen to an SS Sturmbannführer named Berger, a sour-faced Prussian with a saber scar and eyes like ball bearings.

"And so, as you see, Herr Generalmajor," Berger said, in a tone that decreed the end of the tour, "the Forschungsamt concentrates on the collection of communications intelligence. To do so, it utilizes various techniques, most of them highly technical—the interception of radio traffic, both diplomatic and commercial; the tapping of telephone lines; the deciphering of codes. We—"

"Berger," Stachel interrupted, "do yourself a kindness, eh?"

The SS officer said, "Sir?"

"Look at me when you're talking to me. Otherwise I might continue to think that you're a supercilious ass who puts too much importance on his social connections."

Berger's pale face reddened slightly. "I don't understand, Herr Generalmajor—"

"You and your boss are not the only ones who know Göring. So be kind to yourself. Stop talking down your nose to me. Look me in the eye. Or I'll hang your balls on a wash line."

"I meant no offense, Herr Generalmajor."

"I'm sure you didn't. I can now see it in your eyes, eh?"

Berger had been rattled, and, as it was with so many of the Nazi satraps these days, his hauteur proved to have little durability when met by bona-fide challenge. And, in the manner of a bully put in his place, he turned his arrogance into fawning. "Perhaps," he said, suddenly oily, "the Herr Generalmajor would be interested in the fact that his name has figured in several intercepted transmissions recently."

"My name? What transmissions?"

"One of our B posts is charged with monitoring coded radio traffic. Several times recently, messages from a fist in Bavaria have referred to you. You are a famous person."

Stachel considered this. The SS officer, by revealing a fact that most certainly had been classified as secret, either was actually seeking to make amends for his snottiness or hoping to put the fear of God into the Herr Generalmajor. The latter was more likely to be the case, Stachel decided.

"A fist in Bavaria? What's that mean?"

"A fist is someone who sends out wireless messages on a key. Someone in Bavaria named Dagger is sending to someone named Sauerkraut. The transmissions are in code. We've broken it. Your name has been mentioned."

"In what way?"

Berger had taken on the air of one who has said too much and now regrets it. His metallic eyes became indirect again, and there was a diffidence in his voice. "It's not clear, Herr Generalmajor. But the sense of the sendings seems to be that you are considered to be heavy in some way, if you'll pardon the term."

"Who would be judging my weight, Berger?"

"I can't say, sir. We're working on it."

"Who is receiving the messages?"

"We have no way of knowing, Herr Generalmajor. There have been only three sendings. No acknowledgments."

"Would you say these are Germans talking to each other? Or foreign agents?"

"Again, sir, we don't know."

"This Sauerkraut—has the name appeared in any other intelligence summaries?"

The Sturmbannführer shrugged. "I have no way of knowing, Herr Generalmajor."

"You don't know a hell of a lot about anything, do you, Berger?"

"I'm not highly placed, sir. I see only the reports I need to see to accomplish my assigned mission in the Forschungsamt."

"I'm assigning you an additional mission."
"What is that, Herr Generalmajor?" Berger said warily.
"I want continuing reports on this matter. And I want transcripts of the three sendings you describe."
"I'll have to obtain permission from—"
"Wash line, Berger. Remember the wash line."

Stachel, on the theory that attack is better than doing nothing, dialed the inside M line and got Göring at once.
"Stachel here. I'd like to see you."
"Well, comrade, I'm off to Karinhall for some bird shooting with that jellyfish von Ribbentropp and some Arabian sheiks. Want to join us?"
"No thanks. I've got too much to do."
"What's on your mind? Tell me now. This line's secure."
"Those radio transmissions."
There was a moment of silence. Then: "Radio transmissions?"
"Those intercepted by that grotesque pal of yours, Berger, at the Forschungsamt. I'm told you read virtually everything the agency hauls in, and it's unlikely that he'd kept a juicy tidbit like this away from you."
"Oh. You know about those."
"Only because Berger shot off his mouth. I don't know about it because you were nice enough to tell me, God knows."
"Watch your tone, Stachel. I don't like what you're implying."
"Implying, hell. I'm saying it right out: You can use your private intelligence service to spy on me if you want, but I expect to hear what it says about me."
"Who in hell do you think you are, Generalmajor Bruno Stachel? Who in hell are you to give me orders?"
"I'm the old comrade who saved your skin in Munich, chum. You wouldn't be partying around with Arabian sheiks this afternoon if I hadn't put that Munich cop to sleep. And the Führer has given me a medal to prove it."
"Somewhere—someday—my debt to you will have been amortized, Stachel. You should realize that, and proceed carefully."
"And you should realize that, without people like me, you'd be out of a job. If it weren't for me, you wouldn't know what a bigmouth you have working in radio intercept, for instance."
"Berger? I'll take care of Berger, you can count on that."

"And if it weren't for me, you wouldn't know that there are serious deficiencies in the Luftwaffe's performance and morale in Spain. You wouldn't know that Udet is now a trembling addict who's making a lot of wrong guesses. You wouldn't know that Milch does not have faith in the Führer's production forecasts and expansion program and is looking for ways to scale it down and revamp it without going through you. You wouldn't know all you know about Canaris and the Abwehr."

"Hold on. Milch's doing that?"

"How come your little pal Berger didn't provide you with that morsel?"

"Berger is radio intercept—"

"And I'm the one who knows what's going on everywhere. So don't threaten me, Göring. I remember you from the squadron days. I remember what you look like on the toilet. And I'm in a position to keep you safe and happy today. And tomorrow."

"You're still being very offensive. And I have a good mind to take you down a peg or two."

"Go ahead. I have a good mind to let the Führer see my privately collected photos of you in action with a very distraught Frau Raechel Silberstein, the once-beautiful heiress to the Jewish department-store fortune who now languishes in a concentration camp."

There was another pause, and Stachel could hear Göring's breathing. After a time, Göring said, his voice conciliatory, "We've got to stop this schoolboy wrangling, Stachel. Blood Order comrades don't threaten each other like this."

"Right you are, chum. That's my point. Trust is a two-way arrangement. I'll tell you what's going on in your life, if you do the same for me, eh?"

"All right, Stachel. All right."

After another interval, Göring said, "It looks as if the Sudentenland thing is about to happen. There might be some shooting. Do you want to go into Czechoslovakia with an operational unit? Just for the initial penetration?"

"Thanks. But I don't think I will. My Spanish junket cost me too much in time lost and work left undone. I think I'll sit this one out."

"All right. As you wish. How about dinner tomorrow night? Here, at the Air Ministry. We can watch some American films. There's a new one with Cagney."

"I'll call you."

"Good. I'll be in my office at noon. Are we still friends?"

"It looks that way."

He hung up and sat back in his chair, rubbing his eyes. The afternoon was only half gone and he was already weary. A syndrome of life in the Third Reich, he mused acidly; it's tiring to be forever looking over your shoulder.

Outside, the day had turned dark and gray, and there was the promise of heavy rain. He was about to ring for coffee when Feldwebel Ruger came in to announce a caller.

"It's Police Inspector Laub to see you, sir. Are you in?"

"Don't tell me I've overparked, Ruger."

The sergeant grinned. "They don't send out inspectors on traffic details, Herr Generalmajor. Have you murdered anyone today?"

"I'm not sure, Ruger. But I've been thinking about doing you in. The coffee's cold."

"Sorry, sir. I'll fix it right away."

"Meanwhile, send in our cop friend, eh?"

Dieter Laub was wearing the expected gray suit, white shirt with starched collar, and carefully knotted tie. He had a face to match: tidy, barbered, bland, and forgettable. He looked, Stachel thought, rather like someone in the back row of a group portrait.

"What might I do for you, Inspector?"

Laub adjusted his weight to the chair and fingered his necktie. "I won't keep you but a moment, Generalmajor. My visit is actually meant as a personal service to you. It's not truly official."

"How so?"

"You served in the World War in the squadron led by Otto Heidemann, did you not?"

"I did," Stachel said impassively.

"And you are friendly with his widow, Frau Elfriede Heidemann?"

"We're acquainted. Nothing of significance."

Laub raised a brow and touched his tie again. "Oh? I'd thought that you were somewhat more than acquaintances."

"What are you getting at, Inspector?"

Laub said nothing for a moment, taking the time to gaze out the window at the rain-spattered street. Then, clearing his throat, he asked gently, "But you do care about what happens to her?"

"Well, of course. She's a nice lady. A good nurse. Honest. Decent. Why?"

"She's been observed taking part in some questionable activities. If she continues, she could very well find herself in trouble with the Gestapo."

"Activities?"

"She's active in Christian church circles. I have noted that her group seems to be, ah, smuggling unpapered Jews and other political criminals out of the country. This is, of course, contrary to the wishes of the Führer, who, while he wants to rid Germany of its Jews, insists on doing it legally."

Stachel sighed. "The little fool. She knows better than that."

"It's a very dangerous pastime, General. She could get in considerable trouble. I thought you might want to approach her as a friend, warn her. Make her stop."

"Why me, Herr Laub? Why are you coming to me with this? She certainly must have closer friends than I've been to her—"

Laub decided, apparently, that his mission had been accomplished. He made one last adjustment of his tie, then stood up abruptly and made for the door. Standing there, with his hand on the knob, he seemed as colorless as suet. "I've always been interested in flying and fliers, Generalmajor. I tried to serve in the Imperial Flying Corps, actually, but I failed to qualify. Even so, I followed the exploits of our air heroes—yours included. I am a great admirer of yours. I was a great admirer of Otto Heidemann. I simply thought that, for old-time's sake, you'd like to know of the danger to Frau Heidemann before the Gestapo does. Good day, Generalmajor."

He stood by the window for a while, watching the rain and thinking about the day and its peculiar admixture of boredom, vitriol, and revelation. There had been a special sense of hidden forces at work for some time—ever since the award of the Blood Order and the maddening puzzlement triggered by the American-secret-device incident. A medal for a street uprising in which he'd participated not at all; a promotion for "exceptional service" he had no knowledge of, or, indeed, belief in: these were persistently irritating, like unresolved chords at the end of a tune. And now new dimensions of annoyance had been added, with the bizarre radio messages and the unimpassioned intervention of a policemen in the interest of Frau Heidemann, who was doing naughty things, like helping Jews get out of a country that hadn't wanted them.

Who had convinced the German military attaché in Washington that Bruno Stachel had done something splendid by crashing a plane which, he was absolutely certain, had no such thing as an automatic bomb-aimer aboard? Who was now talking about him on a clandestine radio? Why would a police inspector ask him to persuade a lawbreaker not to break the law? Police inspectors don't do things like that.

What was going on?

He was suddenly angrier than he'd been all day. The feeling that he was being manipulated was very strong.

RADIO TRANSCRIPTS

Forschungsamt

Berlin
16/VIII/38 file: 337A

Memo to officer in charge:

1. Station L intercepted coded wireless message this date.
2. Transmission began 08:10 hours, ended 08:10:53.
3. Code, having been broken, provided following text:

   To Sauerkraut from Dagger: Good to have you back as management, Re your query, Stachel is very heavy. Current rank, Luftwaffe Generalmajor. End.

4. Will keep you informed of further transmissions.

Dietrich
Radio Intercept

Forschungsamt

Berlin
17/VIII/38 file: 337B

Memo to officer in charge:

1. Reference preceding memo, this file.
2. Station L intercepted coded wireless message this date.
3. Transmission began 13:45 hours, ended 13:45:31.
4. Code, having been broken, provided following text:

   To Sauerkraut from Dagger: Have determined Stachel ripe, needs picking.

5. Will keep you advised of further transmissions.

Dietrich
Radio Intercept

Forschungsamt

Berlin
19/VIII/38 file: 337C

Memo to officer in charge:

1. Reference preceding two (2) messages, this file.
2. Station L intercepted coded wireless message this date.
3. Transmission began 19:48 hours, ended 19:48:27.
4. Code, having been broken, provided following text:

   To Sauerkraut from Dagger: Plan under way.

5. Will keep you advised.

Linck
Radio Intercept

55

"This Hirtenspiess garniert is absolutely fantastic," Randelmann said, eyes half-closed and chewing with slow pleasure.

Stachel smiled. "The food is somewhat better here in the Air Ministry than it is at squadron level. I know. I've had lunch a time or two with the recon squadron at Staaken."

"You should have tried it in Spain," Randelmann said.

"I did."

The major opened his eyes and regarded Stachel with amused curiosity. "You were there, Herr Generalmajor?"

"I was there. But only for a few days. I'm a big shot now, you see, and I don't have to stay around when things get grubby as you line-squadron fellows do."

Randelmann grinned. "If you'll pardon me saying so, Herr Generalmajor, you're the first Herr Generalmajor I've ever been around that doesn't make me as uncomfortable as a cat in a new house."

"I'm glad, Randelmann. *All* generals make me uncomfortable. So you're one up on me."

Randelmann laughed openly and reached unabashedly for a second helping of potato salad. "An awful lot's happened since that rotten time at Johannisthal, by God. I never thought either one of us would survive that stacked-deck court-martial. And now we're both, ah—" He paused, looking for the polite term.

"Gainfully employed," Stachel said helpfully.

"Yes, that's it," Randelmann chuckled. "My God, Generalmajor, do you find it hard to comprehend—all that's happened, I mean? There we were, all chained down by the Versailles Treaty, with no planes, no nothing, and people like you and me subject to the whims of creepy court-martial authorities and all, and now look at us. The Führer's kicked out the creeps, blown a kiss at the Versailles horror, taken back the Saar, rearmed the Fatherland, reclaimed and fortified the Rhineland, won the support of Mussolini, put Franco in power in Spain, returned Austria to Greater Germany, and seized the Sudetenland. Fantastic!"

"Don't forget the Volkswagen, Randelmann. He invented the Volkswagen, too," Stachel said with mock seriousness.

"Oh, God, yes. The Volkswagen. Did you ever see an uglier vehicle, Herr Generalmajor?"

"Well, I'd say it's on a par with the Stuka."

"The Stuka's funny-looking, all right. But it does its job."

"You like flying it?"

"More than anything." He paused with elaborate second-thought. "Well, there's one thing that's a bit better."

Stachel smiled again. "Spoken like a true flier, Randelmann." He sipped his coffee and watched the major's happy eating. It had been a good idea, he told himself, to invite Randelmann to the General Officer's Mess. This way, prying eyes would assume he was merely having a reminiscent lunch with an old flying chum, whereas if Randelmann had been called from his squadron for a closed-door meeting in Stachel's Richterstrasse office, suspicions would have followed. As in the old saying, Stachel mused: if you want to hide something—to keep people from seeing something—put it on the mantel in the parlor.

He decided to get on with it.

"I have a special assignment for you, Randelmann."

The major looked at him quizzically. "Oh?"

"A most secret assignment, which can be handled only if you are to go on two weeks' leave."

Randelmann put down his knife and fork and took a sip of wine. "Well, now," he said, dabbing his lips with his napkin, "as my dear mother used to say, the stew gets thicker."

"Will you do it for me? Go on leave and then do a piece of work?"

"You know I will, Herr Generalmajor. When do you want me to begin?"

Stachel was pleased by the answer. Randelmann had asked when, not what, or who, or why. "At once. I've already determined that you're eligible for a leave and I've already put through the authorization. In anticipation of your application, that is."

Randelmann chuckled again and shook his head. "Amazing. I don't even know I'm going on leave until after lunch and I'm authorized to go *before* lunch. Dare I ask where I've decided to spend my leave, Herr Generalmajor?"

"You'll start in Berlin. At this address." Stachel handed him a slip of paper. "I want you to watch everything that goes on there. You have rented a room across the street, with a window overlooking the house's front entrance and service driveway."

"I'll spend my leave in a rented room in southeast *Berlin?* Good God. I take it back—you're just as bad as all the other Generals. Absolutely sadistic."

Stachel said, "It won't be so bad. The lady you're watching, Frau Elfriede Heidemann, is quite good-looking."

"What am I looking for?"

"I'm not sure. All I know is that a certain inspector of detectives of the Berlin police has suggested that Frau Heidemann and some associates are smuggling Jews and other unfortunates out of Germany, using false papers, and so on."

Randelmann nodded. "And you, in your capacity as an intelligence officer, are afraid that the people being smuggled include in their number certain spies carrying stolen plans for the new Volkswagen, eh?"

"You are very perceptive, Randelmann. But not altogether correct."

The major fell silent for a time, using the interval to lather a slice of bread with what seemed to be several kilos of butter. Then, once he was munching again, he asked the obvious question: "Why are you turning to me for this job, Herr Generalmajor? I'm no counterintelligence agent. I'm a Stuka pilot."

"Because you offer two qualities I can't find in anyone else.

First, you are what the intelligence community calls an untainted body. You have a new face, you have not worked in intelligence before, your presence on any scene does not ring warning bells. Second, you are uncommitted. You have no axes to grind. You do not care enough about me personally one way or another to have ambitions for or against me; And this is important, because I have reason to believe that someone close to me is planning something against me; someone plans either to railroad me—as they did in that old court-martial action you mentioned—or kill me. And my way to the truth, the opening clues, are to be found, I think, with Frau Heidemann. But I can't afford to investigate the matter personally because that may be exactly what my, ah, enemies want me to do. So I need a surrogate to snoop around a bit. I need you."

"So," Randelmann said, "since you don't know what you're looking for, I'm expected to watch everything and report everything to you for a period of two weeks. I'll not be expected to evaluate the information, only pass it on to you. Right, Herr General?"

"Precisely. I'll decide what it means."

"What if I run across something obviously big—important? Significant?"

Stachel handed him another slip. "Call me at this number. Leave your number, then wait at least five minutes. I'll call you back."

Randelmann pushed away his plate, sipped his wine again, and hid a small belch behind his fist. "You're wrong about one thing, Herr Generalmajor."

"What's that, Randelmann?"

"I do care about what happens to you. If it weren't for you, I'd still be sitting on my ass in that officers' candidate school in Stuttgart, teaching fuzz-faced kids how to march and salute. You took me out of that godforsaken nowhere and put me back in a squadron. And so you can be absolutely sure that I'd do anything you want at any time. I'd watch Frau Heidemann's house hanging upside down by my balls, if that's what you wanted. You're the only real friend I've ever had."

Stachel found himself unable to say anything.

"Now," Randelmann said airily, "I want payment."

"Oh?"

"You owe me a piece of that chocolate layer cake I see on the sideboard."

"Hugelmeier's Delicatessen."

"I'd like to price your Sauerkraut."

"Who's calling please?"

"Laub."

"This is Sauerkraut. Eighty-eight."

"Seventy-seven."

"Hello, Laub, old friend. What's new?"

"Regarding the Stachel study—indications are that he isn't being sucked in."

"Too bad. We'll have to move on to Plan B then, eh?"

"Right. I merely wanted your permission to do so."

"That's all on this study?"

"Yes."

"Thank you. Sauerkraut ninety-nine."

"Jasmine."

56

The view was so stupendously beautiful it looked fake, like one of those gaudy, overly articulated backdrops in a Berlin musical.

Stachel had heard many stories about the Berghof and how the Führer had developed it from a simple Tyrolean-style cabin into an incredibly elaborate mountain retreat. Yet he'd always tended to discount them, not only because they had originated with people he knew to be fond of hyperbole but also because the press photos—the Führer resting in the sun, the Führer greeting foreign dignitaries, the Führer playing with his dog—showed only a mountain here and there, a veranda, a distant cloudy sky. But the truth, the reality of the Berghof, perched as it was on the roof of *everything*, defied comprehension; the place was simply more than could be accommodated by a newcomer accustomed to the real world.

His invitation to attend the meeting here had come as a surprise. The common thread in all the gossip was that Hitler received only the most important of his chieftains in the privacy of the aerie, and, while he was indeed a general and a protégé of Fat Hermann, Bruno Stachel could hardly be considered to have enough horsepower to carry him into the Berghof's heavily guarded splendor.

Göring was there, of course, as were Himmler, Heiss, Goebbels, and the ever-present Martin Bormann. He'd not seen Bormann for six months since a drunken brawl at Udet's apartment in Charlottenburg, and was therefore mildly surprised at how even more gross the man had become. But the larger surprise came when, after he'd shaken hands with Bormann and the others, he was taken by the elbow by the Führer himself and led into the garden. Hitler was wearing a gray Alpine walking suit, with knickers, patch pockets and horn buttons and climbing shoes and knee socks. A Tyrolean hat sat rakishly on his head, and he looked every millimeter the country squire. He was very warm and informal, a fact that made Stachel inexplicably ill at ease.

They went down a path bordered by careful plantings. Hitler's large wolfhound snuffling at their heels. There was a raw wind coming off the Alpine peaks, and it hinted snow, and Stachel, feeling the sadness of a dying year, wished he had worn his overcoat.

At a turn in the path, Hitler paused, broke off his murky monologue on music and why Wagner epitomized the German national propensity for great themes, and regarded Stachel amiably.

"You wonder why you are here, alone on a mountain path, with the leader of Greater Germany, eh, Stachel?"

"Of course, my Führer. It's a singular experience."

"Experience? Most men would have said it's a singular honor."

"I'm not most men. I am not a fawner."

"What if I were to command you to fawn?"

"You wouldn't, my Führer. I would have to play-act, since fawning is alien to me. And alien to you is a willingness to put up with the artificial. You, as one of the great figures of history, have no time for anything but pragmatic truth, reality. Therefore you would not indulge in such uncharacteristic sport."

Hitler laughed. "My God, Stachel—you should be a lawyer, the way you twist things around."

Stachel offered no answer, standing quietly, as if appreciating the titanic scene around and below, but actually trying to find a more comfortable position for the weight of his undeniable duplicity.

Hitler raised his walking stick and pointed to the north, across the great valley, to the distant pastels that marked the barely visible city. "That's Salzburg, Stachel. And that way, to the east beyond the horizon, is Vienna, where, as a lad—as a returned war veteran—I lived in abject, humiliating poverty. Have you ever been poor, Stachel?"

"Only in spirit, my Führer."

"Ah. Blessed are the poor in spirit, eh? For theirs is the kingdom of heaven. Christ said that. Christ was wrong. The kingdom of heaven exists only in fairy tales, and I say this with no equivocation born of my childhood Catholicism. The closest we come to heaven, Stachel, is when we reach out—achieve, rise above ourselves.

"The world will soon be mine," Hitler added deliberately. "My heaven will expand to include all of the governable world. Why? Because the rest of the world really doesn't know what to do about me. There is no will to go against me, because the English and the Americans—the only worthwhile nations beyond our own—secretly welcome me as their most effective protection against the Russian menace. I am their outer wall against the Soviet threat. I make the world safe for their capitalism. And while they live in this delusion, I will destroy them. I will destroy both communist and capitalist by turning the force of their own pipe dreams against them."

"Indeed, my Führer," Stachel managed.

"Let's go back. It's getting cold."

As they walked, Hitler said, "I've called you here, Stachel, because I want you to take on a very important assignment. I want you to be the air attaché in Washington."

In a day of surprises, this was the most surprising. Stachel gave the man a quick glance, afraid he might find that it was all a joke.

"Surprised, Stachel?"

"No, sir."

"Oh? Why?"

"Because I'm the best man for the job. The most qualified."

"You're also an egotist."

"No, my Führer. Like you, I'm a pragmatist."

"I see. You have the audacity to compare yourself with me?"

"No. Only with your practical nature."

Hitler gave Stachel a glance at this, his amusement apparent.

"By God, Stachel, I like you. You've got nerve."

"What will happen to General von Boetticher? He's been in Washington for a long time doubling as military and air attaché."

"I'll leave him there awhile, because he charms the Americans. But I need a younger man, ostensibly his understudy, who will tell me what Roosevelt is really doing."

"The Americans are the key to your expansion plans, my Führer. They are, next to the Russians, the only force that can impede you."

"They can do nothing without rearming. And I say they can't rearm in time to give me a problem in my plans for Europe."

"What does von Boetticher say?"

"He agrees with me on this, naturally."

"Then he should indeed be replaced."

"You don't agree with me?"

"No. I know a lot about the Americans. They can accomplish astonishing things if they have a mind to. And I think that if we peeve them enough, they'll swing into rearmament with a speed that could knock our socks off. You and von Boetticher are both wrong."

Hitler nodded reasonably. "All right. Despite my reputation I can take your opposition. I might not be persuaded by your adverse opinion, but I'll listen to it. That's why von Boetticher makes me uneasy. He always agrees with me. With a man like you, if you agree with me I know you truly agree with me. In a game with such astronomical stakes, I need a devil's advocate. Marshal Göring concurs. In fact, it was he who recommended you for this assignment."

"I see. I'm most grateful to him."

"The necessary orders are being drawn. Von Ribbentrop is being advised to facilitate your appointment."

"Very well. When would you like me there, my Führer?"

"As soon as possible. There are certain diplomatic niceties to be observed, and so on, but we're getting along with the Americans pretty well these days and there should be no problems."

There were hot chocolate and sandwiches waiting in the study with the tall windows. Sipping the thick brew, Stachel stood apart from the others, trying to assimilate the shock of his new status.

Göring, enormous in a pale-blue uniform, sauntered over to him eventually. "The Führer's told you?"

"He has. He says I have you to thank for it."

"There's a slight price, Stachel. I like you, of course, and I am much impressed with your technical proficiency, both as an airman and as an intelligence functionary. But even so, a plum like Washington carries a price."

"What's the price, Herr Reichsminister?"

"Those photos you mentioned."

"There are no photos. I made that up to rattle you. I heard some gossip at one of Udet's brawls. The word was that, in an earlier orgy at Ernst's place, you had the Silberstein heiress brought in and tied to a bed, where you raped her publicly to show your contempt for the Jewish race."

Göring's features darkened with undisguised anger. "You've been toying with me?"

"No. Simply trying to live with you."

"Someday, Stachel . . . someday, you'll push me too far."

"Don't hold your breath until then, as the Americans say."

An SS man materialized beside them, ahem-ed, and said in grave tones, "Pardon me, General Stachel, but there is a phone call for you. You can take it in the foyer."

"Very well. Lead on. Excuse me, Herr Reichsminister. You will excuse me, won't you?"

Göring turned away in ruby outrage.

"Stachel here."

"This is Randelmann, Herr Generalmajor."

"Randelmann? Are you out of your mind, calling me here? I gave you the routine—"

"But every minute counts, Herr Generalmajor. A terrible thing is happening. Your parents—"

"My parents? What are you talking about?"

"They are fleeing arrest. The Gestapo called at their home, but the Heidemann woman's group had somehow found out beforehand. She and some friends got to the house first and they've taken your mother and father to Schloss Löwenheim. I trailed them—"

"Are they all right?"

"They seem to be."

"They're very old, Randelmann."

"Yes, sir. And frightened, I think. But they seem to be safe for now."

"Where are you?"

"At the castle."
"I'll be there."

Randelmann hung up and turned to regard his captor. "All right. So it's done."

Laub shifted his pistol to the other hand and nodded agreeably. "Yes. And you did very well. Very well indeed."

"You know that call was monitored, don't you? I could hear the Berghof security people breathing, for God's sake."

"Mm," Laub smiled. "I sincerely hope so. I'm planning on that fact, you see."

"You're framing Stachel?"

"Not exactly. I'm simply making sure that Reichsmarschall Göring has the pleasure of finding General Stachel *in flagrante delicto,* so to speak. To catch him red-handed in an unforgivable, treasonable offense."

57

The sense of unmanageable forces closing in was especially strong as he taxied the FW biplane along the Strip—a military airfield under construction in the Bavarian foothills as a service facility for the security and supply forces stationed at the Berghof. It seemed fairly evident that he had taunted Bormann once too often and the man had begun the process of framing revenge. There was no other logical explanation for trumped-up wireless messages and police harassment of two good old people who spoke their minds too freely.

The irony struck him as he waited for a JU-52 to lumber in for a landing and another, ahead of him, to take off. Less than an hour ago he had been dazzled by his appointment to Washington, one of the most coveted of assignments. And now, sitting in the dust and snarling of a covey of housekeeping planes, he was on the raw edge of arrest. Bormann's palace intrigue seemed fairly clear: Set up Stachel and his parents as sympathizers, if not direct helpers, of an illegal underground aiding enemies of the Reich. Stachel realized he would have to utilize every shred of his rapport with Hitler—he would have to wave his Blood Order under every nose in sight—if he were to survive a prima facie case of treason. Hitler liked him, to be sure, but how much was a question soon to be asked under the severest of circumstances.

The fact remained, though: his parents were in real trouble, and he'd have to see to them at all costs.

He regretted now having told Göring that he planned to fly to the Berghof conference in his FW. Göring had invited him to make the trip from Berlin in the SS executive transport, but he'd declined, since he wanted to make a side trip to Schloss Löwenheim for a visit with the Baroness, whom he hadn't seen for three years.

Well, spilled milk . . .

What made the developing mess more melancholy was the fact that his mother and father had played so thoroughly into Bormann's hands. They, too, being Stachels, were afflicted with the curse of iconoclasm, and so they had, presumably and at long last, said the wrong thing to the wrong person, giving Bormann the legal authority to move against them. Even worse, though, was their apparent willingness to be helped by Frau Heidemann and her group of religious cranks and Jew smugglers. A big mouth could cost a heavy fine these days, but fleeing arrest with enemies of the Reich could bring a long stretch in a KZ, and he doubted that his parents would last a minute in one of those god-awful places. He'd visited one as an official escort for a Swedish Red Cross do-gooder, and although the camp had looked clean and orderly enough, it had had an oppressive, institutional air, and its communal living and military regulation were precisely the wrong circumstance for Ludwig and Emilie Stachel, each of whom had a passion for personal privacy.

Randelmann's naïveté in calling the Berghof had, in a bizarre way, worked to Stachel's probable advantage. Bormann had no doubt been planning some kind of elaborate scene to humiliate him, and now that the Stuka pilot had alerted Stechel, Bormann—tied down as he was in a Führer conference on the Czech crisis—would have to improvise on the theme. Stachel judged that it would take about two hours.

The security system at the Berghof was, according to reports, complex and fast, but human nature favored careful going when officers of general rank were involved. The man who monitored the phones would make a transcript of Randelmann's call, then his superior officer would take a few minutes to evaluate it. This fellow would, in turn, hurry with it to the watch officer, who, being attuned to the Berghof's sensibilities, would hesitate for a time, struggling with the protocol of what to do when a general officer dashes off to see how and why his parents were in trouble with the police. Any man of any worth would rush off to help his parents. So why should a war hero and Blood Order recipient be any different? Do you run, panting, to the chief of Berghof security, and make an ass of yourself? Or do you think it over carefully, amble down the hall to the security office, pour a coffee, then mention, "By the way Chief, look at this odd call that came in for General Stachel during his chitchat with the Führer. Think we should do something about it?" And by the time everyone had agreed that this delicate question should be tried on Himmler, chief of national security—who would then himself deliberate its implications before acting on it—the better part of two hours would have elapsed.

The JU-52s had either come to rest on the strip or disappeared in the sky, and so he booted the biplane into a half-turn, then opened the throttle wide. Skittering along, bouncing, the ship cleared the trees and took him to a thousand meters, where he picked up a westerly heading for Kempten. Settling in his seat, adjusting his goggles, he tried to pick up radio traffic indicating pursuit. There was nothing but the normal gabble, so he began to go over the whole dismal problem again.

He remained deep in thought all the way.

Circling the Schloss twice, he peered over the side for evidence that the Gestapo might already have arrived. The castle, brooding in the cold sunlight atop its craggy island in the grasslands, looked abandoned, lifeless.

He wheeled the ship into the wind and began the descent, realizing with forlorn resignation that he hadn't the foggiest notion what he would do about all this.

Elfi heard the circling plane and, after applying a fresh compress to Herr C's lacerated eye, went to the window to watch it land. It was a silver biplane, and it waggled its wings importantly as it turned at the far end of the meadow and came trundling back.

"It's Bruno," the Baroness said. "That's Bruno's machine."

Elfi glanced at her. "He certainly picked a fine time to visit. Three injured KZ escapees, two clients for Mulhouse, and he comes to say hello to his old lady friend."

The Baroness continued to sponge Herr B's face with water. Her expression was one of complete indifference, and Elfi felt a touch of guilt over having been so testy. The poor woman was still in a shadow world of withdrawal, and even the slightest sign of normality from her was cause for cheer, not irritability. *I should be above my little angers,* she told herself. *A nurse must forgive the sick their little tyrannies.*

"You can stop that now, Lotte. Put down the pan and sponge and go to your room and rest for a time."

"It's Bruno, and I must see him."

"Of course. But first get freshened up a bit, or something. I'll bring him to your room. All right?"

"Bruno is a good man."

"Perhaps. But he does come at an awkward time."

Laub turned from the window in the gatehouse and smiled at Randelmann, who squatted beside the ancient wall and looked sour.

"Well, Major," Laub said, "your friend has arrived at last. Once I settle with him, I'll release you from those leg cuffs and let you stretch a bit."

"Who are you, Laub? Who in hell are you to push me around like this? All I did was rent a room in southeast Berlin, damn it."

"Tut-tut, Herr Major. Easy does it, eh?"

"If I ever get out of this ridiculous situation, I'll haul your lardy arse straight to the cops. To the Gestapo itself, by God."

Laub laughed. "Oh, my. Such an impetuous fellow." He drew a flat folder from his inside jacket pocket and held it open so that Randelmann could read the ID card there.

"You can relax, my dear Randelmann. As you see, I *am* the Gestapo."

"Do those other people out there know that?"

"Certainly not, Randelmann. It's a secret that only you and I share."

58

He swung down from the plane and trotted toward the car as it came to meet him. Ziegel was in the front seat beside Klaus, who was at the wheel.

"What the hell are you doing here, Stachel?" Ziegel said, his face showing good-natured surprise. "Why aren't you in Berlin, running Germany?"

"Where are my parents?"

Ziegel traded meaningful glances with Klaus, who shrugged a shoulder and showed sudden interest in his fingernails. "Aha. So you've heard, eh?" Ziegel said. "How did you hear?"

"Never mind. There's no time. You're due to be raided within the hour."

Klaus showed real interest now, and the way Ziegel looked at him, the subtle air of concern and deference intrinsic to his action, revealed just who was the leader. "Would you explain that, please, General?" Klaus said, his eyes narrowed against the autumn glare.

Stachel climbed into the car's back seat and said, "Let's go. There's no time to debate things out here in the grass."

Klaus apparently caught the sense of urgency. He ground the gears and sent the battered old Horch bouncing over the ruts, squeaking and snorting in rusty protest at being alive after all these years. Stachel leaned forward, placing his hands on the back of Ziegel's seat, noting irrelevantly that Ziegel looked very much the same as he had in the squadron twenty years earlier, except that there was gray in his black hair and deep creases around his raisin-colored eyes. There was also a scar on his lower lip, testimony to the violence that had brought him to this lonely place in the lee of the Alps.

Stachel felt a dreary sense of infinite time and the futility implicit in it.

"I know what you're doing here," Stachel said, trying to keep accusation from his tone. "But the problem is, the SS and the Gestapo also know it, and they're on the way to put a crimp in your hose."

Klaus, his eyes on the castle gate ahead, said, "What *do* you know, Herr Generalmajor? Tell me exactly." There was challenge in his voice, the sound of a man who recognizes the fact of oncoming calamity and tries to delay it with pointless defiance.

"Enough to ruin you. How's this, for instance—a handful of idiotic Christian do-gooders has set up a chain of safe-houses—a kind of underground railroad—by which Jews and others being roughed up by the Nazis can be shipped out of Germany to places where they can claim political asylum. You people are in on all this. You're probably the southern anchor point, or staging area, where the fugitives are given clothes and papers and money for the jump into France or Spain or Portugal or wherever."

The silence of the two men in front was confirmation. Stachel felt he could see the shock and despair in the angle of Ziegel's shoulders. Klaus pulled the car to a halt in the cobblestoned courtyard and, turning in his seat, gave Stachel an evaluating stare. "And," he said, "you say that the Gestapo also knows this?"

"That's why I'm here. To retrieve my old folks before Himmler does." He paused for a splinter of time, then said, "Incidentally, I think you have a hell of a nerve, arbitrarily making fugitives of my people. There's still law in Germany. Still some good lawyers."

Klaus ignored him. Stepping out of the car, he jerked his large head at Ziegel and said quietly, "You know what to do."

"Right. How about A, B, and C?"

"Put them in the farm truck. I'll be along to tell you how to handle it from there." Klaus moving for the castle door, motioned to Stachel. "Come on. We'll have to hurry if you're to see your parents before they leave."

"Leave? They're not going anywhere with you. I'm packing them into the front cockpit of my airplane and flying them out of this hole."

Emilie Stachel was seated beside the bed, an expression of concern on her face as she watched her husband's struggle for breath. He was pale, and his eyes were closed, showing blue lids.

"Hello, Mama," Stachel said from the doorway.

She looked up pulling the shawl more snugly around her thin shoulders. "Bruno? You're here?"

He stood beside her and leaned over to buss her forehead. "How is Papa? Ziegel says he's been sick for two days."

"I'm worried about him, Bruno. He has a fever, and Frau Heidemann says he could have pneumonia. She's watching him closely, although I don't know what she can do without the proper medicines."

"I'm taking you both away from here. I'll get you to a good doctor." He sensed his mother's fear and aloneness, and he was heavy with a great pity, indefinable yet insistent.

"I don't think Papa can be moved. He's so very sick."

Stachel looked down and saw how truly old his father had become. In sleep, he seemed smaller somehow, and Stachel remember how the dead people he'd seen had always appeared to have shrunken from their life size. Perhaps his father was already dead, and the difficult breathing was an illusion—wishful thinking born of a desire to say all the things that had been left unsaid in the irretrievable yesterdays, to speak of his regret for all the little indifferences and dismissals and tacit contempts that had outnumbered the good times between them. "He can't stay here, Mama. The police are coming. They'll take him away, and he'll have no chance to get well."

"What has happened to us, Bruno? Why have Germans become so cruel to each other?" It was the same question she'd asked years before.

"I don't know."

"We've done nothing wrong, your father and I. We've helped people. Our hotel is a place of rest, and who is more weary than those poor, battered, frightened people—"

"You used the hotel as a safe-house? You and Papa were members of the underground?"

"Of course. For two years now."

"Oh, God."

He called down the stairwell to Ziegel, who was packing food in cardboard cartons in the butler's pantry, and together they fashioned a kind of litter from bed boards and sheets. Getting the carrier to the ground floor was an exercise in ingenuity, but they managed it finally, and once outside in the cold sunlight things went a bit easier. With the old man wrapped in blankets on the truck bed and his wife in the cab,

Ziegel climbed behind the wheel and, looking down at Stachel, said, "Coming?"

"Take them to the plane, will you? I've got to look in on the Baroness and Frau Heidemann. I'll be only a minute."

"I'll wait. I'll need your help to get your father into the cockpit."

"By the way, Ziegel—where's Randelmann?"

"Randelmann? Who's he?"

Stachel paused, feeling the freshening wind and catching the scent of the winter coming. For a moment he had the impression that presently he would awaken and this would all prove to have been a touch of delirium, a dark-brown aftermath of temporary madness, like the hangover he'd have in his days of sodden rebellion. We all have to die, he told himself, but how strange it is that a man can die at a place and time so out of context with all that has preceded. "Never mind," he murmured. "He's a man I knew. He's probably dead now."

"Was he supposed to have been here?"

"It doesn't matter anymore." He looked into the cab. "Are you all right, Mama? Are you warm enough?"

"Yes, dear. But hurry. Your father—"

"Only a moment, Mama." He ran inside, calling for the Baroness. He looked for the women in the great hall, in the kitchen, and in the library, but a young woman, apparently a maid, paused in hurrying to say that Frau Heidemann and the Baroness were in the attic of the armory wing, across the courtyard.

He knew there wasn't time.

From his vantage point in the gatehouse, Laub had heard every word spoken by Stachel, Ziegel, and Klaus as they stood by the car in the courtyard below. And so he was now struggling to retrieve a situation that was in no way following the scenario he'd developed in his mind. It should have worked, but he hadn't planned on Stachel's unlikely decision to overrule his parents' intentions to make for Lisbon.

"I'm going to ask you to remain here quietly for a time, Herr Major," he said pensively. "I'll have to gag you and replace your leg cuffs with wrist cuffs. Not comfortable, I know, but we must do what we can with what we have."

Once Randelmann was securely manacled and gagged, Laub gave him a mocking little bow, then let himself out the door, which he padlocked behind him.

Following the tunnel to the ancient drain under the west wall, he left the castle and, keeping close to the hedge line that skirted the lower meadow, he was able to reach the landing strip unseen.

There, lying in the frosted grass under the silver wings, he drew his commando knife from its leg holster and slashed the tires of Stachel's biplane. The machine settled into the turf on its rims, tilted and lugubrious in its sudden uselessness.

When he reached the castle again, Laub found himself hoping that he hadn't made a dreadful mistake.

59

"What do you know of a man named Laub?" Stachel demanded of Ziegel, who stared, flabbergasted, at the airplane's disfigured tires.

"The only Laub I know at all is a Lutheran minister who works with the chain in Berlin. He comes, he goes—"

Stachel, struggling to contain his anger and alarm, said, "Was he here today?"

"No more than an hour ago, I'd say."

"Where is he now?"

Ziegel hunched a shoulder as he always did when puzzled. "I haven't any idea. I heard him say something to Klaus about going to the village to pick up some tobacco. But I don't know. Why?"

"Laub's a cop, you idiot."

"That's absurd."

"I'll bet you haven't heard the bastard praying."

"Well, no, but—"

"Did you ever know a clergyman that didn't break out in prayer at the slightest provocation? My God, man, it's reflex with them. They pray like you blink."

"You think Laub cut your tires?"

"Does anyone else stay with you here at the castle?"

"I don't think I ought to say. Look at you—all sparkling in your Nazi playsuit; medals and all. It just doesn't seem that I should be talking to you about any of this."

"Come on, you imbecile—who *else* is here? We'll be up to our wattles in the Gestapo any minute now."

Ziegel regarded him gravely for a moment, his narrow face the color of saddle leather in the afternoon glow. "Well," he said finally, "besides your papa and mama, there's let's see: Elfi; the Baroness; the Munsers—that's the butler and his wife; the Effelmanns, who work in the kitchen; the two upstairs maids, Gerda Rolf and Sophi Wilke; Alois Steiner, the chauffeur and his wife and two kids. Then in the attic we have three gentlemen we call A, B, and C, because we don't know their names."

"Why not?"

"They're escapees from a KZ—Dachau, I'd guess. They were found in a swamp near the Starnberger See by friends of Alois who work in the Harlaching safe-house. You wouldn't believe the shape they're in. I don't know how they're still alive."

"Why were they brought here?"

"Because Elfi Heidemann is a marvelous nurse, that's why. She could really be a doctor. She's kept a lot of us alive."

Stachel stepped around the truck and, opening the door, took his mother's hand and squeezed it reassuringly. "I'll ride in back with Papa," he said. "To be sure he's comfortable."

"Will everything be all right, Bruno?"

"Certainly. Just be patient, eh?" He peered through at Ziegel, who was climbing behind the wheel again. "Let's go. I want to get a look at A, B, and C."

The attic was an enormous cavern of crisscrossed beams, cobwebs, and shadows lighted only by the reflected glow from ventilation louvers in the gables. They had reached it by climbing a series of narrow, dark stairs, and at one end, near the jut of a chimney column, there was a cleared area with a solitary electric bulb dangling above it. Stachel did not recognize the woman who knelt there, rolling up some bedding, until Ziegel said, "Where did they go, Lotte?"

She looked up at them, her face half in shadow, and Stachel experienced a great internal sinking, a kind of subsidence of the soul. For him the Baroness had always been the statement of eternal womanhood, an articulation of the abstraction Goethe had labeled "das Ewig-Weibliche," and to see her now was to lift the lid of hell. Her hair was bone-white, held back tight in a peasant's bun, and her eyes, once so animated and full of teasing wisdom, were like old coins. She was thin, and her hands showed blue veins in the stark illumination. "The men came," she said in a toneless voice, "and let them down on the ropes. They are being put in the wagon."

"Hello, chum," Stachel said softly. "I've missed you."

Ziegel touched his elbow. "Come on, Stachel. Leave her here. There's a lot to be done below. Every minute counts now."

Stachel bent to take her cold hand. He looked into her eyes, seeking a trace of the ancient laughter, the soft knowing, the essence; somewhere behind that flat and colorless stare was the amusing, moody, intensely alive woman who had given him her warmth and understanding and indulgence, but for all his peering, there was nothing left of it all, and he was unspeakably sad. "Good-bye, chum. I'll see you soon, perhaps."

They went down as they had come, through the long corridors, across the upper foyer, down the grand stairway to the banquet hall and, from there, through the terrace doors to the steps leading to the driveway. Ziegel said nothing as they went, and Stachel suspected that the silence was a calculated decency, a period of grace to enable him to absorb and tame the distress of old memories revised by new truth.

There was a truck in the driveway, heavily loaded with hay, and three men on stretchers lay on the ground beside it. Elfi Heidemann, Klaus, and two men in Tyrolean farm clothes fussed at them, tucking in blankets and making gentle, reassuring sounds.

Ziegel said, "The Herr Generalmajor wants to inspect our wounded."

The others paused to look at Stachel, who suddenly felt as if he had perpetrated a grossness. Hating the apologetic tone he heard in his voice, he said, "I'm just counting people. I'll only be a moment."

They were ghastly. Each was so grotesquely marred, so cruelly bruised, as to be a caricature. One had lost an eye; another's nose was split from tip to bridge and his lips were like slabs of bacon; the third's ears were missing. Their heads were shaven, and they were cadaverous from malnutrition. They'd been washed, but there was a smell about them that was barely tolerable.

"God, oh God," Stachel said, feeling nauseated.

"Herren A, B, and C," Elfi said beside him. "They are no better or no worse than others I've seen."

Ziegel said, "Now you know why I'm so grateful to you Stachel. You can see for yourself what you saved me from."

"How did they escape in this shape?" Stachel managed.

"I don't think they did," Ziegel answered, his voice low. "I have an idea they were dumped off a truck or something. Who knows?"

Elfi sighed. "One thing for certain—they'd not been fed or treated for days. I'm not sure they'll make it."

"Who would do something like this?" Stachel said, realizing at once how silly he sounded.

"Welcome to the Third Reich, Generalmajor Bruno Stachel," Elfi said without emotion.

"Where are you taking them?" he asked Klaus.

"Cross-country to a small village inn, where the proprietor is friendly and has a large attic. We would not be able to exist today if it weren't for attics."

"The others?"

"Each of us has an assigned vehicle that will take him to his assigned hiding place."

"Well, you'd better be about it," Stachel said nodding at the eastern sky. "Those who disagree with you are about to arrive."

A JU-52, a burnished gray, rumbled in a wide turn above the valley. The black crosses on its wing showed briefly as it came about into the wind, descending with flaps extended, propellers glinting as three matched discs.

"Quick," Klaus shouted, "get these stretchers on the truck. You, Alois, get to the Horch and be sure the Steiners and their kids are in it." Looking harriedly at Stachel he said, "How much time?"

"Another five minutes. He's making his approach too high for that strip of grass. He'll have to go around again."

"Good. Are you with us, Generalmajor? Or are you going to sit this out and wait for your buddies up there?"

There it was, Stachel thought. The question. The question that had been murmuring in the back of his mind since that steaming Saturday morning on the lawn at Wannsee, when Rudi had gurgled and smelled of blood and called for his Mutti. All of his life had been a statement of protest against double standards, against the hypocrisies of a society laying claim to Christian ethics but operating from a base in diabolism. And, eventually, when it seemed beyond resolution or compromise, he'd tried to drink it away, only to find that it was still there, bleak and baleful and malignant, in the cruel dawn of the hangover. He was a soul-brother of that wretched crone in the attic: he would someday most surely have been her counterpart if he had, as she had, succumbed to the need for release from the impossible conflict. Yet here he was, still weighing, still deliberating, still wondering where he stood in the eternal contradiction of Word and Deed. Do you, Bruno Stachel, believe that there is a God and he loves you? Well, then, Bruno Stachel God loves Germany, and he is with us in our struggle against the French and English and American infidels. We are God's beloved, while they are spewed from God's mouth; we are righteous, they are sinners. Gott mit Uns! Do you, Bruno Stachel, believe that Adolf Hitler is the savior of the Fatherland, the architect of a thousand years of peace under a world ruled by an all-wise, benign Germany? Then why do you question Rudi's death, the bombing of sleepy Spanish villages, the splitting of Jewish noses, the theft of other lands, the bullying of old people who open their homes, their hotels, their lives to succor the bleeding and the lost? Where is the conflict in what the Führer says and what he does? Eh? More precisely, Bruno Stachel: Do you want to struggle to keep your privilege and power and material comfort? Do you want indeed to go to Washington as the military plenipotentiary of what seems destined to become the most powerful nation in Europe, perhaps the world? Or do you want to ally yourself with this pathetic band of malcontents, and thereby lose it all?

"What are your plans for my parents, Klaus?"

"Alois will drive them to Freiburg in the Mercedes."

"What happens there?"

"They cross the Rhine and enter France, north of Mulhouse. Via potato barge."

"All right. I'll go with them, then."

"To France? Then to Lisbon?"

"To France. Then to Lisbon."

Klaus gave Stachel a long, speculative look, his eyes traveling slowly over the uniform, its ribbons.

"It's a big step for you, eh, Generalmajor? Giving up your career, your honor?"

"Honor? What honor?"

"All right, then. Let's go. We still have time, I think."

"Correction, gentlemen," said someone behind them. "You have no time at all."

They turned, quickly, surprised, to confront a tall man with sunken cheeks, an aquiline nose, and eyes like peeled grapes. He was holding a Luger pistol on them, and he was wearing the crisp black uniform of an SS Obersturmführer.

Behind him, standing with rifles at the ready, were four helmeted troopers, silent and unmoving like black ghosts.

RADIO TRANSCRIPT

Forschungsamt.

Berlin
13/IX/38 file: 337K

Memo to officer in charge:

1. Reference proceding 10 (10) messages this file.
2. Station L intercepted coded wireless message this date.
3. Transmission began 14:30 hours, ended 14:30:34.
4. Point of origin: Kempten area, co-ordinates A Map: 17N16E.
5. Code, having been broken, provided following text:

To Sauerkraut from Dagger: Situation grave. Stachel on hand but not, repeat not, conforming to plan B. Apprehension and collapse of system imminent.

6. Will keep you advised.

Linck
Radio Intercept

60

The SS officer's name was Pohl. Stachel learned this when he heard one of the troopers reporting that the castle was being searched and stragglers would be brought at once to the courtyard, where the other prisoners had been assembled. Pohl had nodded absently, standing silently in the fretful

Alpine breeze, smoking a cigarette and pondering what must have been matters of great significance.

Stachel had removed his jacket and placed it around his mother's shoulders. She'd complained of the chilly wind, and he had heard her sneeze twice—a bad sign, because she was given to colds that hung on interminably and caused her much distress. His father was half awake in her arms, apparently recovering, since he no longer babbled about the need to polish the floor of the lobby in the Bad Schwalbe hotel.

The others sat on the cobblestones in the deepening shadows of the courtyard, mute and disconsolate. Only the children—a boy about eight and his sister, a year or so younger—showed any animation, asking Pohl if they could go to the bathroom, but getting no answer and finally doing their business behind the rain barrel. Elfi had sought to attend to the motionless men on the stretchers, but a trooper had shoved her away and ordered her to sit down and be still.

Once the airplane had landed, Pohl sent two men to meet it in Alois' Mercedes touring car. Snarling and flattening the meadow grasses, the big trimotor made a final turn into the wind, roared for a full five seconds at full throttle, then subsided into a soft ticking and a conclusive gasp. Its door opened and a uniformed man stepped out, importantly, to enter the car.

When the Mercedes pulled through the castle gate, the newcomer's face was easy to see in the lowering sunlight.

It was Bormann, of course.

The SS squad, assembled in unit front, crashed to attention.

Pohl strode to the car, opened the door, stepped back, and gave a stiff-armed salute. Bormann climbed out, grinning.

"Well, Pohl, you did well. Very well indeed." Bormann regarded the little knot of captives with a jolly glance and then considered the ramrod Pohl again. "At ease, man. At ease. Did you have any trouble?"

"No, sir. As soon as we got your call at Kempten we brought a squad truck as far as the village of Ringhausen, just beyond that ridge over there. We came in deployed, cut off escape routes, and watched the suspects from cover until your plane arrived. We then arrested the principals and held them for your personal instructions. Quite routine, sir." Pohl's voice was softly hoarse, as if it hurt him to talk.

"Good, good. Göring will be pleased. As will the Führer himself, of course."

Pohl, a good soldier, said nothing, letting the compliment speak for itself.

"Tell me, Pohl—is there a good car available to take me to Munich this evening? I brought the plane to return the captives to Stadelheim prison, and, since it's rigged for paratroop duty and uncomfortable as sin, I certainly don't want to ride with them."

"Of course not, sir. The touring car there belongs to the castle owner, I believe, so I'm sure it won't be needed here."

"Good. Good." Bormann paused, then turned to beam at Stachel. "Well, now," he said, "you've certainly got yourself in a pretty mess this time."

Stachel said nothing, keeping his eyes on the valley beyond the castle gate.

"Göring has some very special plans for you, Stachel. He is, I must confess, terribly upset over your phone call at the Berghof and your incomprehensible associations here. He has asked me to tell you that he will visit you at Stadelheim for long chats on the matter."

"See that cow there in the valley, Bormann? Why don't you toddle on down and shove your head up its ass?"

Bormann was about to answer when a Scharführer hurried down the steps, puffing, to show Obersturmführer Pohl a short-wave radio.

"I found it under the eaves of the south tower, sir," the man said triumphantly. "It was hidden between some beams. A weird old woman was up there, too. Schulz is bringing her down presently."

Stachel glanced at Klaus, who gave a barely perceptible shrug and shake of his head.

"Ah," Bormann said, examining the radio and turning its dials, "the plot thickens. We now have evidence of espionage. Excellent work, Scharführer. Please place the radio in the Mercedes and wrap it in the lap blanket so it won't be damaged. Our people in Forschungsamt will like to have a go at it."

Bormann gave Stachel a calculating stare, sardonic amusement in his eyes. "It would have come to this soon, Stachel. You were heading for trouble, you know. I've become very irritated with your condescension, your contempt for me, your blindness to my real importance."

"Your importance? What importance does an errand boy have? Hitler's the man I watch, not his flunky."

Bormann laughed. "That's been your mistake, Stachel. Your inability to read me. I might be in the background now. But 'Dolf listens to me. He hears what I say when all the others can't get through. Nobody but 'Dolf takes me seriously. And I assure you, Stachel—when 'Dolf is gone, I will be there. Germany, the National Socialist world, will take me very seriously indeed."

There was a stir and two men emerged from the gloom of the archway leading to the stable house. One, who was wearing a Luftwaffe uniform, had his hands cuffed behind him, while the other man, who was dressed in a gray suit, brandished a pistol and looked uncomfortable doing it.

"I'll be damned," Bormann laughed. "Laub. What in hell are you doing here?"

The man in the suit nodded pleasantly. "Hello, Bormann. What else would I be doing here? Gestapo business, of course. I've trailed this Randelmann character all the way from Berlin. An elusive bastard. He's a top priority suspect in the Sauerkraut thing Reichsminister Göring's been looking into. I'd like permission to place him on your airplane. You are flying to Berlin?"

"Munich. Stadelheim prison," Bormann said amiably.

"How did you escape our search, Herr Laub?" Pohl wanted to know. His manner was that of one who has been upstaged.

"I did not escape it. I introduced myself to your sergeant as he was investigating the hay barn."

"Is that so, Sergeant Baumer?"

"That is correct, Herr Obersturmführer. He showed me his credentials."

"Why did you not tell me of his presence?"

"I do not readily interfere in matters concerning the Gestapo, Herr Obersturmführer. And Herr Laub asked me to keep his presence confidential until he could find his suspect. It appears he has done so."

"I found him cowering in a wine cellar," Laub said cheerily. "Don't blame your sergeant, Obersturmführer. He did well."

Bormann said, "Laub, can't you place your suspect overnight in Stadelheim with the others while you and I drive up? We can stop for a good dinner on the way, then you can fly on to Berlin tomorrow."

"That would be capital, Bormann. But I've chased the man so far and long I don't want him out of sight for a minute.

I'm going to keep him manacled and under my pistol the whole way. All right if I take this plane on to Berlin after it unloads your group?"

"Certainly. There'll be a couple of troopers aboard to guard the prisoners. By the way, do you have a set of cuffs for Stachel? I'd hate to have a famous ace with his hands free when he's near a plane."

"I have some leg irons. That should do it."

Bormann glanced at the SS officer. "See to it."

Pohl snapped his fingers at the Scharführer. "Baumer, drive Herr Laub and his prisoner to the plane. And tell the pilot to start the engines. We'll be loading shortly."

"What's the disposition of your other men, Pohl?" Bormann asked crisply.

"Besides Baumer, I have these three men. A fourth is bringing a prisoner from upstairs. The remaining five are with the truck at the foot of the hill, guarding the only road access to town."

Bormann nodded. "Very well. Leave the truck where it is for the moment. Have these men march the prisoners to the plane. Except for Stachel's parents. Have a man take them into the castle and hold them as hostages." He gave Stachel another amused wink. "This will doubly assure that our brave general will remain docile throughout the trip, since a move from him will bring disaster to the old gray heads he loves so well."

Stachel struggled to deal with despair. He watched dully as Laub and the Scharführer bundled Randelmann into the old Horch and drove off, clattering down the lane to the meadow. *Poor Randelmann,* he thought. *How badly he's been used.* The feeling deepened to the point of physical pain when he saw a broad-faced trooper, rifle slung on a shoulder, haul the elder Stachels erect and push them roughly through the gate to the castle's shadowy cellars. His mind went to his childhood and the day his parents had gone to the funeral of a friend in Stuttgart; he had felt an unbearable loneliness as they boarded the train at Idstein, leaving him on the platform with Frau Gruber, the neighbor lady, and the absolute sureness that he'd never see his mother and father again. *We never truly grow up,* the memory told him. *We are all children who fear abandonment.*

The wind had died, and in the stillness Stachel heard a footfall on the stone steps, a whisper of fabric, and he looked around to see one of the SS men descending with a woman. It took a moment for him to absorb the fact that it was the Baroness. It was seeing the past as one sees it in a museum: the mink turban with stole and hem to match, and the stately calf-length coat; the mink muff held demurely before her; the prim stepping in the elegant pumps. She'd done something with her hair, too, and her lips and cheeks had been rouged. She looked, Stachel thought with a crawling of his skin, rather like a waxen figure depicting the Roaring Twenties, stiffly articulated and energized by storage cells.

"Sir," the SS man said to Obersturmführer Pohl. "I came across this lady in one of the attic rooms."

She crossed the courtyard and stood before Pohl, her face blank, her eyes opaque. Drawing a hand from the muff, she took what appeared to be a folded paper from under her arm and handed it to him. "I'd like you to read this," she said tonelessly.

Pohl opened the paper and Stachel felt a crushing sense of foreknowledge—an in-rushing of horror.

It was a copy of the *Illustrierte Zeitschrift*, and as Pohl looked up questioningly at her, she said, "It's a magazine. Like the one my son was reading."

Pohl sighed, riffled through the pages again, and told his man, "Get this old hag out of here."

As if he were watching a slow-motion film, Stachel saw the Baroness remove a pistol from the muff. In a stiff outthrust of her arm she aimed and fired six shots through the magazine—six flat-sounding snaps that sent little pieces of paper flying and tiny curls of dust lifting from Pohl's tunic.

Pohl dropped the magazine, peering down at his chest as if checking for lint, and then half-turned, seeming to look for a place to sit down. He paused to regard the Baroness with great seriousness once more, then crumpled in on himself.

There was no sound.

Stachel sensed, rather than saw, the store-dummy immobility of the men and women, the curious stares of the children, the shocked rigidity of the troopers.

Then suddenly Bormann was there. He raised his pistol against the mink turban and fired, and the Baroness spun around in a final pirouette.

There was a scream, and the stop-action motion continued, with Ziegel running to the fallen woman, holding up a hand and shouting, "Stop! Don't shoot anymore. She's—"

Bormann fired again, twice.

"Jesus God," Stachel whispered, watching Ziegel's bloody sprawl.

Bormann, eyes glazed with outrage and bloodlust strode across the cobblestones, slamming a new magazine into the grip of his pistol. "Let's remove some more excess baggage, shall we?" he rasped. "Let's lighten our planeload by a Jew or two."

He emptied the magazine into the three stretchers, the tacky arenas for the mute and anonymous strugglings of Herr A, Herr B, and Herr C.

"Goddamn your eyes," Bormann said to no one in particular. "No one shoots my officers. No one insults me in that way."

The sounds of firing had brought both the Horch—with a concerned Laub at the wheel—and the SS squad truck careening into the courtyard. Laub swung out of the car, eyes wary, pistol poised. "What in hell's going on?" he demanded.

Bormann, pale with the aftermath of fury, waved a reassuring hand. "It's all under control, Laub. One of the prisoners resisted, and there was some shooting."

"Are you sure you don't want me to take Stachel to the plane with me?"

"No. I want him to walk. With the other swine. His days of special treatment are over."

"Very well, then. I'll get back. I can't risk that shifty Randelmann's being alone too long."

As the Horch backed around and headed out the gate, Bormann returned the stare of the young officer stepping down from the idling squad truck. "Who are you, Untersturmführer?"

"Siegfried Lehr, sir. Section leader in Obersturmführer Pohl's command, sir."

Bormann shoved his pistol into his topcoat pocket. "All right, tell your driver to move the truck out of my way. I've called the Berghof and the Führer wants me to return there at once. Remind Laub, the Gestapo man who was just here, that I'll see him in Munich tomorrow. Stadelheim prison at eleven hundred hours."

"Yes, sir."

Bormann's small eyes traversed the courtyard slowly, as if he comprehended for the first time the fact that he had just slain five people. Then, collecting himself and sneering a bully's defensive sneer, he threw the car in gear and drove down the lane to the driveway, disappearing eventually in a drift of dust.

Untersturmführer Lehr nodded at one of his men. "Wiegel,

I'm going to call headquarters for instructions as to what to do with the corpses. Meanwhile, you and Knabe and Hassler get these people on their feet. And if we're to take the dead ones to Munich, they can carry them to the plane."

"As ordered, sir."

To the men in the truck, Lehr said, "You are not at ease. I don't expect any more trouble from these ragamuffins, but keep your eyes open and your weapons ready."

The sky had taken on the blue of autumn, and the clouds running before the winds aloft were lacy and pink with the sunset to come, and Stachel felt a chill.

He knelt beside Elfi and touched her shoulder, but she continued to ponder Ziegel's chalky face.

"Elfi?"

"Yes, Ziegel."

"Is that your hand?"

"Yes."

"I love you."

"Dear Ziegel."

"I hurt. Very much."

"It won't last long, Ziegel."

"I'm afraid, too."

"Don't be. God loves you."

"Do you believe that?"

"I know that."

"Nobody has ever loved me. Why should God?"

"If somebody as bad as I can love you, Ziegel, why shouldn't somebody as good as God?"

There was a long interval, and then Stachel said quietly, "Come on, Frau Heidemann. He's gone."

"Dear Ziegel."

"He was a good man."

The children were whimpering, and one of the women—what was her name? Frau Steiner?—made brave little sounds of reassurance. The others walked in silence, their shoes rustling in the meadow grass. Stachel brought up the rear, feeling the coming snows in his bones and smelling the distant pines.

The plane's engines ticked softly, propellers making silvery flickerings in the darkening afternoon. Scharführer Baumer leaned against the fuselage, watching without interest as the knot of prisoners and the three guards made their halting approach around the Horch, parked in dusty solitude near the big plane's wing tip. "Come on, Wiegel," he called grumpily, "let's hurry it up. If we get to Munich before nightfall I'll arrange something for us with Gretl."

"Just so it isn't a something that looks like the one Gretl set up for me last time. What a beast she was."

They shared laughter over this old intimacy, and then Baumer turned to clamber up the ladder and disappear inside the plane. Wiegel and the other two troopers stood to one side and motioned the prisoners aboard. Stachel held back to take Elfi's elbow.

"Are you all right?"

"I think so," she murmured.

He saw that she was still in shock. "Hold on to me."

"Ziegel is dead. He was there. He smiled. And then he wasn't there."

When the others were aboard he helped her up the ladder and then followed her into the plane to find two Luftwaffe pilots and Scharführer Baumer huddled on the floor, tied together and gagged, amid the silent, impassive collection of church workers.

Laub smiled at him and said in a low voice, "Welcome aboard, Herr Generalmajor. The Refugee Special is about to leave for la belle France."

As Stachel was about to speak, Laub held a finger to his lips. Then he stepped to the door and called, "You men—come aboard for a moment, will you? Baumer and I need your help to tie these people up."

The SS men clambered up the steps to be met by Laub's machine pistol. "Thank you, gentlemen. Now please place your rifles on the floor and hold your hands to the wall. That's it. Very good. Tie their feet, Klaus, then their hands, as before."

"Who are you, Laub?"

"Later, Stachel. First we must jettison these pieces of SS baggage so Major Randelmann can get us airborne."

"Randelmann?"

"He's in the cockpit, waiting for you to join him."

"My parents are still back there," Stachel said calmly.

"There's nothing we can do to help your parents. Every second counts."

"Take these others to France, if that's what you want. I'm staying here."

A redness appeared on Laub's bland face. "You, Generalmajor, are the reason for all this. It's you we want in France."

"We? Who's we?"

"Klaus," Laub commanded, "roll these soldiers out the door as the plane starts to move. Alois, go forward and tell Randelmann to take off."

Stachel shook his head. "Not yet. Give me five minutes."

"Sorry."

"Well, chum, if you went to all this trouble you surely won't shoot me. And that's what you'll have to do to keep me from driving that Horch to the Schloss and retrieving my mama and papa."

"Stachel—"

"Wait if you want. Take off if you want. But I'm taking five minutes."

Laub sighed and rolled his eyes in exasperation. "Well, then, you'll need some help. But let's hurry."

"Who are you, Laub?"

"Be quiet and keep driving. I'm thinking."

As they rattled into the courtyard, Laub said, "Make a U-turn and park the car facing the gate. Let me do the talking."

The Untersturmführer tossed away a cigarette and motioned his men to the ready. He left the squad truck and strode officiously through the blue shadows to peer at them through the Horch's side window. "What are you doing back here, Herr Laub? And with Stachel?"

"I've decided to take Stachel's parents with us on the plane." plane."

"Well, now," Lehr said hesitantly, "Herr Bormann was quite specific. The old people are to be hostages."

"I'm under the direct and special orders of Göring himself. If you'd like to call him and ask if Bormann's instructions are to have precedence over his, please do so. He won't like it, of course, but at least you'll know."

There was a mixture of suspicion and anxiety in the officer's steel-blue eyes as he struggled with the classic human problem of which unbending force to bend to. He took the logical course and gave in to the force most immediately at hand. Over his shoulder he snapped, "Zimmerman, run inside and tell Kruger to bring the old people out."

Stachel said, "I'd like to give them a hand. They're quite old, and my father's ill."

Lehr glanced at Laub, and the Gestapo man nodded, "It's all right. Have your man lead Stachel in. Meanwhile, I'll join you for a smoke."

He went into the damp cavern under the Schloss, and with the two SS men ambling behind, he managed to get them into the daylight. His mother had been crying; her eyes were puffy and inflamed, and her arm trembled when he took it.

"Can we go home now, Bruno?" his father asked.

"We'll see, Papa. Just come out and get in the car." He felt a sadness, as he tried to keep the old ones from seeing the still ones in the shadows of the great wall. Ziegel, with the thin shoulders and the thoughtful dark eyes; Lotte, with homes all over the world, and nowhere to feel at home; Herren A, B, and C, silent nobodies no one would miss, lying there now because they had sinned against the Great Gray God in the Berghof. Such a silly thing to be shot for, after all.

Suddenly a voice called out in the distance. As his eyes followed the sound, he could see a man in black staggering away from the airplane in the meadow, waving his hands and shouting.

"Escape! They're escaping! Stop them—"

There was a faraway popping, and the man went down in the grass, kicking.

Laub and Untersturmführer Lehr dropped their cigarettes to face each other in an odd, side-stepping crouch. Without removing his eyes from Laub's, Lehr shouted to his men, "Something's going on—seize—"

Laub's machine pistol stuttered, and the officer and one of his troopers collapsed, sacklike.

"Quick, Stachel!" Laub roared. "Into the car! For God's sake—get into the car!"

Stachel, unseeing and devoid of thought or emotion, shoved his parents into the back seat. Then he leaped into the driver's seat, groping for the gear shift. There were cracking sounds, and he felt the car rock as a tire went flat, and glass tinkled. His mother began to call on the Father, Son, and Holy Ghost.

Raised on an elbow, Lehr called, "Halt! In the name of the Führer!" He aimed his machine pistol and fired, but Laub leaped to fill the window beside Stachel, precisely in time to catch four shots in his chest and belly.

His words were part moan, part command, part plea. "Get out of here, Stachel . . . hurry . . ."

Another burst of fire lifted Laub from his feet and hurled him against the car with a wet slamming noise. And then he was gone, and Stachel had the Horch in a screeching lurch for the gate.

As they boarded the plane, Stachel saw the SS squad truck bouncing and skidding across the meadow in full chase, its machine gun knocking. A heavy answering chatter sounded in the airplane's topside gun station, and Stachel saw tracers smash the truck's radiator to steaming junk.

"Nice shooting, Klaus," he called from below.

"Stop the speeches and get this thing in the air. The truck's out of commission, but those troopers aren't."

Randelmann was in the pilot's seat, swearing bitterly, and Stachel thought distractedly that it must be very offensive to these good church folk to hear such foul language. They sat on the paratrooper benches, holding on to parts of the plane to steady themselves against the jouncing. The little girl was still crying, the sound of it lost in the engine roar and the clanking and squeaking as the huge metal machine taxied into the wind.

"Son of a bitch!" Randelmann said. "Son of a bitch!"

"What's wrong, Randelmann?"

"That SS man shot me when he escaped from the plane. I always get a little irritable when I've been shot."

"Where were you hit?"

"How in hell do I know? What do you think I am, a frigging surgeon, or something?"

"Alois, take hold of Randelmann and pull him out of the seat," Stachel shouted over the noise. "I'm taking over."

Stachel felt the wetness of Randelmann's blood on the cushion. He managed to get the airplane around, heading upwind along the field's long axis. Easing the throttles to full open, he sent the large machine hurtling along the grass strip, and it seemed forever before the buoyancy could be felt. Somewhere in the mad racing was the sound of hail rattling on the wings, and the windshield suddenly displayed two holes surrounded by silvery starbursts.

They were aloft finally, but one of the engines was losing power and ejecting an oily mist.

"Why are you flying southwest, Stachel?" Klaus shouted in his ear. "That way is Switzerland. France is west by northwest. Our friends—our work—are in France."

Stachel kept his eyes on the unfamiliar instruments. He'd had an hour or two on JU-52's, but long ago, and he was feeling his way now. "There's an outside chance we can make Lehr think we're after asylum in Switzerland. That's only sixty kilometers from here. So—if he bites—he'll assume we're out of reach before he can arouse the Luftwaffe into doing something about us."

"What else might he think?"

"That we're doing what we're doing—flying southwest to fool him. He'll expect that when we're out of sight we'll head for the nearest piece of France, about two hundred kilometers from the Schloss. And so he'll try to set up a fighter interception somewhere near Freiburg on the Rhine."

"Does the Luftwaffe have time for that?"

"It depends on how good Lehr is on the phone. The nearest fighter stations are at Karlsruhe and Stuttgart. The trick is to get the fighters in the air in the next fifteen minutes. If he does, and the pilots are lucky, they could spot us just this side of the Rhine east of Mulhouse. In time for one or two good passes at us."

"That's a jolly thought."

"How are things among the passengers?"

"Randelmann was grazed in the buttocks. Bled a lot, but nothing serious. The little girl's head was badly cut by a splinter. Elfi's doing what she can for them."

He had read Lehr correctly.

Over the village of Hinterzarten, about thirty kilometers from the Rhine, two dots appeared in the sky off their starboard wing. The setting sun caught their surfaces and sent out dull sparklings as they came around in a long turn from the north.

They look like pale minnows in a pond, Stachel thought.

"Have you ever shot birds, Klaus?"

"Some."

"Lead them as you would ducks."

Stachel took the airplane down to fifty meters, flying contour with his wheels barely clearing treetops, power lines, roofs. He knew that there was no way to outfly the fighters coming at them, so the alternative was to make it impossible for the MEs to slide under him for a belly attack and to keep them off balance elsewhere by harassing fire from Klaus's topside machine gun.

From there on, it was up to Elfi Heidemann's God.

Klaus began to fire too soon. But it made little difference because the MEs seemed suddenly to be all around them, darting, little twinklings of yellow at their gun ports. The hail sounds were savage, tearing at them, and Stachel felt the ship's trembling. Then the fighters were beyond, climbing out for another gunnery run.

He heard shouting and wailing in the cabin behind, and for a mad moment he thought that his passengers were cheering their own impending destruction. But a glance showed them cowering together, and he found it possible to think: *Poor devils, they've had a terrible afternoon.*

Insanely, he wanted to laugh.

"Are we going to make it?"

"Why have you left the gun, Klaus?"

"No more ammunition."

The cockpit was suddenly lighted by a yellow flare.

"We've got a fire," Stachel said. "The starboard engine is afire."

"Good God," Klaus groaned.

"Tell everybody to brace themselves for a hard landing. This airplane is finished."

"Get us across the Rhine, Stachel. Please. I don't want to die in Germany. I don't want to give those people the satisfaction."

"Hurry, Klaus. Tell the others we're going in."

From the corner of his eye, Stachel saw the MEs attempting another pass for the *coup de grâce*. But they held their fire—presumably because of the nearness of French territory—and, lifting in a giant, arching turn in the golden twilight, disappeared in the eastern dusk.

The fire was burning intensely now, an incandescence that trailed in a roiling brown smoke. Over the water, the plane bounced badly, and Stachel feared for a moment that its aerodynamics were succumbing to the heated air and there would be an uncontrollable falling away. But then they were on the other side, and, after a seesawing descent over a row of farm buildings, he let the ship settle into a broad pasture—bouncing, swerving, rising for a last time, then sliding sidewise to a halt against an embankment.

With the help of Klaus and Alois, he got everybody out before the wreck erupted in a towering bonfire.

61

Strange, Doubet thought, how we assign to people certain broad characteristics from which they must not stray. The English: excessively formal and bland. The Spanish: glib and artful. The Dutch: stolid and aloof. The Italian: voluble and naïve. The German: coarse and egocentric. Yet for each of these stereotypes he had himself seen more exceptions than the rule, and even in France, where the world expected all natives to be excitable and emotional, there were the slow-moving inhabitants of Picardy, the sharp-bargaining Normans, the moony Celts of the Breton coast, the glum and hostile Lyonese, the raucous connivers of Marseilles. In fact, the only truly excitable Frenchman he had known was his brother, Etienne, long dead in the mud of Verdun, and the excitability had really been little more than the effervescence of boyhood, which Etienne had never had the time to outgrow. No, if he were to assign a single trait to the Frenchman—a trait common to most—it would be solemn reserve. And if he were to label the essence of his country it would be with a single word: politic. France and her Frenchmen were politic, and therefore cool and wary and tactful and cunning all in one. And for all his square, blond, biggish, German construction, it was precisely this quality he espied in Generalmajor Bruno Stachel, late of the Nazi Luftwaffe and now a refugee extraordinaire.

Stachel, crisp in a soft Harris tweed jacket, turtleneck sweater, and flannel trousers, was standing by one of the high windows of the Mulhouse government building watching the morning traffic below. He turned and regarded Doubet with a level, noncommittal gaze.

"Good day, Generalmajor," Doubet said in German, feeling oddly like a bellboy greeting a wealthy guest. "You're looking fit today."

"Thank you, Colonel. And thank you for arranging some clothes. How are my parents?"

"The clinic advises me that your father is recovering from his influenza. Your mother," he added wryly, "is sitting up in bed and asking for something to read."

Stachel showed a faint smile. "And the others?"

"Otto Munser and the young lady, Gerda Rolf, were, as you know, rather badly wounded by aircraft machine-gun fire. They will recover. One of the children, the girl, has a nasty head cut from a flying splinter. The others are doing well after treatment for shock."

"How about Major Randelmann?"

Doubet permitted himself a smile here. "His wound was a graze, which today, apparently, he views more as an embarrassment than anything else."

"I'd like to look in on them all again."

"Of course."

"But first, you want to interrogate me?" Stachel's question was actually a statement, Doubet noted.

"You are not a prisoner, Generalmajor Stachel. You are free to return to Germany at this very moment, if you wish."

"I see, Colonel Doubet, that, in addition to your duties as an officer in the French Air Force, you are also a comedian."

Doubet spread his arms in a small, disarming gesture. "On the contrary, Generalmajor, I am quite serious. I have no way of knowing what occurred before your crash-landing near the canal north of Mulhouse. You could very well have been forced to fly there by the others." He wondered if the German could really see through this posturing, as he suspected he did.

"It's quite simple. My parents were to be arrested by the German authorities for participating in a clandestine effort to assist political and racial refugees who are looking for sanctuary in foreign countries. I flew to Schloss Löwenheim, where they were hiding, to see what I could do to salvage their situation. By doing so, I caused the Gestapo to consider me to be one of the conspirators. And to save my life, along with the others, I commandeered an airplane and flew directly to France."

"Under fire, of course."

"You've seen the bullet holes, I'm sure."

"You are seeking political asylum, then?"

"Are you granting it?"

"France was the first of all nations—a century ago—to recognize the principle of political asylum. You have no need to fear involuntary repatriation if you claim political persecution. Especially you, Generalmajor."

Doubet saw the calculating glint in Stachel's eyes. "What does that mean, Colonel?"

Ah, Doubet thought, *he has begun to smell the underlying aroma. Intrigue carries its own ineradicable scent.* "There are certain parties who are not exactly sorry to see you leave Germany, Herr Generalmajor,"

"Certain parties? Why would Frenchmen be glad to see me leave my homeland?"

"Well," Doubet said, watching the high, enameled door behind Stachel ease open. "Let us say that you have certain—What is the word? In English, it's 'fans'—in several nations."

"There are Stachel-fanciers? I find that hard to believe."

"Stachel-watchers. People who have been observing you for some time."

"What have they seen, Colonel?" Stachel asked impassively.

"A disenchantment. A disapproval. A restlessness. Open disdain, in some instances. All of which could eventually have spelled personal disaster for you in the Third Reich. You were showing signs of rebellion, Generalmajor Stachel."

Stachel lifted an eyebrow. "Somebody must have been watching me, all right. Seeing things I wasn't aware of myself."

"Precisely. The human is always the last to recognize his own, his personal, problems."

Stachel remained silent for an interval, seeming to be in deep thought. The mist, which had blanketed Mulhouse since dawn, had begun to lift, and beyond the window the city was showing its spires and towers and gentle Renaissance textures. Doubet waited, observing the German with concealed amusement. *The man is indeed one of our kind. He's about to ask the question.*

"Are you," Stachel said suddenly, "the one who calls himself Sauerkraut?"

"No." The door opened widely. "I am Sauerkraut."

Doubet was compelled to smile. These were the little vignettes, the fleeting adventures, that made this work so enjoyable, he told himself. It was good form, of course, to maintain a cool façade and to represent oneself as being jaded and beyond emotional involvement in the denouements of secret intelligence. But still, he, as all Doubets before him had been, was fond of surprises and practical jokes—within reason, naturally, and in good taste—and so he had to concentrate now on suppressing his urge to smile openly at Stachel's blue-eyed astonishment.

"Polly Loomis Duncan," Stachel said.

"Polly Loomis," she corrected. "There's been a divorce in the family."

"You are Sauerkraut?"

"Mm-hm." She crossed the room, sat in one of the fancy carved chairs beside the desk, and selected a cigarette from the tray there. Glancing at Stachel, she winked. "Got a light?"

Doubet produced a silver lighter and snapped it alive. "I shall leave you two now," he said amiably, setting Polly's cigarette aglow. "I've a great deal of paper work to do, thanks to your spectacular entry into France, General, and I'd like to have it done before you leave us."

Stachel's surprise turned to curiosity. "Leave you? Where am I going?"

"That depends," Polly said, blowing smoke at him, "on how this conversation turns out. See you later, Georges. And thanks for all your help."

"Certainly, my dear," Doubet said, disappearing behind the closing door.

Stachel examined Polly Loomis with undisguised interest, as if she were a specimen on a slide. He saw that the years had not been harsh on her. She had gained some weight, and was pleasingly round in all those places where, in the early times, there had been flat planes and boyish angles. She now appeared to be more womanly, mature, clear-eyed, smooth, and—as always—glib. Her German had become exceptionally good, virtually devoid of American inflections.

"Let's speak English," he said. "I haven't used it for some time."

"Okey-doke."

"What's all this Sauerkraut business? Those radio messages, and all that?"

She crossed her legs and settled back in the chair, drawing deeply on her cigarette. Exhaling and watching the smoke rise toward the gilt ceiling, she said, "Sauerkraut's been my codename as a U.S. secret intelligence agent since I joined the embassy in Berlin back in the twenties. I was running a chain of informants, and one of the best covered was a detective in the Berlin police, who, in turn, had his own chain going."

"Dieter Laub?"

"Laub, code name Dagger, was on the American payroll as early as 1922. He carried a big torch for his dead wife, was disillusioned by Germany's defeat, and smothered both pains with intrigue and moola. He hated all political parties, particularly the Communists and the Nazis, but eventually resented the Nazis more than any for the way they took over the Prussian police force and warped it into the Gestapo. From the very first—and for very high pay, believe you me—he and his chain ran a surveillance for us on the comings and goings at German army headquarters. The Allied Control Commission suspected von Speeckt of organizing a secret force in violation of the Versailles Treaty, and so we were watching everything. Well, Laub picked up your assignment there, and I added you to the individual studies we were doing on German brass hats. As time went by and the Hitler thing developed, we became increasingly interested in you. You showed signs of disaffection. The higher you rose in rank, the more critical your jobs, the more you showed evidence of political distemper. We decided to cultivate you, and, eventually, we decided to subvert you—to precipitate your leaving Germany—before you got in deep trouble with the Nazi chiefs. We felt you'd be more valuable working on this side of the Rhine than going to jail or getting shot on the other side."

Stachel felt a heat, as if there were a small sun glowing behind his cheeks. "You mean that our relationship—the language lessons, the little dabblings in bed, the work you did for me—were simply a contrivance to seduce me into leaving Germany?"

"Mm. You thought you were cultivating me, but I was cultivating you. Surprise."

"The so-called secret device on that Curtiss I crashed—that was an idea of yours?"

"We felt that we should do everything we could to induce Hitler to promote you, give you greater exposure to the workings of the top-echelon Nazi establishment. We wanted you to be the most informed of our informants, you might say." She smiled. "And the most protected. There were times when our friend, the late Dieter Laub, had to work his head off keeping you alive and out of trouble with both the Nazis and the anti-Nazis—each of whom began to suspect you as working with the other, presumably."

Stachel left the window and stood before her, his face growing hotter. "You keep saying 'we.' Who's we?"

"French Intelligence. American Intelligence. We continued our collaboration after the Control Commission expired. And it was good we did, too. Because—I admit to you quite candidly—we see Hitler as starting a war against us both within a year or two." She stubbed out her cigarette. "And what you know about Hitler and his machine promises to be of great help to us, both for getting ready and for the actual fighting."

"John Duncan was in on this, too?"

"That dummy? Don't be silly. There was a time, when I was married to him, that you were being managed by our friend Doubet, who eventually decided that your case required closer, more knowledgeable handling than he could give it. So Doubet—code name Schnitzel, incidentally—tried to get John to withdraw from his Senate re-election campaign and hire on as your manager. The theory being that he had the necessary personal insights to deal with you intelligently during your subversion. But John had tasted the sweet life and he didn't want to give it up—even for three times the salary. Which was a break, because that left only me, and I know you better, and am a helluva lot smarter then John. So Doubet rehired me."

"And Duncan was defeated anyhow."

"Poor John. He always was a klutz."

Stachel considered her with great deliberation. "Was it you who decided to set up my parents for arrest?"

"We decided to suck you into helping Frau Heidemann escape. But Laub found that you weren't all that passionate for her. And, since Bormann was showing signs of increasing annoyance with your, ah, irreverence, we knew we'd have to act fast—force you into a situation in which you had no choice but to leave Germany and work against the Nazis if you hoped ever to get back. Sorry to use the old folks, but what the hell."

He stared at her, realizing that he hadn't the smallest bit of patience left for this outrageous woman from a pip-squeak culture who dared to meddle, to tinker, to decree do-gooder solutions for a nation whose motivations and problems and yearnings stemmed from the Huns and beyond. He heard questions in his mind: How could you expect someone like this to grasp the essence of a bloody history in which generations upon generations have been trampled, victimized, exploited, hated without cause—all in the name of social order or religion or politics or economics, or all of them together? Why should you expect a naïve wretch from a naïve, smugly virtuous new world to comprehend the centuries-long erosion of individual conscience and communal ethics that simply must resolve in a Hitler and his Bormanns?

Ziegel. Anna-Marie Elsbet Karlotte, the Baroness von Klingelhof-und-Reimer lying on the cobblestones. Herr A. Herr B. Herr C. Frozen old people. Crying children. Elfi Heidemann. A guileless Randelmann, forever alienated from his world. His own apartment in Berlin, silent this morning; ransacked, perhaps. All the little things of his life, the traces of his existence that would never again provide that context: cuff-links; combs; snapshots; letters; his Blue Max and Blood Order stuffed away in a jewel box in the second bureau drawer.

All of it gone, thanks to this dilettante and her serene conviction of righteousness.

He turned slowly and regarded her somberly. When he spoke, it was with the soft cool voice of mourning. "Who are you, Miss Loomis, to fuss around in my life, to manage me, handle me, to drag my old people through hell? Just what right do you have to decide whether I should be in Germany or not? What absurd stretch of your imagination enables you to think that I, a German officer, would turn traitor to my country?"

"Don't push, Stachel. I'm as tough as you are."

"I think not."

"We're two of a kind."

"Then God help us both."

"You'll calm down. And when you do, you'll see how I can help you. You'll see what you really are and what I really am."

As he made for the door, she said, "Your road back starts right here. There's going to be a war, anytime now. We'll be fighting Hitler, not the Germans. We need smart, tough, patriotic Germans like the Stachels, the Heidemanns, the Laubs, the Randelmanns—the others—to get Hitler out of Germany and give it back to the Germans."

Stachel made a sound of exasperation. "I've got a better idea. How about me enlisting you and all the other patriotic

Americans to get Roosevelt out of America and give it back to the Americans?"

"You miss my point. You'll need lots of help—"

But by then he'd left the room and was in the corridor, calling for Doubet.

"Doubet! I want to see my friends."

He saved Randelmann for the last, mainly because he was at a loss for a means to convey his real regret to the man. So it was late in the day before he could bring himself to sit down beside the major's cot, which the clinic people had placed on a piazza overlooking the town. The evening glowed warmly against the mellow buildings, and the air was sweet with the smells of baking bread and Alpine breezes. A great cloud of pigeons swirled in a clatter of wings, and somewhere in the purple shadows of the streets below an accordion moaned.

"Hello, Randelmann. I hope you're feeling better."

The major gave him a sidelong glance from under lowered brows. "Promise me something, Herr Generalmajor. Please don't ever invite me to spend a leave with you again."

Stachel smiled. "You'll have to admit, though, that you haven't been bored."

"Ha. That's what the cannibal said to the man in the pot."

"I'm really very sorry, Randelmann. You've been rather badly used. I didn't intend it to be that way."

The major's face, golden in the setting sun, tried bravely to register indifference, but Stachel could see traces of self-pity and anxiety behind the bravado. "Apologies won't do, Generalmajor," Randelmann said with forced lightness. "I've instructed my attorneys to bring suit."

"I concede my guilt. How can I repay you?"

Randelmann, his expression serious again, said, "Just what in hell did happen, Generalmajor? I mean, what was all the yelling and shooting about?"

"The Americans and the French expect to be attacked by Hitler, it seems. They've watched me over the years and have decided that I'm anti-Nazi and will be willing to help them in their efforts to defend themselves."

"Are they right?"

Stachel sighed. "Politicians bore me. The Kaiser; the Bundesrat; the Reichstag; the Weimar thing; Hitler. They're all the same. Every government, everywhere, at any time. The same. Every charlatan who ever wore a cutaway promises peace, prosperity, greatness. And he sucks in us clods, and we start believing him, and then, instead of peace, prosperity, and greatness, we get taxes, war, poverty—the works. Hitlers? Bormanns? Hell, we'll always have them around. But I don't know who's the larger fraud—the Hitlers, or the Stachels who play along with their rotten little games. I've got a lot of sorting out to do, Randelmann."

The major said in mock awe, "The Americans and Frogs must think you are a very important fellow indeed to have gone to all that trouble to get you over here. They must think you are Herr Super-German."

"I can forgive the Americans. They're children. But the French should know better."

"They're correct in one respect, though," Randelmann said. "If we expect ever to return to Germany we'll have to put the Nazis out of office first. My God, when I heard what that man Bormann did to those people at the Schloss—did you see it?"

Stachel gave him a look. "I saw it."

"It was murder. Unvarnished murder. Any man who can do those things—"

Stachel completed the thought. "—can steal a bicycle."

"Eh?"

"How about you, Randelmann? Your personal history card shows you to be a bachelor and all that, but how will this unexpected exile work on you?"

The major looked thoughtful. "I'm a German. I want to go back to Germany. I don't have anybody there. A girl friend or two. Nothing big. But I live there."

"Want to tag along with me?"

"Where do we start?"

"Bormann. We start and end with Bormann. He's the plumbline."

"He's got a lot to answer for, all right."

"So do I, Randelmann. So do I."

62

There was a small café in the clinic's garden wing, a place where visitors could stir a thoughtful cup while adjusting to the blind haphazard that had stricken their dear ones upstairs. At this hour it was empty, except for a tiny waitress wearing a starchy uniform and an expression to match.

Stachel ate his supper slowly and, afterward, sat for a time, gazing at the pale arc of moon hanging delicately above the darkening town. The waitress came to ask primly if there would be anything else—she obviously disapproved of Germans—and seemed sourly pleased when he shook his head.

He was preparing to leave when Frau Heidemann appeared in the doorway, glancing about the room with tired, unhappy eyes. Standing beside the table, he held a chair for her in silent invitation.

When she was settled, she sighed and touched her hair with an exploratory hand. "I must look a dreadful mess."

"You look fine. How about something to eat?"

"Some hot chocolate and buttered bread, please."

The waitress survived her disappointment sufficiently to see to the order, and in the quiet, Stachel considered Frau Heidemann with undisguised interest. "How long has it been since you've rested?"

She shrugged. "It doesn't matter. The others needed me. The nurses here are marvelous, but they speak no German. My voice, my being around, seemed to help."

"It probably helped you, too. It's better to be busy after a heavy loss."

"Loss?" Her eyes showed curiosity.

"Ziegel. I heard you tell him you loved him."

Color came to her cheeks and she looked away, seeming to grope for a way to answer. "Of course I loved him. He was a dear, gentle person, with surprising virtues and endearing weaknesses. He was very fond of you, incidentally."

"I could never understand why."

"He said once that you are the walking portrait of all that's wrong with man. He said you wear your humanity on your sleeve."

"How touching."

"He meant it in a kindly way. He said you're like a cross-section diagram of the contradictions, the needs and impulses, in all of us. He said to watch you helped him understand himself. He said it helped him to endure the war."

"That's too deep for me. With all due respect to your departed lover, Ziegel was a very peculiar fellow."

"He wasn't my lover. I loved him as a sweet human being and trusted friend."

"That isn't what I saw in his face."

"Probably not. But he needed my kind of love more than he needed a lover."

The waitress brought the chocolate and bread, and, while Frau Heidemann ate, Stachel studied the lights of the city and wondered where Ziegel was now. He tried to imagine a transparent Ziegel, all beatific and gauzy, drifting among the clouds. He couldn't.

"What will you do now, Frau Heidemann?"

She put her cup in its saucer and, with shadowed eyes, peered at the night beyond the casements. "I don't know. It depends on what the French require of refugees like us."

"I don't think they know themselves at this point."

"What will you do?"

"The Americans want to give me a job. I might be going there. If they'll let me bring my mother and father, that is. And Randelmann."

"What if they don't?"

"Then they can stick their job in their ear."

She gave him a glance, a quick movement of her green eyes. "Would you take me, too?"

He sat in the stillness, trying to achieve a detachment, a sense of indifference to the implications in her question. Yet he knew that, since their dinner in Berlin twenty years before, there had been a union between them—an elusive, tacit, insistent bond that had never been given word or substance. He had tried to find it, identify it, in his visit to her shabby apartment on the night of his denunciation by von Brandt. But then, as always, it remained beyond his grasp, and he'd left, her rejection of his overture a bitterness that was with him even now.

"In what capacity, Frau Heidemann? As a trusted friend?"

"That will do for a start, wouldn't you say?"

"I don't think you really like me all that much."

"I suppose I don't. But I trust you."

"Why?"

"I saw you go back to the Schloss for your parents—your unhesitating willingness to give of yourself. Ziegel was right: Like most of us, you're unlikable because you do unlikable things. But then, showing through for only a tiny moment, there'll be the thing that links us all to the divine. It's that quality in you I trust, Herr General."

"It's a long road ahead, Frau Heidemann."

"I have none other to follow."

"All right, then. Finish your chocolate, and we'll be about it."

ABOUT THE AUTHOR

JACK D. HUNTER is the author of *The Blue Max* (which was made into a major motion picture), *The Expendable Spy* and *One of Us Works for Them.* He resides in Maryland with his family.